Atone

Copyright Dec 6, 2006

ACKNOWLEDGEMENTS

This is for my brother. Sorry.

ATONE

BOOK ONE: Escape

Prelude

The light began to return to the sky,
Atone perched on the roof to greet it. In the
morning light, her orange hair seemed blood
red, the thick shoulder length hair framing the
soft pink skin of her face. Her eyes looked out at
the rocky horizon, at current a dark black,
purple. Her fishbone-thin claws absently
scratched at her ankle, the tiny barbs on them
flicking off old, expired scales that covered her
body in rare patches. She felt the hot breeze
across the unprotected skin, the exposed back of
her sweat-moist baby blue shirt left room for the
two broken bones to protrude from her
shoulders. She looked down from the silo
shaped home beneath her. Nothing existed to
ease her night of toil. She scanned her
surroundings, watching the blowing dust create
savage dirt swirls that revealed the jagged rocks
hidden underneath. Her eyes focused on the
army assembling near by. Her eyes narrowed as
she studied them before settling on Lihatiel. Her
gaze left him, surveying instead the huge metal
gate behind the front line. In the courtyard,
another unit of demons and damned waited, and
beyond that the parapet.

Atone

The Order and the Diablonians. It seemed forever since their minuet truce was obliterated though it was only two weeks, she thought. The Order of Flies was known by many in Hell as optimistic dreamers. If it were not for their incredible efficiency in battle, their numbers would have been destroyed eons ago. Their leader was Beelzebub, once one of the three biggest names, here. It wasn't until Jesus, so legends go, blessed him on his three-day visit that their objectives changed. Atone thought about that day, watching the Diablonians assemble in the distance. Beelzebub enforced the safety of the Mortal's savior. He decided then that the goal of The Order was to tempt mortals to strengthen their resolve for a better life; to make strong the souls that would join their lord in the heavenly realms. Those foolish enough to be led astray would be tortured for their folly. The truce signed by Diablos would have merged the two forces, The Order to tempt and the Diablonians to punish. The Diablonians, for their part, were jaded by their fall and were all too happy to exact pain from the wicked. Atone remembered what the good days were like, or maybe that was Beelzebub's plot all along; to trick those that may still be trying to do some good into doing bad. At least that's how things were beginning to look.

She didn't know what ended the truce. Several weeks ago, the first wave of Diablonians' invaded the fortress of Sheol. Lihatiel, one of Beelzebub's head officers and in Atone's eyes the most corrupt, held them off. Since then The Order's men have had little rest. It was all falling apart and she could feel the worst of Hell's tortures unfolding in the chaos. She looked down at her weapons. She would have to hurry to get behind the front lines before the beasts could tear through them. She knew what she must do.

"Longing and Mercy" laid next to her, balancing on the edge, dangerously close to falling inside, past the many cabinets that lined her walls. There was no roof to her domicile. Longing and Mercy, the finished products of her pain-wracked night of forging, were no longer mutilated and horrific humans, their gleaming metallic sheen picking up the crimson sky. They were now two exquisite statues of death and lost love. The first, Longing, appeared as a man with legs twisted in a diamond that would, when worn, hug her arm. He held his forearms together ahead of him, for her to grip her hand around. His hands and feet extended outward in a fan of blades but his greatest weapon was the long Mohawk arching out from behind his wretched face. The second, Mercy, was his female counterpart that accompanied Atone's right hand. Like Longing she was a human shaped weapon, looking upward, though her eyes and mouth where covered with carefully carved bandages engraved into the metallic body. Her hands and feet, like Longing, fanned outward though she was twisted with her face and breasts facing away from Atone's arm. Her forearms were twisted savagely behind her head, pulled back in an unnatural way for Atone's grip. Her inner thighs hung down with toes pointing out from her elbows. She slid them both on when she heard Lihatiel's men ready their frontline.

Bael's army could be seen on the horizon through the burning mist of morning. The two armies would fight soon and she would be a part of it. The end would come soon.

The shrill sound of the trumpet drew Lihatiel's army to attention. The beating drums and roaring of demons answered the horn from beyond the fog. Atone leapt from her perch, her tattered baby blue skirt fluttering in the breeze as she descended onto the broken rocks below, taking the duration of the fall to ready herself for the fight to come. She would have to hide her true desires before joining the ranks. She barely made it halfway to the front lines before the blast of the trumpet rippled the air around her. With the trumpet sounding the charge began. Her heart pounded at the sound of the Balefire Army roaring like a wave threatening to drown the fortress Lihatiel defended. She swerved between Lihatiel's forces as the Balefire Army raced at her heels.

Bael's men, if 'men' they could be called, collided with the front line of The Order, their wave breaking against Lihatiel's more disciplined Order of Flies. The savage, near animal, soldiers of Bael didn't even notice as their comrades died next to them. So impassioned was their frenzy, their rage whipped to overflowing as though Bael himself was behind them, that they fought on through severed limbs and spilled intestine, little noticing or caring until they collapsed only after sustaining too much damage to do anything else. Discipline did little to sustain The Order in the same condition.

Atone dropped down as the blade swung over her. Blood splattered from above in a morbid rain. She rolled to her back kicking out with both feet. The Balefire soldier took only a step back before chasing after her again. She scrambled for safety. An arrow whizzed past her grazing her shoulder in its path to the beast behind. The sting hurt. She tumbled between an Order knight and a boar faced beast, losing her hunter only to gain another on the other side.

She found her feet. The Order knight's head toppled to the ground next to her, his bleeding stump of a neck coating her leg as his body collapsed. Three beasts now pursued her. The blood collected the unmerciful dust and ash slowing her escape as it clumped around her legs. She let out a cry. She was almost at the gate. She just needed a few feet more. A wall of archers greeted her and she dropped in the dirt rolling toward them. Arrows blackened the sky above her. The sound of the pursuing beasts groaned as the arrows dug deep into their flesh. She rolled to kneeling. The impact took her from her feet. They were still charging. Her heart pounded with each rampaging footfall. There was a second volley. They were still charging. She crawled backward. Outlast them, she told herself. The boar face lowered to gore her. She screamed, arms out to shield herself. The impact sent her sliding several yards, the jagged stones slashing her naked feet. The sound was gruesome. It wasn't a sound she made. She opened her eyes, not realizing she closed them. The beast was dead. Longing and Mercy had punctured the monster's skull. The others clawed their way on failing limbs toward the archers.

Atone scrambled free of the beast and made her way to Lihatiel's side. She stayed close to him, fighting by his side, letting his men take the brunt of the beast men. The beastly Balefire Army, though untrained, outnumbered them. Soon the archers were reduced to their blades. Metal clashed with bone. Claws swung, Atone ducking to evade them while whittling away at their forces. The battle was savage. Limbs learned to fly. Blood joined with the mist of the red light of dawn. Several of Lihatiel's comrades collapsed to the sheer might of the Balefire Army. "Hold your positions. Show them that the fortress of Sheol will not easily fall," Lihatiel bellowed. Atone watched as Lihatiel gave out commands beyond the understanding or caring of the Balefire Army. The bulk of his forces retreated to the large stone stairs leading to the walls that overlooked the courtyard. Fewer soldiers stood between her and the masses of destruction. Now, she thought before you don't get a chance. She had meager seconds, sizing up Lihatiel before being swept from her feet to fall to the earth. Lihatiel turned to see the black bristle covered beast over her. She kicked outward. She felt the lower jaw crack from the blow. The beast hoisted her up by the leg. Her skin tore as its claws dug deep. A whoosh of a sword sent her back to the ground, rocks impaling her back. The beast turned to Lihatiel. Then the archers returned to their onslaught. The tide of war turned and Lihatiel's forces slaughtered the beasts like the swine they resembled. Though pushed back to the main wall, Bael's crazed forces where put to death.

"We have victory!" Lihatiel cried out. No cheers called after him, making his hair rise along the back of his neck.

"You have nothing," the venomous hiss spoke, before Bael himself drifted through the fog. Lihatiel and Atone watched as their own army turned against each other. Order killed Order, arrows felling friends, swords slaying their comrades in arms. In an explosion of fury and confusion Bael's army regained the upper hand.

"Bael? Bael himself is here?" Lihatiel faltered.

"Scared, Lihatiel?" Atone asked. The remains of Lihatiel's men began to march, their mind no longer theirs. Their purpose was clear and focused onward to their former leader. There was nowhere for Lihatiel or Atone to go.

"We have to get out of here!" Lihatiel urged, fear coating his words.

"No," Atone corrected, as she plunged her weapons into his turned back. "I have to get out of here." Lihatiel struggled but her first strike was enough to win the fight. Lihatiel's struggle was futile; soon he lay at her feet squirming like a dying fish. "Now you'll pay the price for underestimating me. I will be yours no longer!" she hissed. The orange coal like chains hung around her and she reached for them to burn away the guise and reveal the true form of Lihatiel's soul. She could feel the Balefire Army surround them; feel them hesitate at the treachery they were not a part of. If Lihatiel's soul was exposed she could kill him but there was no time left for her to kill him completely. There was no time for torture, no time to make him suffer. She killed him quick without the chains and cursed herself for the lack of time. She couldn't let the army deny her even this small victory. A powerful warrior approached, stepping forward from the crowd.

"Deception in the ranks. How favorable… for me," he said. She turned to face Bael as he bowed over her, nearly two feet taller than her when standing. This of course was only the smoke of the mirror. Bael's cloud thin body was rippling, giving the appearance of thick, knotted muscle. His face was the visage of a bat, including the large ears. These were haloed by swirling black horns.

"You're welcome. But I didn't do it for you." Atone spat the words on the ground at his feet. Her lips curled up in repulsive anticipation watching his arm rise to prepare his men.

"Then you won't mind when I finish this," he said. "After all I can't use someone like you. It's a shame really. That body and power. I would love to be inside you. But I'm sure you would just lock me away in some strange mental prison." With a motion of his arm his men swarmed the fortress and trampled her underfoot to seize the prize. The agony of their razor's edged hooves cutting and crushing their way through her from one side, the jagged shards of rock tearing through sinew and shattering bone from the other, was comforted only by the joy of watching Lihatiel's corpse undergo the same. She could feel her soul, mutilated in kind, and knew that this was the end. Crushed under the boots of the army that was once Lihatiel's seemed fitting, she thought as she lay there dying. At least now it was over.

Chapter 1

Bael, his rolling body of smoke coiled tight to solidify into a tangible form. Retaining the thick obsidian color his body became darkness, absorbing the meager light that reached him. His men waited patiently as he entered the heart of the fortress.

"So this is it," Bael said, eying over the massive leather bound book; the driving goal of the battle. The front cover was battered and torn, leaving nothing to indicate a title. The back was held together loosely, the binding refusing to let go. Several newer stitches, made of sinew aided its death grip on the back cover. "Somehow I'm not impressed. But if this is what our lord Diablo wants then it shall be what he gets," Bael continued, handing it to one of the many soldiers. With a wave of his smoky arm he motioned them to move, taking their spoils with them.

Dust and ash worked diligently in their passing to conceal all that transpired here this day. Atone's body, like Lihatiel and the rest of the fallen, lay broken with their weapons and armor, slowly covered by the ever-present debris. A blue beam of light descended through the red haze piercing the dust to encompass Atone's trampled corpse. A tanned human form followed the light down, long black hair swirling through the air. Large silver wings remained open and motionless as it floated through the air to land next to her. Though feminine and youthful his square jaw showed signs of stubble and the knot of his Adam's apple protruding from his neck hinted something else. His long fingers reached up to the buttons on his mandarin style collar. He hovered a few inches from the ground looking down at the unrecognizable mass of bones, organs and skin his face twisted, fighting back tears. What could have been but what never was. Death was harsh here in the pits of Hell. No ascension to a heavenly field, no rest in the garden. Death for a devil was much harsher. Soul remained, trapped in the black nothingness of its own oblivious husk. There was no peace to be had in a death like this, he thought. There was only the constant annihilation of its own existence. True death, the letting go, was never an option here. The soul's fragments never remerged with the creator to be remade. But this soul was still needed, he thought, letting out a sound that sounded like a sob. He distracted his thoughts by unbuttoning his collar and clasping his side where similar buttons ran under his arm to the waist. With a savage pull he exposed his chest, deep engravings in his flesh showing a glyph that began to swirl and glow, until a vortex was born there. A similar glow ignited in Atone's eyes as they forced open beyond death. Bones popped in place, lungs filled with air. Organs reformed and she struggled to rise. Her caved in skull pushed outward, her brain once mush squeezed through the cracks restoring itself inside. Her heart once more began to pump by the power of this angel. Her mouth opened, jaw mending, to accommodate her screaming new start. After The brunt of Atone's restoration, her pale pink skin was free from bruises and torn skin, even the blood and gore was removed from her revealing blue skirt and top.

"No... don't... All I want is..." she gasped, fumbling around to grasp at things only she saw. In a moment she regained her bearings. Her eyes, wide, focused on Zopheal and narrowed. Her open mouth closed and curled into a snarl. After the pain subsided she straightened her orange hair with her fishbone claws, restoring its pear shape and order, with her scaly hand she wiped her tears away. Zopheal rebuttoned the top part of his dress.

"Arise, Atone," the angel spoke, tranquil but with authority, like his form between the sexes his voice was indistinguishable. He touched her arm to ease her pain.

"Zopheal," she said, rising to her feet. She scowled, and hissed as her body finished healing. The look she cast on him told him she was anything but happy to revive. "To what do I owe the resurrection?"

"God has need of you."

"You mean you have need of me," she said, barring her teeth.

"It is one and the same."

"What is it then?" she asked, bowed down like a disciplined and scolded dog. But at least a scolded dog has the opportunity to fight against its chains, she thought.

"I sent an angel down here. I need you to find him," Zopheal requested. His face seemed disinterested, but smiled in an attempt to ease Atone's defensiveness.

"Why was he sent down here? Did he say the wrong thing? Screw up a prayer? Drink a little too much ambrosia?" she jested, sarcastically.

"He's not here to be punished."

"Then you're the one that made a mistake. What else is down here?" she asked.

"Two angels. They were sent down here before him. They were going to or have succeeded in starting a war between The Order of Flies and the Diablonians. The goal was to prevent them to combine forces and keep Hell's forces divided."

"That's would definitely be 'have succeeded' Zopheal, just in case your blind devotion can't see the major battle that happened here," she said, pointing a thumb behind her with an unhappy smile.

Zopheal ignored her lack of cooperation. "Rumor has it that they were hunting out a fallen to end a prophecy before it begins. If that's the case they've interfered with God's plan. That's why I sent him down here."

"So who's the unlucky one I'm looking for?" She relaxed, admitting to herself that she was curious why Zopheal would risk so much to come down here and talk to her.

"Axael."

"Axael?" she asked. Everything was focused on what he had to say now. "You mean my Axael?" she said, feeling the weight of the universe fall down with all its force, inside her chest, crushing the heart inside. She gasped for air. Not here. Not him. This wasn't right. She couldn't let him see her like this. It was bad enough when… But he might need her, for there were many dangers at every turn here. These thoughts coiled around each other tightly until they merged into a new emotion, that of maddening rage. She cursed Zopheal in silence. He should never have made that mistake. He never should have used her Axael.

"That's why I thought it was best to use you for this," Zopheal said, oblivious to her inner thoughts, twisting, extending a hand to help Atone to her feet. Atone resisted the urge to pounce. She rose by herself, brandishing her weapons. For the first time Zopheal's expression changed. Eyes grew large and his mouth turned into a wide-open frown. He felt like retreating but didn't for fear of provoking Atone's baser instincts. Atone thought about the treaties, how angels weren't fair game until the end days. She thought how easy breaking them would be. She calmed herself by thinking subjectively about the situation. An angel asking a fallen to take one for the team, since history proved how much they could be trusted. She laughed beside herself though the thoughts of Axael made it strained, even forced. Zopheal eased as well, a tentative smile creeping back to his face. After all these years she still felt the need to comply. She laughed again, free and loud this time but the laughter cracked and bled and the similarity to the sound of sobbing could not be mistaken or overlooked. The sound of Zopheal forced reality back to mind and killed what mirth remained of laughter instantly. She stared bitterly at the angel.

"How dare you send him down here? I should flail you alive where you stand. If you were so concerned then why didn't you do something about it yourself, hmmm? Or get one of those pathetic Doomsday watchers? Why not send in Israfel's forces? They always like fucking us." She hissed the last part, reflecting her distaste. She turned quickly away, knowing that if she spent too much time in his face she would strike. Even so she could feel Zopheal worry about Axael and it comforted her slightly. She hated her empathic curse but focused on Zopheal's concern to calm her and resist punishing him for his oversight. Zopheal started to speak but she cut him off, a snarl still in her words. "I'll find him, Zopheal, but not for you. Don't think I've forgotten what you did. What you all did. You all stood there when he passed that judgment. Every one but Axael. He alone stood up for me, tried to stop me. He thought there was some way, some thing we could do to evoke God's mercy and have him change his most unfair verdict."

"You made your choices, Atone."

"Don't give me that." She swung her arm out, the blade catching the tip of his chin. A loud exhale warmed Atone's hand, Zopheal inching ever so slightly back. The blade didn't follow, and another exhale graced her flesh. "What choices did I have? Hell or Oblivion? What would you choose? I didn't see a choice. I did nothing to deserve that sentence, that choice."

"Just find him. Please. I need to know what's going on down there."

"Whatever." Atone shrugged it off. "I guess you'll just have to trust me."

Zopheal rose, wasting no time in his departure. He was gone in a moment, disappearing in the dark red storm clouds brewing above, to leave Atone alone mulling over the gravity of the situation. Of all the angels he sent Axael. He sent her angel. Second only to God in her heart when last they were together. She thought of all the horrors, all the atrocious things he most have seen her do to survive. Then she realized that he was down here, lost. All the horrors, all the atrocities were now all around him. She knew the kind of beasts and bastards down here. She knew what they felt and what they were capable of. Many would not be as forgiving as she. The treaties only covered two factions, The Order and the Diablonians. The legion of the abyss and the free lancers had no such treaty. Her heart beat harshly, in her chest thinking of the possibilities. She had to find him. Find him before the others. Find him before it was to late. Atone scanned the lands around her for anything useful. Longing and mercy were still with her, but the trace amounts of useful goods proved any further scavenging fruitless. Ash began to fall, blanketing the ground in a thick, snow-like layer as she made haste to leave the battlefield.

Night was an even more dangerous time to be out in the open, but she had to keep going with only her two fist daggers and the thought of Axael needing her again to comfort and protect her. "No," a voice inside her called weakly. She needed him. She needed him safe, even if it was far away from her. Heading south she saw a strange neon-purple glow in the distance. As she drew nearer she saw an establishment emerge through the thick darkness of the stormy night. The purple light was like a beacon to wayfaring damned. The sign formed from the purple light read, *Asmodius's*. She emerged slowly from the shadows to stay in the meager light of the sign. Every step was spent looking for traps, anticipating an ambush. She felt uneasy as she reached out empathically for any signs, afraid of what she might find. What she didn't find made her freeze. She felt nothing. There were no emotions near by. There was either no life in the building inside, or whatever lay in wait was beyond emotion. She looked back at the darkness, knowing whatever dwelled within it was already beyond such things. Stepping up to the door she took one last tentative look around before entering the safety that was not guaranteed.

Chapter 2

Heavy boots crushed the battlefield debris as they stepped through the ruins of Sheol. The bodies once paving the courtyard were now barely visible, the demons showing no regard and even less respect to the fallen warriors. They walked to the vault wall, seeing the doorframe broken, the door several feet away. A corpse of one of The Order's trampled leaders lay across the opening. The boot kicked it harshly.

"Get up, Lihatiel," the large demon that belonged to the boots growled. A glowing orb formed in his massive hand mixing with the poisonous ichor that dripped from his talons. It fell from his grasp burrowing its way into Lihatiel's ruined body. As if pulled by a string the corpse began to wobble awkwardly upward, moving in a way damaged tissue and broken bones wouldn't normally allow. His body twisted repairing only what was essential to survival, leaving the rest as it was. His mutilated body floated in front of Beelzebub awaiting his judgment

"You were in charge of holding this place. What happened here?" the Demon growled again. Lihatiel's eyes opened in fear and surprise, taking in the sight of his superior. Beelzebub's thick red hide moved, the muscles slithering underneath it like serpents as they tensed to reflect his rage. His thick black horns shielded his face from any light save for the sinister green glow of his eyes. The skin pulled away tightly from his lips exposing the bones of his powerful jaw, leering in a skeletal smile. Dark triangular bones jutted out from his back weaving their way between tight, powerful muscles. Gargantuan Dragonfly wings protruded from his shoulders concealing even more of the light. Lihatiel mumbled for a second, formulating something quick. His mind raced to come up with something to avoid what horrible fate awaited him.

"It was Atone, Sir. She turned on us at a crucial moment allowing Bael to win the day, Sir."

"Atone? Don't be stupid. She wouldn't dare even if she could turn against us. You on the other hand…" He smiled with his skeletal face. With his mighty fist he grabbed hold of exposed organs crushing them anew. Lihatiel yelped in agony. He fumbled with his freshly crushed tissue trying to free it from his master's hold.

"I swear it, Lord Beelzebub. Atone has turned against us," he pleaded, crying rivers of tears from his battered skull's eyes.

"Sir," a demon called, emerging from the inner vault. Beelzebub turned releasing his hold of Lihatiel to focus on the new comer.

"What is it, Cosmacrater?" he asked. Lihatiel coiled up, trying to protect his weakest areas while Beelzebub was distracted.

"The book of prophecy was taken," Cosmacrater said, twirling a thin silver dirk and then slipping it back into its home between the other blades on his belt. Unlike the others he appeared mostly human, his thick red hued skin the only real give away. His sorrowful grey eyes hid under a thick mat of black hair that covered his neck and forehead.

"Can you locate Atone?"

"I cannot." Cosmacrater's stern muscles tensed in his jaw as he spoke. He bowed his head, slipping his hands in his pants pockets, the only article of clothing he wore that didn't house his weapons. Belts hung from him laced with a multitude of intricate blades. "She is too far from here. I can say at least that she is not one of the dead that lay here."

"Well find her. I want that book," he said, trying to conceal his ever-building impatience. He redirected his focus back to Lihatiel. "And as for you…"

Lihatiel's screams echoed through the stony walls of the ruins chasing Cosmacrater and his best soldiers from the palace and warning them of failure's price. The hunt was on, and they were the hunters.

Chapter 3

    The door opened easily. The inside was dimly lit from lights in the ceiling sheltered for ambiance. She could hear the beat of the bass line and the seduction of a saxophone though no band was present. The entrance looped around so that at first entering you couldn't see what lay ahead. Pictures covered the wall, all naked dancers in suggestive posses. This was the bait of course. As she entered the main room two burly demons rose, noticed that she wasn't human, and sat back down. She looked them over as they reminded her of the small tan toads she made when she used to be an angel. These heavy hideous brutes were much bigger. A smiling jester of a soul stood behind the bar cleaning glasses. Small nub horns peaked out at the hairline and a ridged, triangular goatee surrounded his toothy grin. He rubbed specks of blood off the drinking glasses using the front of his red vest that covered a white shirt. He looked up and nodded, straightening his small bow tie before returning to cleaning this time using a rag. She looked out away from the guards and the bartender to see the majority of the populace. A woman cleft in twain was on the stage, each half entertaining the clientele on either end of the catwalk. Her lacy black bra and crotch less panties were soiled with blood but she continued on gyrating with the music. Her hands, devoid of flesh and muscle ran through her hair, her face well practiced at hiding the pain she was in. Her legs opened wide in front of the back half of the room as she pulled her bra down to rub her breasts against the face of the nearest patron. Her intestines squirmed between the two halves. The wound that divided her was ragged and fresh. Atone kept her distance trying to avoid feeling what the entertainer had to endure.

She studied the patrons at the side of the stage, pins and hooks piercing their groin, keeping their eyes open and nailing them in place. A twisted smile was carved into each face, though their eyes told a very different story. This whole establishment was clearly to entertain some other much more deviant client.

She stepped back, feeling sick both from the visual imagery and her empathic curse to those suffering souls. She tried to compose herself and restrain the desire to vomit. She turned her back on the perversion and sat instead at the bar. The bartender stepped over, dutifully pouring a glass. Atone took it and held it close to her nose, breathing in. She could smell the iron, protean and alcohol of booze rich blood. She eyed the bartender who waited diligently on her, the only real client in the bar. She smiled weakly scanning his surface emotions. Though disgusting, the mixture was untainted. She nodded and drank it down quickly, trying to miss her taste buds. Forcing the rest down, she set the glass in front of her. The bartender advanced and she slid her hand between his fizzy gun and the glass. He looked up, smiling warmly. His eyes looked confused. Going back to his cleaning he left her to her own devices, her own thoughts. Her thoughts inevitably drifted back to the task at hand. She wondered how she would proceed. She had no leads, no starting point. She couldn't even go to Beelzebub for help. The fact that she turned on her leader Lihatiel made her a marked devil and if anyone looked beyond the surface of the battle to learn this she would be tortured or worse before even getting to him. He might forgive her actions but it was even more likely that he would never get the chance to. Even if she could reach him and he did forgive this Hell worthy sin, he wouldn't offer to help hunt down Axael. Even if he did it would take to long to organize their efforts, leaving Axael in this damnable place. Her heart feared for Axael and she sighed, sinking lower in her chair.

Axael was perfection in her eyes. Everything from his soft, shoulder length light brown hair, his chiseled masculine jaw, firm, muscular chest, lightly dappled with feather soft hazel hair and his majestic and expansive wing size was the ideal. His very presence here threatened that perfection above and beyond any physical damage. She tried to avoid that thought but it was inevitable. She wondered what wickedness held him here. She also wondered what she would do once she found him. No, thinking like that wouldn't help him. She needed to help him. If it were the only thing right she did since the fall, she would make him safe. The bartender returned gesturing with his fizzy gun. She shook her head in the negative. Then she looked into his face with a weak smile. Like the mortal world, if you need advice, find a bartender.

"I was looking for someone. Who would I talk to for information?" she explained her situation, her smile strengthening when she felt his mood. There was eagerness, a craving for secrets. He wanted in on whatever was running through her mind. She knew his curiosity, and that meant possibly getting help. He retracted his offer of a refill and she took her hand back leaving it close to the glass just in case.

"Cronos runs this place. He's entertaining the sisters right now but I'm sure your company would be welcome," he said, the words coming from somewhere beyond him, his smile and countenance never changing. He set his things down, raising the side of the bar for her to enter. She froze for a moment then cautiously stepped across scanning for traps. The bartender remained patient. "We don't generally get your kind over here. Cronos will be pleased."

"I'm glad," she lied, convincingly. The bartender opened the door then motioned for her to enter. She didn't. For the first time the bartender's face changed, the permanent smile struggling against itself to frown only to shrink and wither instead. He bowed and stepped inside first to show that all was well.

"Marcolf, what is it?" she heard a deep, powerful voice call out from inside the other room. She looked inside to see four people around a table. The Bartender, Marcolf, Stood next to a large, dark haired man. Similar to the frog like bouncers at the gate, his pale skin was thick and though very large she could tell that strength lay underneath the folds of fatty tissue. His head was also froggish, flattened and spread out, with large nostrils breathing deeply above a wide toothy mouth. Two massive horns curled close to the skull on either side of his head, square holes bored through along the length of them. The tips of the horns appeared to curl back into the flesh concealed by the fold that replaced the neck of him. Three women occupied the seats next to him, all beautiful in comparison.

"There is a demon here to see you," Marcolf answered dutifully.

"A devil, actually."

"What's the difference? So you fell instead of being born here. It all boils down to the same thing," Marcolf said, under his breath so that Cronos wouldn't hear.

"Devil, humm? Send her in then." Atone held tightly to her weapons as she finally stepped over the threshold. As she stepped closer to the four she could make out what lay on the table. A girl, apparently mid twenties, long, light red hair, gnarled and unkempt. Her arms and legs were clasped to shackles at the four corners of the table. The four beings around the table would carve little pieces out of her between discussion, the skin peeled back to create a diamond shape over her abdomen in which the four removed nonchalantly the parts they craved inside. Atone stopped half way up locking eyes with the tortured female soul on the table. Utmost terror pushed the poor girl beyond screaming and fighting proved useless a long time ago. Atone knew she tried though, seeing her ragged flesh torn by the shackles at her wrists and ankles. She winced as each piece was cut but refused to close those wild, horror-stricken eyes. One simple word echoed in Atone's mind. Help.

Atone felt what little was in her stomach surge upward and clasped her belly, willing it back down.

"If you're going to be rude and not introduce yourself…" Cronos bellowed, his voice freeing her from the eye contact but not the emotional link.

"I'm… My name is Atone," she said, trying to compose herself. The words came out weak, quivering.

"Atone. Humm? Come have a seat," he gurgled.

"Yes do come in. We don't often entertain," one of the women with raven colored hair stated chewing on a piece of kidney. "It would be nice to finally get some other opinions."

"Allow me," Cronos said, interrupting their chatter. "I am Cronos, and these three beauties are Lillith, Naamah, and Agrat bat Mahlat."

Atone scanned them over focusing on anything but what they were eating. Lillith was youthful, almost a girl if not for the obvious maturity revealed by her tight leather bustier and dirty prom dress skirt. Her hair was red, an excessively turbulent river of cascading curls that covered her slender shoulders and eventually ended near the small of her back. Naamah seemed plain. A simple grey pleated skirt and a matching grey blazer that was open to reveal a white tank top. Her hair, boy cut was white clinging close to her head. Agrat sat across from Cronos and had black hair that blended in to the raven feathered and black furred cloak she wore so that on observation one wouldn't be able to tell where her hair began and the cloak ended. This look was enhanced by a slinky dark red dress that had little trouble showing off her feminine assets.

"Pleasure," Atone said, plainly. Any efforts to sound more gracious would threaten to empty the contents of her stomach, and ruin any chance at negotiations.

"Please, have a seat. You must be famished," Lillith said, with the innocence of a child.

"No. I'm good."

"So what is it you do, Ms. Atone?" Naamah said, turning her chair to get a better look at their new guest.

"I am… I was an Akia," she said, squinting.

"Fabulous. We could really use a soul forger. Excellent," Lillith hissed sliding from her chair to go for the head of their dinner. "These new arrivals could do with some beauty enhancements."

"Girls are so self distorting now days," Naamah said, nodding.

"Please ladies, gentle host," Agrat asked of her company. Agrat rose from her seat concealing some gesture she made to the group. There was a silence over them. Agrat moved over to her bringing a chair. Atone took a step back and studied the seat, not daring to bend her knees. Agrat waited patiently before seeing the distrust in Atone's eyes. She took the seat herself. "An Akia with an empathic curse. No wonder you don't come any further. Now, Atone. You have business I believe?'

"If it pardon's. I was looking for an angel."

"There seems to be so many recently," Cronos scoffed getting a playful giggle from Lillith. Atone pulled her eyes from Agrat. She took two steps forward towards him before jerking back.

"So you've seen him?" She blurted, the pitch in her voice rising, for a moment showing a sign of weakness. They were quick to pick up on it like savage jackals.

"Lillith, do you hear that? Eagerness and craving…" Naamah caught the scent of weakness. "What is this angel to you?"

"He was something. He is nothing," she stated trying unsuccessfully to control the affliction in her voice.

"You're a sweet liar," Agrat said, nodding to Naamah who started untying the woman from the table. From outside the sultry music was coming to an end. The door opened behind Atone. "It's O.K. to speak your mind here. We are not exactly affiliated."

Marcolf emerged from the shadows leading to the bar. "Is she ready?"

"She'll do, Marcolf," Agrat said, Naamah helping the half-eaten body off the table. She slapped at Lillith's hand as she tried to steal a few more pieces. Lillith comforted it sniffling. Naamah smacked the woman on the behind. "Now shake that money maker. Don't be afraid to just let go and have fun."

"So what about this angel lover?" Naamah said, following the woman before stopping in front of Atone. Atone grasped her stomach turning from the woman who shot her a pleading glance before being jerked forward by Marcolf. Atone's knees bent and she held a hand out to steady herself. Naamah put a hand around her massaging her back, leading her toward the table to sit. Atone didn't resist and there was no point in acting normal now. Naamah smiled warmly, taking her own seat and slid close to her. She swept the hair from Atone's face. It wasn't until Naamah's comforting hands reached her thigh that she jerked away. Naamah smiled playfully scrunching up her nose. Strangely, Atone half believed her when she asked, "There. Are you feeling better now?"

"Yes, thank you."

"Now tell us what is so special about this angel?"

"He's involved in some conspiracy. I'm kind of in a hurry." Atone firmly pushed her hand away, but Naamah stayed close to her. She tried to look at Cronos but suspicion forced her to keep an eye on Naamah. Agrat returned her seat to the blood stained table and faced it backward sitting down with arms folded along the headrest.

"What's his name, this angel lover?" Lillith mimicked Naamah, plunking her elbows on the edge of the table to support her head, not seeming to care about the blood that splashed across her chest with the action, or the blood that pooled around the portion of her arms that rested on the table. Agrat and Naamah both shot her a scolding look before returning their attention to Atone. Lillith pouted.

"Lillith please, she's concerned," Agrat said. Atone watched them all in the reflection of the bloody table before looking back to Agrat, then Lillith.

"Axael," she finally said, simply.

Lillith's eyes lit up at Atone's gentle smile. "Axael, what a lovely name."

"Lillith, Please," Naamah, said, looking from Lillith to Atone and back again.

"Clean this up, Naamah," Cronos cut in and Naamah bared her teeth at Lillith before getting the bucket. As Cronos spoke she began to clean the gore and viscera from the table.

"You should know the routine, Atone. Information is traded in exchange for a service. Now Naamah has suggested beautician work."

"I said that," Lillith whined. Cronos ignored her.

"I really only make weapons," Atone said, gesturing to display Longing and Mercy. He leaned forward appraising the quality of her handy work. Satisfied he smiled and leaned back into his chair that groaned against the weight.

"You make art, Atone," he huffed, the smile quickly fading. "All I ask of you to do is make more. There are fourteen new arrivals in the other room over there. All I want you to do is doll them up, make them art."

"And I get the information first?" She blurted, and then retracted, trying to find some scheme, some plot that he had to screw her. It was, after all, the nature of this place.

"We are not going anywhere," Cronos said, slowly. She thought about it. She couldn't find the hook. She waited longer, feeling that if she waited long enough the trick would reveal itself. But time wasn't something on Axael's side or hers.

"Fine," she said, through clinched teeth, expecting the small print clause that would bind her in servitude once more.

"I understand your mistrust, Atone," he croaked with a low belch of sound. He patted her shoulder as she looked at the ground. "Two angels came in for a night to let the darkness pass then left taking the road south. Then a single angel came in, asked some questions regarding the others, and then pursued them. Three out of three angels all heading south. My guess, and a knowledgeable one, is that they were going to the Camael and Assaih Crossroads between Diablo and Beelzebub's respective kingdoms. I'm afraid that's all I know. Where they went from there is beyond me."

"Thank you," she sighed rising from the chair. "Well let's get started," she breathed out in a sigh before heading for the back room that held her workload. His arm snaked out quickly to take hers and pulling her to a stop. She tried to pull free as he nudged her toward the bar and the way out. She fought against him confused.

"I think your quest is more important at the moment," he gurgled, indifferent to her mad flailing. When she calmed down he let her go. "As I said, we're not going anywhere."

"Thank you," she said, with a grin rivaling his own. "Thanks a lot." She scanned the area, eying the sisters before heading for the door. She locked her eyes on Naamah; there was something, an angry, pained expression. It was the look she had seen from many people, every time she took a life in the name of God, every time they cursed his name to the heavens when they were betrayed. The same look she had to bare by uncountable humans, before their lives, their souls, were snuffed out by the raging waters she helped rise. Only this time the bitter loss and hatred was different. Naamah pulled her gaze free and her eyes fell to Cronos instead.

"Hurry back, Atone." Naamah feigned a smile glancing back at her briefly before looking back at Cronos. Atone nodded and left. She cast her gaze down avoiding the dinner from minutes ago, now dancing provocatively on the stage, her hands clasping the four corners of her cut flesh, trying to keep the tears from showing weakness to her captive audience.

Inside Cronos' chamber Lillith's eyes followed her departure. When she was out of sight she glanced between Naamah and Cronos. Naamah felt Lillith's eyes on her and clenched her teeth, growling. Lillith didn't notice the change. "Naamah, is he really going to let her leave?"

Cronos answered for her. "Of course. She's a bigger part of something." He rose from his chair. Though a large creature he showed no sign of problems as he walked around the table, and opened the door for the final act of the night to be prepared for her number. He took her hand carefully. Agrat closed the door behind her. She stroked the fair-skinned girl's dirty blonde hair, feeling the nerves tighten muscle as Agrat's fingers graced her skin. She whispered something to the girl that tried to sooth her. Naamah set the bucket back in the closet before looking over her shoulder at Cronos and the rest. Lillith was already sitting at the table smiling with her active desire manifesting itself by a playful, unstoppable swinging of her legs.

"There you go with your cryptic demigod babble again," Naamah bit the words. The room looked at her sensing the hostility of her words even with most of the bitterness swallowed.

"Naamah, if you're that interested why don't you go with her?" he belched back. Agrat and Lillith worked carefully binding the woman's arms. She started to fight, realizing the trap. Her mind raced at the sick depravity these new employers demanded from her. She should have known better. Cronos reclaimed his seat, her legs kicking out at him. Her heel caught him across the face, another to the large bulbous eye. Nothing seemed to help. He clasped her legs one in each hand with the most gentle of caresses spreading them to either side of the table's edge. Her muscles tensed to kick out but they were held firm without any chance at freedom. Lillith and Agrat took to clasping the shackles firmly making sure not to tear the flesh.

"Well I do so hope she comes back," Agrat said. "This one is all wrong."

Naamah walked over tossing a scalpel toward her. The silver, shining blade twirled in the air. Closer and closer it flew. The woman turned her head watching the blade as it whistled toward her, she fought violently, futilely as the blade neared her neck. It sliced through the flimsy strap of the woman's top. With a hard *thunk* it sunk its way into the wooden table, the handle resting along her neck. With every gasp she felt it, cold against her skin. Lillith pulled it from the table, making the woman jerk away. Naamah stood over her now, taking her head in her hands. She bared her teeth. Every time the woman tried to look away she would force her to look in her eyes. Not taking her gaze from the women's face she ripped the thin fabric from her prone body. She smiled, watching the shame and fear in her eyes. She could feel her own cravings; her lust as she leaned against the woman's restrained hand making her feel the moisture of Naamah's arousal. She pivoted her hips, grinding against the captive hand, taking satisfaction in her control, her dominance over her. Lillith played with the knife flicking it carelessly close to the woman's eyes. Her gaze, locked on Naamah, was broken only by the dancing blade. Too afraid to move her head the rest of her squirmed against her restraints only succeeding in causing more of Naamah's twisted affection to coat her clenched fingers. Cronos absently stroked her calf calling in a loud bellow for Marcolf. The smiling bartender appeared swiftly to the beckoning of his master.

"Marcolf, Atone will be leaving shortly. After she leaves Set someone after her. Tell them to watch her but make no move until I say."

"Yes, Sir," Marcolf nodded leaving the room to fulfill Cronos' wishes.

Chapter 4

"Those are pretty weapons," Marcolf said, watching her as she readied for her search south. "They must come with some story."

Atone looked down at her weapons feeling a tear well up in her eye. She thought of them and their history. Longing and Mercy were two ornate fist-loading daggers. Her mind drifted to Axael and herself. How similar they were to her weapons. "Not really."

"Well if you don't want to talk about it…"

"It's fine, really. It was just a long time ago." Her thoughts drifted to their first meeting…

"Where are we going?" Nathaniel Longley asked the woman leading him. His battered leather duster flapped angrily against the wind, the ends torn and shredded like an old flag. The sky, a harsh red, turned hazy by a thin dusty fog that clung to his duster and faded jeans. His shoes had worn thin from travel doing little to protect his aching feet from the jagged rocky path, occasionally interrupted by razor sharp brambles. The tangled thorns and ridged stones were unmerciful against his already weary clothes. He looked ahead to the woman he followed. At least they weren't in the salt fields any more though the terrain was little comfort. She never seemed affected by the surroundings, soldiering on through the harsh environs without any sign of fatigue or agony. Her pale skin seemed to glow an unearthly red to match the blood colored sky. Her light orange hued hair closed around her head like the hood of a cape, ending just before her delicate shoulders. The wind that fought so unmercifully against him seemed only to tease her periodically as she scouted ahead. Her attire was primitive. Her thin frame was covered sparingly. Her top hugged around her firmly below the breasts and above the abdomen and was simply tied behind her neck leaving the majority of her back exposed. The sparse fabric ended in tassels that danced mockingly below her breasts. They seemed to laugh at his misery. The skirt, a matching blue though purple in the light, was slit high, showing most of her shapely, athletic legs as it billowed, a peaceful, graceful, and hypnotic pattern in the midst of the roaring wind. The thin dust began to thicken in its efforts to conceal them. Nathaniel quickened to a brisk walk, then a jog. The woman in front never changed her pace nor did he shorten the distance between them.

"To someplace safer. It's not far," she said. Her voice sounded distant as she disappeared from sight into the blowing dust. The sound of animals grew closer, an unseen scurrying through the underbrush, the scream of prey being devoured. Nathaniel's eyes grew wide but nothing helped penetrate the blood like fog and the dark twisted shadows, undistinguishable from one another but all menacing.

"Nathaniel, Where are you?" She beckoned, when the sound of his struggling footfalls could no longer be heard. She turned to face back the way she came but was also blinded by the dusty, ash-laced fog. He heard her voice. She was close but the rocky terrain bounced her voice endlessly, first in front, then behind and so on until her position was impossible to find.

"How the Hell would I know?" he shouted back, after the rippling echoes of her call subsided at last.

"Follow my voice," she said. Nathaniel stumbled through the unforgiving terrain falling into jagged rocks that tore at the knees and hands. Straining against the greedy, grasping vines of the thorn bushes he could feel the sting of the wounds followed by the burn of his own sweat pouring salt in them. Wrenching free he heard her call again. A vague shape becoming that of the woman appeared before him.

"It's not much further, Nathaniel. Come," she beckoned waving for him to follow her. As he stood on shaky, unreliable legs she turned away to lead him once more.

"Hold on, how do you know my name?" He said, partially from a nagging doubt gnawing at his stomach and partially to by some time to steel his resolve. When he realized she wasn't going to wait he took his chances with her rather then the surroundings and took up his ragged, weary march behind her.

"Candice told me," she said, not turning to face him. She seemed to slump for a moment as though wounded by the words from her mouth.

"You know Candice?" He blurted in disbelief the sound of her name stopping him in his tracks and sent an electric surge up his spine.

"Of course, who do you think sent me?" She shrugged, a growl of annoyance forming in her voice. "It's not like I enjoy being here. It's dangerous for me out here as well. We can talk when we are inside."

Atone

Nathaniel's brow furrowed down. His whole body tensed, forced against his will to face some buried pain. His voice was starting to waver as he began to speak. "Candice is dead."

At the words even now he could feel tears welling up in his eyes, the agony of her life pulled violently from his fingers against his will or his desire. He clutched his chest, as if trying to scratch a wound that never healed. "She's been dead for seven years."

She took his hand and he could feel the slenderness of it calloused by hard work. She smiled at him and he saw her eyes, void of any color, and he could feel himself floating, lost in the dark nothingness of oblivion set in her glistening black orbs. Her attempt at a comforting smile faded from her lips noticing his slipping soul. She jerked her gaze away closing her eyes tightly. She held back a pain all her own. "Nathaniel, I... Where do you think you are?"

She could feel his hand go limp in hers and she released it, the fact of his plight dawning on him. She took a step from him. The fog turned to ash, blinding him and burning his lungs. The sound of savage animals grew close. He felt his heart pounding.

"Nathaniel," she called. Staggering through the darkness, breathing in the burning sky, he tried to follow her voice. Plumes of ash thick smoke clouded the air around him, confusing him as he stumbled lost in the dark. Each noxious bout of tainted air sent him wandering in another direction, Nathaniel trying to protect his lungs from the vicious air that attacked him. The sound of baying hounds grew closer and he heard long bony nails clattering against the rocks in a rapid beeline for him. He ran in the corrupt darkness blindly. The heat to the base of his neck made his hair rise. He turned only to see darkness. But this darkness was close. Very close. He smelled the rotten gore, felt burning, dripping saliva on his face. He opened his mouth to speak but the guttural rumble from the creature in front of him drowned out his sound. He inched back but the dark form stayed in front of him.

"Go away!" he backed up only to feel the cold, solid stone behind him. On impulse he pulled back from it, so freezing that it made even more torturous the searing heat in the air. The stone wall, chill to the touch, frosted his forearm, the heat making it boil from his arm. Nathaniel screamed provoking the beast to act. Two orange orbs opened to stare at him, and then a blast of blistering heat as it roared an exhale, the growl deafening him. Nathaniel bowed low, closing his eyes, fear bending his body to expose as little flesh as possible. His mouth opened in a twisted, silent scream. He felt clawed hands pierce his flesh pulling him upward. His flesh tore and he dangled helpless, his arms trying feebly to defend himself. He grabbed the creature's arms to find them soft.

"If we linger here we're both doomed," the mysterious woman said from behind, close to his ears. Her soft gentle touch comforted him as she entwined around him. Her soft flesh and gentle urging were a moment of ease in a ceaseless torrent of pain. It was a moment that passed too soon. She drew her clawed fingers from where they grabbed him. An eerie, unnatural glow emanated from the wound allowing him to see her fingertips. Thin fish bone like claws refracted the light creating a prism effect that shined back at him. Tiny barbs clung to the gory pieces of his flesh. His mind tumbled madly, trying to figure out just who or what his savior was. This was quickly followed by where the light came from. An agonizing tremor traveled through his body when he gazed inside his open wound to find nothing. She left him on the icy rock to resume their travel. He leapt unsteadily to his feet in a burst of adrenaline and took hold of her arm.

"What the Hell is going on here?" He shouted forcing her to look at him. She tried to turn her gaze away to avoid locking eyes but his resolve outweighed her effects.

"I'm sorry Nathaniel, but it's a fact. You're dead," she said, giving up to his will. He deserved that much. He stood there gazing into her eyes for any sign of deception any hint that she was tricking him in some way. After finding nothing he at last released her and she turned away. Her voice faded, as though she herself had to face the truth instead of him. "We have to keep moving."

They walked on in silent darkness. She no longer kept her distance. There was no point now. After many heavy footfalls the silence was broken. She jumped at the sound. The creature had found a way past the stone and had returned to their trail.

"What is that thing?" he asked, finding it a strain to speak. He felt her claws take his hand, clasping it tightly, painfully as she broke into a run. He jerked along after her desperate to keep up. With every step Nathaniel's lungs burned. His chest was wet with sweat and it burned as he clutched it with his free hand. Even in death he was out of shape and despite the urgency he couldn't help wonder why he still felt all this torture, if it was how she said it was.

"Can't... go on," he wheezed. She took hold of something and nudged it hitting him with a cold refreshing breeze that made him gasp. He tried to breathe, the air scratching his throat. In the meager light he could make out a door marked with sorrowful angels in armor, swords held in both hands in front of them. The dim green glow made the decorative carvings on it warp; creating haunted shadows that shivered furiously with each ragged breath Nathaniel took. The woman creature let go of him needing both hands to open the door fully.

"We're almost there," she encouraged though the beast was closing in fast. Another roar so close that Nathaniel had to cover his ears. So close.

A light shattered the dark, forcing Nathaniel to shield his eyes. The agonizing yelp of the beast made Nathaniel cower. It moved on retreating to the shadows.

"Who are you?" Nathaniel asked the woman as she stopped, gesturing for him to enter, then stepped inside herself. He stepped in after her, not daring a moment of thought to steal away a chance at safety. The open door led straight into a kitchen.

"My name is Atone," she spoke soft, her eyes downcast. He watched as she walked to the sink to clean the grime from her hands. An eerie combination of moans echoed through the house, accompanying every step she took. The room was narrow and roughly circular with a passage leading to another room. The chamber was lit with a soft and yellow glow that seemed to rise out of the ground by some mystical means that Nathaniel was not knowledgeable of. A second light was on in the other room leaving the thin gap between them in ominous shadow nearly concealing what appeared to be a closet door. The kitchen was sparsely decorated, only a lone white table and some chairs carved to depict twisted images of faces. Half melted candles from above tracked melted wax along the walls and left splotches on the ground in a corner. Several simple wooden cabinets climbed up the seemingly endless walls eventually disappearing into the darkness and the rafters. There thin white paint, now yellowed and aged, crumbled off at the slightest touch leaving a fine white powder on his fingertips.

"So you knew… know Candice, huh? Is she here? Is she O.K.?" He trailed off as he saw her tense up. Bowing his head low he stepped over to her, each step provoking a moan from the floorboards that seemed to add more misery to his host. "Hey are you O.K.?" he asked, reaching around her comfortingly. She turned into him, crying gently into his arms.

"I'm sorry. So sorry," she spoke in sniffles, her arms wrapping around him, navigating him slowly to the dark corridor.

"Why? You got me out of there right? You got me to safety," he urged as the shadow engulfed him. A strange rustling clamored in the darkness.

"Safety. No," she said, her eyes wallowing in tears. "Safer."

Chains twisted around him pulling him from her. She fell to her knees sobbing and retreating back to the light of the kitchen. She collapsed in on herself not wanting to face what deception she weaved. "I'm sorry. Sorry I have to do this. It will be better for you."

As Nathaniel fought against his chains he could see her shake and jerk savagely from some foul attack deep within herself. Two broken remnants of wings forced their way from her back, her skin grew red with fine scales covering patches of flesh.

"Please, whatever you do don't scream. You'll only make it worse. Worse for both of us."

"What the Hell?" The sharp blow from the hammer knocked the rest of his words from him. The second hammer swing made her scream and cry, tears burning down her face like liquid fire. The third sent them both to their knees.

With each swing, each collision, she could feel his pain, not only from the mallet in her hand but the life that he lived. He began to scream as the chains started their flesh-melting glow, a blinding bright yellow. The violent glowing chains scorched his skin and muscle tissue charring it black. The chains tightened as they worked, slicing off crisp chunks of flesh that crumbled in their falling to the ground like burnt parchment exposing the raw soul underneath. Raw and malleable.

"Shut up, just please shut up," Atone cried hoisting the hammer high to land squarely on the translucent green image of his skull. It flattened pushing outward like splashed water frozen in time. She recoiled, holding her head "These images," she gasped clasping her temple. He looked up at her, eyes distorted by the blows of the hammer each swing drew more

memories to his mind and hers in unison.
Memories like his soul, distorted with every
treacherous impact. Bent folded and mutilated
before becoming nothing but a forgotten
nightmare.

The seventh swing. Junior High after a
football game where he got beat up behind the
bleachers.

Ninth swing. Making out with Candice
at her parents' house he was trying in vain to
slip his hand up her shirt.

Twelfth swing. Succeeding, feeling her
warmth against his skin as they shared their first
time.

Fifteenth swing. Staring up at the sky
wondering, dreaming of what their life was
going to be.

"Stop this. Don't you see what I have to
do? It's better this way," she tried to console
him or more honestly herself, trying to ease her
own tortured mind. "I'm sorry," she repeated
over again. The tears mixed into him as she
forced his essence to a shape. The physical pain,
long since numbed, was made fresh mentally as
every memory was twisted with his shape. Her

vision blurred and she drew back to clear her eyes.

"Why are you...?" The mutilated soul wanted to plead, only able to release a pain wracked wail. "Why are you taking my life away?"

"You are already dead, Nathaniel," she answered him without hesitation. Realizing she could understand his wailing he took advantage of the meager break.

"My memories, Why?" He pleaded.

"Why don't you tell him, Atone?" A voice drifted from the doorway. From the darkness outside a robed man, bone armor guarding his shoulders and chest stepped in. Drawing back his hood he claimed a chair by the table. The newcomer flung his head back running a clawed hand through his thick black hair to shake out the dust and ash. Unlike Atone's his claws were thick and black growing lighter as they merged with his fingers, armored in a crustacean like exoskeleton. The line of his jaw was bearded with several small yellow spikes their tips stained dark green. A cleft lip revealed several severe fangs, reminding Nathaniel of a Shark he caught with his father... Where... lost... His skin was dark, a shade lighter than blood, eyes were sunken in and seemed like yellow sparks crawling from the shadows.

"Lihatiel, I told you not to bother me when I work," she scolded. The force of her voice was betrayed by the tears she wiped from her face.

"Of course," he said, turning his attention to the twisted form once Nathaniel's. He claimed his chin with his claws looking studiously into Nathaniel's eyes. "This kind of work is hard on her. She's too emotional. She's a former Akia after all. She has a closet full of unfinished projects. Rest assured it hurts everyone involved. Even her. Why your little Candice... Oh but I forget myself," he taunted turning Nathaniel's face to the closet door.

"Don't you dare, Lihatiel!" she said, putting herself in front of him. A loud crack sounded as the boney ridges of his hand collided with her jaw. Blood splattered from her mouth and chairs knocked over as Atone fell to the ground sputtering from her raged wound.

"You may be a soul forger, Atone, and that makes you a prize for our lord Beelzebub but never forget that I am a general. I will not let a subordinate deny me!" Lihatiel towered over

Atone her bloodstained hand clutching the shredded pieces of her jaw and neck. Satisfied that his subordinate realized her place Lihatiel turned back to Nathaniel. "Women, Nathaniel. So sweetly they bring a man down. So softly they bring him to ruin, so gently they try a man's patience."

She began to rise. That was one big mistake. A blur… swift, blinding motion cracked bones before she even saw. The kick landed solid to her stomach, sending bile and acid charging outward through the blood. She struggled to retreat under the table the only meager safety she could get to. "Know your place!" Lihatiel shouted smashing a fist down on the table, making her cower into an even tighter ball.

"Now I believe we have a reunion to get underway." Lihatiel threw open the closet door. The room flooded with the sounds of agony and despair. Words and phrases poured out in waves, many incomprehensible but their agony could all be felt. "Where's mother… My eyes, I can't see… No, daddy, please. Don't…" Every echoing plea and mottled wail was a memory stolen and corrupted.

"Oh, Candice. There's someone here to see you," Lihatiel called, poking his head into the black shadows beyond the closet door.

Lihatiel pulled back from the moaning madness to look back at Nathaniel sneering. "She's not finished putting on her face." Lihatiel faded into the darkness the sounds of wails growing stronger. "Candice I'm sure he doesn't care. He's come all this way to see you…"

Nathaniel twisted around in his chain struggling for freedom. Atone rose to her feet supporting herself with a broken chair.

Enough of this," Lihatiel roared in the shadows. From the darkness flew a form. Nathaniel rocked jarring his bound arms and legs against the chains. The flung form collapsed beneath him releasing a muffled groan. Nathaniel could here scratching, thudding as it struggled to escape its revelation. Nathaniel stared at the door to the closet not wanting to face the thing that scrambled for cover behind him. Lihatiel Emerged from the doorway, arms crossed in self-gratifying satisfaction.

"Aren't you at least going to look at her? Your precious Candice," Lihatiel sneered waving a hand. Nathaniel swallowed hard tightly closing his eyes. Remember her like she was, he told himself trying to wake himself from this ill and unmerciful dream. Lihatiel unfolded his arms, muscles rippling under the bone armor, as he took a step forward the humor gone from his face. "I could always make you."

Nathaniel readied himself. Whatever was to come it wouldn't affect him he told himself. But as Nathaniel looked down to see a naked soul half formed, all his attempts to will everything to an acceptable fate shattered in the face of what he saw. The mutilated creature's bladed and pronged former hands shielding its mauled face. Her legs were crippled by the sledge and struggled in vain to crawl away. The forged limbs made it impossible to save her modesty, her legs broken at the hip to keep the legs apart while the arms where forced upward and could not reach below the neck. Her twisted legs were no longer good for escaping and it wasn't long before she collapsed, exposed to anything that wanted to bear witness. Tears streamed endlessly over its… her face. Her long fiery red hair soaked up the salty beads as they tumbled unceasingly from her eyes. Her full lips cringed back in a silent cry. Her nose an unmistakable slope jutting upward at the last moment. The small dent in her ear lobe and the pencil eraser mole at her neck were unmistakable. Nathaniel's eyes widened.

Atone

"Beautiful isn't she?" Lihatiel said,
twisting her hands back from the disfigured part
of her face displaying its wretchedness in
contrast to the purity of her naked and shivering
torso. Her legs raked across the floor trying to
find stability. Candice gasped at the sight of
Nathaniel, tears beginning their torrent anew.
Her thorny bladed arms reached out to him.
"Well this has been fun. I see what you find so
attractive," Lihatiel smiled sniffing in the scent
of her, "she's gorgeous."

She squirmed as Lihatiel's war calloused
hands groped her breasts savagely, and then
slithered low across the taut muscles of her
torso. He could feel the muscles tighten, the legs
unable to protect her as the barbed fingers found
their way between them. Her mutilated mouth
squealed and her breathing grew rapid as her
womanhood grew moist. Blood and erotic juices
flowed across her thighs joining the melted wax
on the floor. "Yes, does this make you angry?"

"Very much so," Atone hissed claws
piercing through the muscle under his ribs.
Lihatiel's eyes opened wider. His fingers
retreated from Candice, the barbs leaving torn
flesh in their passing. Before he could counter
attack, the broken chair leg was driven
downward from the base of the neck avoiding

64

the armor to find what meager heart dwelled inside his chest. "As I said before..."

"I know. I'm just trying to put your mind in the right place that's all," he tried to joke through the pain and blood. Composing himself despite the awkward position he staggered for the door. "I'll be taking my leave then," he said, taking a mock bow before disappearing once more into the outside world.

Atone slammed the door behind him then set to the task of reorganizing her tables and chairs trying to loose herself in the meticulous placement of her ruined items. Too much was ruined. She couldn't find peace in the wake of Lihatiel's chaotic destruction. She hoisted up her mallet.

"He makes me so angry," she fumed. Candice shuffled over to the wall but Atone captured her hoisting her up adjacent to Nathaniel. Like him the chains bound her to the will of Atone.

"You will always long for each other but you will always be this way," she spoke in a growl, her humanity bleaching away to nothing, the colors in her eyes bleeding out until they were a pure white. "So near to each other, so close but never one. Never will you be united as before, you are the tools to wage my war. You will be my strength. You will be my servant souls. Mine and no other until your penances are fulfilled. Then and only then will I release you. Only then will I let you be at peace, together."

The hammer swung hard and three souls as one squirmed in agony. "Your souls will be sentenced to Hell until your sins are burned from you. Serve me and your sentence will be paid." Fire raged in her eyes, glowing in her mouth as she spoke. Steam rose from her body as she forced the souls of her victims into shape.

Her body quivered at the blow to Nathaniel's back, chains rattling. Atone fell to her knees, roaring and writhing around in pain, a mirror reflection of the torment of Nathaniel's rattling chains above her. After a moment Atone rose up panting and hissing trying to sooth her pain. Candice and Nathaniel stared at each other in sympathy a glimmer of color returned to Atone's eyes before fading and departing once more. "I promise your freedom in time."

"…and that's about it," she said. "Two lovers separated forever." She looked at her weapons. One had to watch the others decent, to watch her suffer for her sins. She thought of what Axael had felt when she plunged from the heavenly heights that fateful night. How he must have hurt for her sake. "It's nothing special, really."

She turned her head, a tear falling to the ground, out of sight from the always-smiling bartender. "Nothing at all."

Chapter 5

      The week Atone spent walking from the bar toward the crossroads seemed like months. Atone walked through the desert heat, the rocky hills shrinking in the distance. The red haze grew brighter as the demonic sun heated the scorched earth. A shrill trumpet of a wounded horse broke the mind numbing silence and overwhelming heat. Atone turned, grateful for something other than excessive heat to occupy her attention. She climbed the sandy dunes following the sound of the horse's trials. The whinnying grew in volume and she knew she must be close. As she crested the burning sand dune she saw the beast entering the plant growth for shade disappearing from sight. Near the meager, inhospitable oasis rotted, sun cooked food and corrupted water sprung from the harsh unforgiving sands. The tainted food was marked in their evil by the collection of sun-bleached bones. She raced for the edge. Knowing the dangers did nothing for her grumbling stomach. As she neared towering ferns and twisted palm trees a rustling warned of something approaching. She dropped down instinctively, blades at the ready. The bushes crashed outward as the dark horse burst loose. The tangling of a savage vine in the underbrush twisted around one of the horses legs. Atone rose, hands out and blades pointing away. She wondered how such a magnificent animal made it this far. She also wondered about the last time she had a decent meal.

"Easy, easy," Atone encouraged submissively bowing her head and avoiding any direct gaze to the eyes. It snorted violently, kicking with one leg, the rest tense, but stationary. "You're hurt. How did you get all the way out here?"

The sinister call of the harrowing beasts made her pull her attention from the animal. The horse whipped its head in a craze searching for the cause of such a noise, or a safe place that seemed increasingly rare. The sky clouded over and ash filled the air, a symbol of their approach.

Atone rubbed her blades together turning slowly for any sign of them. Darker shadows moved through the fog, distorted by the concealing ash clouds. A feral growl caught her attention, making her twist in the dark to find it. She sprung toward it colliding with the oncoming beast. An ashen crust broke lose from its coal skin, the red glowing of molten magma burning under the surface ignited her flesh as she assaulted it. She caught it with her blades.

Atone

Slashing through the surface she ignored the sparks and liquid fire that spewed outward in the wake of her onslaught. The beast yowled in agony clawing out at her. Longing cut through the right wrist, the molten claw thumping into the sand along the toxic pool. Mercy chewed through the left forearm leaving it hanging loosely by a charred layer of harrowing beast flesh. It cried out, molten fire splattering from its jaws. It turned to flee. She leapt over it to deal the finishing blow.

She took one in stead. A second beast hit her sending her tumbling with the corrupted food toward the pool edge. A rotted gourd fell into the pool causing its tainted waters to splash her. The acid burned her. She yelped in pain trying desperately to get it off her. The new beast pinned her, each claw clamping down onto a hand. Her flesh burned. She struggled to avoid its snapping teeth as they tried to take her head. She twisted under the beast, bracing her feet against the monster's midsection. She kicked savagely, throwing it over her and rolling with it to the sinister pool. She freed her hands stabbing into the beast now under her. It was the monsters turn to scream as the acid ate away the creature under her. Mercy and Longing began to wail in agony as the mass under Atone began to give way and bathe them in acid. The beast entered its death throws, telling Atone that her job was done. She leapt from the pool before the rest of the beast dissolved. She checked her weapons. Mercy and Longing, their forged bodies more resilient to the acid, did not have any serious damage.

A third beast appeared, descending like a bomb from the sky. Atone rolled on her back kicking outward to intercept it. She felt the skull cave in as it collided with her, kicking the corpse into the pool to join its brother. She turned, seeing the Harrowing beast that started it all clawing its way toward the horse. She used the new corpse to run across the dangerous waters to the far side of the pool were the horse fought against the vines. The harrowing beast pulled back, yowling. Atone pushed outward with both hands, sinking them deep into its chest. It flailed, violently burning her with every wicked strike. The damage was already done. The harrowing beast slumped low in her arms. She pulled her arms free. The Harrowing beast's intense heat and the acids damage had burned away her mortal seeming, showing the glowing light from within. Her soul was now vulnerable. She was now vulnerable. As the burnt flesh began to cool her seeming began to return, leaving no sign of damage. There was only the painful memory of the event to remind her.

Atone

She approached the horse bringing with her the scent of blood and devil. The horse struggled more against exhaustion than with the vines holding its foot. Atone could see the scars on the horses body, marking a history of a previous demon's attempts to claim it or worse. She didn't blame its hesitation. She represented everything evil it had to face. She spoke softly, gently. It wanted to kick but with its tangled hoof it could only trot in place. Atone was always cautious calling gently. The horse conceded, bowing its head, tired of resisting. She shook its main and patted its neck.

"I see why you've gone so far from the salt fields of Appolyon," she said. It nuzzled her looking for food. She patted its nose checking it over. "There doesn't seem to be any permanent damage. Once you have rested we can get to the cross roads," she said, trying to ignore the grumbling of her craving stomach. "We should probably move to safer places though. This place will only bring us ruin."

Chapter 6

The Order set camp just outside of Goap's labyrinth. Cosmacrater set up his tent pausing every now and then to take in the impressive structure that lay before them, admiring the massive work of art. It was too bad such a creation was here; too bad it had such a diabolical purpose. Finishing his task he entered the tent setting up his belongings so that he could spread open his maps. Most of the land outlaying Sheol was searched with no useful information gleaned. He looked out at Lihatiel, who met up with their group. If he was lucky, Beelzebub would continue to take out his wrath on him. His thoughts were disrupted by the flap to his tent opening. Focalar stepped forward. Lean wiry, muscle twisted tightly around bone concealed by yellow hide. A face, like a lean feline looked back at Cosmacrater. With one look in the eye Focalar bowed his head.

"There is a visitor for you, Sir," he said, submissively.

"Who could possibly…?" His words trailed off at the sight of the white clad beauty stepping into his make shift chamber. She pulled the hood back to reveal her long brown locks shining like coils of copper. Her large, dark doe eyes watched him. He bowed to her. She appeared just as he remembered her. Like him, she appeared as a normal human, though her skin was soft and her scent was a garden of flowers never smelled by human noses. Her presence made the room light in comforting soft yellow glow. She removed her cloak revealing her perfect female form to him. He pulled his eyes away from her focusing instead on Focalar. He saw also the men outside, their mouths watering.

"Focalar, leave us and close the flap," Cosmacrater ordered sternly.

"Yes Sir," he bowed again with a low growl escaping his throat. Cosmacrater shot him a deadly look and Focalar shivered leaving them in peace.

"Hello, Cosmacrater," she said, fighting back tears. He touched her cheek. Noting the demonic features, he pulled it away quickly. He took a fast step away from her as though her very presence hurt him. In a way it did. She took his hand and replaced it to her cheek. Closing her eyes, she tried to remember the way it was. "It's like a strange dream."

"This isn't a dream, Barbellos. You are here," he said, the strength in his voice failing.

"I am only here to visit," she said, softly, opening her eyes to face the truth. A tear managed to escape and he caught it.

"It seems like such a long time ago," he said, softly.

"I come down here to you once a month," she corrected with the attempt to smile at him.

"I know. Things have been trying lately," he spoke struggling in vain to spare himself the pain of looking at what he couldn't have. "I'm sorry it slipped my mind. Please," he motioned to a chair his voice strong again only for her sake. She didn't sit. He smiled with pain, shedding tears of his own. He bowed his head away from her gaze, hiding his tears. "I've missed you Barbellos."

She walked silently to him, cupping his averted head in her hands, and turning it so that he faced her. His eyes were clenched tightly closed as she kissed them. "It won't be much longer. The Penitent is on the path. Then you and the others will be judged."

"And that's good?" he asked, suspiciously, his voice so loud it surprised himself and her.

"Fear not Cosmacrater. All shall return to him," she said, kissing his forehead, hugging him. "Now shall we begin?"

She set up the pedestal so that it sat in front of her and before him as he sat on the side of the bed. "Bow your head. Lord we pray you deliver us…"

He sat there, listening to her words as she continued on. Tears flowed from his eyes hearing her gentle voice pledging fealty to God on the highest. He cried for the memories of God in all of his goodness. He cried for the pain he caused against his father. He cried for the reminder of her, here in the flesh, only to leave again and cause all his pain to bleed anew. He cried for the love they shared and the love he violated.

"Cosmacrater?" she asked, stopping her sermon. Instinctively he sunk his head lower, hiding his shame from her.

"Cosmacrater," she said, taking his head in her hands and gently lifting it for her to see him. "Cosmacrater, I'm sorry. We don't have to do this."

"It's alright, Barbellos," Cosmacrater choked on the words. Composing himself he went on. "I was just…"

"It's O.K.," she said, kissing his tears. "Everything is going to be fine."

"I'm sorry Barbellos," he spoke into her ear, shielding himself from her gaze by getting in close. "I'm sorry I seduced that human. She was so much like you, Barbellos."

"Stop this, please," she said. It was her time to let honesty bleed out in her voice.

"I just wanted you so much I couldn't resist. I corrupted her…" Cosmacrater confessed.

"Don't," Barbellos warned him but her voice weakened to a near whisper.

"…to save you," he finished. It was only after his confession that he dared to look at her. Their lips danced close to each other.

"Don't glorify or sugar coat it," she said, pulling away from him. Her eyes were lit by a deeply seated wound. "You didn't sacrifice yourself. You defiled yourself."

Cosmacrater covered his eyes as a waterfall of pain cascaded through his spread fingers.

"I can't say I'm not grateful. If you hadn't… We might both be here," she stated, holding her pain and her desire in check. "…but no. I can't, I won't. I should go."

"Wait," Cosmacrater pleaded reaching out to her. He caught her in his arms as she turned back to face him. Their lips collided, locking in a longing kiss. Cosmacrater's hand slipped low to the small of her back feeling her soft, gentle flesh. Her leg hooked around his. She smiled, but pushed herself away with unexpected force, pulling them apart. "Have you ever wanted to?"

"Still asking the wrong questions after all these years," she said, kissing him gently but briefly on his cheek. "But the answer is it doesn't matter what I want."

"But what do you want?" he asked, his voice growing stronger.

She reached out for the flap to the tent. He resisted restraining her again. "You," she said, her voice craving, wanting. It quickly grew stern. "But I need him. I have to go."

"Take care, Barbellos," he said, showing her out. He looked savagely around his eyes settling on Focalar whose hands stayed firmly to the fletching of his arrows. He could see the hatred on his archer's face. The cape of Barbellos danced in the breeze wrapping around her. Arches of translucent light pushed through from her back and in one fluid motion of this light she rose from the ground leaving a whirlwind of dust. Cosmacrater kept his eyes on her. "Don't ever, Focalar. Ever."

Chapter 7

Atone and her new friend rode south to the two huge cave systems known as the crossroads. A strange pale green glow came from inside, radiating from some subterranean fungus. The horse neighed and gnashed its teeth. She absently patted its neck, her gaze watching for any movement of shadows in the light.

"I don't have a good feeling about this either, Faust," she agreed stroking it more trying to calm the black steed beneath her. She could feel its tense muscles bulge under its scarred skin. "Come on."

As they entered the cave, she saw the thick brambles of a thorn bush; its wide, broad leaves covered the vines that snaked out along the ground and up the cave walls.

"This doesn't look like demon made foliage," Atone said, quizzically. She slid from the horses back to get closer to the twisting vines. She sheathed her hands into her weapons in case it was more than it seemed. Faust, her steed, sniffed cautiously as well before nipping at the leaves with his teeth. The horse coughed as the leaves scratched his throat. Atone looked over and smiled sympathetically. "Eat up, pal. This is the closest you're going to get to something edible." The horse seemed to agree and kept eating the harsh, abrasive plant. Atone left him venturing further along the vines to the brunt of the plant. The trail led to a wall of flora at the intersection of the two massive cave systems.

"Show me your secrets, little plant. What brought you here?" she asked, poking around. As if on command she heard the sound of metal hitting rock. She froze, her eyes looking for the creator of the sound within the foliage, her hand squeezing for a tighter hold on Mercy. At the base of the bush lay a broken sword. She pulled it to her, studying the engraved hand guard. "Israfel's symbol? I should have known," her voice grew to a growl. She spat, the very sound of his name on her tongue growing foul and bitter. It may have been God's judgment to cast the 'rebels' out but it was Israfel that wanted even more than that. His men patrol the gates in Gehenna that deny any form of communication from lord Beelzebub's emissary seeking retrial. It was Israfel that sent spies into Hell to plot and scheme his own filthy desires, and commissioned the first Electors to arrive. Her hand clasped tight to the metal handle in her palm trying to crush it with her hate. She spat again.

Putting the broken sword in her belt she used Mercy and Longing to chop away some of the foliage. In moments a foot appeared inside. The vine retreated at the onslaught pulling back to show all of Axael, dead and bound by the heavenly shrub. A wail of agony tore free from her lungs and echoed from her mouth, so horrendous that the plant itself recoiled farther still from the sound. She clawed out trying to reclaim the angel, only to trip over the vines. She collapsed to her knees ignoring the jagged rocks that dug into them. Her hands danced toward her face, but refused to cover her eyes. She balled them into fists. Her pain fueled her rage. Tears streamed from her as the wail turned into a roar. She dove at the plant attacking savagely trying again to reach the dead body. This was Hell and he was trapped inside. A rustle echoed through the caves overtaking her raging screams. Then the bush retaliated. Atone duck and wove trying in vain to reach Axael's body. Shrieking fanatically as the plant pulled it away, she followed after it, mindless of whatever trap it may have in store.

"No!" She roared in defiance slashing furiously at the ever-increasing danger. "You can't take him away from me. Not again. Axael!" Soon the vine would overtake her. The foliage pushed her back, and she could feel the thorns dig deep into her flesh. She pushed against them, watching as her angel was pulled deeper into the heart of the beast. There were too many vines. She couldn't see. She could no longer see him. If she could only reach something, a finger, a lock of hair, she could find the strength. She only felt more vines and the ever-growing weight in her heart. She broke her arms free slashing furiously against the angry plant. She roared as the brambles became an impenetrable wall. Through her rage she saw the bush closing in around her. She struggled to reach him, plunging her weapons into the foliage finding only more thorns and vines with no sign of her angel left. Logic pushed past her primal yearning and she at last let the vine take him away from her. She had no choice, again, but to leave him behind. Tears streamed from her eyes as she fled the vengeful plant.

She reached the outlaying vines watching Faust fight with his diner. "Time to move, Faust," she called running toward him. She slipped Mercy from her arm, strapping it to her belt. Vines snaked out after her. Slashing them away, she saw Faust galloping toward her. She sprung from the ground landing on his back as Faust passed her. Taking his mane in her right hand she slashed out with her left still armed with Longing. The vines coiled closer, Longing fighting valiantly. Soon the vines gave up retreating to their home. After a safe distance was between them she turned to face the shrub. "A sword made with Israfel's symbol and an alien angel killing plant. Axael…" She trailed off. Sniffling back her tears. She busied her mind by thinking of the facts and the enigma they presented avoiding the emotions she didn't want to face. "Two other angels. We'll need to find one of them. I will make them pay, and their master. Hear me, Israfel! I will bring a fate to you worse than death!"

Chapter 8

Atone swept open the door to Asmodius's knocking off the dust. Faust snorted angrily. He pranced at the entrance trying to enter. "No. You have to stay outside. Its O.K. Harrowing beasts won't come here and anyone who will won't bother you for fear of who you might belong to. It will be O.K."

The horse snorted pawing at the step leading up to the door. It even dared rearing up at her in retaliation but Atone held her ground and convinced the animal to stay. Entering the establishment she saw Marcolf's fixed expression. Lillith was crouched down in front of one of the restrained patrons. Naamah, sat at the bar having the house special, a intricate mix of blood alcohol and Styx water known for its unique properties of forgetfulness. It was popular for that reason alone. There wasn't much here a person wanted to remember. Naamah turned to face her, smiling warmly and motioning over. Thankfully no dancer was on the catwalk and the patron's, along with Atone, were spared a degree of pain. Naamah patted the seat next to her, running her finger along Atone's leg as she took it.

"I have a friend outside. A horse." Atone furrowed her brow. "Can you find a place to shelter him? Maybe food and water. No torture."

"Marcolf. Take him to the kennels. I know that it isn't a stable but it should be more than enough space for his needs."

"I said no…"

"He'll be fine, I promise on my own soul. I wouldn't dare hurt you, and it seems to be important to you," she comforted, smiling, caressing her neck. She took a drink feeling the blur run through her mind. She searched her memories trying to find what they were talking about. "Now tell, how did it go?"

"Marcolf?" she asked, pointedly, getting a snarl from Naamah. Marcolf bowed.

"I'll wait, and take you to the kennels myself, ma'am."

"Thank you," she said, jumping at an unwanted touch to her leg.

"Now talk. What's up?" Naamah coxed. Naamah fixed her a drink and offered it. "Unless you want to take your mind off it."

Atone

"He's dead," Atone answered flatly before turning her full attention to Naamah.

"Who's dead?" Lillith raised her head from the tortured patron's lap. Her pretty features were blurred with blood distorting her confused expression even more.

"I'm sorry to hear that, Atone," Naamah said. "Need a hug?" She said, breathing in her ear. Atone, cringed in disgust. She slipped further from Naamah, keeping her distance.

"Is Cronos here?" Atone said, her voice firm, dominating.

"He's in back with Agrat. They'll be there a while," Naamah said, stroking the hair from Atone's face and running a hand along her neckline. "But I've got time if you want to talk about it."

Atone rose from her seat, feeling Naamah's eyes memorizing her from behind. "Not really. But thank you for your concern." She walked toward the back room.

"Atone, I'm sorry," Naamah called after her. She pounced from her seat to intercept her from reaching the door, her empty glass clattering on the bar threatening to fall off. "I don't think you want to go in there." Atone opened the door with her still standing in front of it. Naamah dared to put a hand up against her chest, now not interested in seduction but protection. Atone gave her a confused look feeling this new concern but pushed against her. Naamah bowed her head, moving her hand away. She stormed toward the bar to reclaim her seat.

"Who's dead?" Lillith continued to ask as Atone entered the back room. She could here Naamah vent her frustration on her.

"Shut up, Lillith."

Atone followed the passage to Cronos' chamber. He sat at his throne by the table; Agrat sprawled on top of it holding a wine glass up to catch the droplets from above. The metallic scent of blood filled the room, Atone's eyes following the droplets up to find the source. She saw an ornate chandelier, impaled within its metallic fingers the form of a naked man, now weak and drowsy from blood loss, the fingers collecting the punctured vein's treasures to the center that produced the drip. Agrat looked over to Atone as Cronos ran his tongue along the exposed skin of her plunging neckline. She purred as a thin stream missed the glass and ran down her arm seized immediately by Cronos. "Atone. How fairs the hunt?" Agrat asked.

"He's dead," she said, flatly, brandishing the damaged weapon. "I have a good idea who killed him."

"Israfel's mark," Cronos belched taking his attention from Agrat immediately. She hissed in distaste at the uttering of his name. "That filthy swine. He is no angel. If anyone should be down here it's that loathsome tyrannical prick!" His powerful arm slammed down on the table shaking Agrat violently. Agrat reached out her arm, cooing softly for him to calm himself despite his righteous anger. With his words spoken he reclaimed her arm, his tongue licking hungrily at the renegade stream of blood that dribbled from her arm. Though Agrat motioned to enter she stayed near the door. Agrat looked up at the body and nodded taking a drink from the glass.

"You said there were two other angels, do you have any way of finding them?"

"I can put my runners out. See what they can find. I wouldn't get your hopes up. Angels rarely stay down here long. It's not exactly their kind of place," he croaked leaving Agrat to her own devices. He rose from his chair with surprising ease and stepped toward Atone. "Marcolf."

Atone instinctively took a step back only to find Marcolf there. "Yes, Sir."

"Take Atone and set out the hounds," Cronos said, talking past her to the jester faced barkeep. He took a raspy breath before turning his attention to Atone. "We'll send them after those angels and get you on your way. Now if you'll excuse me…" He trailed off turning back toward the table where Agrat waited, letting the dripping lifeblood cascade down her cleavage. Atone watched, transfixed as she peeled her dress down, letting him claim the streams of life's essence from her. Atone's attention was pulled free by Marcolf.

"If you'll come with me," Marcolf said, smiling. He looked down at the broken sword. "Was that the killers item?"

"Oh, yes," she said, turning away from the macabre embrace of the lovers at the table. Marcolf followed closing the door behind them.

"I'll need that, for the hounds to get a scent," Marcolf asked, awkwardly.

"Sure, take it," she murmured absently handing him the busted sword. He replaced her in the lead escorting her from the main building. Faust was there waiting eager for her company. Marcolf looked up ever smiling. Atone could feel for once since their first meeting that the smile on his face was matched by his true emotion.

"He is truly a magnificent animal. It's a pity they are judged the same as man," he commented more to Faust than Atone. She smiled as Faust followed the two to the kennels. Again Marcolf spoke. Again it wasn't to Atone. "I am truly sorry that our accommodations could not be better. There isn't a stable here. My... Cronos' hounds are very well disciplined. They will not dream of hurting you without my command."

"You have a soft spot for animals, Marcolf?" Atone said. Marcolf jerked his head to notice her as though she surprised him. She smiled softly, genuinely back to him.

"Don't tell Cronos. I don't think the master would understand. He does however understand their usefulness. And it gives me secret joy to train them. I've spent much time with all my hounds," he smiled, confiding in her. "Come let me show you."

Behind the dance hall was little more than a shed, though a large one. Inside could be heard the faint whines and occasional barking, muffled by the insulated walls. The door swung open at Marcolf's touch and no sooner than it moved a towering tan blur of muscle and bone leapt onto him tackling him to the ground. Atone and Faust both jumped back, Atone crouching to a combative stance while Faust trotted eying her for protection. Growling was heard as the hound jerked and pulled viciously at Marcolf's prone body. Another sound reached her ears. Laughter.

Atone relaxed as she heard Marcolf laughing joyously. She reached out for Faust trying to convince him that it was all just a game. More eyes peered out from the kennel but made no move to interfere. Marcolf's laughter subsided and he pushed the animal back to pull himself from the ground. Jagged stones dug into his back and he pulled them free without so much as a sign of pain.

"Jerrod, back. You're making me look bad in front of our visitors." Marcolf chuckled. With the commotion over Atone could see the beast better. He was large for a hellhound almost the size of Marcolf on his hands and knees. Strong thick muscles rippled away from the spine where a row of long spikes protruded from tail to the base of his neck. His ears were long and angular pointing out like horns from the side of his head. His powerful jaws curled back to reveal razor like teeth.

"I am most sorry, Master Marcolf. I was unaware we had company," Jerrod chewed the words. Atone gasped. He looked at her and lowered his head submissively.

"He talks?" She said, surprised. Marcolf patted him on the head lovingly.

"Only Jerrod. He is very special." He led his hound back into the kennel. He stood at the door waiting for Atone and Faust to enter. "I have to admit with Jerrod it's easier to train the others."

Inside she saw many hounds, half the size of Jerrod, a medley of colors between white and black. When they saw Faust they bayed quizzically. Jerrod turned to Marcolf.

"They wonder if they can eat the horse."

"No, Jerrod. This horse is property of Atone. But tell them I have a special mission for them. Tell them that they are to look for two angels," he instructed, holding the sword out for them to smell as Jerrod translated. They sniffed at the weapon in his hand and then one growled and yelped.

"Bonshiva asks if then they can eat the horse."

"No," Marcolf answered followed by a low fierce growl from Jerrod. Bonshiva, a ragged dark brown hound with tattered ears whimpered and stepped back submissively.

"This is by order of Cronos," Marcolf said, sternly. Faust pranced around violently. Atone turned her back to ease her panicking steed. Jerrod led a baying howl that seemed to organize the many hounds. They streamed from the shed steering clear of Faust and his uncontrolled hooves. Jerrod waited eying them as they passed the horse letting out a low growl each time one got to close. When the shed was empty Faust was consolable. Pacing around the room, Faust stayed from the walls where the strongest hound scents lingered. Snorting in dissatisfaction he stood stoic facing the door.

"This is the best we have to offer I'm afraid," Marcolf said, patting Faust's nose before Atone could comfort him.

"It's O.K., Faust," she said, but gave him a concerned look as she left him to follow

Atone

Marcolf. Lillith greeted them as she carried a
large bundle of foliage from the bar. Atone
searched the leaves, vegetables and vines. She
shot Lillith a suspicious look but let her pass.
Lillith was nearly knocked down from the force
of Faust's hunger. Her curses were blanketed by
Marcolf's chuckling. Lillith slammed the door
behind her.

"Don't laugh, Marcolf. I'll tell Cronos,"
she threatened making his mirth fade instantly.
As she stormed back to the main house Marcolf
turned to Atone.

"I'll bring some water out later," he said,
as they walked. When they entered Asmodius's,
Cronos was waiting at the bar. Marcolf
shivered.

"So what's the deal, Cronos?" she asked,
feeling a weight settle on her heart. He looked
up, his toad like features twisting into a smile.

"No deal. My hounds will chase the
scent and inform us of the location of this angel
for you."

"And what do you get?" She hissed,
waiting for the weight to prove itself.

"Whatever you wish to give during your stay," Cronos responded kindly. "Your company at the very least. Of course there are those new arrivals to work on but if helping you is going to hurt Israfel then I am very glad with my decision to help."

"Where do you want me to start?"

"In a moment. No rush." Cronos led her to his chamber. Agrat stepped off the table to head toward him.

"Agrat, go to your sisters," he growled.

"But..," she protested, eyes reflecting pain.

"Go," he ordered, Atone shivered as he appeared to grow larger, more imposing. Without another word of protest she left them closing the door behind her. Though the menacing power he displayed faded away her fear did not. Her mind wondered what devious cravings he expected. Her heart pounded anticipating some ghoulish sinful desire he would force from her.

"I realize our first impression must have shocked you. I want to show you something special," he said, warmly. She readied for battle as the walls rotated, concealing the doors to reveal new ones. She flashed her blades toward him but was surprised that her menacing posturing got no response. In fact he didn't even seem to notice. This made her confused, which made her vulnerable. "Come with me," he chuckled heading for one of the new doors.

She followed him through the doorway. Inside was an amazing garden, flowers and trees spreading outward, with no end in sight. A bright yellow sun shined down on them, and prey animals lounged sleepily next to predatory animals without any fear in their eyes. Birds flew through the air, singing peacefully. In a moment she recognized the lay of the land. It was God's playground. Her heart lifted, the harsh memory of the outside world fading into a terrible dream. She breathed in the rich wilderness scent feeling her spirit lift. This was Eden. This was home. Cronos touched her arm and she turned to face him seeing the Hell behind. She turned away trying desperately to reclaim the illusion. It was gone, the illusion shattered. She clenched her fists tightly her nose crinkled in disgust. Movement distracted her. Cronos pulled her down into the bushes. The leaves parted. From the gigantic ferns stepped a girl.

"Her name is Janie," he whispered. "I found her in the salt fields. When I met her I thought, if I could save just one soul from torment, give one soul peace…"

"Why are you showing me this?" Atone grumbled standing up. He caught her quickly pulling her back toward the door and out of the sight of the girl.

"Out of all the scum, the twisted freaks that come through here, you were different. You've been in Hell and still you do God's work."

"What are you talking about?"

"Who set you on the quest to find this angel?"

"Why do you want to know?"

"After all you've been through, all your time here, you still care."

She rose stepping past him toward the door. He caught her arm. "I felt your pain your disgust at the sisters dining. In many ways you're still pure. Like Janie. All she wanted to do was survive. She did what was necessary.

Yet by doing so she ended up here. Why? Why are you here for that matter?"

"To survive," she hissed pulling her arm free. "Can I get to work now?"

"Tell the sisters none of this," Cronos croaked harshly. Atone growled having enough of this.

"If you want to save her from all of this why don't you just absolve her?" He pulled her through the door her heart partially yearning for the comfort of the false Eden.

"What do you think I am, a Fallen? I'm as much a fallen as you are a human."

"So what are you?"

"You don't know? You must be younger than I thought. Before God used angels he tried to run a world vicariously through demigods."

"You're a demigod?"

"I was."

"So are all these demigods down here?"

"No. God noticed the demigods that were supposed to rule his world were instead squabbling amongst themselves. He knew then that he had to take control. When he appeared most realized their mistake and returned to God. They were remade into the angels that must have sired you," Cronos explained rotating the room again. "Do you see? God showed his true power with the gift of Absolution. Only those that sided with him gained that power. So you see I can't absolve her regardless of want."

"I see," Atone nodded. An emotion overwhelmed her. It was an emotion that wasn't hers. It was the feeling of Cronos missing his opportunity for redemption, a feeling of self-loathing and sorrow. "Don't worry about the sisters," she said, weakly, reflecting his pain.

Chapter 9

Atone felt herself move as she slept. She was rocking back and forth. She was young again just a wisp of a youth, little more than a baby. She was with her parents. The angels that brought her life and in so doing, committing to their own sacrifice. They were standing on a ledge, the playful breeze kissing her eyes awake. It was dark, the full face of the moon shining fully on the family. She saw the skeletal trees of winter, but it was not cold, only a comforting chill to her skin. Below them at the foot of the grand, magnificent pillar of earth was the frozen waters of the depths below, the raw materials of souls known as the guff now frozen over. The sound of ice rubbing against stone, wanting to flow free, was heard from the cliff as the tingling of a chime, gentle and peaceful with no hint of the anger it felt in its restraint. She cooed at the sound pawing at her ears to welcome it. Her mother, realizing that she was awake smiled lovingly down at her, smiling despite the tears that rolled from her cheeks, freezing before leaving her face and turning into little ice spears that pierced through the thin layer of snow on the ground. She let out a *shhh*, soft and quiet. Atone reached up from her mother's arm to touch the ice forming on her skin. It hurt. She wanted to cry, because her mother cried. Instead she turned her attention to her father who soldiered on with no sign of emotion. This silenced any sob she would have made. Her baby brow curled into a confusing bump, her face frozen in a frown. She returned to her mother's face, and felt her mother's arm around her trembling. She felt the cold. She felt the fear. What was this feeling? She thought. Why was mother feeling this? She never wondered why she felt it herself. She watched as her mother faced the bright orb ahead of them and she followed her gaze to it. The moon was gone, replaced by the warmth of the All Maker. Her mother raised Atone into the sky holding her away from herself. Atone squirmed uncomfortably wanting to remain close to her mother. Regardless of want she felt herself pulled from her to drift in the air between her mother and the face of God.

"You know this was forbidden," the voice spoke loud but without hate or rage, if anything it was pained and sorrowful. "Not only the proof of child but of the sign of your sin between your legs. You shall be punished. But you have served me well until this day. I will be merciful. You shall join the princes of earth, never again to step foot in Heaven." Atone turned in the air to see her parent's heads bowed low their hands trying to shield their sex from the eyes of the Lord. Diana looked up, her face a blurred mask of pain. Atone realized that it was not for their punishment but her desire for the child suspended in the sky in front of her.

"What of our child?" she asked, with her voice choked by her sobs.

"The lack of her shall be your punishment. The reward of your lust is mine to cherish. Now go."

The memory aged, until once again many years later Atone stood on this ledge. She smiled through the tears. She saw the face of God. Taking her eyes from him she leapt from the edge rocketing toward the ground.

She awoke, jerking up in a flash at once feeling the strange softness of her new surroundings. Faust snorted near her, sniffing her sweat-drenched flesh. She reached up absently stroking his nose.

"It's just a dream, Faust. It's alright," she said, laying back down facing him. "Just an old memory."

Chapter 10

The hounds raced across the salt fields, ran feverishly across the endless desert, through the dangerous swamps they prowled. They searched the living graveyards and navigated expansive canyons, their nose ever to the wind. Their paws danced cautiously through the burning wastelands and left prints in the snows of the harshest, blizzard burdened barrens. Through every cave their noses, eyes, and feet covered, they pushed on endlessly through the hostile realms of the underworld. Jerrod growled turning his nose to the air to howl his frustration to the ash-laden winds.

It was at the ruins of Goap that Cosmacrater heard the angry howl. He led his troops from the wreckage they caused. He held a hand out to signal his men to stop. Lihatiel brushed against it unaware as he searched the horizons for the owner of the howl. Cosmacrater's face twisted painfully, pushing outward to lengthen his nasal passages. The visage of the beast was one of many demonic abilities Cosmacrater possessed. His nose broadened with an agonizing popping as bones bent to fulfill his needs. His face took on a darker, almost black tint, eyes changing to that of an animal. Indeed his visage began to reflect the hounds he searched out. His powerful nose breathed in, seeking a scent.

"What is it?" Lihatiel asked, impatiently, getting an elbow to his chest from Cosmacrater's outstretched arm.

"Those hounds. They have her scent on them," he said, in a low growl. His eyes met Focalar's. With a subtle nod of his head, Focalar scanned the horizon seeing the vaguest outline of the beasts on the prowl. "Take aim to wound."

"Yes, Sir," he said, with an eager grin. He drew an arrow silently from his quiver. Notching it to his bow with equal sound, he pulled it back, his eyes steady on the horizon. The arrow raced for miles high into the air. Reaching its apex it began its descent plummeting to the jagged rocks with such speed that it glowed, igniting as it fell. Without a sound one of the small images of the hounds collapsed, the other forms taking a quick turn away from their comrade. Cosmacrater's men charged forward with a wave of his arm. The small figure grew ever larger as they covered ground. Focalar was the first to reach it, notching a second arrow. The hound interrupted its whining to make a futile attempt to growl at the assassin at his head, only achieving a chuckle from Focalar for his efforts. The arrow severed its spine rendering the hounds back legs useless. Cosmacrater stepped up next to the wounded animal, lowering himself in front of the hound locking eyes with it. It fought savagely against the gaze but Cosmacrater's mesmerizing eyes held him fast. All the dying hound could do was snap out at the air between them. Lihatiel arrived to see the hound as Cosmacrater's eyes weakened him. The hound's hide shriveled and cracked painfully. Its eyes dulled to a lifeless grey. It gave one last weak snap at the air before it was too weak to move. Cosmacrater on the other hand seemed stronger, wiser.

He rose from the ground, flexing greater muscles than he started with. His skin seemed to radiate with youth and vigor. He smiled with the heady feeling of his mystic gains. "Atone has this hound looking for angels."

"Angels? What for?" Lihatiel demanded. Cosmacrater thought searching his new found memories. When they failed to provide an answer he used his own. "The book. It has to be. She made some deal to deliver them the book."

"Where is she now?" Focalar asked, pulling his arrow from the dead beast and cleaning it off on its still body. Cosmacrater looked at him his smile gone at the disregard his archer showed the felled animal.

"I know where," Cosmacrater said, kneeling down to pet it softly. "I have all the information I need. March on due east. We'll make camp at Garson's then head north."

"You here that boys? Move out," Lihatiel cheered leading the march to Garson's. The jovial nature of his men made Cosmacrater's smile return. They've worked hard enough for a night of debauchery. It would only make tomorrow morning that much harder on them. He laughed inwardly but trailed behind until they were a safe distance away. The men were too eager for a moment's peace to notice their captain lingering at the corpse of the hound. Cosmacrater put a hand on the hound, feeling its lifeless flesh and dusty fur.

"You served well your masters. You served me as well. Go your way in peace," he said, in almost a whisper taking the animal's head in his hands. The animal's eyes opened as it began to glow a soft blue. Slowly Cosmacrater felt it grow softer and softer between his hands until the animal's physical nature itself faded into a translucent, ghostlike body. It yelped defensively at the strange experience, alien to such a primitive mind. It fought against Cosmacrater violently unable in its current state to damage him. He was between worlds now. It would be free to roam much happier terrain now. The soft light consumed it entirely as it disappeared. In one brief moment Cosmacrater glimpsed heaven so fast that it seemed more like a feeling than actually seeing. In a silent prayer he was finished and walked quickly to reach his men.

Chapter 11

The Hounds paced the gates to the Elector's Hell. From the edge they could see the carnival rides and the Ferris wheel. A serpentine roller coaster coiled around the lethal amusement park. Everything in view was an illusion concealing the dark atrocities the electors used this pit to perform. Though the large heavy gates were twisted, unable to close the hounds whined their anguish to the construction. Even their animal minds knew the sent of blood and disease. They whimpered sensing the sinister ghoulish joy from the elector's inside who caused the wretched odor they smelled. Jerrod prowled along snapping at the heels of his hounds.

"Cowards!" He growled biting down hard on one hounds back leg snapping at another's tail, who quickly tucked it protectively between its legs. With a bound he jumped the gate himself. The earth gave way behind him. He broke into a run, as more ground was consumed by an unseen foe. His back claws danced dangerously on falling earth his front claws struggling to close more ground. His front paws sunk deep into solid earth and he clawed at the surface to secure his back ones. He desperately struggled against the wicked sounds he heard from the newly formed pit behind him. Each inch he gained in ground made the beast beneath him roar angrily. One back paw claimed the surface. A serpentine tendril snapped from the depth. He kicked out awkwardly. He felt it try to twist around his leg. Pulling free he tumbled to the safety of solid earth. Looking back he saw snake heads retreat back down to the depths from where they came.

With the first peril of the electors done Jerrod shook it off, visibly displeased at looking foolish to his comrades. He walked along the seemingly vacant Carnival dreamscape. He could hear the Carnies barking their twisted versions of more innocent earthly games. Ghouls hurled darts at mortal prizes then took their bounty to do with as they pleased in the dark shadowed alleys between stands. Another stand displayed ghouls armed with water guns spraying their fluid into a tube that was forced into their victim's feminine genitalia. They worked diligently to fill their bloated victims beyond bursting. Jerrod stayed cautious as he avoided the carnies while investigating the air for the scent he wanted.

Walking past the arcade he found it. A faint familiar scent caught his nose. Poking his head in the tent he sniffed. A handful of the machines were played by mindless drones drooling and tapping buttons blindly. Their random button mashing continued even more pain for the video victims trapped in the machine. He sniffed eagerly as he prowled the arcade searching for the smell that teased so gingerly across his nose. It may be trapped in one of the machines, perhaps. He searched onward unable to focus the smell. A growl caught his attention. He turned only to yelp as he was attacked, fangs biting his hindquarters.

"So you guys finally decided to come." He growled back at two other hounds that braved it past the gate. He boxed them with his forepaws provoking a playful fighting. It was no real contest. Jerrod as large as both of them combined made them both submit as they bared him their throats. "All right then. Enough games."

They resumed their search of the tent. With three working the job of one they quickly decided the angel was not inside. It was close, real close, but they had trouble pin pointing it. One hound bumped one of the ghoulish arcade gamer's legs. It turned, eyes void of sight. The hound whimpered at the sight of it. He jerked backing away but awkwardly bumped into more things.

"Play with me," the ghoul moaned drooling. Sparks shoot out from its fingers. The hound yelped as it caught hold of him, the electricity and morphic magic of the domain forcing it to a pixilated mockery of itself. The two remaining hounds bolted from the tent forsaking their comrade to a life and many painful deaths of video madness.

The smell was stronger out here. Jerrod and his comrade both raised their noses, focusing to its location. They took their first tentative steps toward that direction. Jerrod looked around for attacks as they followed the sent. The freak show portion of the amusement park made a gauntlet between them and the possible end of their destination. Each step was cautious, their tense muscles shivering with anticipation. Each movement forward Jerrod looked around eyeing every glass case of abominations with suspicion. He sniffed for other more sinister traps lurking beyond the glass.

Each case showed the Hell-twisted victims as they suffered on display. One had thick metal spikes driven violently through his head, removing any ability to hear, see, or speak. Another case housed a woman being slowly devoured as larvae and maggots chewed their way from her privates, mouth and eye sockets. Jerrod shook violently from a chill tickling his spine. He looked at another case where serpents wriggled under the skin of a young woman like the muscles used to. Jerrod let out a small growl in his hound-tongue. *We're almost through, just two cases left to the end.* He eyed the two cases in question. Unlike the others that lined the wall left then right, these two faced each other. One was of a man trapped under water, thin razor edged leeches swimming by him to slice thin cuts from his bloated, and water logged flesh to spill the blood within. The blood-thinned pink, sending the leeches to lap at the stream before fading to match the yellow tint of the water he floated in. His head was in a harness to feed him oxygen and keep him staring out to the case across from him. Jerrod followed the man's gaze to the other case. The other was a woman naked, her skin stretched by a myriad of hooks distorting her once beautiful form. Like the man her head was forced to witness the others pain. The tension in one of the hooked cables broke the flesh making the woman wince in pain. A bat flew in feasting on the wound it left, and with it another hook burrowed into her to even the suspension, pulling tight a new patch of flesh from her body. Each time the hooks gave way a new bat feasted and a new hook took its place puncturing the flesh and causing more pain.

Jerrod heard glass break and turned to see his follower grappling with the leg of the serpent-infested woman. Jerrod stalked over jerking on his ear to make his subordinate whine. Jerrod growled. *We don't have the time.* The follower growled back. Jerrod let go of his ear and stepped back toward the scent. "I know you're hungry. But…"

His words ended when he heard the yelp from his friend. The serpents under her flesh escaped through the freshly opened wounds from the hound's fangs. It twisted against its devourer, tangling the hound it its coils. The hound whined as its breath was forced from him. His stomach began to twist with tiny serpents of its own. He looked at Jerrod for help, the larger stronger hound petrified by the sight of his friends demise. Its abdomen ruptured letting serpents slither to their freedom. Jerrod jumped backwards. They slithered blindly in every direction. The hellhound kicked its last, as it died. Jerrod raced away in a panic and found himself in a different part of the freak show. It appeared to be some storage room. Two more cases waited here. He scanned the floor with his ears perked up for any sound of the snakes.

One was a restrained man being slowly devoured by several bats, rats and other rodents.

Fluid pumped into his body to force his body to heal the new wounds just to have it eaten away again. His mouth was gagged restricting his screams to muffled noise. The last case was only a frame that seemed to work like a picture window. Jerrod looked behind it carefully to find nothing but wires that held it in place. Passing in front of the case he saw another tortured victim a woman struggling to climb an ever-increasing slope. She neared the top only to slip and tumble painfully, her bones snapping and flesh tearing at the vicious fall down. Again she renewed her climb some savage creature in the darkness driving her on. She saw the hound as it peered down at her.

"Please. Help me. Help… Just end it… end it all…"

Beyond this he saw two workers standing in front of monitors that maintained the freakish amusement displays. Their suits, sanitary, protective biohazard suits concealed any observation to their form. They were yellow, tinted orange by the red glow of monitors. One of the workers tapped angrily at the side of the machine.

"Damn it. Gluttony's busted again. See if someone can round up those snakes and get Ms. Roscoe some medication. And remember not to get to close. Those snakes will go after anything," a thin, attractive nurse said, as she entered, shoeing away the workers to deal with the problem. His nose perked up sniffing madly. That scent. It was her or rather the smell of it on her. His muscles were tense and ready to flee. He watched as she saw him in the corner of her eye. She didn't bother to turn, or to draw attention to him as the rest of the workers left keeping her eyes on the monitors. Once they were gone she relaxed. The hound lowered his gaze risking the slightest of growls to alert her of his presence. She looked over her shoulder smiling innocently at him. "Don't growl at me, Doggy. Your friend did it to himself. You even warned him. Speech capabilities. Your masters must be proud." She stepped closer. He hunched down ready to fight. Unafraid she petted his nose disregarding his barred teeth. "Don't worry, I don't work with animals."

"What about angels?" Jerrod growled denying his urges of biting or relaxing. Stay focused he told himself. "Do you work with them?"

"Wow. News does travel fast," she chuckled. Crouching next to him, he got confused. This was not a battle position. It would be simple enough to kill her like this. She was making a gesture, he thought. He convinced his muscles to ease a little, a gesture as well, but trust was never given fully. She continued to speak as if the two had known each other for eons. "Yes, we have taken on an angel patient. He's at the hospital."

"As a patient?" He whined.

"Of course," she said, stroking his back. There were gunshots followed by the sound of static. The small machine by her hip vibrated making her jump. His muscles tensed and he tackled her sinking his teeth into her throat. "Relax. I have to take this call," she said, her countenance surprisingly unfazed. He knew better. Her expression may not have changed but her hearts rapid, panicked beating and the salty taste of sweat on her skin told him how scared she was. He licked it with his tongue. His stomach growled. She would be so tasty. Slowly she drew the crackling radio from her waist. She knew any more sudden moves would have her day go from bad to worse so she remained focused and calm. Better not to make him more excited, she thought. She pushed the button. "Yes?"

"Snakes are taken care of. They were after one of the ticket vendors. Luckily she trapped herself in her booth."

"Well keep searching. Just one of them can close this place down for a massive overhaul. Make it your chief concern for the next seven hours. Be thorough. Nurse Kimberly out," she said, turning off the radio and leaving it set on the ground next to her head. She smiled at Jerrod submissively. He let her go. She rose back into her crouched position stroking his back ignoring the puncture marks in her neck. "I'm afraid your search ends here. The hospital doesn't allow animals. You can go back to your master. You know what you can know for whatever your masters wanted you to find in regards to the angel." She raised and turned her back on him. "Go and tell them what you learned."

"I could always kill you and go in anyway," he growled.

"More sinister creatures dwell inside, creatures much more dangerous than little ol' me. Will you kill them all by yourself? You've made it this far. You're very good. But you'll go in there and get killed and then no one will relay your findings. Is that what you want?"

She gasped as she felt fur brush against her, the first time her mask of emotion failed her. He licked her hand to relax her. She stroked his nose. "He isn't a friend of yours is he?"

"No," he barked, readying his muscles for the dangerous trek through the elector's funhouse. "I will report back," he growled.

"If you're looking for an easy way out there is a service entrance over here. It'll take you right out. He followed her close as she led him through the freak show exhibits. They reached a door in the shadows, lit ominously by the red exit light. Jerrod stopped at the door as she opened it. She looked at him and rolled her eyes. "Fine. Come on, look."

He watched her as she walked through, and the smell of the salt fields teased his nose. He dared to take a step forward. When the world didn't collapse his muscles burst, overtaking her he raced for the relative freedom the outside world offered. Exploding from the mouth of a cave he found himself on a steep slope. The ground was gone from his feet before he could stop. Falling he braced himself when he hit the ground. His legs jarred on the impact and he fell over, tumbling down the slope. His bones broke, unable to bend with the impact of the earth around him. Sharp rocks cut him. Bruises ruptured. Landing in a thick choking cloud of salt his body burned. In moments he burst from the heap howling in the stinging agony. But howling meant survival. He was alive.

Atone

Nurse Kimberly watched from the cave mouth. Her face was twisted up in a sneer, looking out at the world below her in disgust. She watched the hound get up and run on awkwardly with broken bones. "Take care, doggy," she breathed to the salty wind, feeling the sting in her throat.

A moth flew toward her, following the words on the wind to their source. The black wings and body where streaked white in the pattern of skeletal bones a skull image resting behind the large compound eyes. It flew toward her. Fluttering in front of Nurse Kimberly's nose it took her attention from the running hound. "Oh, Miriram, it's you. Welcome. I think you'll like what we've accomplished so far. Please come in."

Chapter 12

The cliff. Birds flew past Atone, teasing her hair happy for the new found warmth of spring. She breathed in the sweet smell of the flowers carpeting the ground between the trees. She could feel the warm spring breeze carrying with it the hum of insects. The wind wrapped around her like a comfortable coat. She looked down the edge of the cliff getting drunk off the splendor of the world around her. Opening her arms wide she leaned forward as if to embrace her whole surroundings. The water of the Guff crashed against the rock its voice a roar as it called her, asking her to come down from on high and enjoy its mysterious depths. She closed her eyes and let herself fall. The wind that was her friend screamed for her to stop, roaring in her ears. She tried to ignore the wings on her back. *Open them*, the wind whistled loudly in her ears; *open them before it's too late. The water's getting closer. Hurry.* Plummeting to the grounds she screamed out in fear. A hand reached out catching her arm and spinning her through the air.

"I'm here. I'm with you," he said, his silk like voice caressing her.

Atone

"Axael," she breathed heart beating fast with the exhilaration of her rescue.

"Everything is going to be O.K.," she heard him say through her closed eyes.

She felt herself hit the ground, the bones in her flesh shattering leaving her a mangled mess across the jagged rocks.

Her eyes snapped open, jarring herself upward from her slumber. The door was open. Atone saw eyes shining in the doorway and their owner's silhouette casting a shadow over her. In an instant her blades slid into her grasp, ready for a fight.

"It's alright, it's just me," Naamah's voice drifted into the kennel. When Atone wouldn't back down Naamah stepped in to reveal herself. "Are you alright. Want to talk about it?"

Atone held her head, shaking the loose straw from her hair. The threat over, she felt the drowsiness crawl back into her. "Why are you here?"

Naamah stepped up to her, touching her arm gently, calming her. "I know you've been having problems. You need to let this out. Come on," she said, her hand sliding down to her leg. Atone's eyes went to her leg as the hand caressed it working its way to the inner thigh. She held Longing and Mercy in the ready, hovering over Naamah's hand until she withdrew it. Atone eyed her as she rose. Naamah's eyes worked upward from Atone's legs to her face accompanied by a wicked smile. "Tell me what's troubling you?"

"At the moment?"

"It's just a tension breaker. You need to relax." She looked around at the living quarters. "And better sleeping arrangements would definitely help."

"I'll be fine," she said, heading to the bar. She could feel Naamah's eyes follow the swish of her thighs.

Atone took a seat at the bar, Marcolf pouring her a drink. She took it absently taking a drink before realizing what it was. Her insides retaliated at the taste. She strained to swallow down what little was in her mouth. Marcolf took the glass with an evil chuckle. "Sorry." He poured another drink and she sniffed it cautiously. She took a sip. It wasn't much better but she drank the whole glass. "You're a strange one friend, a demon favoring tomato juice over alcohol rich blood."

"You know I'm a devil," Atone said.

"Right," he said, jokingly.

They looked out at the establishment. The place looked cleaner, despite the blood crusted dance floor. The girl on the stage was dancing. Some skeletal musicians were positioned near the stage giving a sultry rhythm for the erotic and disturbing display. The supplier for Cronos found them fighting against the rivers of Styx. Atone found herself unwittingly swaying to their musical manipulation counting herself fortunate that their talents were not stripped away by the mind erasing waters. "I guess it's true that music is the heart of the soul," she said, to no one in particular. The quality of their music out matched the former tunes that lingered before. The old music was an incantation from the former owner before he left that had faded beyond its quality. The music now was impressive and Atone often found herself tapping and swaying as she thought about her plight and the hounds that haven't returned. She soon found herself lost in thought again until Marcolf spoke again.

"The new girls are a big hit," he said, motioning to the stage. The girl dancing was armless with portions removed from her cheeks to reveal her white, sparkling molars. She finished another tomato juice.

"It's a shame the sisters eat half your work," Cronos said, taking a seat next to her at the bar with a tired sigh.

"Yeah," she said, motioning for Marcolf to fill another glass.

"Some times I think I would be better off just getting out of here," Cronos said, off hand. She turned in her seat focused on him. She sipped at her drink nursing it.

"Give all this up?" She said, with a laugh, half-joking. He smiled taking his drink from the bar. Marcolf checked on an imp that had wandered in leaving the two to talk in more privacy.

"That's what Asmodius did. He found a way out."

"Out," she stated her wandering thoughts now drawn in to one focus. "What do you mean out?"

"A way to escape Hell," he said, simply. He took his time with his drink. She slid closer to him waiting. Her attention was fully on him. She still waited. She wanted to ask but not seem disrespectful. She couldn't take it. He was doing this on purpose. She took a breath readying herself to urge him on but he began again. "That is of course without a possession and without unlocking a gate. At least that's what I'd like to believe. You know he never came back at all."

"Did he say how he would do it?" She said, casually. If he was going to play with her then she would with him as well. He looked at her as she watched the woman at the bar exit. The lead musician said over the crowd that there would be a brief intermission. Cronos Turned back to watch the empty stage as Lillith, the only one still hearing music went over to claim the pole. Naamah, entering from outside and took off her outer garments to reveal skimpy leather. She took the stage behind Lillith and dominated her in front of the captured crowd.

"Yes. He was keenly studious when it came to possession. He said the key was timing. Possessions are short term as the demon fights to destroy the original soul, which in turn causes too much damage to the physical body. Possession of a corpse requires no such combat but let's face it, your already deteriorating. He said you have to take the body at the moment of death when the soul is weakly attached. Then the trick of course is to stop the body you've just stolen from dying."

"Interesting," she said, watching the two sisters do more kinky things than she wanted to witness. She caught the eyes of Naamah, grinding Lillith's exposed buttocks in her groin she smiled blowing a kiss to Atone. She smiled forcibly and gave the slightest of waves. Cronos seized her seat spinning her around to face him. She was taken aback, her shock visible to him. His face was stern.

"Take a body when it's still warm. Your empathic, it should be easy if you were so inclined," he suggested letting her go he rose from his seat and motioned to Marcolf to get Naamah and Lillith off the stage. By the orgasmic look on Lillith's childish face their show was near its end anyway. He headed for the back room to get a new girl. At the door he looked over his shoulder. "You may have to once this whole angel conspiracy unravels."

"Speaking of which…" Cronos froze at her words expecting this sooner or later. "Any word? Of the hounds I mean?"

"Not yet," he smiled weakly. "Have faith."

"Yeah," she watched him leave, and then turned back to the stage where Lillith collapsed in ecstasy, quivering on the ground. Naamah cleaned her weapon of choice. Atone grimaced her heart sinking low in her chest matching her spirits. "Yeah."

"Like what you see? I noticed you barely took your eyes off me up there." Naamah stepped toward her. Atone took her tools, from under the stool. Some of the torture machines were getting old and she was going to fix them, which explained the slow torture day. She escaped her seat before Naamah could box her in. Marcolf had a drink waiting for her and Naamah took it before pursuing her prey.

"I was just waiting for your performance to end so I could get to work, impressive though it was. I'm sure the captive audience would agree." She motioned for Marcolf to give her the rest of the tools behind the bar. She made her way to the aged devices bringing out her chains and hammer from amid the pliers and ratchets.

Atone

"You know I don't get you," she hissed towering over her as she kneeled by one of the patron's chairs.

"That's the point," she answered under her breath. Naamah threw her glass across the bar, the glass shattering across the wall. Naamah took hold of her shaking her sternly. Face to face Atone saw the desperation in Naamah's eyes concealed by her mask of bitter depravity.

"You're in Hell; don't you have the brains in your head to realize you're evil, you're sick? My God! You're pathetic!"

"And you're in my chains," Atone said, as they coiled around her. Naamah screamed as her flesh began to burn. "Where are your brains?"

She clutched her hammer tight getting a sick feeling of satisfaction mixed in with the pain she received from Naamah. She steadied for her first blow. She swung hard. Naamah flinched in her captivity. The hammer hovered next to her. Atone forced herself to laugh against her own pain. It was Marcolf who stepped up to intervene.

"Girls, girls. Should we really be wasting our time fighting against ourselves?" he asked, placing a calming hand on Atone's shoulder. Naamah whimpered in pain. "Naamah, I think you've learned your lesson. Atone, please."

The chains uncoiled freeing her. The burns from the chains cooled replacing exposed soul for flesh. Marcolf stood between them staring Naamah down. Atone paid little attention to her glad someone was here to stop this. She shimmied her way under the stage to work on the light fixtures for the stage. Naamah went defeated to the bar, pouring herself a drink.

"How is that?" she asked, after tinkering with the small parts. Given the tools she had to work with it was awkward to say the least. Marcolf walked over her as she watched him through the small space between the floodlights and the stage.

"The third one is still flickering," he stated pointing to the light in question. She shifted under the stage to reach it. Lillith rose from her place on the stage to stand near him.

"I like the flicker. Like a hypnotic code," she mumbled mesmerized.

"That is all the more reason to fix it. Lillith, could you make yourself useful and find

Agrat," he asked, pushing her to draw her attention back to reality.

"I already know where she is," Lillith giggled falling over. "She went hunting."

"For new victims," Naamah intercepted pouring herself another drink. "Since Atone used some of them to fix the place up she thought we may need more," she said. Lillith rose from the ground looking at her puzzled. Naamah growled back making her retreat on all fours slinking away like a wounded dog. Atone made a popping noise that brought Marcolf's attention back to the task at hand.

"There. I think that should do it. What do you say?" she asked Marcolf.

"Good."

"Yippy," Lillith said, clapping excitedly. Naamah finished her drink and her sulking to walk back toward the stage.

"Damn you're annoying," she grumbled to Lillith. Atone shimmied toward the exit to find Naamah blocking the route. Marcolf stared her down again and she stepped out of the way. "Sorry."

Atone escaped the confines of the stage to stand again and flexed out her muscles. She didn't pay attention to Naamah's slight instead focusing only on Marcolf. "If you don't mind I was going to take Faust out for a ride."

"You know you don't have to ask," Marcolf answered. Naamah and Lillith made nervous glances at each other. Naamah tried again to intervene but was stopped again by Marcolf. She whimpered slightly as Atone left the bar. When she was gone he turned her to face him. "What's up with you lately? You're up to something."

"No I'm not," Naamah said, pulling free to look painfully toward the door. She sighed. "Just unreturned desire. That's all." Marcolf gave her a suspicious glance ever smiling despite himself. Shaking his head he returned to his bar.

"Must I remind you she is Cronos' guest? Leave her in peace."

Chapter 13

Agrat perched on a stony ledge, long leathery wings extending out from her shoulders, watching the horizon as the hound raced toward Cronos' land. It grew close and it slowed sniffing the air. Glancing around nervously it tried to find her. She watched amused from above. As it grew close she jumped down to stop it in its tracks.

"Have you found anything?" she asked, with cold icy words. Her wings slid into her back, completely concealed. The hound looked up at her baring its teeth but not daring a growl.

"That is information for Cronos," he stated firmly. In a blur of motion a spike left her hand, hammered down into the hound's spine. It yelped in pain. Agrat studied the injuries this hound endured in its journeys. She studied the path of injuries painfully with her fingers making the beast yowl in pain.

"What severe injuries you've sustained. Wounds like that will not heal on their own. You say this information is for Cronos. Then I suggest you give it to me." It tried to snap at her but, unable to move, it was a futile attempt. She drew another spike from her belt. A simple weapon it appeared as a large pin, a spike on the end with a weighted ball for a pummel. A simple ripple in the spike barely passed as a hand guard. She held it backwards, sending the weighted end down hard to shatter the bones in its right forepaw. It yowled. The dog did its best to curl up, trying to protect its wounds. This too was fruitless. "Tell me or else."

The hound eyed her bitterly; she hoisted up the spike for another strike. "Very well. I'll talk. We found the angel at the electors. They're holding him in some warped version of a hospital."

"That wasn't so hard was it?" she said, pulling the spike from his spine. She held it up in front of her eying it with a vicious grin. "You do realize that I can't let you go home." The hound looked up with a growl brewing in his throat. The spike locked it there driven through his skull and pinning him to the ground. With a turn of the knobby handle the Pin began to glow a pale teal. Agrat smiled knowingly.

"What a harsh growl you've had, Dog. But it's over now."

Chapter 14

Atone carried a saddle over to Faust. His bridle was already fit past his teeth, slung comfortably over his head, the reigns tying him along side the entrance to Asmodius's. She positioned the saddle on the blanket that covered Faust's back. As she tightened the cinch Lillith and Naamah came up behind her.

"So… going out, huh?" Lillith murmured getting an elbow from Naamah.

"It's dangerous out there, Atone. Are you sure you don't want to stick around here," Naamah said, uncharacteristically concerned. "If this is about me, I mean… I'll back off."

Atone could feel Naamah's concern. She turned from Faust with a weak, forced smile. "I'll only be gone for a little while. I'll be back," she said, putting a hand on Naamah's shoulder. She clasped one of her own over it.

"But the harrowing beast population is at an all time high," Lillith said, looking between Naamah and Atone. Atone, in turn looked back and forth between the two sisters.

"All right, what's going on? What are you guys up to?"

"It's just…" Lillith started getting elbowed by Naamah to stop her. Naamah started where she finished.

"We're only looking out for you, Atone."

"Thanks, but I'll be fine," she said, pulling free the reigns. She slid in the saddle. Looking out she saw a shadowed form flying through the darkness.

"Yeah, she's a tough one," Agrat said, landing on the roof. She left her wings out letting them fold up but remain out. Naamah and Lillith looked around sheepishly.

"Of course, Agrat," Naamah mumbled.

"How was your hunting?" Lillith asked, innocently.

Naamah smacked her in the back of the head. "Shut up, Lillith. She obviously didn't get anything."

"That's right," Agrat said, flexing her wings to adjust to the sudden change in the

wind. "Diablonians had the salt fields covered.
There was no point in trying." Atone saw the
pin shaped spikes at her belt. She studied Agrat.

"Hunting with pins, Agrat?" she asked.
The strange tools of hunters that siphon a soul
from the body allowing for easy transportation
were widely used until they were banned by the
three factions.

"How else would I get them all the way
back here? We have a resurrector come through
every now and then. Are you going to punish
me?"

"Why?" Atone, said with a half smile.
"I would only seal my own fate then. It would
be pretty foolish, wouldn't you agree?"

"Yes indeed." Agrat mused to herself.
Faust, catching the scent of death on her,
fidgeted, madly looking around. "We can talk
later. I'd like to get some riding in before it gets
to dark."

"Enjoy your ride," Agrat shouted after
her. Atone rode off leaving the sisters to their
own devices. Naamah looked over at Lillith then
they both turned to their sister as she left her
perch on the roof to land near them.

Atone

"So how did your hunting go?" Naamah asked. Agrat's smile was answer in itself.

Chapter 15

Atone rode across the ashen hills. She wanted some privacy, time to think. A dusty fog rolled in concealing the ground. She heard the distant marching of an army and turned to see soldiers advancing on Asmodius's. Faust bucked madly snorting. His head bowed to the left staring crazily into the darkness. He smelled something. There was something that was spooking him. Atone tried to see or smell what Faust did but was unable to do either. With another furious kick Atone toppled free from her seat, Faust tossing her to the ground. He trotted several paces away. Atone moaned feeling the jagged rocks in her back and neck. She jerked upward from the ground gasping sharply. She resisted the urge to scream not wanting to spook Faust any more. She reached back to pull the sharp stones free each one creating a new, tormenting surge of pain through her body. She stayed away from Faust trying to calm herself before calming him. Taking several deep breathes she turned back to him. Faust looked over to her snorting cautiously.

"What's up with you, Faust?" She said, her eyes catching the dead carcass of a hellhound, a deep hole through its head. "One of Cronos' Hounds."

She studied the scene she stumbled into. "What is going on here?"

Chapter 16

Lihatiel burst through the door, Cosmacrater and Focalar following close behind. Marcolf looked up as he mopped up the counter. "Oh, more guests. How delightful."

"What the Hell are you doing here?" Marcolf growled through his grinning teeth.

"Nice to meet you too, Marcolf." Garson said flatly.

"We're looking for an Angel." Cosmacrater intervened, ignoring whatever problems they have had in the past.

"Join the club. It seems to be a popular trend," Marcolf said, starting to get more glasses. Lihatiel grabbed him pulling him over the bar. Marcolf's eyes were wide and panicked but his face, as always retained its mocking smile. He clawed at his face trying to conceal it. Lihatiel's violence subsided but not by Marcolf's attempts to conceal his features. Cosmacrater pulled him back roughly both freeing him from Lihatiel and taking him for himself.

"No games you grinning Bastard!" Lihatiel said, putting his hands on Cosmacrater to reach out to Marcolf. A lethal arrow pointed under Lihatiel's chin and he eased away leaving Marcolf's questioning to Cosmacrater. Lihatiel grew silent, an absence which was quickly filled by Cosmacrater.

"I'm looking for an angel who goes by the name Atone," he asked. His hands, gentle in comparison to Lihatiel's, smoothed out Marcolf's lapels. Marcolf glanced around nervously, all eyes in the bar not forced to watch the stage were turned on him. He could only babble getting a frustrated grimace for his trouble. The Lapels began to smoke, Marcolf's vestments ignited. "Tell me, where is Atone?"

"Atone?" Lillith asked, from the pole in center stage. She hung upside down her legs twisted into a lock around the pole. She watched Cosmacrater, as he walked, radiating authority with each step. "She rode off, went far away."

Cosmacrater looked up at her smiling gently. His gaze continued up and she giggled from the attention. "And where did she go, Little Girl?" he asked, when his eyes returned to hers.

Atone

"To Goap's In the North West," Cronos bellowed entering the room. He made his way quickly to the stage paying no heed to the soldiers. He knew the one in charge was his only threat. "Don't mind Lillith, She lost more than her soul to this place long ago."

She laughed, innocently releasing one leg from its hold on the pole to lie across Cosmacrater's shoulder. He felt the soft skin across his neck and cheek. He looked over to Cronos with a poker face. "I was talking to her."

"At your own expense. But if you only want information then I'm afraid I've given you all we have," he croaked nonchalantly playing the indifferent host. Cosmacrater smiled again rubbing Lillith's leg. He enjoyed the soft texture so uncommon for a soldier. He kissed it softly, happy that she didn't shy away. Cronos waited wondering how long this game would last. Cosmacrater began to speak but to no one in particular.

"No. You give to easily."

Cronos' guise shattered as Cosmacrater's men began to destroy the bar. "What is the meaning of this? I told you what you wanted." Devices became wreckage. The bar's countertop was hacked apart to get the inventory of the very best underworld spirits and alcohol available. The room took little time to destroy. What they didn't drink they shattered across the stage and patrons. "Stop them this instant!"

"You told me what you wanted me to believe. Now I'll ask again. Where is Atone?" Cosmacrater asked, remaining calm, as calm as Cronos pretended to be when first he entered the room. He was the calm in the eye of the hurricane that ensued upon Cronos' bar.

"I've told you North West."

"Sir, look what we found," two beastly soldiers growled dragging Janie into the fray. Cronos lunged to stop them but several of Cosmacrater's men held him in place. He instead inspected her, unable to do anything else. She was still unbroken, but for how long. "A real looker. This could be fun."

"No please. I'm telling the truth."

Lihatiel looked at Cosmacrater then spoke. Cosmacrater didn't intervene. "Well boys, she is precious," he said, running his crushed hand over her. He could feel her nerves, a myriad of trembling butterflies under her skin. Her eyes wide sweat running from her brow. He looked back at Cosmacrater his face still unaffected, He folded his arms in front of himself. Lihatiel smiled turning back at her. His smile grimaced only briefly as the fact that his mutilated body made his preferred torture impossible. Lihatiel pulled his gaze from Janie to focus on the men holding her. "Tie her to the pole."

Cosmacrater picked up Lillith gingerly spinning her with ease to set her on her feet next to him. She took hold of his arm with a wide grin. "You're really strong," she purred taking his war weathered face in her soft, delicate hands and bringing Cosmacrater's face to look down at her. His brow crunched up studying her for some angle.

"You're really dense. Do you even know what's going on?" Cosmacrater grumbled. He returned his attention to the men near the stage. "Take them outside."

"Yeah, a field trip." Lillith clapped excitely falling in next to Naamah. Naamah growled rolling her eyes.

"Be quiet, Lillith."

Cronos fought against the soldiers as they herded him and the sisters out. Cosmacrater

145

Remained inside for the first time alone, with Janie and the patrons of the bar. "Do you know where you are?"

"N… No."

"You're in Hell. Your Savior is a Demon. He should have known better than to try to save you. You must be cleansed of your sins like everyone else. No exceptions. For what it's worth I think it sucks too. I can sympathize with your savior. But no one gets out unscathed. Do you know what I must do now?"

"Y…Yes," she said, her blue eyes tear-blurred. She couldn't help but twist against her restraints. Cosmacrater bowed his head, concealing a single tear of magma that streaked across his face. She watched. Time slowed. The tear of fire fell. Splashing across the floor the tear ignited the alcohol that spread out into a wave of fire. She fought harder, but was bound fast. The fire grew closer. She screamed. She looked, hoping, preying against the odds that Cosmacrater would help her. He swallowed hard, turning toward the door. "No. Please. Help."

The flames crawled along the stage. Fire danced around her. She felt the heat. She gasped as it licked her feet, shrieked as it blackened her flesh. She screamed as the flames, like worms, crawled up her skin.

The scream chased Cosmacrater from the bar. Cosmacrater left, burning footprints marking his passing. The screams could be heard above the roar of the fire. Cronos was held firm by four of Cosmacrater's men, Focalar with Arrow trained to the base of his bulbous neck.

"You monsters," he cursed under his breath as Cosmacrater walked over to them. His face returned to the straight unfeeling mask he often wore.

"Tell me the truth and her pain, their pain can be over."

"I've told you," he croaked in a sob. Cosmacrater paid his truth little attention.

"Do you hear her? The flesh burning and blistering in the heat? The skin bursting to ash as the flames consume her?" He baited. Cronos fought against his words, fought against his desires. He fought, and lost against himself. He hung his head low.

"She went south to the crossroads. I swear it," Cronos said.

Lillith, unaware of Cronos' confession, swayed back and forth watching the flames mesmerized. "Pretty."

"Shut up Lill…" Cosmacrater kicked the last syllable back into Naamah's throat.

"Let her enjoy it. Don't talk down to her," he commanded. Cronos growled violently, pushing against the men that held him.

"I told you what you want now end this!"

Cosmacrater shot him a disinterested gaze, nodding his men to release them. "Men, let's go."

"What about the fire?" Cronos continued. Cosmacrater began to follow his men south. Cronos seized him. His hand burned from the touch and he pulled it away.

"If you want her that bad go in and save her," he said, not stopping his march or slowing his pace. Lihatiel laughed as he led Cosmacrater's men. Lillith watched the fire until feeling the absence of The Order's soldiers. She pulled her gaze away to look around.

Atone

"Hey they're leaving," she said, jumping to her feet and running after them. "Wait. Wait."

"Lillith, stop," Agrat said, watching helplessly as the fire devoured the building.

"Let her go. She's one less problem to deal with," Naamah snapped, holding her throat.

Chapter 17

Atone saw the fire ignite in the distance, Asmodius's burning down to the foundation. Faust forgot about his fear of the harmless dead to snort nervously to the fire instead. She waited, watching The Order march south. She waited, making sure they would not see her slipping back into the camp. She slipped into the saddle when she could no longer see the army's black shadows on the evening horizon. By the time she reached the remains of Asmodius's the bar was reduced to a dull red glow of angry coals. Darkness closed in around her leaving the coals as the only beacon to lead her. She could hear the baying of Harrowing beasts in the distance. They were probably attracted by the blaze and the smell of the hound's body that sat in the saddle behind her.

"We have to go back, Faust. Come on," she said, urging him on. Faust nodded catching the scent of the beasts in the dark. Coming up to the ashes they found Cronos cradling a savagely burned body.

"It's all over now. My clever deception ruined," he sobbed trying to separate the ash and coal from the crisp, blackened flesh. "I'm so sorry, Janie."

"Those were your friends!" Agrat said, descending to attack Atone. Atone raised her hands in reflex. The blades made her stop short, flames fanned to weak life by her wings. Atone dismounted hanging on to his lead. Naamah sat on her haunches noticing with a gasp the spike and the hound on her saddle. Agrat noticed it too backing off to land behind Naamah. Atone knew what the hound made Agrat feel. She felt the sorrow of Marcolf inspecting his fallen friend. She felt the pain of Janie and Cronos. She felt the fear in Naamah. Atone tried not to let this affect her as she knelt beside Cronos or Janie.

"This is Hell, Cronos. Suffering is Law. You should know this."

"I tried," he sobbed, his face distorted to accent his suffering all the better. "Tried…"

"…To spare just one soul." she finished for him. She moved his arm and pushed him back to examine the full extent of Janie's wounds. "I can spare her."

Cronos slithered back, the wind twisting around Atone nearly picking her from the ground. A blue light pierced through the ash and debris that blew in the wind, encompassing the remains of the bar. Agrat went for the spike at her belt but Faust, spooked by the souls escaping the wreckage, jumped, throwing the Hound in the air to topple onto her as she advanced past him. He bucked and kicked furiously. His eyes were wide with fear, his breath ragged. Marcolf tried to calm him unsuccessfully. A hoof caught Agrat adding insult to her injury. Atone floated in the current of ascending souls rising off the ground. The very remains of the walls twisted and bent, breaking apart in the beam returning to the vague shape of human souls. The burnt husk of Janie ripped apart crumbling away to reveal the soul within as it rose to join the others. Her pain was over. She turned in the current to face Cronos.

"You did what you could," she smiled weakly before being carried away. As the pillar of light collapsed in on itself Atone collapsed, drained, to the ground. Agrat pushed the hound from her legs, her right arm useless with a horseshoe shaped bruise.

"Just great, now where are we going to live?" Naamah asked. Agrat rose shakily to her feet, clutching her bruised arm.

"Now's not the time," Agrat grumbled turning her attention from Naamah to Atone. "That stupid horse of yours freaks at everything."

Atone walked over to Faust. Faust stayed only close enough to the group to avoid the beasts in the darkness. He sniffed at her then walked slowly to her. "You're not stupid, are you Faust." She stroked his nose, easing him. "Besides I wouldn't be worried about Faust's bravery. Someone took out one of your hounds."

"Those bastards that did this?" Marcolf asked, motioning to the meager remains of the bar. His blood boiled with misplaced rage.

"No. I don't think so. It had this stuck in it. It's not an Order's weapon," she said, while drawing the stake from her belt. She held it out in front of Cronos. "You recognize it?"

"Agrat, explain yourself," Cronos bellowed. Atone felt genuine anger rippling off him like sweat. Agrat shot him a defiant look. Atone looked at Naamah, and felt the fear for her sister, her emotions so strong that Atone saw as a child watching mother and father fighting.

"Information is power and you give yours away to her, for what?" Agrat barked back at him. She was about to say more when Cronos grabbed her. His speed was blinding. Agrat was thrown off balance. Her eyes widened, body trembling. She had seen what could happen before. Atone couldn't help but feel sorry, her curse of empathy echoed remnants of other fights, Cronos and Agrat's emotions slipping easily into their roles, exposing their abusive past.

"You have no idea what you're messing with," Cronos roared his form changing from sorrow to rage. Agrat struggled against his tight grip unable to escape his massive form.

"I'm sorry… I thought…"

"Which sin made you do it? Greed? Envy?"

"Please, don't be mad. I'll make it up to you I swear." Her words grew weaker as one hand wrapped around her throat.

"Cronos…" Atone intercepted. She stopped when Cronos shot her a wicked glance. She stepped back ready to jump on Faust at a moments notice. Cronos' attention was brought back to Agrat by her strained words. Naamah slunk deep into the shadows all but disappearing in the darkness of night.

"Cronos… Please… I'm sorry…"

"Why…"

"I thought if no messages came back to Atone then she wouldn't leave."

"…Should I show you mercy?" he asked, raising her from the ground. She dangled helplessly in his massive paw. She flinched as His other hand rose over her for a strike. The blow sent her tumbling from his grasp, sputtering for air she scrambled away from him. He stepped over her and she stopped, knowing there was no place safe to crawl to. "What did you learn? What did my hound tell you?"

"He found the angel. The electors have him."

"That repays your dishonesty to her…" He croaked, pinning her to the ground with his foot. He was larger here, his anger making him swell, making him more imposing. She felt his weight slowly force her skin to sink into the rough, blade shaped stones. She felt her flesh pop loose allowing the blades to sink deeper into her flesh. She coughed up blood. "…what shall you do for me?"

"Anything…" She coughed adding a sick, wet splattering sound to her words. "Just don't…"

"You will rebuild this place," Cronos commanded before turning his attention to Naamah. "And your sister also, which no doubt had some part in this."

"Yes… Of course…" Agrat sputtered. Satisfied Cronos removed his foot and his weight. Naamah reemerged from the shadows tentatively.

"Lillith was in on it too," Naamah grumbled.

"Silence," Cronos ordered. "Now get to work."

Cronos tried to calm himself as the sisters scurried away, his shadow from the waning coals growing smaller. He sighed, letting his rage fade. Atone froze watching it all from the edge of the coals. He turned to her and she stepped back again. He smiled trying to undo what she witnessed. "I am terribly sorry for all of this. I again thank you. I know Janie is at peace. Once we are up and running again you are welcome any time." He reached into his maw finding something buried deep within. Retrieving an ornately carved gem he held it out to her. "A boon so if we move you can find us again."

Atone readied Longing cautiously, taking the boon in her right hand, still armored by Mercy. The gem sunk through her skin, burrowing into her like a carnivorous insect. She winced at the sharp sudden pain but it faded quickly with no sign of ever happening. The gem was gone from sight but she knew it was within her, ready to use at a moments notice. "Thanks. Please don't be too hard on them."

"Suffering is Law. I wouldn't worry about them."

Chapter 18

The Electors were angels of heaven sent to punish the wicked in Hell to purge the souls of evil before returning them to heaven. This was their original purpose but Hell had long since corrupted the Angelic and they have since become the craziest, the sickest, and the most vile of Hell's occupants. Atone's heart sank as she rode to the gate. She sat there on top of Faust hoping that the angel would just come out. Hope didn't bare fruit. She sighed. There was no point in stalling. She slipped from the saddle and stroked Faust's nose.

"No reason both of us have to go, boy," she said, close to his ear. She stepped up to the gate a large metal monster that was twisted into a door. She looked up at a metal plate above it that read: Abandon all hope, yeah who enter here."

The gates opened freely as she approached as if it expected her, but the unexpected movements made her stop her approach. The sound and stale scent of the fun house carnival drifted forebodingly to her ears and nose along the wind. She tested the ground carefully. She walked slowly, testing for safe passage. The ground heaved as she left the safety of the gate. She leapt back as the ground gave way. The ground she leapt to disappeared and she fell into the dark dank pit Her hands caught hold of the edge of the metal gate jerking her arms forcibly trying to pull them from their sockets. A reptilian screeching drew her attention behind her to the snakes in the void slithering toward her.

Risking one arm she prepared Longing for the fight ahead holding him tightly. She slashed but the serpents went for her lower legs away from the reach of her weapon. Her hold on the metal slipped as they jerked her downward. She held fast to the less reliable ground that her talons and Mercy's blades dug deep into. The serpents caressed her legs holding her tight while working gently upward. Her hold gave way. She fell free. Falling she slashed free of the snakes around her legs, only for another serpent to grasp a leg again. She drew her focus on it kicking it in the head with her free hand. Two more snakes came for her arms. In a fluid motion she decapitated them but still more snakes headed from the darkness. Six more snakes went after her. One claimed her head, its fangs sinking into her face and the back of her head, its tongue tasting her left ear. Her free leg was captured by another. One headed for her right side and she cut it through, the useless remains falling in to the depths below. A fast snake coiled around her left arm getting a swift death for its speed.

More kept coming and soon she ran out of options. She struggled against her captors made difficult with both arms now claimed by slithering serpents. Two snakes hovered around her head threatening to strike. She watched them helpless as they danced around her. They bobbed and weaved hypnotically until one struck. She screamed as it drove into her eye socket. The second coiled around her neck. The snake squeezed to silence her. She felt yet another slithering up her leg to plunder the secrets of woman. She fought, useless as it was, jerking her serpentine jailors around but causing little else in the void. She felt the head enter, pushing past her meager defenses of womanhood. She felt the true violation begin as the serpent twisted against itself making smooth scales twist into rows of serrated edges. She tried to resist her body's natural response by squeezing down. Resistance only intensified the pain. Then she felt herself rise and bob. Something big was stepping toward her or drawing her to it. She couldn't be sure. She pivoted in her captivity to witness the new threat, only to find it the old one. Snakes slithered from everywhere around him their tails becoming various parts of him. Amid the incredible mass of Serpents was one massive python head.

"A devil visitor? What a privilege," it hissed at her his voice deafening. "Please come in. Make yourself at home," it said, twisting her upward and over his gargantuan maw. She lowered helplessly toward it. The tongue wriggled around her. She gave one last attempt to struggle. The snakes held her tight. The mouth closed around her, the snakes only retreating at the last possible moment leaving her with only the reek of its foul, fishy breath to keep her company in the dark. She screamed inside herself at the pain of the newly exposed wounds that the snakes left in their passing not wanting to give this abomination the satisfaction of hearing her. It was bad enough it could feel and taste her pain. Atone stared blankly trying to focus. She felt the tongue harsh, abrasive as it lashed upward to taste the blood of her rape. She punched downward refusing any feeling of shame. There was only rage for a beast such as this. She felt the tongue try to evade her jab but it made the error of going between her legs. She held it tight with her thighs, stabbing the tongue in place with Longing forcing it through to push outward through the lower jaw. A second tongue ending in a mouth of its own rose up from the esophagus to attack her. She heard the beast roar making her footing shake. She released Longing as the second tongue attacked. She slashed it with Mercy then with all her might went skyward with an uppercut forcing Mercy through the soft pallet and carving a path to the brain. The second tongue pushed at her, its massive maw opening. It pushed, bit and twisted around her to squeeze her. She reached down to grab Longing, holding fast to Mercy. In the dark she severed both tongues in half, blood spraying out to coat her. She slipped but Mercy did not, remaining lodged in the roof of its maw. She held tight to her weapon. Soon Longing and Mercy worked toward the brain of the sinister beast. Crawling like a worm she reached the maggot riddled brain and a sickening green glow of the monster's soul. Boring through it she continued worming her way to the surface.

As she pierced through the skull she heard clapping from the shadows to greet her. She cleaned what little of the gore she could off; keeping her eye focused in the dark to find the clapping's origin. She couldn't take it for long. "Who are you?" She called out.

An impish character, two feet tall and thin with skin a sickly yellow-gold, stepped out. He was emaciated except for the small potbelly and had a large hooked nose and tiny wings. A few fires took the places where his feet left the ground, creating a weak light to combat the darkness. It bowed nobly. "Just a humble Imp, madam. You can call me Ralphy."

"Your name is Ralphy?"

"No. I said you can call me Ralphy."

"Superstitious?"

"It's not superstitious. How do you think I came to be in the service of Cronos?"

"So Cronos sent you?"

"Well honestly I don't know why. I would have to agree with Agrat on most of this. But he's the boss not me. That's one thing she forgot," he said, with a violent shudder. He scurried over and up her to take a seat on her shoulder. The smell of brimstone that oozed from him was strangely welcome blanketing out the far worse smells of the pit. "Besides since now we're both here we'll have to work together to get out."

"Sure. That sounds good."

The path was lit periodically by Ralphy's fire bursts and she could see a door along the wall. Carefully entering they found themselves in a sterile room, with a man sitting, chained to a chair. Maggots and bugs were eating trough his flesh, mostly centralized around the abnormally swollen abdomen. The stomach rose, squirming with insects until they erupted from their prison running to the top of a platform. This platform was little more than a ramp that led to a funnel crammed into the man's mouth down the throat, creating an unusual taper to the man's neck. Atone paid this man little attention. Instead she was looking for the operator.

"Where's the boss? There's got to be someone running this show," Atone said, scanning the surroundings. The insects turned to face them marching toward Atone and Ralphy. Atone stepped back toward the exit. The door slamming shut by a mass of crawling insects. The army of bugs began to form a pile that grew to create a giant insect form, made of little ones. Ralphy ran out in front of her, his hands spread outward and low.

"Walls of fire rise," he said, raising his arms high above his head, fingers outspread. The floor ignited between them and the large insect beast. It stopped at the edge pacing like a wild animal behind bars.

"What brings you here?" It chirped. "Why do you resist your punishment?"

Atone

"We want information, Elector. An angel came through here." She paced just as impatient as it was.

"Yes. He suffers," it said, happily chirping and clicking. "He is here, not like it will do you any good," it chattered, leaping up on grasshopper legs to overcome the flames. Atone jumped up to greet it, slashing out at it/their unarmored underbelly. The heap gave way breaking back up into tiny bugs that rained down on her, biting savagely.

"You will pay with your life, forever, devil one," its voice called from the broken up mass insects flying to portray the moving mouth.

"Fire of the soul burn," Ralphy called whipping his left hand out to create an intense wave of heat. The insects ignited, their tiny little souls exploding from their shell. A thousand little fires sparkled and crackled around her, their bodies bursting like popcorn away from her. She stomped a few of the bigger ones that seemed to hang on then turned her attention to Ralphy.

"You have quite some power, Ralphy."

"Yes but it has a price. I don't have very much energy left. If we get into too much trouble I may have to bail."

"Well at least you've given me a heads up."

They left the room entering a hallway. They followed it to the nearest door. Listening outside, they heard the sounds of moaning pleasure rather than of pain. Entering the room they saw nothing akin to pleasure. Two electors in razor lined sadomasochistic leather outfits did their own breed of torture. One was male one female each with a specimen of the opposite sex. Their significant others however were in worse shape. Their mouths were sown shut, their arms and legs amputated and assimilated to the electors wardrobe to make it seem as though they were still attached while the electors did their work. Atone gasped then quickly ducked as the electors ears picked it out from the moans. One turned her head trying to find were the noise came from. Shaking her head she returned to her helpless basket case. Her tender caressing and craving womanhood shredded his flesh. The male didn't bother to look instead working feverishly on his own tortured soul. She slid from the shadows ready to strike.

"I've had enough of this," she thought in her mind, remembering her own violation. It was the same violation of Candice, and later as Mercy. It was too much. She couldn't be a part of it any more.

"Really? You haven't even started," the female said, turning its head to face her. She slashed downward with Mercy severing the throat to the bone. Her four legs tried to run but there was no chance for it. The male pulled itself free of his victim ripping loose internal tissue along the way. It grasped at her arm but she twisted her wrist letting Longings blades carve deep into the wrist of her would be captor. Then it showed up.

"What in Hell..." She gasped. It belched smoke and electric sparks as it moved in on her. The machine rolled toward her. It reached out for her with barbed tendrils. She thrust her blades into the elector pulling it in the way of the ravenous machine. The barbs caught him, pulled him close, and sent the elector through the machine. Screams and banging gave way to a mutilated body, void of arms and legs, safely sown and surgically treated to avoid certain death. "That..."

The machine chugged onward toward them. Atone looked for a place to go but every

turn she made it countered. She had to shake it.
She had to slip past. It followed regardless.
Damn, she cursed. She slipped around avoiding
the ravaging tongue like barbed tendrils. It was
a trap. It closed her off in a corner. There was
nowhere to run to, nor was there a way to evade
it. The barbs wisped close, toying with her. She
hissed in pain as one of the barbed tongues
slashed across the thin fabric of her shirt,
making it tumble free from her shoulders, baring
the skin underneath. An angry red welt formed a
line were a thin layer of flesh once was. The
machine seemed to laugh, burping out noxious
smoke that made her light headed. Another coil
of barbs snaked out to finish what the first one
started but Atone was able to slip away at the
last moment. The machine belched in anger
redoubling its efforts to strip her before
consuming her. "Damn. Where the Hell is
Ralphy?" The machine belched mocking her
plea as it slashed furiously at her tattered skirt.
She pushed against the wall unable to get any
farther away from the beast. It was over. She
forced her eyes closed having no other option.
Then there was a ping. The machine made a
ping that seemed out of place. Atone opened her
eyes. The machine slowed its assault. Though
the tongues still lashed out at her they seemed
blind, attacking randomly. A dark, foul burst of
smoke plumed out from inside the metal beast
then, mercifully it clanked to a stop. The

tongues of blades skittered in their death throws on the ground in front of her.

"You called?" A chuckling voice came from inside the machine.

"It took you long enough," Atone retorted as if she never had need of him in the first place. If she didn't know better he may have been hurt.

"I had to find a wrench," he chuckled holding out his hands. Inside were several nuts and bolts. "Take out enough and it's got to stop."

Atone carefully stripped the female elector, the blood from her throat growing cold. Her head rolled back still trying to talk. She was still alive. You would be surprised what someone could live through here. She was useless for her, unable to talk. She took the bladed shirt from her and putting it on. Atone stepped up to the male Elector whose arms and legs were amputated. "I'm looking for an Angel."

"You found one. I am Chimdael."

"I'm looking for a real angel. It might have come through here not to long ago."

"Nothing went through here." He smiled back at her. Atone went to the female again, She pulled the bladed sleeve off her slipping it on to her own arm, putting Mercy on her belt. She then returned to the more communicable elector.

"No riddles. No games. I can make this take as long as necessary," she said, gently caressing him. The sleeve was as dangerous as it looked, the slightest touch ripping ribbons of flesh from the source. "Is this what gets you off? Or maybe this?" She breathed seductively, playfully torturing him in ever more uncomfortable locations. Inside she felt her own skin flake away. She closed her eyes to narrow slits and focused only on his suffering, trying against fact that she wouldn't have to feel it too.

Luckily he broke quickly. "He's in the room down the hall. There. Three doors to the left."

"And what's waiting for us in that little torture room?"

"The Doctor. He's in there. He runs the show." He squirmed as she peeled away flesh with every passing touch. "There's a nurse too. But she's nothing, really. She's barely an Elector. Her only purpose is to make sure the sinful don't die."

She nodded scanning the room for any threats between here and the door. She sunk Longing into Chimdael avoiding any major organs. He screamed as she dragged him with her down the Hall. Ralphy hopped along in front to make sure there were no traps. No tricks.

"What are you doing?"

"I'm taking you with me, in case your lying," she said. As she neared the door she hoisted him up, putting him against the door. With a twist of the doorknob and a kick the door burst open leaving her ready, with Chimdael as a shield ahead of her. The opening door didn't seem that obtrusive to the Doctor, sharply focused on his patient. She shivered as she neared feeling her skin peeled back. She wanted to coil up, protect herself. The woman reflected the pain she was feeling. Atone watched her, as the Doctor skinned her alive.

"Now Mrs. Sanchez what we're going to do is go right to the root of the problem. Your bone structure is what keeps you from being beautiful. So we'll have to fix that," he explained as he carved into her. She jerked her body entering a forced spasm as the knife dug deep into sensitive flesh. She screamed from the pain. Atone nearly dropped Chimdael, her face burning from the incision the woman suffered from. "Mrs. Sanchez, please be still. Nurse, some anesthetics."

"Right away, Doctor," she said, plunging a needle into the doctor's spine. The patient watched on, her skinless face watching them terror-stricken. She flailed wildly as the Doctor resumed cutting.

"Thank you, Nurse Kimberly," he gave her a slight nod. Mrs. Sanchez jerked up grabbing his protective cloth mask from his face. Beneath gleamed exposed bones. He continued his speaking unfazed. "After repairing your bone structure we'll work on your skin. Those liver spots and wrinkles are disgusting. We'll have to take it all off." Atone squirmed, bumping into a table of saws, scalpels and swabs. He looked over his shoulder for the first time aware that someone unexpected was in the room.

"Who are you? Can't you see I'm operating?" He growled angrily plunging the knife down hard, making a wet slush. Atone winced.

"Where is the Angel, Doctor?" she said, flinging Chimdael to the ground to free up her second weapon.

"Angel? Oh, the angel. He's in room 212," he said, turning to face her. He pointed angrily at the door she came from. With a heavy sigh he returned his attention to Mrs. Sanchez. "Sorry about the distraction Mrs. Sanchez. Where were we?"

Atone looked back to the door before returning to him her face curling up in a feral toothy grin. Before she could fight, Nurse Kimberly intercepted her attention smiling warmly back at her. "I can take you there if you'll follow me."

"But we just came from that way," Ralphy fumed. The nurse hurried past them through the door they just entered. Where the hall once stood was now a hectic hospital complete with a packed emergency room. She smiled over her shoulder, absently weaving her way through the sea of burn victims and a gang shooting. "Right this way. Satan will be pleased. We don't often take on affiliated clients but this was an offer the doctor couldn't refuse."

She opened the door to room 212. Inside there was an angel deteriorating from some hideous ailment. Boils covered its face puss coating its feathered wings. Sweat burdened hair stuck to his skin. His eyes wallowed deep in their sockets. Atone watched as he gasped, hoses worming out of his nose and along the side of his mouth to join the tangle of needles and wires keeping him monitored. Atone felt like vomiting at the atrocity. She wondered then what she was hoping to accomplish when she found him. Would her hatred against this once faceless angel have driven her to such horrible things for revenge? The answers where staring up blindly from the hospital bed. She breathed hard, pained gasps as she looked on. "Satan's legion wanted this?"

"Yes. We're quite pleased. A disease that only preys on angels."

"What about devils? Wouldn't that disease kill them too?"

"That's the beauty of it. Our tests indicate that devils are infected just like any angel, but the atmosphere of Hell over time alters the disease's affects on devils, making them only carriers," she cheered triumphantly. When there was no shared response she caved in on herself, looking with wounded eyes at Atone. "We worked very hard on this. Are you not pleased?"

"What?" Atone said, pulling her eyes from the blasphemous image ahead of her. "Oh yes, very impressive. Has Satan told you of his plans yet?"

"Yes, somewhat. A source says that a Penitent Angel will escape Hell and reach heaven. His plan is to infect the Penitent Angel before that happens?"

"How contagious is it?"

"Very," nurse Kimberly said. Atone felt a pin prick in her side and turned at once piercing Longing into Kimberly's stomach. Atone's right hand grabbed Kimberly's right shoulder, Atone's razor edged forearm braced across Kimberly's neck, lifting her off the ground with the impact of Longing. Her momentum drove Longing deep into the wall holding Kimberly in place. The razor edged sleeve cut vicious strips of flesh loose from her face, neck, and shoulder.

"What did you just do to me?" she asked, practically foaming from the mouth with her rage. "Explain yourself?" She demanded her eyes fading white.

"It's an antidote. You are here to transport the body are you not? Since there was a small chance that a devil might catch the sickness in its dangerous form Satan had express orders to vaccinate the deliverymen. That puss bag is really important to him. He wanted to make sure his delivery arrives. It's simply a safety issue," she insisted. "I just made you immune."

She flung the nurse down, leaving her free to clutch her throat. With many years of practice Kimberly quickly went to repairing herself. Atone entered the room with the angel. The doctor's clipboard had the angels name as Malach Ra. She pulled the syringe as it clung to her and tossed it aside. Ralphy looked at Kimberly and then the diseased angel. Finally he settled his eyes on Atone.

"You seem to have everything covered. If you don't mind I'll take off." He said avoiding Kimberly and her needles. "It's not that I don't… But…"

"I understand, Ralphy." Atone said plainly. Atone took a deep breath focusing her mind against the angel's pain. She took another to steady her fast beating heart as she entered the sterile room.

"You, Angel. Tell me about this?" she asked, pulling the broken sword from her belt and tossing it to him, leaving it to rest in his lap. He eyed it lacking the strength to reach for it.

"What business is it of yours? Do your worst."

"Alright." She turned her back to him heading for the door. "I'll leave you here, forever in agony, a diseased, worm eaten corpse kept alive only to feel the pains of the death your denied. Tell me what I want and I'll let you die." There was a silence save for the breathing Machine and the heart monitor. She knew he was going to talk. She also knew that there was no way she would be able to kill him in a way that Nurse Kimberly couldn't bring back. Even redeeming him was impossible. It would only aid Satan's plans by turning the disease loose early.

"Israfel sent us down here; he said some fallen angel will ascend marking the beginning of the end. We were sent to get this angel killed. Unable to do so directly both because of the doomsdays watchful eye and that the identity has been hidden we engineered a war against the Diablonians and The Order. What little we know of this angel is that it was affiliated with one of these groups."

"Why would Israfel turn against God? Doesn't he remember what happened last time?"

"Israfel has grown powerful. He has only one weakness. A prophecy. He will be the first to die in Apocalypse."

"If he…" She began figuring it out.

"If he could get rid of this angel he would end the threat of Apocalypse…"

"…thus leaving nothing to stand in his way," she finished. She shook her head not believing the words slithering from his mucus-coated mouth. "And he actually thinks he can get away with it?"

"Who knows? I agreed to this to try and save Isis from Lucifer's evil clutches," he began to ramble on. Most of it was unintelligible but there was something about When the pantheon of ancient Egypt was about to assimilate… return to God, Lucifer… Satan took hold of Isis and one of her two books of Prophecy… though the book was lost somewhere Isis was dragged deep into the abyss.

"That's all very interesting but not what I want to know," she urged him on taking another step for the door "Who killed Axael? Why?"

"I did. He was trying to interfere."

"So you cast your faith in Israfel, not knowing if his foolish plan will even work."

"I would give it all up to see Isis one last time. If you suffer without the one you love then you would understand," he gasped, looking into her eyes, though milky white in near death he could see her shed a tear. She returned to him picking up the broken sword and holding it over him. She understood, but knew there was nothing she could do. She ground her teeth trying to think of a way. But there was nothing she could do. She took his blistered hand. She put the broken weapon in it, folding his fingers around it. Her rage against him was gone; he did what she would have.

"If you are able, you'll do your own death." She left the weapon in his grasp. When she walked away the nurse was waiting, bandaged from her wounds.

"You're not taking him today?"

"Not yet. Let him suffer here a little longer," she said. The nurse, nodded making sure to keep her distance.

"Then the exit is over here. No doubt you'll want to report to your master."

"No doubt." Atone left, feeling the weight of the issues stoop her body. There was no saving Axael; there was no vengeance to be had on Malach Ra. Zopheal wanted answers, he would get them. Find a way to take the body right before the moment of death. She would bring his information straight to him. And then she would face Israfel. If her fate was in some way twined to the end of days then she would be the one to bring Israfel to Hell. A scheme began to brew in her mind. If there was a way… She was so lost in her thoughts she never realized the moth fluttering by. It fluttered in to Nurse Kimberly.

"Excellent job. Everything is coming along quite beautifully," it clattered as it built up to human size, its insect like body softening into a black human form, robed in skeletal wings. His face was that of a skull, painted over his dark flesh.

"Thanks Miririm. I thought for sure she was on to us for a moment there."

"Don't worry, Kimberly. Everything will be fine." He stepped closer to her making Kimberly shake, unable to control her fear. "Now it's time for your reward."

Atone

"Reward, me… No," she said, her words choked off as a spray of blood splattered across the sterile hospital wall.

Chapter 19

She was on the cliff again. She saw herself, as if looking over her shoulder only partially bound to this entity that bore her name. It was the end of summer, and the first leaves began to turn, a menagerie of yellows, oranges, and reds. She was fully grown now, the innocents of youth violently pulled from her features to show the stern sorrow of maturity, no less attractive but with her beauty a sense of agony that was blissfully absent in younger days. The waters, invisible underneath, nonetheless echoed her anger, her betrayal, crashing savagely against the rocky outcropping as if in some ways trying to tear it down and bring it all crashing into its depths. She looked up at the sky, a grim swirl of dark blues, purples, and grey. Nothing of this day reflected the heaven they were in, the violent wind tore at her, the environment frightened her, and the face ahead of her dealt the most cruel blow.

"Are you ready, Atone? Oblivion awaits you," it asked, in that infuriating, nonjudgmental boom. Her face was not like her parents, stricken by grief, hers was a face marred by rage.

"I'll see you in Hell first," she cursed running toward it. Her feet left the cliff. She wanted to dive at him, to hurt him like he hurt her. Instead she dove downward escaping his judgment and his sight. She felt her wings unwrap in an attempt to save her from this decision. She fought against them keeping them tight to her body though they seemed to resist her own desires. Then something caught hold of them jerking her to a halt in the air below the cliff. She looked over her shoulder to see his face, lost in hoping against hope that it could be some other way. She felt her resolve slipping. She didn't want to lose him.

"Don't do this, please. Maybe… We could…" he began, his mind trying to formulate yet another attempt to redeem her. Then her emotions caught his. He wanted her to stay, not for God or for her own sake, but for himself. This weight, like a black stone began to weigh down in her chest.

"He won't change his mind, Axael," she said, drawing the sword from his scabbard. "…and neither will I. I won't have you coming with me."

She swung the sword overhead, severing the wings from her back. She tumbled, helplessly left to the angry winds and the law of gravity. A steady stream of blood flowed from her severed stumps, forming morbid wings of their own. She saw Axael frozen in disbelief, astonished at her own resolve. She was to far away to know what he felt but had a good idea. They would never be together again. In this she spared him the same fate, the same resolve that sent her spiraling to the wet water beaten rocks below. The rocks rose closer, closer. Cracking bones resounded around her, from her, as she tumbled through the rocks, and beyond. Falling again she saw the first red lights of Hell's dawn. Jagged rocks like serrated teeth rose up to bite her.

In a start she lurched forward. She quickly tasted the salt in the air. Oh yes. She was in the salt fields of Appolyon. Faust was near by ready for any trouble that might have come. He was why she allowed herself a moment of fitful rest. Shaking the salt from her body she resumed her body searching. This quickly grew tiresome. What was this now, she thought two, three weeks or so?

"Simply exchange places with a newly deceased. Take their body while it is still warm," Atone muttered, sitting on a salt dune overlooking the Appolyon Salt Fields. "Your empathic, it should be easy for you," she snapped sarcastically to herself. Faust lingered around, behind her, periodically walking up to her. The saddle and the bridle sat next to her. Though she let him go when she got here he wouldn't go far and she stopped trying to chase him away. Boredom had long been a constant antagonist here and now she moved around to try and shake it from her. Talking seemed to help. "This has to be the most useless place in Hell. I mean it. Aside for soul hunting there's nothing here. How does this punish anyone? I mean what's the point. It's more just irritating than…" She trailed off. The small hairs along her body began to rise and she could feel the tingle of death in the air. She rushed over the dune she just left to see the first shimmering of a soul. It wasn't secured to this plane yet, nor was it completely free from the host it barely clung to. She charged toward it but froze in her steps. Past the soul's translucent form was The Order army that hunted her. "Fuck," she breathed out. She saw them as they saw her. She charged on taking the risk. She saw Focalar go for his bow. Cosmacrater held his men back and she could here his voice, saying something undecipherable to her. She was nearing her soon to be host. The arrow whizzed through the air. Her mind screamed as she ran toward her certain doom. The impact came from behind sending her down. She looked up confused as the arrow flew over her harmlessly. Faust galloped past her careful not to step on her. With no time left she darted forward.

"I missed," Focalar said, shocked. "I…" he gasped. Cosmacrater was shouting at him to fire again but the fact overwhelmed him. Cosmacrater took hold of Focalar's bow and drew an arrow. The arrow sung as it flew and Cosmacrater gave the order to charge.

"Hang on. Don't you die on me," Atone urged wishing she still had her wings. She struggled to reach the spot where the soul was waiting, the arrow spinning toward her. Cosmacrater's men started a full charge. The Salt became her enemy. It seemed to pull at her, slow her from her destination. With the elements against her she would soon be overtaken. They were coming. She collapsed into the ghostly form. She saw Cosmacrater's face stop, not feeling the arrow pass through her. She saw him call out to his men to stop, pulling up his men short right before the salt sucked her down. It burned her flesh. Her head sunk below the surface. She couldn't breathe. The stinging of salt made her itch. No. Not salt. It was too wet. The moisture warm, growing tepid. She tried to open her eyes. She saw red.

Then she felt it. There was a heartbeat, slow and weak. She opened her mouth to gasp for air. Water and blood rushed in leaving the taste of metal in her mouth as she choked on it. No air. Her lungs burned. She pushed against something smooth behind her. It was slippery. She broke the surface of the water, gasping. There was a light, bright, and painful. Hands tried to block it out. They burned, fingers stiff. There was blood. It pumped slowly from her wrists. Her wrists were a pale white. She swept them of blood. They soon produced even more blood. She slipped falling downward. Water splashed washing the walls and floor pink. Her hands went out to stop her. The pain made them curl inward toward her body. Blood water painted the simple white camisole, now pink. Her body shivered underneath. She crawled to her knees. Blood followed her like a faithful hound. She was so weak. She tried to open the bathroom door. I can't get it open. There. There was a hallway. Her vision became blurred. Head sore. There was ringing. Was it in her head? No. It was coming from somewhere outside of herself. She put an arm to her head to try and block it. Her legs felt stiff. Numb. Try to steady yourself, she thought. A coffee table. There was more ringing. She steadied herself feebly against it. She looked behind. There was blood everywhere. All that blood. Her head pounded. There was nothing but blood. There was only blood and that constant ringing. She didn't feel the fall. She didn't feel herself hit the ground.

She barely saw the shattering glass of the coffee table. The ringing stopped. Only silence. There was only silence and blood. Silent, nothingness. Death.

She lay there dying in the hall, shards of glass cutting into her. "Life sucks." She tried to speak. It came as a harsh whisper. "I've had it for less than... and it's over again." The world went dark. She slipped into oblivion. A part of her welcomed it.

Then the screaming. The high-pitched wails making her want to cover her ears. Her arms felt heavy. She felt rough straps around them. She could feel hands on her arms and legs. She was rising. Lights intruded on the darkness, even with her eyes closed. Something grabbed her head, covered her mouth. Her defenses said fight but she couldn't move. She felt the wind chill her exposed, wet skin. She shivered despite the loss of blood. She forced herself from the darkness. She forced herself to open her eyes. It took all of her. There a small room. It rocked back and forth. Hoses and wires poked in and out of her straining against the odds to save her life. A face blocked the brutal brightness of the light above. His face was shadowed, the outline hazy.

"Axael," she gasped. Her eyes fluttering closed again.

"What a shame." The voice was not his. "It all seems so God-damned pointless."

"Ours is not to reason why, Walters. Our job is to keep people alive whether they like it or not."

The ambulance rolled on. She had made it. Keep it from dying. She was free. Free... free...

BOOK TWO: Betrayal

Chapter 1

A Ray Charles song played across the intercom as Heinrich walked through the halls of the St. Bridgette's psychiatric ward in Preston, Colorado. He drew a pen from the pocket of his white lab coat. In his other hand was a clipboard he flipped through noting the new arrivals. He liked to get to the new comers first, So that he could start the healing quickly. The familiar faces weighed on him. That was another reason to get to them right away. After marking out key points to look into he held the pen in his mouth like a cigarette as he smoothed out the wild patch of hair above his left ear that seemed to rebel against the rest of his light brown, nearly blonde hair. He straightened the frameless glassed that protected his dark blue eyes in this action undoing his efforts to smooth his hair.

"Rebecca Van Ness... Suicide attempt... Brought in yesterday. History of mental illness. Room 142." He muttered to himself as he headed for this room. Inside the folder attached to the clipboard were a photograph of the wounds to her wrists and a mug shot style photograph. She was a cute girl, with long blonde hair, though the roots showed quite obviously black origins. In deed it had been some time since she fixed it with at least three inches showing. It almost seemed like it was a look she was going for, a brilliant yellow fire raging out to the smoky black top. Her small heart shaped nose and full pouting lips rested perfectly in her smooth almond shaped face. His heart weighed heavily in his chest. She was such a pretty girl to be driven to such an act. The photograph was not the best of sources since she was withdrawn probably still doped up or suffering mild blood loss.

He opened the door and stepped inside. The room was small and incredibly sterile for safety reasons. It only had a simple single bed with a thin sheet. The patient, a Ms. Rebecca Van Ness, lay over the thin sheet in the hospital's standard issue grey T-shirt marked with sweat, her hair wet and sticking to her face and shoulders. She also wore the standard issue string-less pajama pants. She was curled up in a tight ball facing away from him but she heard him enter and rolled over with a smile. In a slow, fluid motion she shifted to sitting, leaning toward him. Her hands, wrist still bound with bandages, clasped between her legs to the edge of the bed. Twisting her legs around she moved to perch at the edge.

"Good morning, Mr. Shrink. How are we this morning?" Rebecca's voice spoke Atone's desires.

"My name is Heinrich Gordon. You can call me Henry if you wish," he said. She was kind of taken off guard by the way he carried himself. She reminded him of a teacher very proper in speech and authoritative, his words carrying a weight to them that they didn't in themselves have.

"Heinrich. What a lovely name," she said, pawing outward towards him. "Unique. But you haven't answered my question."

"Rebecca. We're supposed to talk about you, here," he said, stepping back.

"What about me?" She snapped, taking hold of his shirt in a speed his eyes couldn't capture. She smiled as the look of shock spread across his face as he was gently pulled closer. "What about you, handsome?"

"Why did you try to kill yourself?" he stated, quickly getting a hold of himself and gently removed her hands from his shirt. He smoothed it out and stepped out of her reach.

"I see," she recoiled as if hit she shook and leaned forward confused, before leaning back to restore her balance. "A man of authority. Stern but fair. I like that."

"You know the longer you draw this out the longer you're stuck here. Make it easier on yourself," he said, again smoothing his hair and straightening his glasses in the wrong order. She watched him do this twice before she responded.

"I'd get to see more of you? Sounds good to me," she purred seductively, Heinrich standing over her. There was an awkward silence as they stared at each other, Atone smiling at him. Heinrich in turn didn't know what face to wear and was left with a slightly slacked jaw and wide eyes. The stare down broke with Heinrich stepping back. "Fine. Let's negotiate," she said, standing up and countering his retreat with a step forward. "You give me something and I'll talk. We could even make a game of it, like strip poker."

"What do you want?" Heinrich questioned his calm voice unable to conceal the sweat on his brow.

"Your tie and top button. For starters," she said. Heinrich mulled it over in his head and as he dwelt on it she sat back on the edge, realizing now the weakness of blood loss and drugs. She concealed it better than he concealed his nervousness evident by his constantly moving fingers. Heinrich shook his head, his hair getting more ruffled as he came to his senses.

"Excuse me? I can't give you my tie you're suicidal," he exclaimed stepping closer to her. Even so he struggled to loosen it having trouble breathing for some reason.

"Then put it in your pocket, simply taking it off will suffice," she said, leaning up against him, with a quick pinch sending the button skipping across the room. He backed off to retrieve it, picking it up, and tucking it into his pocket. She was suicidal and it was a choking hazard. This was a warning he should listen to, he thought, but maybe he could get somewhere with her, mentally speaking. He didn't want to see her here on a permanent basis. "Eyes like a hawk. What's a matter, think I'll choke on it? I've…" She stopped at the look that twisted his face. She didn't want to push him too far, and there was no need to. He got the hint without it. She knew he was good at separating himself. His stern look relayed it all. But she did know what secrets lay beneath even though her strong connection to others emotions was lost to her. Good intention often suppresses darker impulses. It bothered her that she couldn't feel the emotions around her, but it also brought with it a calming peace. Her angelic form of claws, wing bones, and scales were lost too. This bothered her most.

"Then you'll talk?" Heinrich asked, quizzically returning to fighting his tie and getting some air as a reward.

"Scouts honor," she said, gaining an unsure look from Heinrich that he let slip before he could reign in his 'in charge' guise. He removed his tie and tucked it into the pocket with the loose button. "That's more like it."

"So why did you do it?" he asked, crouching down to her level so that they were on even ground. He felt it best not to be intimidating.

"Before I answer that have you ever considered that maybe someone else did this to me?" She couldn't help but get somewhat defensive. Deception was an option the doctors would not take account of in her favor.

"You're saying someone else did this to you?" Heinrich asked, calmly, looking briefly over his notes then back at her and again at his notes, rereading her file.

Atone

"I don't know. I don't remember. All I know is going to Carmina's party, having some drinks. That's it. Everything else is hazy," she said, accessing her alternate's thoughts. Heinrich was dwelling over it doubtfully.

"We talked to Madeline. She said Eric Sinclair dumped you and you went home alone, very distressed. She called your place and you fell, knocking the phone over. I know what happened."

"That makes one of us," she lied remembering full well Rebecca's memories. It was not exactly how Cronos explained it. She found that both Souls seemed to be merged strangely in this their one vessel. She tried to manifest her physical traits, broken wings, extended claws. For some reason the physical body was less tolerant of change than an angels. She knew if she could show him something tangible then he would have to let her go. She had to try something fast. Heinrich was loosing interest. "So automatically you take her word over mine. For all I know she did it," she hissed narrowing her almond shaped eyes making them grow dark with her thick lashes concealing most of them.

Heinrich's brow in contrast, rose. "I'm not sure who's right and who's wrong. But you do have a history of mental illness where Madeline doesn't. Now since we're starting to evaluate your case we have to start somewhere. If it turns out otherwise your case would go to the police again. But for this to happen you need to cooperate."

"Cooperate with a man who's trying to convince me that I'm insane," she wailed rolling her eyes skyward, defeated hands raised over her. She began to cry.

"I'm not trying to convince you of anything. Try to understand that's all I have to go by." Heinrich tried to comfort her while maintaining a professional veneer. Rebecca sobbed, remembering the last psychiatric wing she was in. Atone cried in frustration, her most useful tools concealed from her, the most obvious signs of her demonic gifts hidden from him. She curled up tightly her sobbing growing in intensity.

"I can see we're not getting very far this way," he stated hoping for something more. He rose to leave. From her weeping she felt her skin and muscle tighten defensively, rubbing against inhuman bone. She flexed her shoulders feeling the wing bones. She charged ahead of him, a blur of speed making Heinrich prepare for tactical holds to protect himself. She barred the door instead of attacking him directly which made Heinrich second guess waving over back up. She didn't mistake his slight eye contact and steady open hand. She knew he told the man behind her to wait, but for how long, she wondered. She realized she was running out of time.

"Wait. I'll show you something. Please," she pleaded. She felt the skin push outward along her scapula but it was weak, maybe only in her head. She was panicking, hoping she could pull it off. Heinrich waited. It was now or never. She started to remove the grey T-shirt, which quickly prompted Heinrich to act.

"No. No," he demanded, restraining her.

"If you don't trust me, how can I trust you?" She inquired softly. She stood there frozen in action waiting on him. He released his hold on her. "This better go somewhere."

"When I was dying a fallen angel took my body and merged with my soul," she said, removing her shirt. She tried to picture her skin breaking free from her shoulders and setting free the bony wing stubs. She also pictured how the good doctor saw this if it didn't work. Making her wings show in reality was not only necessary but absolutely crucial. There was no other option. There was a long pause her mind giving in to the fear that they were not going to be seen.

"You needed to take your shirt off to tell me this?" he asked, his voice reminiscent of a parent to a young child. As a young child her answer seemed innocent and delusional.

"I'm trying to show you my wings," she said, blushing then turned angrily around.

"All you're showing me is... well... not wings," he said, taking in the sight of her then pulling his view away. She was a patient, and possibly hostile. Using peripherals he kept his eyes on her in case she would strike. She knew he was still looking by his blush matching her own. "This is an interesting development, however. Angels, Huh?" He said, uneasily.

"You don't believe me?" She hissed made angrier by the lack of claws to strike. Instead she fumed keeping her distance.

"Honestly, No," he said.

"Look, I thought maybe I had enough control, but I haven't yet," she started. This only made it worse and she continued to talk to make it sound less crazy. She babbled knowing that the longer she carried on the less likely she would ever get out of here. She found it impossible to shut up. The more nervous she got the more she talked and with every word that escaped her mouth the more nervous she became. She bit into the side of her tongue and swallowed, formulating a simple phrase to sum up her chain of babble. "Give me a break, I've only been here a couple of days and spent most of that time in the hospital."

There at least it was over. She sighed exhausted.

Heinrich headed for the door, turning his back on her for her own decency. He heard enough crazy from one person. "I'll be back here tomorrow. I think our preliminary evaluation could have gone better but we'll spend more time together, tomorrow. I usually check in with new arrivals to see what plan I have to follow. This should prove interesting."

"Do you think I'm crazy yet? A nympho that's suicidal and thinks she's a demon?" She spat, still trying to manipulate the situation. Maybe she thought if she could convince him she was trying to seem crazy he wouldn't think she actually was. Heinrich didn't seem to change, his demeanor finally under control. She studied him quizzically, like he did her.

"I haven't passed judgment," he said, turning back to face her with a less than authentic smile. For the first time she noticed that her being topless might give the wrong idea especially with how she played with him earlier. She caught herself, concealing what she could from him, better late than never. "You could be, or you could be trying some clever reverse psychology. Either way we'll both find out tomorrow." He locked the door as he left, closing it behind him.

"Hey," she shouted from behind the glass. "You never said…" She gave up, watching him walk away. She picked up her shirt but decided there was no point to modesty. There was at least that benefit here. She had her own room and any one coming would be used to far worse. The tiny lens of a camera over the door would more than likely keep her safe from any would be violators. She lay back down on the bed, the shirt in her hand strewn across her stomach. Her mind drifted to her changing, or lack there of.

She understood the mortal body's rigid structure but an angel's power, even a fallen one's, should be more than enough to break it, bend it, or change it at least. Granted this wasn't exactly a possession, she thought, and there was no telling what state her soul was in after merging with Rebecca. She closed her eyes and tried to change. She tried not to force it but simply wanting it didn't seem to make it so either. Even the effort of trying, combined with hospital drugs and blood lose seemed too much and soon she was asleep.

She awoke when it was dark, the eerie feeling of something hideous pulling her savagely to consciousness. Quickly leaping to her feet she looked around searching for the evil presence. She felt the hairs rise on the back of her neck. Something wasn't right. In a lot of ways this was a good sign, telling her that she still had her connections to others emotions. She was too afraid of the feeling beyond her to be grateful for knowing about it. She stepped up to the door and peered outward from the reinforced window. She noticed that she was still locked in when she tried the door. Returning to the window she thought she saw a form in the dark move. She looked hard to see something, anything out there that would explain this feeling. There, she gasped following the shadow in the dark.

A hand slammed against the glass making her jump back. She cursed herself but noticed the tiny cuts on the hand and thin bloody traces left on the window. A face of a woman with short, boy cut hair matted with seat peered back at her, eyes wide in terror. Her face was flushed as she gasped to catch her breath. Her Grey shirt, like Atone's, was stained with sweat, and clung loosely to her thin frame.

"Let me in, please," the woman that belonged to the hand sobbed. Atone could see small lacerations all over her body. Thin strips were torn from the flimsy standard issue wardrobe. Her voice was muffled through the glass to a tiny quiet whisper. "Please, God, let me in."

"I can't. It's locked," Atone blurted through the glass. She looked into the woman's terrorized eyes. Atone saw the blur down the hall stop, focusing on the woman. "You have to run."

There was no time. The creature, tiring of the hunt, closed in for the kill. It stalked, slow at first, feeding off her fear. Each step made the terrorized woman's heart beat faster. The form, lingered in the shadows just outside of the light. Atone couldn't make it out.

"No, please. I don't want to die. I'll do anything," she sobbed sinking down to beneath the window until only the top of her head remained to be seen from Atone's vantage point.

She wrapped her arms around herself defensively.

"Anything?" Atone heard echo from the shadow in a sinister rumble. The woman's sobbing grew worse. Then a burst of speed sent the shadow into the light in an undistinguishable blur as it collided with her door. Atone fell back at the impact. The woman's head cracked the glass, coating it with blood. Her scream was brief but loud. Her macabre urge to look led her to the door once more, scanning the outside world to find any sign of the woman or monster. Blood pooled under the door making her feet sticky. She stepped back, gasping. The poor girl didn't make it. She looked down at the pool spreading farther inward. She shifted her feet further away seeing a shadow flicker across the floor. A long barbed tongue slithered hungrily under the door. She shrieked and leapt back but the tongue caught her leg sending her backwards. The tongue slithered back, relinquishing its hold. Atone took the opportunity to retreat further in the room to avoid its reach. She sat on all fours in bed, eyes widely staring at the crack under the door. She heard the click of the lock being released. She didn't move. She kept her eyes on the door, her mind trying to figure out how to unlock her angelic powers and what was preventing her from using them. After several moments of fear-petrifying motionlessness she looked at her room for any defendable equipment. There was nothing. She simply sat and waited. When the sun arose her nerves calmed and she slept until Heinrich arrived.

"Rest well?" he asked, flipping through his notes as he entered the room. She moaned as her eyes opened against her desire.

"Not really. I don't like this place," she said, scratching her hair and stretching. She looked out at him with cloudy, sleepy eyes.

"Then maybe you would answer my questions," he said, with his unauthentic smile. "It may help you get out of here sooner." He stopped the rest of his words as he noticed her shirt was still off. He returned to his notes, focusing on her through the corner of his eye as she got dressed.

"You still want to know why I tried to kill myself," she said, sitting at the edge of her bed with her hands to the side of her head. Her head ached and all thoughts of playing with him like their first meeting faded with the throbbing pain.

"Yes. Believe it or not I want to help you," he said, crouching down.

Atone

"You know the deal," she said, looking at the gaudy tie covered in cartoon characters.

"We really…" He began to protest.

"Look, it's just that you don't look like you really care. Like it's all business. I would feel more comfortable if you just…"

"I see. Well it seems reasonable," he said, taking off his tie and unfastening his top button. "Is that better?"

Atone sat Indian style on the bed one hand absently scratching at the bandage on her wrist. "Have you ever felt that everything you put faith in, everything you think real and right and good turns out to be wrong? To have everything you stand for pulled out from under your feet leaving you helpless."

"So are you saying that you depended on Eric perhaps too much?" he asked. Atone curled her nose like a foul stench had invaded it.

"Look you're not listening. I'm saying everything falls out. My mom died. I lost my job. The landlord kicked me out. Eric left me. And God… God's not listening to me anymore. Friends you think you have instead plot against you and the people you depend on avoid you like the plague. I honestly thought that it was over. That there wasn't anywhere left to turn. I really believed there was mostly nothing left."

"Mostly? That's interesting. So what do you think now?" he asked, jotting down a note on his papers. When he was done he turned back to look at her. She couldn't tell if he was really interested or just doing it because it was his job. She paused trying to decide.

"I realize that Life, however terrible, is better than the alternative. I don't know if you are a religious man, Heinrich, but I think I was so close to dead that I saw Hell and I don't want to go back." There was no trickery in her voice only the flat seriousness of someone who's seen too much. This took him a little by surprise expecting more games it was his turn to make a decision.

"It's interesting you brought that up. Yesterday you said you were a fallen angel trapped in this body. Why would you think that?"

"I don't know, really. I've been under a lot of stress lately," she said, taking in a deep breath and scratching her face. Some more notes were written down as his eyes scanned over her.

"I see… Well what I'd like to do…" He stopped, looking away from her down the hall. Thomas, one of the orderlies, stumbled from the hall bleeding harshly from the neck. His coat, once white was horridly transformed with wide stripes of blood. "Oh God! Thomas?"

Before Heinrich could move, a form raced down the hall leaping on the injured man clawing and biting, tearing at the open wound. Heinrich leapt from his stance, waving his hands and calling for aid. Moments later Thomas and his attacker were tackled to the ground. Atone slipped from her room inching closer as tranquilizers were injected into the crazed patient. Peering through the crowd of busy workers she saw the face from the night before, now feral and twisted but still unmistakably her.

"Kara Jameson," Heinrich said, harshly, firmly taking Atone's hand and leading her away from the crowd of people, his body placed protectively between her and the other woman. "I don't get it. She was recovering nicely. We were even going to sign release papers tomorrow," he said, ushering her back into her room. "It's the fifth time this month someone just looses it."

"Have they all reacted this way?" Atone asked, taking her seat, her eyes darting back and forth between him and the doorway. She wrapped her arms around her legs for protection.

"Well now that you mention it… They all became incredibly violent, but this is the first time one of the patients actually bit an employee." Heinrich tried to focus completely on her but there was something about her words that bothered him. "What are you implying, that these reactions are related?"

"I'm not saying anything. It could be a reaction to medicine; perhaps they have the same shrink…" she said, and waited for any acknowledgement. Heinrich looked back at her from the hall and mumbled something before speaking up.

"No. There are four 'shrinks' that work here and we've all had patients go berserk," he grumbled looking at Kara and feeling the absence of progress. "She was one of mine. A couple of Bryce's, and the others were Dr. Sanz, and Maria's."

"Then maybe it's an orderly giving them the wrong drugs or maybe a night watchman," she said, hinting toward a possibly non-crazy explanation for the night before.

"I'm not sure I like where this is going," Heinrich said, squinting. A bitter taste made his face crunch up disgusted. He was starting to turn his attention to other things. She continued regaining his attention.

"…or it could be an outbreak of some crazy cannibal virus. All I'm saying is you should maybe look into it. That's all."

"I will but in the mean time let's get back to you…" Heinrich said, shutting the door to remove his attention from Kara as they bound her and carried her to solitary confinement.

"Great," Atone grumbled. Her mind tried to create a lie worthy of escaping this psychological prison. The beast's face appeared in the back of her mind. She would need one very soon.

Chapter 2

Atone spent the day studying the lay of the psychiatric ward, looking for anything that might help her if the thing returned. There wasn't much. Gone were the days of torturing the mentally handicapped, a fact she both thanked and cursed. Some of those tools could at least be useful.

The hall led to a large recreational room. Couches, tables and a television suspended over the far corner anchored by a metal tray and some cables were the only non living thing in the room the rest of the space being filled by the mildly dysfunctional who busied themselves with playing cards, checkers and of course watching television. Across the hall past the sea of bodies was a reception area or guard post depending on how you choose to term things. There was an empty hall that mimicked the one Atone now stood in, on the other side of the guard post. This sister hall was much more fortified. The dim lights and absence of sound created a foreboding eeriness that made Atone shudder. It was for that reason that she headed toward it.

As she wandered past the desk a nurse looked up. "Miss. Miss, you can't go in there," she shouted her died blonde hair bouncing up and down as she ran around the desk to stop her. She raised one darkly, mechanically tanned hand ahead of her. "Miss!"

Atone stopped to look at her. The sense of the nurse's determination made Atone want to ignore her to see what she would do. She saw how badly the nurse stressed that the area was off limits. Atone smiled at her with the best attempt at innocence.

"What's down that way?" she asked, stepping a single foot forward. The nurse didn't budge from the path instead sternly pushing back. The tanned hand tried forcibly to move Atone/Rebecca back. For a moment they locked against each other non-combatively testing one another before Atone stepped back a pace.

"That's where the really dangerous patience go, that is until they can be transported to a better holding facility. I'm afraid we are ill equipped to handle them properly and though they are confined for your safety it is possible that something could happen. That is why they are in a restricted area." She forced the word Restricted to make her get the point.

"I see, thank you," she said, wandering back to her own room. It could be a long night and she would need the rest. Her sleep was fitful with haunting images of the shadowed figure and strategies on which to combat it.

She awoke, as the night before, in the dark, her eyes on the door handle. A shadow passed and then completely consumed the light that trickled under the door. She let out a gasp despite herself as the lock clicked off. She rose to sitting, eyes steadily on the door. The shadow let the light return as it departed. Atone got up, stepping toward the door. She hesitated as the hair rose on her arms. She felt a breath on the back of her neck.

"Run" breathed the voice. It didn't leave it came in! She tensed, resisting both the urge to face it and the desire to flee as it wanted her to. She gave herself a few seconds to calm herself before doing anything.

"No," she defied the beast. Then, under her own powers and not that of fear, she turned to face it full on, unafraid, her eyes growing darker becoming angry tempests. The Beast did a double take as it looked in her eyes. "I'm not going anywhere."

She felt her torso burn before her mind could register the movement of the monster's claw. Blood followed the burn, coating her clothes. She clutched her chest, falling to one knee from the pain.

"Run," it hissed out again. "Run or die."

Atone felt the fire in her chest grow hotter, reminding her of somewhere else. She watched on in pain as the beast advanced upon her. It grew closer; one step followed another and another. It was drawing out the hunt making it a game. She knew running would only add to its sick pleasure but denying him that meant nothing if you were dead anyway.

Atone burst from the room ignoring all the other doors, heading straight for the recreation room. The shadowed form behind her chased after happily enjoying his sport. Throwing chairs aside, Atone dropped to her knees and slid under the table to the other side of the room. The table buckled as the beast leapt from the hall, ignoring the toppled chairs, to land on top of it. It looked at her, puzzled that she was no longer moving. "Run."

"What are you?" she asked, taking a moment to take in the wretched distortion of this creature. It was obviously human once, but its features were now stretched nearly three feet longer than normal human proportions. The once peach flesh was now a light grey blue. Its features were jagged its ears stretched to long points. Its jaw hung dangling loose from its face, savage rows of teeth long and pointed. She swept her leg out to break the flimsy leg of the table but the creature corrected itself to fast for her to gain an advantage. The beast tumbled off to the side. Atone grabbed the freed leg of the table and took off, running down the dark, foreboding corridor. She could hear the beast rise behind her, throwing the table aside. She began to try the doors. No. No. The beast slowed watching her but still kept coming. No. No. Damn! She could smell the rotten decay of its breath but didn't dare stop. There, the latch gave and she entered quickly. Inside the padded cell a form rocked back and forth murmuring crazily while hugging herself inside her straight jacket.

"Hey," Atone said, nudging the body. "Come on." She kept most of her attention to the door. She did not hear the beast approach and secretly preyed that she escaped it. "Your name is Kara, isn't it, one of the craz… people that faced that thing, right?"

"Something wicked this way comes," the woman murmured, flipping her entire body around to face the new comer. Her features shimmered taking on for a brief moment the visage of the fiend outside. Atone shook her head and saw the image of Kara Jameson, normal crazy person.

"You're Kara, Kara Jordan," she said, shaking her violently. "Snap out of it. We have to fight this thing."

"Dark Father is coming. The vampire lord. All hail Dark Father. Our prince. Our king." Her mystic mumbling almost covered the wisp of sound trailing in behind her. She turned to notice the door ajar. "Dark Father is here."

Atone could feel the shimmering form behind her. She was trapped. Before Atone could turn around, she was hit by a heavy blow from behind that sent her forward into the padded wall. She then tumbled down to the ground. When she tried to move a weight landed on her, pinning her down. She realized when the Dark Father spoke that it was more than likely his foot. "Yes, my ghoulish vixen," it spoke, for the first time like a human. Its voice was rich, masculine, and almost majestic if it wasn't so arrogant. Atone tried to rise again when the weight eased up. The force of his leg came crashing down. She was sent back down for her trouble. Her back made a painful popping noise and she saw a flash of light blinding her in the pain. A long barbed tongue licked the blood his claw found under her skin. "Just as I thought. I know this taste. The taste of my maker, when he gave me new life. Come my queen; drink your first drink of eternal life from the blood so sweet and pure." The horned tongue slithered down Kara's throat his claws shredding the fabric making up the front of the straight jacket. She squirmed happily eager at his embrace. His tongue retracted. "The blood of an angel."

He unclipped Kara's jacket shifting his weight to reach her better. Atone felt almost excluded if it wasn't for the fact they were talking of drinking her life's blood. Her eyes fell on the table leg. Kara was wriggling free of her loosened restraints like a psychotic butterfly. She took hold of the leg pushing Dark Father aside as Kara did the same with her binding cloths. They dove toward each other the table leg forced through Kara's exposed chest. The force of the collision sent Atone toppling out of the room. Jumping up in a flash she slammed the door shut gasping. The Dark Father pounded on the door jerking her forward with every strike. She looked down the haunting hall to see the reception desk. "The keys."

She gasped bracing herself. These deluxe crazy rooms were practically airtight.

That's probably why he was pounding on the door instead of slithering out as a shadow. She held it fast until the banging stopped. When the Dark Father gave up she bolted for the desk rummaging through it for the keys.

"What are you doing?" the nurse asked. Atone was about to explain to her the events of the night when she took in the sight of her. The night nurse's eyes were glowing a sickly blue white. Her features were blank and mindless. She raised a hand up with the stiffness of a marionette revealing a syringe.

"I'm going the other way." She turned to see the Dark Father behind her, nearly colliding with him when she turned. Her heart leapt, lodging forcefully into her throat and making her head pound. The heart in her throat wouldn't let her scream in his face.

"It wasn't very nice what you did to Kara," the vampire growled. Atone struggled but she was already captured by his strong arms.

"No I could be…" She went to bargaining before being cut off by the syringe piercing her flesh.

"What you will be is my prey. You will be mine forever." She felt the fangs tear her flesh, the spiked tongue licking into the wound each thorn sucking hungrily at the injury. The pain and drugs were too much to bear and she fell to unconsciousness in his arms.

Her mind swam in a fog as she could feel the sounds and fears of all the patients and doctors. She could feel the intense fear, the fear of the Dark Father. Her mind reflected faces transfixed in horror. Her eyes opened to see orderlies grabbing at her. She heard her voice but it wasn't her. Her body burned. Her hands and back felt like they were broken and healed only to be broken once more in a savage cycle of agony and mercy. Bones popped in and out of place as the orderlies managed to fit her in a straight jacket.

In the confusion they never saw the bones pierce through her flesh or thin, fish bone claws extend from her fingertips. Her mind tried to catch up to what she missed. The Psychiatric ward was in a state of Chaos. She couldn't tell what was real and what wasn't. She could hear someone screaming in pain and saw the haunting phantasms corrupt the faces of the orderlies that bound her. "I'm not crazy. The Dark Father hunts here. He hunts for Blood. Blood gives him power. It's in the blood… the blood…"

She trailed off as the drugs kicked in. Heinrich stepped back as the orderlies carried her down the haunted hall. She looked out, eyes drained of light as horrid reflections distorted the walls, playing off her fear and the drugs in her system. She tried to fight but the drugs and men held her fast.

Heinrich cursed, "What the Hell is going on here, Bryce? Did you see her eyes?"

"I'm not sure…" He sighed, scratching his scraggly red beard. Bryce's bald head was spotted with tuffs of red hair. He yawned, wiping his hands on his khaki pants and plaid shirt. "I don't know what's happening to this place."

"The blood," Heinrich said, his mind mulling it over. An idea started to formulate in the back of his mind. "Listen, Bryce, I may need your help on something, but I need you to keep it between us."

"Sure, man, what is it?" he asked.

"Get a blood sample from Rebecca, George McAlester, Louis Tabard, and Kara…"

"I can't get Kara's blood sample, Henry," he said, scratching down notes on his palm. He raised his head. "She broke out last night. Beat up the night watch man and fled. Cops are still looking for her."

"All right the others then. Have the lab call me as soon as results get in."

"You got it. What are we looking for?" he asked, suspiciously.

"Anything out of the ordinary," Heinrich advised.

"What's this about?" Bryce wondered out loud. When Heinrich answered him he seemed surprised.

"Just a hunch. I'll be in personnel records for the rest of the day."

"Hey," Bryce said, pointing at his chest with both hands in an exaggerated macho stance. "Who do you think you can count on? Me baby."

"Thanks Bryce," Heinrich smiled falsely. Bryce's grin was wide taking up half his face, like some creepy animated character.

Several hours later Heinrich reached for the last file of the stack of employees. "The

night watch man, a mister Winter Forest Blue…
Hippy parents… last known occupation:
security guard for World Development
Organization."

Heinrich moved to the computer taking a
drink as the screen loaded the WDO search. It
pulled up several files mostly news clippings of
the fateful destruction of its base. P.R. could not
remedy the outbreak caused by the pathological
disease and WDO was bankrupt and liquidated
shortly after the infection. "World Development
Organization lost all employees that worked that
shift… 17 civilians outside the facility lost their
lives in less than 24 hours. The next day
casualties would rise to 76 before the infected
area was properly quarantined. No further
casualties were documented but WDO was
forced to shut down, unable to rise above such a
public disaster."

"Bryce poked his head from outside the
room. Glasses to large for him sat awkwardly on
his nose. The myriad of tinted lenses making
him look like a bug. "I'm leaving for the day.
Are you coming?"

"In a minute, Bryce. Hey, do you know
anything about the WDO?"

"Yeah, a little. They had a factory not twenty minutes out of town. Why?"

"I don't know. This thing has me rattled, that's all," Heinrich said, shutting off the screen. "It's probably nothing."

Heinrich left with Bryce before parting company in the parking lot. Heinrich was headed for home but stopped at the light. "I must be crazy," he said to himself, turning instead down a rubble-covered road away from home. He drove past a bullet-ridden sign that read: Restricted! Property of WDO.

He parked his car and squeezed between the tin sheet barriers. Something rattled near him and he turned his head. The wind banged a part of the barrier into a bush. A particularly strong gust of wind agitated a raven from his slumber making the night colored bird squawk in agitation. He heard a moan from the building ahead and froze, his eyes looking for where it came from. There, he thought, breathing again. The wind blew across a broken window making the noise. He advanced on the building trying to calm his nerves. Soon he was opening the door to the abandoned factory, a loud screech of rusted hinges echoing throughout the complex. On impulse rather than logic Heinrich said, "Hello?"

Atone

A strange rustling carried across the breeze growing louder. Heinrich reached for a light switch and the lights snapped on then several exploded from years of neglect. A fury of fangs and fur attacked him. Heinrich's scream was muffled by fluttering wings. The broken light shot out sparks, raining down on the multitude of the fleeing bats.

"Fucking bats," he cursed, missing the human form in the flickering light. It was gone by the time he turned back. He wandered through the dimly lit and flickering halls until coming to the time clock, next to the break room. "Winter Blue. If he worked that day his badge would…" He looked through the names by the clock. Winter Blue had one punch. There was no punch for leaving. He slipped the punch card into his shirt pocket before a scrapping sound caught his attention.

"Great, more bats," he said, looking over. The light in the hall flickered and went out. Each light followed in turn until only the end of the hall remained lit. There he saw a man.

"Oh, I'm sorry. I thought this place was closed down," Heinrich explained. The man only moaned, disinterested. The lights flickered back on. Inches from him, emerging from the break room was a severely injured man, wild eyes peering out of flayed flesh. Heinrich chirped a scream, leaping back a few paces. The man clawed out at him then fell to the ground as Heinrich retreated. It growled fiercely, broken legs and spilled intestines trailing after it. "I'll be leaving now."

Heinrich turned to see another mutilated person. Reacting on instincts he punched the crippled man in the face knocking the head off its shoulders. The head dangled along his back upside down. Heinrich froze a moment too shocked to do anything. He stepped past it to see the man's head, mouth still snapping and snarling. Heinrich was ready to leave. Claws brought him to action. He screamed, flailing. He turned to see a third, a woman without a lower jaw and sickly yellow eyes sunk deep in her head. Dodging her grasp he headed for the door.

"No. Stay," came a voice down the hall, He turned against his better judgment and saw Kara beckoning to him, shimmering in the temperamental light.

"Kara?" He heard himself say, for a moment forgetting the gruesomely disfigured people closing in. The light flickered off for a moment then a horde of zombies replacing her radiant form where she stood. Heinrich turned to escape. The way out was blocked. Masses of crippled bodies were at every turn. Heinrich ran ducking down a hallway. He lost the horde as they came after him. His eyes darted around his hand finding a knob. It turned. He closed the door carefully. Behind him something moved, grabbing hold of his shoulder, harshly. He jumped flailing around to strike the thing that attacked him. He turned on his phone to see the vicious mop flung aside. He peeked through the key hole seeing the creatures searching. He stepped carefully back, looking around. There was a ventilation duct in the small room mostly covered with many industrial strength cleaning supplies, many leaking from their neglected containers. He looked around in his broom closet prison. This was his escape route. He searched around for a screwdriver to remove the panel. Then the ringing started. The whole compound echoed with loud moans. The door began to bang as they wanted the prize inside.

"Give me a fucking break," he cursed prying the vent from the wall with his bare hand. The door burst open. In a reactive swing he hit the first with the edge of the vent covering, cutting deep into its skull. "Son of a…"

Chapter 3

Atone shook violently as the drugs wore off. The heat rising from her body was gone, replaced by the chill air. She looked around and noticed unmistakably the padded walls and sealed door that marked her new room on the dark side of the ward. The straight jacket held her firmly, though her wing bones protruded from holes torn from her vicious thrashing earlier. The door clicked open but nothing waited for her on the other side. She felt a strange sense of completion; the drugs helping her wriggle loose her demonic visage and abilities. She couldn't see anything but felt her talon tipped hands cut away the top part of the straight jacket. The strap freeing her hands must have cut her legs free also as she fumbled for her footing. The top of the jacket fell away to her waist and her bare feet curled up under her from the cold of the rubber beneath them. She reached back, touching the bony nubs, feeling the burn as raw nerves touched fingertips. She smiled. She looked at her hands, barbed with thin near translucent claws.

"They're not Longing and Mercy but they'll do," she whispered to her self, barely a sound, not wanting the attention that a louder noise might attract. At this time of night, she thought, no one would care anyway. Then a noise brought her attention sharply to the slightly open door.

She heard another door open and took a fighting stance. She froze there in place until her mind remembered Dark Father creeping like a shadow into her room the night before. If she was going to face something she did not want to be trapped in this small room while doing it. After a moment she stepped outside. She saw a patient wandering the halls. Another door and another opened, each one producing a single patient, each shambling, mindless predators. She turned to flee the suddenly overwhelming odds to see more behind her. There was nowhere to go as they mauled over her. The sheer numbers toppled her and pinned her to the ground, the patients shrieking in psychotic babbling tongues that flooded not just her ears but her mind as well. Her only option to protect herself was to curl up into the fetal position as their gibbering noise harassed her and their stiff, numb fingers groped her. A scream echoed out, drowning out the shrill wail of the psychotics. For a moment even their feelings were absent from her mind. She lay there eyes forced protectively closed a moment before realizing she was alone in the hall. She rose cautiously testing one of the doors to find it still locked and unyielding to her force.

She felt the presence of something in the back of her mind. She tried to figure out if it was the Dark Father or a few remaining traces of the drug that tried unsuccessfully to destroy her brain. Either way these mind games angered her. She walked cautiously, stepping silently toward the Rec. Room. She felt comfortable in the relative space. She and her nerves calmed a little and she looked around the corner peeking out just enough to see the end of the hall. She straightened, scanning her surroundings for anything suspicious. A breeze made her hair billow behind her and she turned following the gust of air. There was nothing there. But then nothing moved.

"I said you would be my prey," the Dark Father, said. "Say you're sorry," he said, stepping closer to her. She stepped back and tried to watch the blur as it darted across the room.

"You're not gong to make me run?" she asked the blur, more amazed at its speed then afraid of its childish threats. Atone was in control, now more than ever. Rebecca, simply a memory, hid in the back of her mind like the normal weak human she was. She heard a guttural hissing from the left side of the hall then a second from the right.

Atone

"There is nowhere to run, Rebecca Van Ness," Winter stated whimsically. "Just give up and except your fate. Make it easier on all of us."

"All of us. The last time it was all in my head. What's to say this isn't?"

"You have no way of knowing, Rebecca. I have taken the precaution of adding Emotion to any illusions that will dance with you tonight. What? Don't act all surprised. You think a vampire wouldn't figure it out. Everything about you is at the tip of my tongue, except for that which still flows in your veins. Blood knows all, You foolish, foolish devil."

Atone stood, watching the crazed patients on either end of her slowly advance. Even in their feral natures they knew what she was. That wasn't going to stop them, but that second-guessing might just give her the edge she needed, her mind calculated. Time for thinking was over with a vicious snarl. They charged, Atone leaping up to kick outward. Her foot landed to the jaw of one, her hands digging deep into the throat of the other. Her feet quickly twisted around his neck. She hung, suspended a moment between them. She rolled her body, the sound of a crack coming from the patient at her feet. The one at her claws gasped as she wrenched free, the head rolling away. With nothing left to hold her up she plummeted to the ground. She landed on all fours, close to the ground reminding the Dark Father of a reptile. The headless body squirmed, spewing blood from the jagged whole. The other rose, his jaw and neck popping back in place.

"You're going down, bitch," he growled attacking again. Atone pushed up off the ground, spinning in her ascent, feet kicking her opponent as she rose through the sky. He flew over the new table landing in a heap at the far end. She followed after him. Leaping in the air, she grabbed hold of the replacement table's edge, flipping it over as she landed on the other side next to the crazed patient. It flopped awkwardly through the air landing upside down near them. The ghoul patient was combat ready when she landed.

"You missed," he said, taking a savage swipe at her with his simple ghoulish claws.

"Did I?" she asked. One clawed hand punched into his stomach the other shredding his throat. Hoisting him up, she slammed him down onto the upturned table leg. He screamed wriggling in agony until lying still. Her eyes searched for the Dark Father when crazy no longer posed a threat. She caught a glimpse of the other patient, headless, start to shrivel in the first rapid signs of decay. Slowly, deliberately she returned her attention to Dark Father. "Are you enjoying the show, 'Dark Father."

"Enough of this!" He roared lunging from the shadow to tower over her from the center of the overturned table. "You are MY prey."

Chapter 4

Heinrich crawled from the vent outside then ran to his car. "What's so damn important to call me here?" He cursed to himself speeding off. It was several blocks before his heart beat slowed enough to responsibly check his phone messages. He parked the car when the gravel road turned to asphalt and he could see the city lights ahead.

The information played back in his ear after he punched in the appropriate numbers. "This is Professor Grey from the blood clinic. The information we've gathered is surprising. There is a significant amount of Excleozine, a strong hallucinogen that permanently damages the brain. There was something in Rebecca Van Ness's sample that seems to neutralize the long-term effects. We're looking into that. Something else was in there too. There was a rare blood born pathogen in each subject that seems to destroy blood at an alarming rate. Again, Rebecca Van Ness seems protected from the long term…" The phone message ran out of time ending with a tinny voice of a computer message prattling off options at what he could do now. He didn't listen to this hitting the familiar button that ended it all and returned to the main screen. With a sigh he put it in first gear and released the clutch to resume his drive to the hospital. He hoped Frankie would understand.

Professor Grey sat in his lab, eyes to the microscope. "Amazing, simply amazing. This is unlike anything I've ever seen."

"I'm going home, Raymond," Bryce said, poking his head in. "Get hold of Henry yet?"

Professor Grey shook his head no. "Kill the lights on your way out. I'll be done here soon."

The light shut off at Bryce's touch before he turned and departed. Professor Grey looked around. From the dim light he made out the Bunsen burner, chemical rack and the body, covered with soiled white linen. "Just you and me now, friend."

He turned his attention back to the microscope. An arm slipped from the white cloth showing the mangled flesh from underneath it. "This DNA is a new strain. I've got to check this out, make sure it's not a hoax," he said, raising from his chair. He looked up noticing the missing body. "What the…" The last words never came as his throat was torn from his body in one blurred motion.

Heinrich parked his car at St. Bridgette's hospital getting as close as he could to the door. He entered the main building and jogged to the elevator pushing the second to last button up to the psychiatric ward. He scowled as he had to change his speed while he waited in the metal box. Winter Blue was on duty. Hopefully he could return before something sinister could again occur. Finally he sighed as he was free to trot the few yards to the door of his wing. Digging the keys from his pocket his fingers nimbly found the correct one and slid it home.

"Pathetic, Rebecca Van Ness. Try harder," Winter Blue hissed. The turn of the doorknob caught the Dark Father's attention. Heinrich stepped in quickly noticing the carnage and aware of what awaited him as he looked at a barely human thing near an inhuman Rebecca. Dark Father turned toward him, dropping Rebecca thoughtlessly to the ground. "Interruptions."

Atone leapt up sinking her claws into his back. Winter Blue growled in frustration. "No more games." He grabbed hold of her and tossed her gingerly to the reinforced window. His extra reach leaving her no real mode to defend save for flailing ineffectually at his arms with her claws. Flying through the air she had no time to soften the landing. The force made the translucent window opaque with spider web cracks. Her boney nubs punched through the glass holding her in place, her blood filling the cracks in the window to create a macabre red cross on a field of white. The pain fired through her like an explosion the force escaping her throat in a wretched scream.

"Stay in your place, angel. I will take care of this." Dark Father turned his attention to the good doctor. Atone swung her legs upward, twisting them around the television and its loose support. He paid her no attention, taking a step toward Heinrich. "Welcome, Dr. Gordon. I see you want in on the party. Nurse, assist the doctor with some medication."

Heinrich looked over at the nurse, with the syringe in hand. A crash echoed through the room, and his head turned back to see the television break loose crashing over Winter Blue's head. Atone hit the floor hard taking Blue down with her impaling him on one of the upturned table legs.

"I'm ready, doctor. Please don't struggle," she said, smiling with the emotionless of her dominated state. Heinrich punched her getting no reaction. He went for it again with more force but she caught his arm and twisted in a well-trained move they often used for out of hand crazies. She continued on unchanging. "You will like it. Trust me."

"Heinrich," Atone said, shaking the fog of blood loss out of her eyes. She looked over in time to see the Nurse about to induce her medication on the struggling doctor. She dove toward them intercepting the syringe. It burned as the fluid pumped into her body. In a fierce growl she snapped the nurse's neck, which then crumpled and fell dead to the ground. Heinrich turned around to take it all in. The drugs began to take hold and Atone slumped into his arms. He held her noticing the bony, now bloody, protrusions along her back. "I told you I was... an angel..."

He held her tight looking around the room at the carnage he stumbled into. The broken television lay empty free of its horrendous prisoner.

Chapter 5

Atone heard water running and 1950's music playing from another room. Bright lights filtered in from the door leading to the origins of the music and water. The smell of dust was a strange relaxant calming her nerves. She peered into the light from the door to see Heinrich rinsing blood from his arm. She looked at her own hands, tipped with claws marked with blood and tissues of flesh. As she rose from the sheet-covered couch the dust kicked up creating a cloud that blurred her vision and tickled her nose. Couches, chairs, and bookcases played ghost, shrouded in white sheets. There were no windows in this room, she noticed. She slipped from the room seeing the hall outside, the dust ending half way toward the 45-degree stairwell to a foyer. The end of the armrest was a pedestal with a flower-filled vase on it. There were pictures on the wall of hand painted and, by the look and age of the pictures, long dead people. As she headed for the stairs a shimmer of light crossed her path.

Atone shielded her eyes from the light seeing between her fingers. There was an elegant hand carved wooden bed with pink bedspreads and canopy. Ballerina figurines, stuffed animals and a large porcelain doll lined a shelf that cut the room in half on three walls. She heard a door open from the other room then close. She slunk backwards from the light toward the shadow and dust. Heinrich opened the door as she stepped behind it.

"Ms. Van Ness?" Heinrich asked, looking for her. His hands were busy wrapping his wounds with gauze. He looked at the footprints in the dust following them. She followed him to where he stopped at the pink room. "Ms. Van Ness?"

"Pretty girly." she spoke from behind making him half jump. He looked back at her with a mock scowl.

"That's my daughter's room. Francine. She doesn't even stay here. When she's over she sleeps downstairs in the den," he explained.

"Where are we?" Atone asked, not interested in his explanations.

"Oh, sorry. Welcome to the casa de Gordon. This is… was the family estate, handed down to me. But when Ingrid left I didn't need such a big house. Two thirds of this house isn't even used," he went on, oblivious to her disinterest, a simple my home would have more than sufficed.

"So what happened?" she asked, gesturing toward his arm. He didn't see it.

"We grew apart. You know how it is. I got joint custody and now just try to rebuild my life," he continued on. Clearly outside of work he had no clue about people, she thought. It was either that or his nervousness talking.

"I meant with your arm," she smiled, half-curious to find out the answer she was really thinking.

"Oh, your claws. You got me when I was carrying you in," he said. She leaned in close to him staring intently, like a predator to prey.

"So…" she said, with lips dangerously close to his. "What do you want in return?"

"Excuse me?" His voice grew shrill.

"For helping me. No one does anything for free," she purred rubbing up against him.

"Sure they do. It's called Kindness. You know, Charity." He tried to squirm past her and she toyed with him a little, playing some cat and mouse. She caught him by the stairway using the handrail to get in front of him. She slithered her body across his, making him shrink back, nearly laying on the steps.

"I know what you want. Your heart rate is pounding, groin bulging. Your mind is practically screaming for me..." she said, the sweet seductive sound of her voice half-joking and half serious.

"That... May be but sometimes we have to follow something more important than instincts," he said, not denying his attraction. This made her smile while she pulled back the seduction, reining her womanly wiles in slightly.

Why?" she said, smiling, but rolled away allowing him to get up. "Like what?"

"Logic. That's what separates us from animals."

Atone burst into a riot of laughter. Heinrich frowned and she tried to restrain herself. "Are you sure about that? All right, Heinrich. I'll let you go on thinking that for now, but be prepared for a surprise when your time comes." He rose to sitting and dusted himself off. He straightened his tie and took a step forward.

"I'll see you tonight, we'll talk," he said, all business.

She felt like pointing out that he did in fact want something even if it was just to talk but restrained the temptation to bait him further. "Where are you going?" she asked instead.

"To work. I still have to smooth over what happened last night," he said. She reached the door as he opened it. "Don't worry. I've got a good idea how to explain this and without this they'll never know the truth," he said, waving a VHS tape. "Do us both a favor and burn this, will you?"

"I know you wanted something from me." She gave in taking the tape from him with a smile. He returned hers and went for his car. His face turned to a frown as he saw the back seat speckled with blood, growing brown with age. He took a few quick sweeps with a shop rag that he kept for car work. Looking at it again the traces were minimal and he convinced himself that no one would be searching his car anyway. Being a doctor had to get you some credibility, he hoped. He slipped the transmission into reverse and rolling out of the driveway.

The drive to work was not interrupted and he arrived a little earlier than normal. The extra time was burned up with finding a parking lot. Several police cruisers were blocking the way and he had to drive around toward the emergency entrance instead. Entering the building and then elevator he relaxed his mind, putting himself at ease. He was calm, as though there wouldn't be bodies to count once he arrived upstairs. He found it unsettling that knowing what to expect made it easier to reach a calm state. There would be police, maybe reporters by the door guarding entry to the crime scene. This was to be expected. He tried to convince himself that he wasn't there to cover up a crime only to steer it away from the innocent. He also tried to convince himself why she was considered such. She did save his life. That was something, at least as far as he was concerned. As the door opened he was genuinely surprised and a little disappointed in his assumption. His look of shock was anything but forced or fake as the police raised their hands to intercept him.

"State your business, Sir!" they demanded. There wasn't any yellow tape or flashing lights. There were only these two officers with raised badges to indicate themselves from everyone else. The lack of the hubbub made Heinrich start to sweat.

"I work here," he said, brow furrowed in confusion. His voice came in stuttering spurts emphasizing each word. Get it together he thought. But the duality of having a police presence while at the same time being so minute threw off his hold on things that took the elevator ride to grasp. The door swung open and a bald, grim looking man in a brown suit half emerged from the room.

"Hey, rook…" He froze mid statement as he looked at the doctor. "Are you… Heinrich Gordon?"

"Yes. What's going on?" Heinrich asked, looking past him to see the upturned table but no bodies to speak of. Maybe they moved them. He smoothed his tuft of unsettled hair and adjusted his glasses before sheepishly smiling at the detective.

"More missing crazies, please. Step inside," the balding officer said to Heinrich waving him in. Then his attention turned to one of the rookies. "Rookie, get me and the three doctors some coffee." Heinrich stepped past them taking the hint from the balding man's gesture. The rookie frowned as the detective listed off flavors and styles for him to retrieve, Erwin asked Heinrich what he would like and he mumbled the first type of coffee that came to mind. Heinrich investigated the carnage as Erwin relayed this information. A smashed television was there and the smashed up window with cross of rust brown dried blood, still marking the events from the night before, as he would have expected. But were the body on the table would have been was what appeared to be sand instead. He almost missed the Officer as he came up behind him. "Weird isn't it. Yesterday one of your patients disappear, now three more are gone and also a night watchman oh, and the dead nurse."

He motioned the pen in his hand to the corner by the desk. Heinrich saw her feet facing him other cops taking photographs. He watched Heinrich as he took it all in. The detective jotted down some notes and Heinrich turned to face him as he spoke again. "Looks like you guys need better security."

"I… I don't know what to tell you," he said, fighting off the stutter in his voice while studying the scene ahead of him.

"Well, I've got theories," he said, making a sweep to the expansive room of wreckage, dramatically. "This room for example. I'm thinking something pseudo-religious."

"Excuse me, detective?" Heinrich turned at last to face the detective. His brow furrowed speculatively, trying to get into the detective's line of thought.

"Erwin, Erwin Marks," the detective said, with a smile that made his eyes crinkle to small black specks and his cheeks puff out.

"Mister... Officer... Erwin. What's this have to do with religion?" Heinrich asked, waving his hand back to the crime scene rather than return his gaze and be caught by it once more.

"Last supper," he said, pointing down to the table. His arm swept up to point at the window. "Crucifixion. If I could tie in the nurse, and figure out the who..." He turned his attention back to the window. "I can find out who it wasn't, when the blood comes back from the lab." His feet unconsciously stepped toward the window, stopping at the Television, muttering about another piece of the puzzle that doesn't yet fit. Heinrich waited and grew agitated.

"Officer Marks. If I'm done here, I've got patients…"

"Patience is a good thing to have. I've got patience; you need it in a job like mine," he said, smiling. When his humor didn't get a response the laughter faded in his eyes. "All right Mr. Gordon."

"Dr," Heinrich snapped, and then thought it best to soften his approach. "Heinrich, or Henry if you like."

"Henry. I've talked to Bryce," Marks said, waiting. Heinrich stared at him confused. "He said you were looking into something. He said you asked for blood samples?"

"Oh," Heinrich said, remembering it at last. Thankfully the absent memory lost from the events of last night made it seem a simple and unimportant matter. "Yes. That's right. What does that have to do with anything?"

"Oh nothing. Except that the three missing patients were the ones you wanted blood from. Four if you count Kara."

"You don't think I had anything to do with their disappearances?" Heinrich asked, after debating the question in his own mind. It sounded like a decent question in his head, but came out worse and he nearly bit his tongue trying to stop the words coming out.

"I don't think anything, that is until all the sides are heard from and the facts are in."

"I see. Well about the blood samples… the patients were the ones that seemed to get worse. Blood samples aren't uncommon. We test regularly to make sure what might be a mental illness isn't actually caused by some foreign ailment."

"And what did your test prove, Doctor?" he asked, flipping through his pocket notebook. "Don't bother. High amounts of the hallucinogen, Excleozine, and an unknown blood born pathogen in each sample with a mutation in Rebecca Van Ness's sample stating that she is immune to both. This sound familiar?"

"Yes. This proves that it wasn't mental problems but drugs, or a disease, or both." Heinrich waved him over to his room and entered. They took a seat in their respective chairs. It made Heinrich more at ease to be in his seat of power, were he was most in charge. "I was starting to get suspicious when patients

lined up for release would suddenly go berserk.
I was working on that last night."

"You think you're on to some
conspiracy? Did you ever think about contacting
us? You know the law enforcement?" Erwin
grumbled, his cheery visage growing more
serious as he got down to business.

"I wanted to have proof first," Heinrich
said, reigning in his most professional
demeanor.

"Well aside from the blood samples
what else do you have?" Erwin asked.

"I was looking for anything peculiar
among the employees, some sort of sign or
something. That's when I found this," Heinrich
explained pulling out the employee biography of
Winter Forest Blue along with the news
clippings of WDO and the punch card he
confiscated from the closed testing facility.
Erwin looked it over and then back at Heinrich,
his face growing pale.

"You went into the WDO building? You
got balls, man."

"I saw… I thought I saw Kara there too.
You might want to go check it out, but be

careful. A lot of squatters are there and they didn't seem to be keen on intruders."

"So you were out last night in an abandoned and condemned factory building. Any witnesses?" He sighed, knowing the answer. Not the best of alibi's for someone, Erwin thought.

"You mean besides the horde of homeless trying to kill me? No," Heinrich retorted sarcastically.

"Right, well do me a favor, Doctor. Next time you get the urge to follow conspiracies contact us first." He looked back through the notes that Heinrich handed him. "Not bad work for a civilian, though. You should think about changing professions if you plan on making a habit of this."

"I assure you I do not, Detective Marks. Was there anything else?" Heinrich said, in all seriousness.

"Yes, actually. You do know that Professor Grey is dead?" Erwin asked, with a sly eye studying Heinrich as he said it.

"Professor Grey? When? How?" Heinrich inquired loudly.

"Last night. Throat ripped out. Guess what?" Erwin said, with a slight smile trying to soften the blow.

"What?" Heinrich asked, on command not really wanting to hear the answer expecting something to point back to him somehow.

"That case has a missing nut ward employee too," Erwin said, eyes focused quizzically on Heinrich. It was an unintentional look that made him seem to judge people. It was a look that he couldn't change but one that has unnerved enough cases into confessions so he couldn't complain, even if people had a hard time trusting themselves in his presence. After letting Heinrich sweat a little he spoke again. "Thomas Shepard comes in looking like his neck was made out of hamburger and now he's gone in less than 24 hours."

"Do you think their related?" Heinrich inquired.

"I don't know yet. I don't have everything, you understand." Erwin rose extending his hand to Heinrich. After the awkward shake he went for the open door. "You know you can't leave town, right."

"Of course. Good luck Detective Marks," Heinrich said, with an uncomfortable smile. Marks nodded and continued on heading to the Grey case below. Heinrich shuffled his papers from last night's research and set them aside getting ready for business as usual. "That could have gone better," he muttered to himself noticing as he said it the Rookie at the door with his Caramel mocha without whip cream. "Thanks."

"No problem, Doctor," he said, opening his mouth to speak then shook his head confused, instead passing to another room.

Chapter 6

Atone walked cautiously through the back alley to her… Rebecca's old apartment. She used the tattered straightjacket and some of Ingrid's clothing that she left behind. She wouldn't be wearing this mixed matched outfit for much longer. If she was lucky they still had her things here at the apartment. She looked up to the fourth floor then scanned her surroundings. The fire escape's ladder was a good ten feet from the ground. She grew her claws back and dug them through the masonry, climbing slowly to the first landing before using the fire escape instead. She looked around for anyone and confident that no one saw her climb she proceeded upward. She didn't know what Heinrich was doing but she did know that taking the front door might draw attention to her. Her feet hurt pushed by her own weight into the metal grating that made up the fire escape. It didn't matter, she had been through worse, and this soft, fleshy shell she was in could use a little toughening up. Atone cursed it anyway.

She found the window to her old apartment open, the curtains flapping wildly from a running fan inside. She hesitated. It seemed rather quick for them to find a new tenant. She plunged her head half inside and looked around. Her things still lay, strewn about in a chaos of her former life. The radio and fan was on indicating that someone was here and she searched the room for something that would clue her in to who. Her eyes fell on an old duffle bag with a decapitated cartoon head attached to the zipper. Next to it was a bowling bag.

Eric. She smiled as she stalked through her apartment. Good, Rebecca thought crawling to the front, I hope he thinks this is his entire fault and he is completely miserable. Atone stopped her kicking her back to an afterthought. She would stay in control. This idiotic thinking was no good and did not serve a real purpose. She took some clean clothes from the pile. Besides, she sensed what he did. He was neither feeling guilty or miserable. The song stopped to begin another. In the space she could hear the noise that was otherwise lost to the music. Panting moaning and creaking furniture filled the silence. The new song began and Atone sprang into action. Dropping her newly acquired clothes she slithered across the floor like a predator, eyes narrowed, and breath coming in short bursts. Her nose couldn't help but sniff for the scent of her prey. She gently, silently moved the beaded curtain that replaced a door to the bedroom. She saw Eric his naked body covered in tribal tattoos and Madeline, who gyrated rhythmically over him. She was lost in the moment of ecstasy her body quivering. She would stay lost.

Atone felt a shattering in the back of her head. A wave of something, someone washed over her, taking over. She walked forward without thinking or feeling.

"Yeah, baby. Like that," Eric encouraged then did a double take as an extra set of arms began to caress Madeline's round perfect breasts before wandering elsewhere. Atone tore open her jugular with one set of claws spraying blood across Eric's chest and face, the other clawed hand went to spilling her prey's intestines. Atone dangled the macabre marionette over him, her dying convulsions finishing what her living body started, bringing Eric to completion. He tried to scream, the fear and shock choking him. Atone let Madeline fall aside still quivering. Blood and gore soaked the bed and covered Eric. He found his voice only to have Atone's clawed hands silence him. Blood squirted in his mouth as her claw held his lower jaw and tongue together. He struggled not to drown on his own blood. She could feel his tongue struggle to wriggle free from her claws.

"You're not done, Eric. Not by a long shot," she hissed escaping from her clothes with one hand. "This is going to hurt you as much as you hurt me." She spun the volume knob to conceal the rest of the noise and took the place Madeline left. She made painful, violent jerks as she crushed him under her. Her hands worked feverishly to make it anything but enjoyable. Knife like claws tore between his ribs filling his lungs with blood. He gasped but her legs held him under her. She jerked screaming and moaning in false ecstasy, her eyes never blinking or removing from him. His flailing hands found a lamp and he smashed it across her face. The pieces of the now broken lamp mixed with the entrails and slid between their grinding bodies, cutting them up. She didn't take her eyes from him, her blood mixing with his and Madeline's. She was oblivious to the physical pain, lost in the emotional pain. Fragments of the lamp stuck in her face, driven deep into her flesh. Some pieces found themselves all the way to the bone.

She stopped playing. Her claws began to carve into his wrists as she forced him to stay down. She could feel, even in his pain, that he begun to swell. She roared, in anguish as she felt everything twice. She was not going to let him find even an involuntary amount of satisfaction. He was going to pop soon. Twisting around, she slashed his throat and severed his member simultaneously.

She leapt free from him, landing shakily on her feet. She grabbed a towel from the pile and rushed to the bathroom.

"That was really stupid, Rebecca," she said to the mirror, cleaning her wounds. "Really foolish, this is so fucked, Rebecca. We can't do things like this here," she chastised, washing the blood from her fingers and face. She pulled the broken shards of glass from her cheek. Then took several deep breathes. Atone looked out loosing control. "O.K. What's going on? What just happened?" Rebecca panicked; Atone meanwhile struggled to reign in Rebecca's mind. Look in the mirror, she willed. Look. Rebecca splashed water on her face to rinse it and took the towel to dry off. "What have I done?" she asked, looking up into the reflection as the reflection changed.

"It's alright. Let me handle this," Atone said, relaxing her volatile nerves.

"Who are you?" She breathed out locked in her own gaze.

"I'll take care of you," Atone asked of her insane, human host. "But you have to trust me."

Atone

"Help me," Rebecca gasped, too confused to give up control. Atone broke her gaze looking back at the post slaughter mess. Atone dressed in jeans and an old shirt the rock band logo faded to barely recognizable.

"You made a mess, Rebecca but I'll fix everything." Atone began to pack the bodies. She knew Rebecca's thoughts and she helped without really knowing how. "He goes camping a lot at Lake Manitou."

She took the blanket carefully off the bed. Luckily the blood mostly pooled up in the thick blanket and sheets. She folded it up carefully and lugged it all down to the green, wired together Volkswagen. She thought meticulously of what to do, at the same time separating herself from the event. She fit clothes over mangled bodies. The lake was shadowed by the large hill that had several dangerous curves. Many people go off them this time of year. It wouldn't be hard for one of these accidents to be fatal. She filled Eric's bowling bag with several changes of clothes and set Eric and Madeline up for the drive to their inevitable destiny.

She sat over Eric's corpse and propped up Madeline in the passenger side. It didn't take nearly as long as she expected. She felt uncomfortable as bones poked her and blood soaked through her clothes. It wasn't that long a trip she thought, trying to focus on the task at hand. She reached into Eric's pocket under her to get the keys and was about to turn the engine over when the door to the lot opened. Atone froze looking back through the mirror. Her heart began to race as it seemed to take hours before a presence was seen. A grey haired older lady with a walker and hand knit clothing shuffled slowly through the lot. She started her engine.

"Who's there?" she asked, as the car inched next to her "Hello?"

"It's me, Mrs. Putnam. Rebecca."

"Oh, Rebecca," she said, adjusting her telescopic glasses. With lenses that could see Jupiter on a cloudy night Mrs. Putnam could barely make out the form of Rebecca and Eric. Gratefully Madeline was beyond her sight. "Is that Eric? Are you two back together?"

Atone opened her mouth to speak but Mrs. Putnam kept going. "It's a shame what happened isn't it, dear? You shouldn't go so extreme. They'll be other chances as I always say."

Atone

"I have to get going, Mrs. Putnam," Atone said, urgently. Her eyes started to seek out any vehicles that might interfere.

"Where, dear?" she asked, meekly asking for more conversation.

"We're going camping. Lake Manitou. You know get away and try to patch things up," Atone said, sweat beginning to stream. There was a long awkward silence as two different generations tried to find something similar to talk about and relate to.

"Well drive carefully, sweetie. You kids drive to fast. Every year someone goes off them cliffs," she said, conceding to the fact that there was no one to remember her and talk to her. Rebecca sympathetically touched her arm the gesture bringing light back to the old woman's eyes and a smile to her face. Atone smiled back.

"I will, Mrs. Putnam. Take care," Atone said, driving off. By now the bones that were before uncomfortable have begun to carve their way through her soft mortal flesh, pushed in by the weight. Mrs. Putnam was left behind murmuring something. As the sun was beginning to descend, the first shades of purple and orange coloring the horizon, she approached the curvy roads signs. She sighed deeply slamming her foot to the floor. Gravel kicked out under her tires. The car fishtailed at the sudden need for speed. She released the steering wheel, and clutched the door handle. Her other hand held tightly to the bowling bag. The car roared like a mad bull as it charged for certain death. It collided with a make shift rock curb launching it through the air. The bump sent Rebecca up, pulling her free from the bones that held her in place. The door swung open and she dove free from the anticipated crash. The door collided with the high branches and broke, slamming it closed again. She flew through the air knowing that nothing was going to make the landing hurt any less. She did remember how to fly. Applying the same rule to landing she curled up avoiding tree limbs. It was going to hurt, but her skill could keep her from death. She used the natural slope of the hill to slow her momentum by tumbling. Rolling would be far better than a flat sudden fall. It didn't feel that way as she pin-balled off tree trunks and large rocks, but she was able to steer her roll from the worst of it. One collision unfolded her and she skid the rest of the way along her back leaving a deep, painful groove exposing earth and tree roots in her wake. Her expendable, cheap clothing was torn asunder, her back lacerated severely by the lashing leaves, brambles, and grass.

Atone

She rose almost instantly the pain forcing her to move or die in agony. Her tattered shirt hung to her like a meager washcloth held only in place by the resilient elastic bands. The jeans were a little more durable, but still remained as several tattered threads held together by the thick seam. Unable to see the damage her fingers searched along her back to see for her. She hissed in pain but continued, her hands finding her broken wings dislocated. The bones dangled unattached and sore. She felt like screaming as she reached back in a feeble attempt to reset them. She wanted to scream to the uncaring heavens but that would draw more attention than the rocketing car already brought. No she would have to do this in silence. The noise of the junk vehicle flying through the air and crashing through trees would soon alert the cops or at least the skinny dipping teens. There wouldn't be many warm days left and several people would try getting the last of it in before it grew too cold. She set both her pain and her observations aside and rushed to the wreck site. There were things she had to finish. The Carnage was horrendous. She smelled gas. The car stuck at a 45-degree angle face down and belly up. She took one of Madeline's cigarettes that lay scattered across the windshield along with the lighter. She took a drag, her nerves a mess. Then she ignited the gas setting the wreckage ablaze. Stripping down, she added her bloody, torn, and useless clothes to the fire.

She could hear, campers coming through the woods. They made no attempt to be quiet and the noise made it that much easier to disappear before they reached the burning wreckage. She left to the lake.

Lake Manitou was actually several smaller lakes that speckled the forest at the foot of this killer hill. It didn't take long for her to find one that wasn't being used. She set the bowling bag aside and washed the blood off from it with her hands. She dove in letting the cool water wash away her sins. Her divine healing made the smaller cuts mere memories and the deeper gashes thin scars. Her broken wings would still need to be set to heal properly. Her healing was not capable of remaking parts she didn't have, and the wings would never grow back. She pulled herself free from her last memory of Axael alive, holding her severed appendages, by focusing on Rebecca. She felt Rebecca, scared, panicked, and hiding behind her eyes and found herself pondering. She was supposed to be dead. Having competition over a body was more than she wanted to deal with. But she couldn't help but feel sorry for her at the same time. Being an empath denied her the ability to be a completely heartless demon.

Feeling the pain of her adversary or in this case a simple scared girl took away her right to be angry. Feeling sorry for Rebecca was the same as feeling sorry for herself.

She thought about what happened and why she did it? She searched deep inside poking through the memories of Rebecca. She remembered what Eric did to her. To say it was suicide would be a lie. The imagery she was able to pry from Rebecca's iron grasp was more than enough to justify the violence, even when Atone wasn't the one to carry it out. She debated if she should stay, to spend the night in the wooded shadows, as if a murder wasn't concealed several yards away. After noticing sirens off in the distance she decided instead to make the long march back to Heinrich's home. She dressed promptly in something practical yet appealing and put on some shoes. They felt strange to her. They were to restricting as they cut her connection to the world around her. They were a necessary evil in a human society so she made the best of it. She made it to the outskirts of town before she had enough. When the gravel roads became concrete and asphalt she slipped her feet free of their restraint and continued on barefoot to the Gordon Estate.

Chapter 7

Erwin Marks sat at his desk looking over the reports of the disappearing crazies. Paul Orlando came by tapping on the wall to let Marks know he was there for him. "Yeah?" He said gruffly. "Oh, hey Paul."

"Lost in a case, Erwin?" He said stepping in. He smoothed out his tan slacks and white button up shirt, as he sat down in a chair across the desk from Erwin. His dark brown arms folded up in front of him in prayer, elbows resting on the edge of his desk. The tips of his fingers touched the thinly trimmed goatee "Guess you'll cancel our golf game tomorrow, then. What are you working on?"

"Disappearing Crazies," he said setting a file aside to take up another. "You?"

"Just two toasted college kids down by Lake Manitou. At least we're not on that call to the hospital," Paul informed with a half smile shifting his position and his hands to rest his powerful, masculine jaw line on one of them. Erwin looked up to see more in his friend's eyes then he was telling.

"What call?" he asked, judging the reaction to the question as seemed to be habit.

"Some strange outbreak is causing mass hysteria. I've heard it's like a war zone," Paul answered, his smile fading and a shudder crawling up his spine. Erwin deciphered the look in his eye and grew even more curious. It was fear.

"That's strange. I haven't heard anything," Erwin said, quietly almost to himself.

"That's because some military units took it over. They got there pretty quick," Paul said, with a scowl. Erwin nodded. Paul sat down knowing Erwin long enough to know he still had something to say. "Any leads?" he asked, pushing the ball to make it roll.

"A few. But something seems wrong. Like, for starters, all the video footage between two and six was looped in the first case, that of missing Kara; I think some underhanded crap was going on at night because the loop was old, say fifteen years or so. Then the new case last night, four missing persons and a homicide, the video tape was taken."

"They are two different crimes or at least two different criminals. Maybe one dropped the ball or something so the second had to make the best out of the situation," Paul replied.

"The dead night nurse and missing watch man?" Erwin asked. "Maybe she screwed up and he had to fix it. Maybe. It's not enough to make it stick."

"What else you got?" He shifted his position again mirroring his former position to the other side.

"Dr. Heinrich Gordon. He's been doing some investigating on his own. At least he says he is. He might be in on it. Could be a threesome with them all turning on each other. Either that or he's a legitimate and concerned human being. Either way, he's casting suspicion on the absent watch man." Erwin passed the file over to Paul. He scanned over the files that Heinrich established.

"The WDO? That sites off limits. How did he get this information?" This news seemed to hit Paul hard, jerking him nearly out of his seat.

"He snuck in. Said a bunch of bums tried to kill him. So he grabbed this and ran."

"Didn't they have armed guards on surveillance or something?"

"Paul it happened twenty years ago. I'm sure whatever bureaucrat was assigned to the problem would have long since pulled out their forces."

"So what's your plan?" Paul asked, trying to hide the quake in his voice. "You're not planning to go in there and verify this, are you?"

"What else do I have to go on, Paul?" Erwin asked, then looked up from the paper work to see Paul's dark brown skin several shades paler. "Are you O.K.?"

"Look, Erwin. People don't come back from the dead 20 years later and go to work for a psycho ward. It's crazy. Are you sure this doctor's right in the head? I mean he works with nut jobs all day. That kind of shit has to rub off on you."

"I'm sure he may say the same for us in our job. Will you relax? I don't know what I'm going to do yet. I'm not going to do something stupid," he reassured more to placate his friends concerns then to actually adhere to it.

"Famous last words, Erwin," Paul said, catching a glimpse of his silver watch with a moon icon faceplate. Then he saw the time and rose to his feet. "I better go. I've got those kids to deal with."

"Hey Paul," Erwin shouted to get his friends attention before he reached the door. "I'll still be in for tomorrow. And speaking of kids, when am I going to see my godsons? I haven't seen them since… well, you know."

"I'll see if I can convince Nicole to let me have them for a week end," Paul said, forcing a smile before resuming his exit. Paul's last visible motion to Erwin was a hand jutting out from the door with a wave. His other hand freed a cell phone from his pocket. He carried it in his hand until he was in the privacy of his own car. The phone began to dial with a press of a button. He waited clenching his teeth. It was a bad habit he picked up from when he quit smoking. You can't smoke if you won't open your mouth. This wasn't exactly true but it developed from the untrue thought. He could really go for a cigarette now. He reached over to the glove box were one archaic pack of smokes lay in wait. He never felt like getting rid of it. He did take it out every now and again when his will was weak. He was about to dust it off and peel the plastic wrapping from it when a voice reached out to him from the small machine next to his ear.

"Dianna," he said, gruffly, tossing the pack aside and starting the car. "We need to talk."

"What about, Anubis?"

"You have an hour and an half to figure it out. I've got a case to work on, and then I'm coming over." He hung up half way through a rebuttal. He didn't want to give her the satisfaction of a quick answer. Besides, he hated machines preferring the option of talking to someone, not something. He smiled with an animalistic toothy grin. Let her suffer a little, he thought. It served her right for not fixing the problem the first time around.

Chapter 8

Little Sally Parker saw the door flung open a form stepping unsteadily in front of the doorway. It shambled for her awkwardly, silhouetted by the light from the other room. "Daddy, is that you?"

The dark form couldn't be identified by her blurry sleep interrupted eyes. It moaned in an angry, inhuman sound as it reached out fumbling for her. She stumbled for the flashlight next to the bookcase. She managed to turn it on as the form grew nearer, standing at the foot of her bed. The meager light revealed the face of her father, ghostly in the weak light. His hair was a disheveled mess and his skin cut and bruised.

"Daddy, have you been drinking again?" she asked, flinching as the words slipped out. She expected him to hit her and say she was just like her mother. He just kept stumbling forward, and she lay there trembling. He took hold of her roughly throwing her back down onto the bed. Her eyes were already crying though she only landed in her pillows. She didn't fight nor would she resist. It would only hurt more and anger him if she resisted. He would take her as he had before, as he would no doubt do again and then he would leave. He clawed his way over her, his mouth already drooling in anticipation. The drool traced a slippery zigzagging line across her legs. She closed her eyes. It would be over soon. He groaned over her then opened his mouth, the drool running to the soft flesh between her legs. Then the teeth sunk into her thigh. Her eyes snapped open wide, screaming in pain and shock. This wasn't right. Blood soaked her sheets. She kicked at him wildly with her good leg making the blood from her bad one pump that much faster. Her heart pounding in her chest was little help in slowing the flow.

"Sally, what the Hell is wrong with…" Darleen said, flicking on the light. Even through her beer battered eyes she could see Earl and the blood. Sally struggled blindly in her death throws her nerves jerking her unnaturally and beyond her control. Earl looked over, face covered in the gore of his dying daughter. The growl from his throat made flecks of blood and bits of stray flesh spray from his mouth as it changed to a roar. She turned to run. She skidded when she reached the kitchen in her socks doubling back for the phone on the stand. Earl staggered toward her. Her fingers typed in 911. The phone rang. With each ring Earl shambled ever closer.

Atone

"Come on. Earl, back off. Back off, Earl.
I got the cops on the phone," she yelled trying to
get through to him. The phone continued to ring
and she was loosing ground quickly. She forced
herself to think quickly. "Hello, Officer, My
husbands trying to kill me."

It continued to ring as she pretended.
Earl was not phased as she darted out of his
grasp. Tears began to blur her eyes. She began
to sob loudly, eyes staring through the haze at
Earl. "Please, God, Please." She staggered back
running at last out of room. Earl quickly
hemmed her in as she reached a locked door.
She tried to get past him, unsuccessfully. Earl
was to close now to avoid. The realization of
being trapped made her cry even harder,
slumping forward in a fetal ball. Her fear ripped
free from her voice through her tear soaked
face. "Somebody fucking help me!"

"What seems to be the problem,
Ma'am?" There came a voice from the other
end. Darleen screamed as the teeth and fingers
tore through her flesh. The force of Earl sent her
falling to the ground completing her protective
fetal ball, the phone clattering on the floor next
to her. "Madam we are going to send some help
right away."

Chapter 9

Detective Marks sat on his standard issue police car hood with an unlit cigarette dangling from his mouth, his eyes looking up to the old World Development Organization building. He knew that going in would break the law and there was no chance in Hell of getting a permit for this place even though no one was using it. He wouldn't have, or be able to get, back up if things got hairy. His thoughts drifted to what would happen to him professionally if anyone found out about what he was going to do. He remembered Heinrich's warning about the homeless in the area. Well if he wasn't going to have back up officers at least he could get back up artillery. He slid from the hood to the ground and walked around to the trunk. Opening the latch, he raised it to reveal his hidden cache of weapons.

Inside the trunk were six various hand guns, an extra Billy club, a shot gun, fire axe, riot shield, gas mask, a can of pepper spray and a few canisters of tear gas. Only one quarter of this gear was necessary for something like this but Erwin liked to be prepared. There was even an old baseball bat, well used with bits of bone and metal indented into its wooden body. His old partner Tony Yuri took it from a street thug as a war trophy. There was Erwin's left upper incisor embedded in it as well. He looked back at the WDO building. Tony wasn't going to save him this time. He was alone, with only these weapons. He thought back to what brought him here. He was looking over the files and the photographs trying to find a clue. Then his eyes fell on the blood reports on the four missing patients. They all had the same blood ailment. The WDO was known both for finding cures and making diseases. Both of these things would need to be tested. This compounded with Heinrich's finger pointing at Mr. Blue pushed him to this action.

He took three of the handguns adding another to his shoulder holster, one in his belt ghetto style and another in an ankle holster. He took the gas mask and contemplated the bat before setting it down and going for a more practical Billy club. He added that to the belt with his other club. He closed the trunk and began checking the wall to get a way in. Finding a broken window he slithered in to the first basement, the noise of breaking glass was concealed by the start of a gentle rain. Broken furniture, busted canisters, and a few traces of dried liquid greeted him. There were four tables in the room something roughly human in diameter laying on them covered in a grizzled sheet, stained black brown with twenty-year-old blood. Each table had a tray with doctor equipment and shriveled, barely recognizable origins on them. At the foot of the tables were doctor's notes.

"Heart… Liver… Kidneys…" Erwin read as he walked past the tables. "What the Hell were these people doing?" Reaching the last table he didn't have to read. On the stand next to the patient was a fully recognizable brain. The only unnatural things about it were the thick black tendrils at its base. It wriggled slowly, feeling for anything that would grow near. Pulling off the sheet a wasted away body of a twenty-year-old corpse remained. Clearly a brain this bizarre and obviously fresh couldn't have come from here. A noise made him draw his gun. In one hand the club in the same hand pointing the path of a bullet if needed. "Nerves," he said, but used his free hand to pick up a scalpel from off the floor. Erwin forced down the lunch that worked its way up from his stomach. He cut a quick sample of the tentacle brain evading the lashing tendrils. He jumped back quickly avoiding the tentacles as it felt around for him. With an unwavering eye on the brain he put on rubber gloves and picked up the twitching sample he cut free. He looked back to see the sheet covered forms begin to struggle against their restraints.

"What the fuck?" He breathed. He stepped several paces away. He was forced to set down the gun and club to open the evidence baggy for the brain creature slice. As soon as the bag was zipped the gun was back in hand. The brain leaked from the wound struggling like a dying animal. He threw back the next sheet nearest him revealing the heartless form facing him with dead eyes. Unlike the lifeless husk without a brain, this body was clearly dead by all accounts, with one exception. It could move. Its chest was cracked and heart removed without so much as a substitute pump to prolong life. The mouth was clamped with a metal plate screwed through the bone of the skull and lower jaw.

"You poor bastard. How are you still alive?" It struggled with its straps fighting, a high-pitched cry coming from under the metal plate. Its fingers clawed at the metal slab it was strapped to. Detective Erwin hesitated, trying to decide if he should try to help these survivors or give them mercy with a bullet from a gun. Finally his sense of duty overtook his desire. "I'm going to try and get these things off you. Wait here."

He shook his head at the last of his words. Where could they go? He shambled through the wreckage to a computer module.

The lights blinked even in these years of disuse. The monitor was destroyed but it was clear that the tower would be salvageable by and large. His hand unwittingly reached for his communicator. Wait, he thought setting it back in the clip. He turned back to the trapped person, its lifeless eyes following his movement. "I'll be right back; I need to find a monitor to this thing."

With club and gun in hand he ducked through the open door and entered the hall. Only patches of light showed thin strips of the hallway ahead. Heinrich left the lights on but most of them were out or broken, leaving small twinkling fractures of light shining off broken glass.

"Erwin," he thought he heard someone say. He began to sweat his eyes wide to take in as much as he could. Strange shuffling noises and quiet eerie moans echoed from the dark patches of the hall, unlit by the remaining bulbs. Erwin moved from door to door until finding one that wasn't barred. The sound was growing nearer. The hair on his neck rose and he whirled around, expecting some nightmarish ghoul that experimented on humans like the ones in the now distant room. Finding nothing he checked the room quickly before backing in, eyes on the darkness. On instinct he closed the door to hinder his building paranoia. The room he was in seemed to be a decontamination chamber before proceeding onward into the inner rooms. With no windows to the outside world the inner rooms were even darker. He peered in through the dark seeing a well-lit room at the end of the hall. A few narrow strips of lights marked the way for him broken by shadows that seemed to move.

Erwin took in a deep breath and left the decontamination chamber. Inhuman sounds echoed through the halls that he walked and his gun was feverishly moving trying to cover everything at once. Erwin's nerves fought violently against his police training. He tried to convince himself that it was just a spooky old dump, but his mind kept going back to the people strapped to the tables. He walked crab style keeping his back along a wall. He felt something, a hand perhaps, grasp at him from the wall. He propelled himself away from it aiming the gun in the dark. He heard moans. Something moved.

"Show yourself!" He yelled at the wall. It in turn moved forward in response. A throng of bodies stumbled forward into the light. Rotted corpses moved on, forced by something other than their own will and volition. They clattered toward him awkwardly, blindly yet with one soul purpose. One collapsed under atrophied legs, its clumsy fingers found the gun around Erwin's ankle. It tried to pull itself toward him and inadvertently pulled the trigger sending the bullet straight through the space between the bones of its left shoulder, directly to where the heart would be. Erwin shrieked as it continued on, only a splatter of coagulated blood pooling on the floor from the shot.

A black stream of fast moving smoke darkened the light then brought it back in its passing. As the light returned the horde of crippled monstrosities sank back into shadow. Erwin pulled himself to the safety of the well-lit room. This seemed to be an inner control room. The room was lined with door locks and emergency override switches giving the room the look of a massive fuse box, levers interrupted in the middle by an overview map of the many floors. A small office chair and Computer faced the door looking away from the switches. The alternate energy supply light was blinking a yellow orange. Erwin went to the computer and turned it on. The lights dimmed as the computer struggled to start, the green screen washing the room in an eerie unnatural light. Several icons appeared on the screen marking projects, security, and employment among others. At the bottom there was a red lined box icon that read Natalie.

Erwin looked around as the lights grew brighter. Sure that he was alone in the room he clicked on the red lined box. The screen flickered and the lights went out. Erwin looked around in the dark, trying quickly to develop night vision or a sixth sense. The lights flickered back on and Erwin whirled around to see if any crazed bums where there with him. Satisfied, he returned his attention to the computer. A three dimensional woman appeared on the screen, from the ribs up, looking around with a frown. He blinked surprised at the curvy woman, with soft features, her two toned hair twisted up into a ponytail. Her eyes were large covering a great portion of her face. Her nose and mouth in contrast were diminutive. Her pupils turned back and forth seeming to look out from the computer screen.

"You're not Yin Quan. Where is Yin?" she asked, pouting.

"Uh… More than likely he's dead," Erwin said, looking outside toward the darkness, paranoia creeping into his bones.

"Systems check," it shuttered in a robotic voice then looked at Erwin with furrowed brow. "Why have I been off line for 20 years, 72 days, one hour and 23.6 minutes?"

"WDO was infected by some… thing. Something they were working on. It was shut down and WDO went under. That's all I know. The police were taken out of the occurrence before we were even involved after a special team took it out the whole thing was buried. Maybe you can find out what happened."

She blinked off the screen and he watched as she opened security files to several rooms, opening up windows faster than he could realize what he saw. He thought he could hear sobbing from the computer console. From what glimpses he caught of the flickering screens made him glad he never caught the whole thing.

"It was project resurrection. Room 27 subbasement 11. Yin Quan death confirmed. Who are you?"

"What?" he asked, returning his attention to the screen.

"What is your name?" She repeated, with a kindly smile.

"Uh… Erwin Marks. Detective Marks if you like," he said, looking for the room she spoke of on the map. "And how come that room isn't on this large map?"

She flickered from the screen opening project files to find Resurrection. Though she was not on the screen he could still hear her voice. "Project Resurrection was initiated when the fallen soldier, Private First Class Rodger Xaphan fell on the field due to massive chest damage, and damaged internal organs. After being declared dead at 08:00 he returned to the mess hall at 17:00, body still burst open. A panicked patrol attacked and in self-defense Rodger Xaphan made short work of them until the commanding officer managed to stop the firefight. Afterward Xaphan was still dead by natural sciences definition, but it was undeniable that he still functioned. He called himself Asmodius and claimed to be a demon. His claim was later dismissed do to possible brain damage while dead.

"At this WDO was notified and Asmodius was taken to our labs. Of this two strains have been developed. One, the pure strain creates a zombie effect on the recently dead. The second mixed with the drug Excleozine creates extreme effects beyond human comprehension but corrodes the brain tissue creating insanity in its victims. In both cases a defect in the blood supply removes the ability to produce new blood forcing victims to crave and obtain blood from other sources. The original hope for this virus was to create a new, non-lethal and non hazardous version of it to, in effect, cheat death. Because of the project being ethically and morally questionable, it was labeled top secret and that's why Room 27 subbasement 11 doesn't appear on the map. Top secret projects are done in exclusive areas concealed so as not to create a possible public relation nightmare."

"I think they dropped the ball on this one," Erwin said, grateful for her to finally answer his question. He glanced to the side of the computer console and noticed the stack of blank DVDs still on the stand under the computer. He blew some dust off and saw that they were relatively unscratched. "If it's so top secret why are you telling me this?"

"Because you're the only one alive here. Who is going to reprimand me?" she asked, in a very non-computer way. It made him do a double take before letting it slide.

"So those things out there..," he said, changing the subject.

"Zombies. If you want to label them," she said, with an unaffected smile. It grew more genuine as his look of astonishment amused her. "Is there anything else I can do for you,

detective?" she asked, with a humorous chuckle
in her voice.

"Yeah," he said. "Can you burn
DVD's?"

Chapter 10

Atone reached the Gordon estates. Checking the watch she produced from the bowling bag its digital numbers exclaimed two o'clock. She saw a figure slinking up along the wall climbing up to the window. Atone slid in the shadows to sneak up on this perpetrator. The figure creatively used its surroundings, a wobbly crate here a lattice covered with flowers and vines there, to navigate upward. At a juncture of unsure footing Atone took the opportunity to strike. She leapt from the bushes to the side of the wall, her claws letting her cling there. The figure screamed falling, Atone jumping down to catch her before hitting the ground.

"So you're Francine," she said, scanning over the girl in her clutches. She had curly dishwater blonde hair, two frizzy to look brushed. Her makeup was to thick, borderline gothic, her eyes peering wildly from the false shadows. She was athletic with youth and energy, her black tattered dress was concealed by an old oversized blue jean coat. Fish net stockings, torn in spots revealed pale, cream white legs ended with black platform shoes, the souls of which plated silver.

"It's Frankie and who, the fuck, are you?" She growled and hissed like a cat with a pulled tail.

"I'm a friend of your fathers, Frankie," Atone said, still clutching the girl to her.

"Let me go." She fought clawing and kicking, the platform shoes clunked against Atone's abdomen. Her fingernails were less effective being restrained behind her. Atone showed Frankie her own claws that made her stop kicking, her angry eyes growing wide.

"First tell me why you're sneaking into your father's house at two in the morning."

"You must be Rebecca," Frankie said, going limp in her captivity.

"Sometimes," she hissed. "Now answer my question." In a surge of energy she kicked out sharply against Atone's knee. It buckled and Frankie tried to exploit the situation. Atone was not dazed for long and held her firmly by one arm.

"Ouch," she grumbled, "Let go, you're hurting me."

"Answer," Atone demanded squeezing tighter. She squeaked in real pain. Her second surge of struggling subsided.

"I wasn't sneaking in I was sneaking out. I just needed to go back for some things," she said, her black, haunting eyes streaking with a few stray tears.

"Where were you planning on going?" Atone asked, not at all phased.

"What's it to you? You're just a delusional my dad brought home," she grumbled in a third counterattack finally pulling free. The lights turned on inside the house making her freeze in place looking at the front door. The sound of commotion inside could be heard where they stood and Frankie stepped back toward Atone.

"Your Dad responded pretty quickly to the scream. Your father must really care about you."

"Whatever." She tried to push past her. Atone caught her by the denim jacket.

"You have a problem with your dad?" She inquired, lifting her off the ground to look into her face.

"You wouldn't understand." She folded her arms in front of her. Atone set her down on the ground. Her claws retracted letting Frankie go. Frankie looked to see her captor's eyes filling with tears.

"Wouldn't I? Has your father ever asked you to kill yourself?" she asked, softly, stopping Frankie in her tracks.

"What, no. God, you're messed up." She inched closer to the door. Heinrich emerged from the front door a flashlight in his hand that encompassed both of them in a circle of light.

"What's going on? Frankie? Running away again?" he asked, holding his robe tightly around him. His pain added to Frankie's made the water in Atone's eyes run free down her cheeks before she could stop it.

"No Heinrich, it's my fault, really," Atone jumped in. "I left to get some of my things and lost track of time. When she saw me she freaked and jumped out of the window before I could explain."

"Is this true, Francine?" Heinrich grumbled skeptically.

"Yeah," she agreed looking back at Atone confused.

"And you had time to get dressed?"

"I was up late watching old movies," she retorted bitterly. Heinrich gave them both a quizzical, half-convinced look.

"Francine, go to your room. I mean your actual room. I need to talk to Rebecca."

"Sure, Henry," she said, walking past him into the house.

"Francine," he grumbled like a low bark.

"You want to be called Dad, call me Frankie," she shouted from the stairs. Heinrich rolled his eyes and muttered something about trouble and worth then led Atone back into his study.

"Did what you say really happen?" he asked, gruffly.

"Would I lie?" She batted eyes at him, getting in close. She knew this confused him enough that maybe he would move on and leave what happened outside alone.

"You tell me?" he asked, gently, yet firmly pushing her back a few inches. When he realized that his hands were cupping soft breasts he gave up and she nearly collided her head into his from the sudden release. She backed up.

"If I told you I don't then I could be lying so why bother?" she asked, withdrawing from him farther.

"Because I'm a potential suspect in 5 missing persons cases, I helped someone, something out of a psychiatric ward under the pretense that they are a fallen angel or something. It would ruin my career if people found out. I mean why even do that? A fallen angel is like a demon, right? They are usually, generally evil aren't they?"

"It depends on who you ask, really. Do you think I'm evil?" she asked, with all hints of humor gone. Tears wouldn't fall from her swirling multicolored eyes but she was surprised that the answer was so important to her. Her face twisted as though she would start to cry. She swallowed hard. She could feel him empathically sympathize with her.

"I think whatever that thing you were fighting, that thing that drugged and poisoned my patients, that was evil. I don't think Evil would spare my life," he said, honestly.

"Well there's your answer," she said, with a musical rhythm to her voice easing his ears.

"So why did you fall?" he asked, sitting down at the edge of the desk in his study.

"God said I was obsolete. He was going to absorb and recycle my essence. I didn't think that sounded like a good idea so I left," she said, quietly, her eyes cast down to the ground.

"You went to Hell?"

"That's generally how it goes when you turn from God. Yeah," she replied bitterly.

"So why come here?"

"You mean besides the up side of not being in Hell? I've stumbled on to a plot against God that his angels are going to try and overthrow him. I've got to warn him."

"But isn't God all powerful?" Heinrich said, the first traces of doubt infiltrating his voice. "Couldn't he just fix everything with a blink of his eyes?"

"Normally I'd say yes but if you catch something of this magnitude could you sit by and do nothing?" She countered the question with one of her own.

"But why try to warn God? I thought you weren't getting along."

"This is more important than my own well being," Atone said, seriously. Her eyes grew dark with the line of questioning.

"Like?" Heinrich asked, ignoring the eerie dark swirl in her eyes.

"Life, for starters. God is all things. Imagine what would happen if He got distracted. Everything he created would be in a state of Chaos and that's just if he wins... Imagine what would happen if he looses."

"I think I get the point," Heinrich said, leaning back. After a long pause Heinrich yawned wide unable to conceal it all with his hand. "Look. You can stay here as long as you like or need to for your quest. All I'd like is to know when you're leaving and that you keep a low profile. The police are still looking for you and the others. Now if you'll excuse me. It's late."

"Working in the morning?"

"No its Saturday. But I have to check on Francine. She can be headstrong and I'm not sure of your honesty. We'll get started tomorrow."

"No good night kiss?" she asked, with the playfulness returning to her voice.

"Rebecca..." his will began to weaken.

"Call me Atone." She smiled. He caught the scent of pine, flowers, and faint traces of smoke. Beneath this was the scent of a woman. His mind went back to the last time a woman was so close to him and she liked to be close. He shook the thought from his mind. He had a responsibility.

"Good night," he said, returning his smile.

Atone headed to the dusty room of concealed furniture and expanded her mind. She was secretly monitoring Francine as Heinrich was talking to her. She knew after Heinrich checked in on her she would try to leave again. The feeling of a caged animal biding its time was unmistakable. She slithered from this room to one that had windows. Crawling out of one she walked along the wall with her claws waiting outside Francine's window. She waited while Francine was interrogated by her father. Heinrich left and Atone waited for the click of the window's latch that would inevitably lead the girl to her once again. She was not disappointed.

"So what's up?" she asked, making Francine jump with a start.

"Are you going to haunt me all the time now?" she hissed her inquiry with bitterness.

"At least until there is something better to do," Atone said, looking at her sideways from the side of the wall. Frankie leaned from the window to look at her watchdog.

"How did you know I was going to…?"

"I'm an Empath," Atone stated. Francine didn't need to know that it was an educated guess rather than a sure thing.

"So you, like, read minds and stuff?"

"No that's a telepath."

"What's the difference?"

Atone

"A telepath reads minds, an empath reads emotions."

"So what else can you do?"

"I can do this," Atone said, placing a gentle hand on Francine's forehead. A flood of emotions and deep sorrow overwhelmed her. Francine started to cry uncontrollably.

"My parents… don't go mommy…" She pleaded through tear-coated eyes and make up streaked face. "I thought you didn't use telepathy?"

"I didn't. It was empathy," Atone responded getting tired of repeating herself.

"But I saw it so vividly," she insisted, her hands giving up on stopping her tears and balled into fists.

"You did. I didn't. I just set you to sad, your mind pulled up the images," Atone explained. Frankie hissed angrily, her manipulation making her seek retribution. This made Atone tilt her head to the side trying to understand why she felt that way.

"But why? Why make me feel sad? Of all the emotions…" She fought against her emotions trying to overcome the magically induced one. The two powerful emotions made her shake violently.

"Sorry. I've been in Hell a little long. You get used to torturing people. Let's try this," she said, brushing her cheek. She could feel her budding womanhood moisten, her feminine juices start to flow. Her breath grew ragged, rasping as her body quivered and her face flushed.

"What did… you… do… to me?" She gasped between surges of indescribable ecstasy.

"Doesn't that feel better?" Atone smiled slyly, patting her on the shoulder.

"Yes," she panted trying to decide whether to suppress her arousal or drive it further "But do me a favor. Don't… ever touch… me… again."

"Well I'll leave you to your own devices. This should last until morning but just to be safe I'm still on to you," Atone said, tapping her temple to give Francine the message.

"Uh huh," Francine murmured trying and failing to compose herself. Atone left as

Francine's fingers struggled not to stimulate the overwhelming emotion further. Her resistance wouldn't last. Atone left confident in knowing that she wouldn't be going anywhere tonight.

Chapter 11

Paul Orlando, Anubis to his business associates in POE or the Princes of Earth, tracked down the scent he picked up at the wrecked car. He would file the police report as a basic accident but POE would need to know about this other scent. They would need to know the truth. The fire department was nearly finished with hauling out the destroyed car and cleaning up the charred mess. Soon Paul would be able to change, and allow new, better senses to hunt. The DNR put out the last of the fire before returning to their make shift camp. In the morning they would check again before conceding to the fact that no fire was left.

Paul crawled down on his hands and feet; his face mere inched to the ground. It was dark and few people were around, scared off by the charred car, or the police barricade. His face began to change, growing more feral, when the phone began to ring. His features snapped back into place. He answered the phone with an angry yelp for a hello. "What is it?"

"Where are you? You said we have to talk," Diana said, confused.

"I'm busy," he growled like an animal.

"You made it sound urgent," Diana whined unable to hide the irritation in her voice.

"There are more problems now. A fallen is here somewhere," he growled stepping even farther into the shadows. "Somewhere here. Killed two people so far."

"And the other thing? Tell me why you called me before so I can get whatever it is squared away. You know this kind of thing is what got you demoted. You can't keep secrets, Anubis. Most of our POE agents are at the hospital, hunting. They've mopped up most of it…"

"Pull someone. Maybe a small team and send them to WDO."

"But WDO is over," she said, through a tired sigh.

"No it isn't," he growled back. He heard a ticking sound from the other end, probably Diana tapping the side of the phone while she thought.

"We've been all over that place. Top to bottom. There is nothing in there we haven't seen or destroyed." She tried again. "We can't keep sending men into…"

"Yeah, well something survived. You want to continue believing that this hospital epidemic and the WDO fiasco are separate events, fine. Then this team won't find anything. Job done."

"Alright, Anubis. I'll set… Poseidon on it," she said, caving in again. Her voice quivered, remembering the WDO. There was always something eerie about those sterile rooms, zombie crawling halls and military test subjects. Anywhere else it was just another job, but WDO had some dark ambience indescribable, some feeling that it slept only, to one day raise again. Even though the team was meticulous in its sweeps there was always that feeling. Search after search brought fruitless "all clear" from the away team before pulling out of WDO, never to satisfy that nagging thought that there was more. They buried it without ever truly putting the mission to rest. "Good luck on your hunt, Anubis. Diana out."

He hung up the phone without any further response. The woods made no sound at all now. He was completely and utterly alone. He was free to change and free to hunt.

Several miles away outside the hospital a phone began to ring. "Poseidon here," spoke the man into the phone. A lupine shaped helmet made of hardened plastic and metal was tucked under his arm. His face was rugged, but handsome, grey hair cut short, but thickly grew from his head. It was early Saturday morning, the sun many hours away.

Two of the survivors were in the plastic quarantine bubble that sat in the parking lot of the St. Bridgette hospital. Guards circled the bubble like vultures, watching them for sign of change, sign that the infection has taken root. Sam, another officer on the site left the bubble guards and ran up as Poseidon spoke. "WDO? But that site is cleared?" Sam waited as the voice on the other side occupied Poseidon's time.

"I understand, Poseidon, but Anubis thinks we missed something. He thinks there is a connection with WDO and what you're doing now," Diana spoke her voice broken by static over the radio. Poseidon grumbled and rolled his eyes, in doing so noticing Sam. His relaxed posture and irritated expression snapped rigidly to cold professionalism. No sense in teaching new recruits bad habits.

"I understand. But I don't know what he expects to find," he said, checking his attitude at the door.

"Humor him for my sake. Dianna out," a sympathetic voice spoke into his ear.

"Poseidon Out," he said, looking over to Sam. "I'll need you to watch the kids and take reports from the cleaning crew. I'm needed elsewhere."

Sam nodded and followed him to the patrol of armed guards around the bubble. "Uthgar, Yuri, you will accompany me."

"Yes, Poseidon," they spoke as one rounding up Poseidon's APC.

Sam took his wolf like helmet off to speak plainly. "Good luck Sir."

Poseidon nodded and followed the two soldiers he called to the Armored Personnel Carrier. The APC rolled forward kicking up or plowing over anything in its path. The Vehicle was bus size in length and an extra half a bus length in width. It looked like a tank without the main turret. The APC chewed its way through the city streets trying to reach the other side. He thought of the WDO building. He remembered finding Anubis there, held prisoner by the evil organization. They saw him change and managed to capture him to add to their freak show roster of experiments. He could understand the perverted addiction Anubis had for the place. How sometimes tragedy attracts their victims and that their torture will never be over. He could understand the fear of Anubis but he couldn't understand Diana agreeing to this. There was nothing left, and never would be.

His eyes caught movement in the sleepy residential area. A woman, bitten and bleeding ran screaming from some unseen assailant. Poseidon's eyes went from the woman on the road to the house she fled. There, at the front door. Two of them exited. Undead were here. The impact of the APC covered up the whispered prayer from his lips. Yuri leaned out of a window in a vain attempt to see if she was still alive.

"You just hit her, Sir," Yuri called out seeing no solid piece of her after the tread rolled her under.

"As I'm no doubt aware, Yuri," he said, in a subtle yet unmistakable way to convey that he should not take it further. He swerved the vehicle to a stop at a ninety-degree angle from its original heading. The zombies stopped moving ahead and began to linger around aimless, seemingly unaware of the vehicle and the people inside. He returned his attention to Yuri's mortified expression. "She was bitten. There was nothing else to be done." Exiting the APC the zombies wobbled around blind to the soldiers. Poseidon used to think that it was because of the uniforms. He used to think that the jackal like helmets and body suits that masked heat and scent using a special material designed by their R and D department hid them from view. He knew that to an extent this was true, but it was never fail safe. He nodded and gestured his hands in a silent message to stay alert.

"Their not supposed to be here," Uthgar grumbled out a whisper, Yuri sitting back in his chair.

"That's a given, private," Poseidon growled a rebuttal before calling Diana. "Containment might be mute. We have hostiles on Mountain Boulevard and Hastings Avenue. Two confirmed undead with one civilian casualty thus far."

"Forget WDO. Begin search and destroy. I'll contact the powers that be… Police and what not, to avoid any errors or entanglements, you know the routine."

"Rodger that. Poseidon out."

Chapter 12

Atone slid from the couch, clutching the sheet around her. Her teeth clattered and her skin rose in bumps despite her best attempts at fighting it. "This is ridiculous."

She left the chill of the room for the chill of the hallway. Stalking the halls she found her way to Heinrich's room. It was nice, here. A private bathroom was visible through an open door. His bed was a king size covered with a comforter and fuzzy blanket with ducks on them. He didn't really have taste, she thought but at least it was clean and almost overly organized. She could see a wooden chest of drawers with an oval mirror on top. Few knick-knacks sat on the counter and even those seemed placed strategically. She looked down the hall to where Frankie was on the couch downstairs. She was strewn out across it in an unmoving and uncomfortable pose, the light of the television static illuminating her unconscious body. She was too warn out, gone to the world for the next several hours at least. Atone gently nudged Heinrich's door open all the way. Prowling like a jungle cat curious by campfire she paced closer to the sleeping body. After inspecting his state of consciousness she decided he was too far gone. Slipping the covers open carefully she began to climb in with him. She could feel the magnificent warmth, so close. She smiled. The bed made a subtle creak and she froze imagining his eyes open. He didn't move, speak or any sign of waking and she tried again. This time he spoke unmoving.

"What do you think you are doing?" he asked, flatly.

"I thought I'd surprise you," she said, playfully her teeth clatter chopping up the words.

"Congratulations, you have. Now go to bed," he said, unchanging.

"All right," she said, snuggling up closer to him under the covers. The warmth was incredible. A delightful humm of contentment escaped her lips.

"In the other room," he murmured. She sneered at the back of his head for the selfishness of his warmth.

"But it's freezing in there," she whined softly. "I won't try anything. I promise."

There was an unsettling silence before Heinrich rolled over to face her. She tried not to smirk when his emotions teased her. He rolled back to avoid staring at her. "All right. You can stay but until we square away the rules of good and evil and finding your place in that system I'd appreciate if you keep your temptation, or whatever it is you do, to a minimum."

"You think I'm tempting you?" she asked, sliding in closer to him, draping one arm over him. It felt natural spooning along his body, her upper most leg wedging gently between his to gain the most heat possible. "I'd be flattered if I wasn't so tired."

He felt her body hugging his, her soft though somewhat scaled skin pressed against his back. He found himself awkwardly lying there, unable to sleep. "Thank you, Heinrich," she said, half sleeping, curled around him for heat. It wasn't until her hold on him relaxed from deep sleep, that he was able to close his eyes and drift from the real land to the surreal world of dream.

It was several hours before the physical world wormed its way into his mind and forced him to wake, groggily. The sound of music, harsh and rough yet with a sensual softness hidden away in the grind of metal, played from the stereo by the door. The midday Sun shined through his window as he stumbled to the bathroom. A billowing blast of hot, moist air hit him as the door swung open; waking him fully in time to witness what greeted him second.

Atone stood in the room with one foot up on the toilet seat a towel wrapped tightly around her hair, and loosely, revealingly around her body. A disposable razor dangled from her hand. Her eyes looked up and seemed to glow in the steam-filled room. She smiled as she looked at him. "Are you always so stiff, first thing in the afternoon?"

"I thought we talked about not tempting me?" he asked, in the brief moment his mouth wasn't hanging open.

"It's not my fault you keep finding yourself in tempting situations," she said, slithering close to him. "You barged in here. The real question is what are you going to do about it?"

He lowered his gaze from her eyes to her lips his mouth watering. It was too early in the day to reign in his self-control. He leaned in closer to her. Their lips were molecules apart. She squealed, jerking back. "There is something here," she said, staring past him at nothing. He turned to see and she worked past him running off.

"What's here? Wait a minute," Heinrich said, trying to figure out what was going on around him. Unable to do so, he went after her instead.

Francine sat in front of the television, a black and white zombie movie flickering back at her relaying the message that bad creatures do bad things until the hero saves the day. Her lap stayed warm with a bowl of freshly made mac and cheese.

"What a crock," she grumbled stabbing into the cheesy goodness. A moan came from the television and received an answering call from behind her. "Henry? The gas guy stopped by to fill the tank. Bill's on the kitchen counter," she said, not turning back. She was answered by another moan.

She heard the shuffling feet dragged across the floor behind her getting closer. The gasping moan escaped its breath again. "Quit trying to be funny, Henry," she retorted but the shambling, shuffling sound continued followed by groans. She growled putting down her bowl of mac and cheese between her and the television. "I mean it Dad. You're not going to scare me."

The shuffling figure stumbled into a lamp knocking it over. The lampshade slapped the top of the couch next to Francine's head, two of the three bulbs busting in a flash of quickly dying light. Francine leapt from the blinding flash to stand facing the fallen lamp.

"Jesus Christ. What is your prob…?" She stopped seeing the bitten, decomposing body stumbling toward her. She screamed stepping back. Her foot slipped in the macaroni bowl sending her back first to the ground. Her shoulder collided with the solid television stand feeling the bones pull loose of its socket. The scream shifted from shock to agony. The zombie, uncaring stumbled closer. She tried to rise but her fear and the pain made any movement difficult. The Zombie moved over her and she kicked at it with feeble results.

A blur landed on its back wrenching its head back as it landed between Francine's legs. Francine inched back and saw Rebecca sitting on the creature her fingers burying their claws through its temples spraying gore across the carpet, the Mac and cheese, and Frankie's thighs. Frankie's screams transformed slowly to sobs as Heinrich comforted her aiding her further from the bleeding intruder. Atone rose over the creature's now motionless corpse. She took a step toward Frankie her claws retracting to about an inch. Frankie looked up frightened and shaking in her father's arms. Atone looked over them.

"That shoulder looks bad." Atone took hold of the dislocated arm. With a few savage jerks she forced it back in place, feeling the bones pop in her grasp. The scream from both of them shook the house, Heinrich forces to stumble away and protect his ears. "Congratulations," Atone said, tears streaming wildly from her eyes before she could wipe them away. "You survived your first zombie attack."

"You just killed someone in my house," Heinrich finally found his voice and used it loudly.

"No. I'm pretty sure his time of death was much earlier," she said, kicking the body to turn it over. Facing the ceiling, they could see the absence of vital organs. Heinrich inched back; Frankie recovered well from the shock and began investigating the holes in the creature's torso.

Atone

"Those things at WDO," Heinrich said, getting up. "At the Psychiatric ward. They were these things?"

"WDO?" Atone asked, then addressed the second issue. "Those things at the psych ward were not the same as these things. They were smarter, with more ability. But back up. WDO? What is that?"

"The World Development Organization. They did experimental medicine, made drugs and stuff. Of course they had to test their drugs obviously, on things with diseases. They got shut down when one of their diseases got loose. Is this what got loose?"

"I don't know. I'm not the doctor here."

"Winter Blue… The night watch man, he used to work there. He was there the night the outbreak occurred. Do you think…?"

"I don't know. Turn on the news; See how bad this thing is. I'll check doors and windows make sure more don't get in. If it seems safe we'll have to get Frankie to the hospital to check that arm." Atone walked off wandering the house. She could feel Rebecca trembling inside. She wanted to run screaming. That was the worst you could do. "We must keep a cool head, Rebecca. Let me keep us safe."

"No. You're trying to trick me," she sobbed.

"Maybe I am but it's our body at stake and I need it in tact," Atone said, harshly back to her.

"You want my body, not me." Rebecca's crying grew worse.

"Maybe so but I have bigger problems than you at the moment."

"Like what?" Rebecca looked out through Atone's eyes.

"Like a zombie horde," Atone said, checking every room for open windows, making extra care to seal off the unused portion of the house. "Don't you see? This plane of existence knows I shouldn't be here."

"So go away," Rebecca demanded.

"I can't do that," Atone answered sternly.

"It's my body I could make you,"
Rebecca threatened growing bold.

"Then who would protect you from
them?" She snapped at herself she saw a mirror
the look of fear and anger staring back at her.
"Look, I need to find a way to God so that I can
stop all of this. But I can't do it alone. I need
your help."

"Why don't you just go to church?" She
heard a voice and both of them turned around to
look. Surprised there was someone else there.

"Oh, hey Frankie…" she said, turning
the mirror aside.

"You need to stop the apocalypse from
happening and Rebecca needs her body back,
why can't you just ask God for forgiveness?
Since you don't have a body wouldn't you just
go back then?"

"It's a little more complicated then that,
Frankie," Atone said.

"Why?" asked Rebecca, the thought
given sound by Frankie.

"A demon, or devil like me, has obstacles that humans don't have to worry about."

"Like what?" she asked, testing and locking a window then advancing cautiously on a closet door.

"Angels mostly. They don't make it easy. Seals also make it hard for a devil to stay in heaven for long. Then there is religious dogma. It says that a demon, or devil, can never be forgiven making it hard for a fallen to go to church or be absolved, what do you call it… baptized by a priest. That's what really pisses me off. Vanity. Humans are so vain they think they are the only ones with a soul, the only things capable to go to heaven and be forgiven for their sins. Well guess what people, that vanity is sin and you take part in it every faithful moment of your life."

"Are you through?" Frankie asked, closing and locking the closet door.

"I'm sorry. It's just I don't have a lot of time to work. If apocalypse is on the horizon I have even less."

"So what about angels? Couldn't they help?"

Atone erupted in a harsh cruel laughter. "Oh no, no, no. I listed angels as part of the problem for a reason. First of all there is Israfel. Not only is his men guarding most of the conventional ways in but if He is turning against God then there is no knowing who to trust and even if the angels I go through are loyalists I can't very well go up and say, 'Hey, it's O.K. guys, I'm just trying to warn God about a plot to take over. Don't mind me.' They'd kill me in such a way there wouldn't be a coming back."

"No reason to get sarcastic," she said. They found an old room covered in dust; years of neglect corrupting the integrity of the wall. Leaves blew in marking unique trails in the dust. A glass case over the doorway had a shimmer of light, Atone sweeping away the dust and cobwebs to reveal a sword underneath. Engraved on the blade were words that Atone read aloud. "Eisenhower Gordon, My knight in shining armor."

Frankie stiffened. Atone looked to see the doorway darkened by more shuffling corpses. "Well time to find out if you are battle ready," she said, smashing the case. She carved her way back to the dilapidated wall. "Frankie, back. The door," she said, edging her way back while fighting off the undead. They escaped the room, Atone holding them off. "Over here,

Frankie, the book case. We need to barricade this room from the rest of the house."

"I can't move it. My arm…" Frankie struggled against it pathetically.

"Suck it up and push, Francine!" The cumbersome bookcase made a vibrating hum as the legless mammoth base cut into the floor, the freshly dug grove making it that much harder to move. Eventually it groaned conceding to Frankie's wishes. Atone finished off three of the nearest Zombies as the bookcase began to cover the hole. "That's it just a little more."

More zombies turned their focus to Atone and the shrinking doorway. Atone flung the sword down to add her efforts to Francine's heavy burden. There was a crunching sound of a snapping limb followed by the impact of the case against the corner wall. A hand wriggled in its own gore and dust, a few nervous impulses before it lay still.

Atone picked up the sword and noticed the shuffle marks heading deeper in the house. She growled. "Give us a break."

Chapter 13

Erwin Marks read the WDO literature as he waited for the disks to finish burning, glancing to and fro every few moments to make sure the zombies don't return to finish him. An animated glyph of Natalie was on the screen, literally burning a CD with a kiss the cook apron on. With the work of the computer the lights flickered between light and dim making reading difficult.

"How much is left Natalie?" he asked, setting the manual aside. Yin Quan was a very creative if severely lonely young computer specialist.

"Just one disk left, Detective Marks." The Glyph looked up to him and smiled before resuming her task at flipping the disk to the other side and setting it back on the animated grill.

"Call me Erwin," he said. He waited several minutes staying busy by putting the three other disks in a plastic sleeve. Then, silently passing the floor, his thoughts wandered to the strange inky cloud the zombies seemed to fear.

"All done, Erwin," she said, cheerily. He took the fourth disk from the tray and put it in its own plastic sleeve. He returned his attention to Natalie.

"Thanks, Natalie. Look I'll be going now. There is a good chance I'll never see you again," Erwin said. This was harder than he anticipated, most of this problem stemming from the hardware on the other end of the conversation. That and the nagging fear he'd never see anyone again, computer program or otherwise.

"Don't be such a pessimist. You'll be fine," she said, squinting cutely. "We'll meet again."

"Sure Natalie," he said. "Well, goodbye." With a touch of a button he killed the power of the computer. The lights returned to brightness, the taxation of the electricity lessened. The light gave him comfort. Like a safe zone in a den of crazy. He wished he remembered a damned flashlight. You always forget one friggin' thing. He rummaged through the room again hoping the extra light would reveal some hidden cache of usefulness, overlooked in the darker situation. There was no such revelation.

He glanced down the hallway, the way he came, the way to safety. He looked through the dark hall, Patches of questionable lighting making a sketchy trail to possibly unravel the truth. He needed to find room 27 subbasement 11.

"Where are you going?" He heard bubbling from the airy nothingness behind him. He twirled looking around. There was nothing. "Why are you here?" It came again this time from the shadows. A billowing shadow faded, teasing his mind as it disappeared before he could grasp what he saw.

"What do you want here?" The voice came again from behind but this time he caught the faintest form of a woman fading into tangible darkness rushing past him, through him, to get behind. He could see it now and spun around to face it as it submerged into the all-encompassing darkness. He rushed out trying to stop it from getting away.

He heard footsteps walking away down the darkened path. The crushing sound of glass as one step led to another. From the shadow emerged a girl. She looked familiar.

"Hello. Hey you?" He dared to shout. She turned smiling adding a swish to her strut.

Detective Marks saw the face. He Remembered her. This was Kara, one of the missing nutcases. She continued to walk away, a bubbling chain of laughter accompanying her steps. He ran after her, Hand on his gun.

"Kara. I need you to come with me. Kara, Oh, shit." He picked up the pace but no matter his velocity her slow deliberate strut was always out of reach. "I need you to answer some questions."

Light, dark, light, dark, light, dark the hallway continued on without end. He ran through the haunting corridor, now at a full run. The laughter echoed in his ears until he wasn't sure if it was her laughing or a noise in his head. Several turns and twists through the labyrinthine compound and soon he couldn't tell up from down. He was lost and all he had was this laughing specter of a woman leading him somewhere. But where, He thought, was she leading him?

She plunged into the shadows and he followed. Reemerging into the light she was gone. He stopped. Her laughter was so close. He peered into the darkness to see nothing. He readied his gun.

"This way," he heard as a light down a third direction flickering on. He waited, and then curiously, cautiously followed. The laughter was all around him louder still and growing until he had to fall to his knees covering his ears with his hands trying to stop it.

"Stop!" He called out. The laughter ended. A form moved ahead of him. It was Kara. She was walking. One foot ahead of the other. She emerged from the darkness smiling innocently. He rubbed his eyes, her form affixed to the ceiling as he stood on the floor. "What…"

"Your answers await you. Freedom awaits you. Release your mind and all is yours," she said, walking back into the darkness, lights now revealing a path down a once shadowed corridor. She walked in a hypnotic spiral up and down the walls ceiling and floor. Erwin followed silently lost in the madness.

As he drifted behind her he managed to pull his attention from her to notice the walls. They seemed to transform into gruesome, horrific corpses. No, he thought. They were ambling along them as if part of them came to life. He could hear them fall in behind him.

She stepped into the darkness; the sound of her foot falls gone. In fact he noticed as she sank again into darkness that she seemed to hover instead. A voice called to him from the darkness as he stopped. He turned to see a wall of dead behind him. "Come with me. Be free of yourself." He could see her in the darkness, an unnatural glow radiating from her body. He stared at her, mesmerized until his gaze lowered, noticing in her light the absence of ground. He noticed that and the cables of the elevator.

"There's no ground," Erwin said, dreamily. "This isn't real."

"What is real? Are you real? Am I? Is what you see real?"

Erwin drew his spare Billy club and tossed it into the abyss. It eventually clattered as it finally hit the ground. Kara frowned. He looked back at her, the spell broken. He could feel the horde of freakish dead closing in on him from behind. Erwin knew what to do. "That was real."

He heard the dead begin to wail and lept to reach her, grabbing the elevator cable tightly. He jerked as his own weight pulled at his arms. She swarmed around him, half-tangible, biting and clawing. He dangled, for a moment helpless. Corpses tumbled to their final death from the open elevator doors, still trying to get their prey.

Regaining himself he felt her fangs sink into his arm. Twisting his legs around the cable he freed his one arm and the gun he still gripped in his hand, firing blindly. A sinister smile crossed her face as she fingered the new holes in her chest. "Is that the best you can do, little human?"

Black smoke filled the wounds and turned solid. Erwin's arm slowly pumped blood, his head getting dizzy. A lone zombie struggled up the cable and he fired downward exploding the head. His eyes felt heavy. Kara's form began to blur. He slipped from the cable slightly, the motion waking him only a little.

"I was going to give you eternal life." She laughed wickedly. "But all you want is death. You shall have it forever." His eyes closed and he heard screaming in the darkness. Then somewhere in a dream he felt himself fall. The voice of his friend Paul was in his ears.

"Hang in there, Erwin. Damn it I told you not to do something stupid."

"Just shows you how well I listen," he heard himself say muffled and distant. For a moment he wasn't even sure it was his voice. Then there was heat, a fire in the dark coursing through his veins, searing his soul. He heard a growl of pain ripple from his throat. Then there was nothing. The darkness was complete.

Chapter 14

There was no time for comfort as the horde closed in from all surroundings.

"Fuck," Poseidon breathed, exhausted mentally if not physically from the killing. There was no longer a cul-de-sac. There was just a throng of ambulatory dead surrounding them waiting to kill. Poseidon stood in the middle, gun blazing with an attractive blonde, though marred by age and lack of sleep, clutching one leg her other arm holding tightly to a young boy. His face was featureless, looking out into the throng at where his parents fell to the masses.

Poseidon stopped shooting, sweat rolling under his helmet and burning his eyes. The APC left minutes prior, full of survivors, Yuri and Uthgar taking those they could save to the survival camp. It didn't look good that they would return in time. Poseidon reloaded his gun and aimed it at the boy.

"Hey, what are you doing?" the woman shrieked taking hold of his hand on impulse trying without success to move the gun away.

"This is over ma'am. I'm sorry," he said, as the zombies closed in. The hammer clicked into place as he began to squeeze.

"No, please," she said, for the boy who was too far gone to care himself.

"I can't let you become like them," Poseidon said, flatly. The blonde closed her eyes shielding the boy who stood in her arms emotionless. "Let me end it." He pulled them closer as space dwindled. "It's now or never." The horde, closed in. He squeezed the trigger. A click. Zombies took hold of his arm and pulled the woman away. With a pistol butt he knocked one over only for another to take her. A Zombie moved in to bite. She closed her eyes. Poseidon struggled to reach her through the masses.

Then a strange wail, different from the regular hypnotic drone of the normal zombies, rumbled like a wave through the amassed horde. They stopped in their tracks. After many painful seconds the blonde dared to open her eyes. The undead stood, like statues all facing off into one direction, one destination.

"What's going on?" She whispered not daring more noise.

"I don't know," Poseidon said, honestly. "Don't do anything." Another call rang out and the horde began as one to depart. Poseidon reached out and grabbed her as the zombie holding her pulled her with. It didn't seem to care that she was no longer in his possession. The boy remained frozen, mystified at the sight he witnessed before Poseidon pulled him along, in the opposite direction of the undead masses.

"Sam," he said, activating the communicator in his helmet. "We have a strange occurrence here. Zombie hordes moving in unison South West anything on your end?"

There was a crackle, faintly, at first then the sound of Sam could be heard. "…Same… thing… They're going South East from our position."

"What's on the south side of our position?"

"Already on it." While Poseidon waited he turned His attention to the blonde woman and child. "Do you have a car, miss?"

"Helen Murdock. Yes. It's over there," she said, her body shaking uncontrollably. She thought it funny that she wasn't shaking when the danger was there.

"Keys?" he asked, clamping one of his hands around her shoulder.

"Inside. I didn't…" She began to stammer. He raised up his hand for her to stop, hearing Sam on the other end of the communicator. "A residential area? High end? No? None of that ringing any bells. We'll rendezvous at your current position, are Yuri and Uthgar there?"

"I see them coming now, Sir."

"Good. Keep them there. Poseidon out," he said, turning back to the blonde. "Well let's go get those keys."

Chapter 15

"Give us a fucking break!" Atone cried out, dueling monsters as she carved her way through the ever thickening wall of death. Heinrich and Frankie followed close keeping an eye on the rear guard. Atone's body was coated in sweat despite the chill fall morning. Her arm and chest burned from the overheated, overwhelmed muscles that swung the sword. She paused for a moment putting her hands on her knees, winded. She hissed between gasps of air. "Damn, Rebecca. You're so weak."

Heinrich and Frankie noticed her lag, a few slashing spasms and the strength was free from her. Heinrich saw the wall lurching forward and pushed them back, taking the sword from her hand. Rebecca screamed in Atone's mind. She could feel Atone give up. She was going to quit on her like everyone else. She felt the walls shatter, found the crack in her armored mind to regain her body.

Atone retreated into her mind, Rebecca pushing her way to the surface, screaming out in terror.

"Rebecca?" Heinrich asked, and He and Frankie turned to face her. Rebecca's legs burst into motion pushing a group out of her way as she ran. Heinrich swung madly with powerful if slow strikes, the zombies shambling in around them, separating him and Frankie from Atone. After moments of uncontested hacking, Heinrich and Frankie stopped. The undead ambled mere inches from them, but didn't even acknowledge their presence, turning to the direction of the fleeing devil lady.

"They're after her," Heinrich said, renewing his attack. It wasn't long before he realized how ineffective and fruitless it was. He stopped swinging to save his energy as more zombies took their place. "Come on."

"What about her?"

"I don't know what's going on but we should get help."

"Yeah, Dad, like the government has a special paramilitary unit for dealing with walking dead," Frankie said, following her father to open ground. Heinrich led his daughter through the abandoned streets. As quickly as the horde of death appeared, it seemed to disappear again. It was only their moans that remained to deny silence. They were like a plague of locusts, coming quickly and stripping down everything in their path before departing once more. Heinrich and Frankie wandered the naked city streets with the distant undead moaning alone to keep them company.

"Why do they do that constant moaning?" she asked. Heinrich, mesmerized briefly by the sound, was broke free from his daughter's voice. The moan changed to a new sound.

"That's not Zombies," Heinrich said, looking in the direction of the new sound. The APC smashed through some abandoned cars blocking its route.

"Holy…" Francine's words were muted by the roaring engine. The armored vehicle rolled to a halt in front of them, the door opening. The light from inside illuminated the soldiers as they filed out. They created a barrier around the APC, their guns waving furiously in Heinrich and Francine's faces. The soldiers faces were concealed with a wolf headed mask.

"State your name!" one barked out.

"Uh…" Heinrich sputtered from the shock. The click made the words find his tongue. "Heinrich Gordon."

The guns motioned sidelong a few inches and down. "Francine. Frankie."

Understand this. We are here to help you. Safety is a key issue." The front man continued raising his gun. The others surrounded Francine and Heinrich "For the safety of all it is crucial that the infected do not reach base."

"What the?" Francine said, as she was stripped along with her father down to her underwear. The lead soldier continued to talk.

"This is standard procedure. I am sorry for any inconvenience you may endure."

"They appear clean, Sir," one of the hound-faced soldiers addressed him, another handing back their clothes.

"Good," he said, then turned to the civilians. "Welcome aboard."

"You ripped my shirt, asshole," Francine growled putting back on the tattered, now slightly exposing garment.

"There was a friend of ours…" Heinrich spoke up.

"Sorry to hear that. Probably dead by now."

"No you're not listening. They were following her. Those, those…"

"Zombies."

"Yes. They were after her. They didn't even try to fight me or Francine."

"Interesting, where is this friend now?"

"She freaked and took off running."

"I'll take note of your information now please take a seat."

"I wonder if mom…" Francine stated and Heinrich paused as they walked to the seats at the back of the armored vehicle. There was a long painful pause as they contemplated the possibility and probability.

"Let's not jump to any conclusions. Simply hope for the best," Heinrich said, not wanting to dwell on the thought. He focused instead on the driver.

"Yuri, here. Calling Diana," the driver, apparently Yuri, said.

"Please hold." There was a long pause and then sounds of clicking heels over marble.

"Yes, Yuri?"

"Diana, I think I may have some information on the Zombies strange behavior, a recent addition to our good ship lollipop says that they seemed to be tracking a girl," Yuri explained. There was a long silence over the communicator. Yuri was about to respond again when he heard a humming from the other side. "Does that mean something to you?"

"Maybe. I'll dispatch air units to the area. Your mission is to escort what survivors you have back to the base then assemble a team to find Anubis. He's not responding."

"Last known whereabouts?"

"We lost his signal at WDO. He thinks this outbreak and WDO are connected."

"So what else is knew?"

"He also said he was picking up a scent. A demon."

"Someone should remind him he's not an active agent any more."

"Regardless, this girl might be connected," Diana said. Yuri knew better than to push her farther. "More importantly She might give us insight into this knew development."

"So why are we going for Anubis? She sounds more important."

"Do as your told, soldier. Anubis's paranoia might actually translate these events into something that makes sense."

"Very good, Diana. I will find Anubis."

"Good. Diana out."

"Yuri out," he growled as the armored car crushed debris and dead bodies on its route back to the hospital the steady thumping beat of the helicopter blades could be heard, already patrolling the sky.

The barricaded door to the roof burst open, Rebecca amazed by her own strength. She kept running. Her legs burned as she ran from rooftop to rooftop. The creatures that were after her still gave slow, methodical pursuit after her. She was granted some moments of peace, restricting the zombie's pursuit by the leap-frogging of buildings. She used them to conserve what little strengths she had left. As she watched, gasping for breath, undead began to appear all over the rooftops. They were restricting her, like some sick chess game where she was the only piece left to fall. The shambling horde grew to close to her and she was forced to flee where she could.

Every safe rooftop became lethal in moments as more zombies pushed her back to other rooftops. Her heart pounded as she was funneled into a thinner and thinner safe zone. The helicopter hovered by looking at the scene from above. The zombiefied corpses worked a successive plot pushing her somewhere. "They're thinking," the pilot sighed. Diana waited on the communicator.

"What did you say?" she asked.

"They're driving her like a sheep to slaughter. They're herding her somewhere."

"Where?" she asked, impatiently.

"It looks like South East. Toward the WDO building."

"See if you can get her out of there. I don't want whatever's controlling those undead to get their hands on her until I know what it is they want her for. That means taking her in alive."

"Will do, Diana."

Rebecca stood on the ledge. Where there were once open rooftops were now small islands of death waiting for her. The horde pushed her back further, now no longer giving her the space to run. She glanced down to an open street and wondered just how much damage she could take to survive. She didn't want to die, despite what the good doctor thought. She would have to find a way. A thought invaded her brain. What if she died when her wrists were slit? What if this is a nightmarish vision of Hell. The lurching forms clawed at her clumsily, groping her ankles. She shrieked staggering off the ledge. The helicopter whirled by, arms grabbing hold of her and hoisting her away into the open holding bay.

The faces of dog men greeted her. Rebecca screamed fighting and kicking out but the shear number of them held her in place. One of the dog-headed men removed his helmet. He was a handsome, older man with nut-brown hair disheveled by the suppression of the helmet. A glow radiated from one eye, a void of light from the other. As she focused she saw that one eye was blue and the other nearly black. He clutched his stomach as though he was going to vomit.

"She's tainted. She's the demon Anubis was talking about." He drew a gun from one of the officers holding her down. A crackling came from over the communicator.

"Don't you dare, Orion. We need her alive."

"She's a fucking demon."

"Don't cross me, Orion," she warned. He could feel bones twist and pop. He fell back, his gun falling from a now hoofed hand. "She comes back alive and unharmed," Orion howled out in pain.

"Understood, Diana," he gasped out through the pain. He struggled as a new wave of pain took over him. His body flexed, shifting back to normal.

Chapter 16

Erwin Marks awoke on the cold basement floor in the dark. A form crouched over him. Erwin squirmed crawling backward away from it. He scrambled on impulse to the meager circle of light that reached this level of the compound.

"It's alright, Erwin," Paul's voice spoke from the massive shadow above him. It followed him toward the light but hesitated at the edge. Erwin could tell by the size of the shadow that it wasn't Paul.

"What are you, Monster?" He shrieked. A hand reached out and he saw it in the shadows. It was a mass of muscle ended with savage, jagged claws. Erwin looked for any weapon that survived the fall.

"Erwin, no. I'm not going to hurt you," it said, from the darkness.

"Stop talking like Paul, you're not Paul," Erwin yelled.

"Keep your voice down. We're in the belly of the beast; someone's bound to here us," it said, its own voice lowering to a loud whisper. "I am Paul but your right. I'm not the man you think I am."

Erwin waited in the shimmering light realizing that the beast did nothing in way of attack. It wouldn't even come toward him. This comforted him a little now that he was able to start thinking again. "Then what are you?"

"I was a God once. Now I'm… stuck on Earth to right my wrongs and such. I'm stuck here to guard the Earth of potential threats to existence yadah, yadah, yadah. Look I'm going to show you something O.K. and I don't want you to freak out."

"I can't make promises," Erwin smirked. He noticed that his wounds were healed and there was another wound at his right shoulder that was not from Kara. It was bigger, deeper with long serrated edges like the teeth of an animal. The figure in the shadows stepped out, revealing a gigantic bipedal Jackal. Erwin squeaked in shock and backed up to the edge of the darkness away from it. The beast stopped once it was visible and slowly condensed within itself into something more similar to the familiar form of his friend.

"I've got some other problems for you. I had to bite you to try and spare you from the undeath you were going to face. The upside to that is you're not a mindless corpse." His face though inhuman was not without remorse, muscles stretched down in a large frown to go with drooping, sad eyes.

"So what's going to happen to me?" Erwin asked, his hand noticing the second gun in his shoulder holster still in place.

"IF you are lucky a mind shattering pain that will be nearly impossible to overcome in one human lifetime." Erwin frowned taking the gun from his shoulder holster. He didn't train it on Paul though kept it on the ready. Paul tried to smile despite the obvious hurt he bore from his action. "Then if you manage to stay in control and overcome the agony of the transformation you get stronger, faster, and healthier."

"And if I can't stay in control and overcome the transformation?" Erwin asked, his voice already starting to grow into a growl.

Paul turned his attention to the ground, looking almost completely like his former self, save for his ears, which extended wide giving him the look of an anime dark elf. "Then I would have to kill you before your mindless, bestial rampages divulged my intervention and jeopardized humanity. I'm sorry about this, Erwin, but you would never get a second chance otherwise."

"I guess that makes sense, you son of a bitch. What are the odds?" Erwin asked, getting a wave for silence from Paul. He motioned for him to follow and they soon found themselves in a hall.

"That room was never there before." Paul ducked into a cubicle pulling Erwin in with him. Two forms, that of Kara and Mr. Blue walked by.

"So the plan is simple. You create a diversion against all the lovely little air-breathing mortals of Reno. I will liberate our masters from the pit," Winter said, again.

"Apple's gate," Kara added. Winter shook his head his hand curled into a fist.

"That's Appolyon Gate… Oh, it don' matter… not for long that is," he said, stroking her hair. She curled close to him affectionately and he stroked the soft, delicate skin of her outstretched neck. Their footfalls were never heard and Erwin looked down to their feet seeing that they didn't even step on the ground.

"Appolyon Gate," Anubis whispered to the wind when they were beyond them. When they were gone they slunk closer to the open room. Inside was a powerful, demonic corpse withered with age and absence of life. From a throne of zombie bodies he rose with zombies working diligently for his pleasures. He knew his associates were combating them from above. They must have thought his ravings the working of an insane mind for no one else to arrive yet. That figures, he thought. Anubis focused on the demon as it reviewed his new minions.

"We've got to get out of here. My superiors will have to know this. Come on," he said to Erwin, working his way from the compound quietly. Erwin looked at the horde and nodded following after him.

"These recruits are pathetic," alone with his zombie minions Asmodius spoke. He waved his hands and the zombies parted like a slow moving wave for him to walk through. In front of him lay a youthful eight-year-old zombie. He stepped up majestically to her and reflected on her situation, scrutinizing and inspecting her body, fully. His hands touched her cheeks and ran them down along the pale, dead flesh until it rolled over her rump to the legs. Sliding his skeletal, clawed hands he parted her legs looking at the chewed edges of a hole in the inner thigh. He hissed out a blast of air. "I hate when its children. So sad. But I have an idea. Tell me your name."

"Sal… Lee…"

"Sally. What a lovely name. Would you like to be freed from this nightmare to start a whole new one? I take your inability to answer as a yes," he said, more for himself than her, knowing that she couldn't comprehend his inquiry. He brushed the blood-matted hair from her eyes, caressing the clammy cold line of the jaw.

"Then get ready," he said, taking hold of her head roughly with both hands. His strength took her fully off her feet. "This is going to hurt, little Sally Parker," he smiled. Her lifeless form stared blankly, uncaring as her face was held mere inches from his. His smile attacked her, transforming into a deep kiss. The dead lifeless body in his hand began, slowly at first to jerk, fighting to free herself. He could feel her scream in his mouth. The light in her eyes returned in a painful spirit-igniting kiss. She pushed free falling to the ground. Her chewed leg twisted in an unnatural way. She screamed, and then trembled from fear in a tight ball. The corpse demon stepped back into the shadows with the rest of the dead.

"Numb," she said, finally in a whimper. "So numb. I can remember. Can taste the blood. What's going on? What is happening to me?" Her voice escalated in volume until she was practically screaming the words. The calm reassuring voice of Asmodius answered her from the throne he reclaimed.

"You died, Sally Parker. You were killed by a zombie but I brought you back. I have a special need for you, Sally."

"Who are you?" she asked, trying to penetrate the darkness with her dead eyes.

"I am your God now, Sally; King of the Undead and you will be my Queen." He stepped from the shadow revealing himself to her. "I am Asmodius." Her small youthful body was easily overshadowed by his massive towering form. "But such a weak, frail form. Perhaps I was wrong to choose such a fragile Queen. Maybe it would be better to return you to the throng and choose another."

At his words the undead fell in line behind and around them. The room came to life. Zombies, like a sea, surrounded her. She closed her eyes tight, shielding herself with her arms. "No. I'll be a good Queen; I'll be anything you want."

Atone

"Do you know what an Elector is? When I was an angel I was sent to Hell, not to be punished but to dispense righteous persecution to the sinful. More specifically, I was there to heal the damned so their torture would last forever," he said, turning to face her again. "You accept your fate, but your body needs some improvement. I will teach you something very important. Be grateful that death numbs the body. But first I have to test your resolve, my Queen."

The Zombie throng opened to reveal a hostage human still uncorrupted. It was a woman maybe 17 or 18. She was a human on the verge of starting her adult life. "You must kill if you seek a new body. Kill and take what you desire. Kill her, my Queen."

Sally stepped slowly, carefully toward her. Her mind was afraid. She killed as a zombie but she couldn't think then. For moments of eternity she stared at the girl. "What's your name?"

"Friends call me, Birdie," she sobbed. "Please, don't kill me."

"I'm sorry but I must," Sally said, flatly, concealing well her fear of murder. "What's one thing you've always wanted to do before you die?"

There was silence for a moment, Birdie getting slowly cautiously to her feet. She relaxed the best she could. For the first time since her arrival here she saw a slim glint of light in her eyes, enough to let hope through. Shakily she began to speak. "I've always wanted to go sailing, Like to Bermuda or Jamaica." It sounded like a question. As she began to talk the desire became more of a reality, like a dream too simple or basic to be realized fully. It wasn't until confronting death in the most bizarre and final way that it brought itself to her realization. Birdie continued talking, Sally getting closer as she talked moving slow, encouraging her to fully flesh out the dream that never was. She urged Birdie on to dream of the Caribbean, to dream bigger. To tell every detail of it she could imagine.

When the strike came it was quick. The bite was only enough to break the skin. The effect would be the same but she spared Birdie the brutality that she had to suffer. Birdie shrank back. "It's O.K. Birdie," she spoke watching her prey. Asmodius sat back in turn watching this scene unfold. "Think of Jamaica. Feel the sand on your feet, the salty cool breeze off the sea. Close your eyes and picture yourself there."

Atone

Birdie realized her doom was evident yet found herself thanking the chance meeting of this, her strange assassin. Death was inevitable, but the kindness it showed her allowed at least some semblance of peace. The numb began to affect her now. Her eyes clouded by death as she slipped away. Sally looked up and over to Asmodius. "It's done. What is it you need me to do?"

Chapter 17

Rebecca Van Ness awoke feeling the cold water and scum, thick along her calves. The sludge sucked her feet downward devouring them up to the ankles, tendrils of it squishing between her toes in the most unwelcome manner. The thread of the ropes dug into her scarred wrists, blood already dripping slowly down her arms. She looked out from her cell, a dark moss covered room with rusted, moldy bars. She couldn't reach them as they lined the far wall, like a massive arched mouth with filthy teeth. The "Mouth" led only into darkness. What light shown was from above through a sewer drain and lights, dim green with mold, lining the walls over her head. Two large gears on either side of her had chains bound around them. She looked above to see the ropes that held her tight twisted around the chains in a large knot. The walls tapered toward each other into an ever-narrowing tunnel above her.

Something made a unique reverberating noise like an alien creature's death wail from the darkness past the bars. From the shadow near the strange noise a voice spoke out. "Who are you?"

"Rebecca Van Ness," she answered. There was a blue glow that formed in the inquisitor's hands, giving her just a small glimpse of what made the noise and spoke the words. Then the blue glow streaked out as lightning toward her, sending her body into painful seizures.

"Who are you?" The vaguely female voice ordered gruffly.

"Who the fuck are you? Why are you...?" She would have continued but another crack of lightning sent her jerking sharply, her teeth nearly severing her tongue in two from the savage thrashing.

"You try my patience, show yourself, Demon!" The third blast of electricity sent Rebecca temporarily out of the water. Atone thought rapidly while the host suffered if they wanted to see her then they couldn't possibly be friendly or trusted. Rebecca growled, the locked jaw of electrocution denying her the scream she craved. Wave after wave of trauma was more than Rebecca could stand, Atone could feel her slipping out of consciousness. Rebecca faded away and Atone was pushed to the foreground of her mind, left to control the body they shared.

"That's enough! What are you thinking, Kali?" A woman's voice angrily reprimanded her torturer. The alien death wail, quieter than before was heard again.

"I was doing my job," Kali answered with a growl.

"Bullshit, you directly disobeyed my orders," the woman yelled to her subordinate.

"Your orders are not my job," Kali demanded back at her.

"I said unharmed." The voices argued back and forth, both feminine and both fighting for authority. There was a choking sound in the dark then the softer, more feminine voice spoke again, breaking apart into four voices at once. "You would do well to head my wishes." The sound was like several humming violins just seconds separated. There was no response from the other woman. Footsteps clicking on stone led the woman to the edge of the cell, her form finally visible. It was a youthful looking, vaguely familiar blonde, with hair tightly wound behind her into an almost perfect ball, held by a straight and narrow black spike. Her body was restrained by a smart and fashionable grey suit with matching skirt hugging her body tightly, delicate thin legs ended with spiked stiletto heels that she seemed to have no problem walking in. The woman looked with her golden eyes, hypnotizing even from there distance to Atone. "I am terribly sorry, Ms. Van Ness. Kali is really dedicated to her work. She is the best at her craft and I'm sorry you had to experience that first hand."

Atone looked up moving anything but her eyes as little as possible. A wicked purple fire burned in her eyes a sinister smile carved a path across her face. "You're calling her off. I was just getting into it."

Diana's faint smile faded to near nothing only traces in the eyes and the lines at the edge of her mouth remained of it. "You're the demon I presume?" she asked, without an answer. Atone looked in at Rebecca curled in a protective fetal position even in the back of her mind, sobbing uncontrollably. "Then we have much to talk about. Mainly I need to know who you are and why you're here."

"Why does it matter?" Atone panted in pain from the electrocution earlier.

"Do you have a problem giving us your name? Why is that?" Diana questioned sounding too much like Heinrich for Atone to enjoy.

"Because everyone I've ever met since coming to this world wants to know who I am and why I'm here," Atone breathed out, feeling weak. Her thoughts drifted back like a half remembered dream. She remembered leaving Heinrich and Francine behind to run in terror. "What about Heinrich and Frankie? Are they O.K. or do you have them locked up like me?"

"They're safe. They're the ones that alerted us to you. They are also the ones that made us break protocol in your case. The very fact I stopped Kali is thanks to them. Your very different for a demon."

"Devil," Atone corrected.

"Excuse me?" Diana said, scanning over her quizzically.

"I'm a devil not a demon," Atone answered again.

"That's not possible. Devils can't get out of..." Diana denied her but then stopped herself. "No devil has ever escaped before now. What makes you so special? Who are you and why are you here?"

"Do you really care? Tell me who you are and what you do here?" She retorted sarcastically. The woman in the suit didn't seem to take it as such.

"My name is Diana, a neutral angel. I run the north western office of the POE organization."

"What's POE?" Atone asked, head swimming.

"Prince of Earth," Diana explained.

"That makes sense. I should have known," Atone spat, shaking her head and then feeling sorry for doing so. She hung limply. Princes of Earth were the fallen angels that weren't evil but neither were they good. God decided that they would best serve on Earth to trouble shoot threats to his order. This was not a good sign for her as many of the demons back from a possession would tell her.

"Now you will answer me. Who are you?" Diana asked, with the authority of a person controlling the situation, like a warden to a prisoner.

"My name is Atone. I'm not special and the only reason I'm here is to warn God of a conspiracy against him, while trying to avoid as much of the apocalypse as I can along the way.

This reminds me…" Diana stopped listening as Atone continued saying something about the zombies and that things are going to get worse the longer she's restrained here. Diana was too thrown by the first sentence. "My name is Atone." Diana began to shake unconsciously. When she realized what she was doing she stepped back into the concealing darkness to hide any sign of weakness.

"You mock me, Devil. I don't know how you got to me…" She hissed from the shadow, her voice turning feral, loosing all authority.

"Got to you how, Bitch? I don't even know who the fuck you are." Atone hung there waiting for a response. She didn't here footsteps leave but the ever-building feeling of overwhelming loneliness told her no one was going to answer her.

Diana walked up the ladder to the roof of the compound. The POE head quarters was a solid building planted inside a dam. She stood on the top. It was nighttime, the stars and moon dazzling in the otherwise barren sky. A thin layer of water pushed ever onward to the smaller stream bellow but the force was not strong enough to move her from her position. She looked up at the moon, it seemed so much smaller from this side. She thought back long ago when the moon, the night, the hunt, they were all hers, her dominion. She thought of God showing mercy on her and letting her stay as an angel. She thought of God showing mercy again, this time letting her come here instead of the darkness of the Hell beyond. This last thought lingered in her mind. What this creature, whether or not Atone, had to endure. This thought made her hope that the devil lied about who she was.

"What do you think, Diana?" There came a voice from the distance beyond her thoughts. She turned to see Orion standing in the water near the hatch that had led her here.

"No doubt wondering about our guest. Wondering about what she is and why the dead want her." There came another voice echoing from the hatch. A head emerged as Orion got out of the way to stand on the dam with her. Diana smiled at the human, so brilliantly smart and overwhelmingly naive at the same time.

"Half right, as usual, Stephan," she welcomed with a sad smile as he emerged from the hatch to join the two. The water proved more difficult for Stephan Marquette being the only human out of the three. He was also the only one to twist his coat closer together for warmth.

"I heard you reprimanded Kali," Orion said, feigning disinterest. "Care to tell me why?"

"Not really," she said, flatly, then feeling the eyes on her she knew he wasn't getting it. "I don't feel I have to justify my actions to you."

"But they must be justified throughout the organization. So I ask you again, why? Why let this one live?" Orion said, looking sympathetically at her. She shivered but it wasn't from the cold.

"She's different somehow. We should find out what unique events made her existence possible," Diana said, attempting to sound impartial.

"No. Our purpose is not to reason why but to prevent things like this from occurring," Orion said, making Diana jerk back stunned like a bad dog getting slapped on the nose. Her eyes widened and looked hurt and bewildered back at the one that made her feel that way.

"And I say we should know our enemies before hand," Diana said, looking away from him after the raising of her fury and voice. She watched the moonlit water flowing past her. "So we know better that which we fight against."

"This doesn't sound like you. Something's wrong," Orion said, reaching out to her. He put his arm around her and she slapped it off with a huff.

"Why did you come up here, Orion?" She growled defensively.

"No reason to get defensive, love. I worry some times that's all," Orion said. She accepted and allowed him to hug her with one arm. "That… and Woten is coming."

"What?" she asked, uncharacteristically unraveling. She turned to face him and nearly slipped from the dam wall. Orion held her safely and she caught her footing.

"Anubis came in here with a cop and they had a lot of information," Orion continued as if nothing happened.

"And the book," Stephan spoke up for his part. "Don't forget that."

"And Stephan's book opened. We learned some more prophetic warnings," he finished.

"Yeah, and with the current problems he thought direct control would be best." Stephan doubled back to explain why Woten was showing up.

"To shove me out of the way while he runs things. Why put me in charge if he didn't think I could handle it?" Diana fumed glancing back and forth between Orion and Stephan.

"This is a bit bigger than ego, doll," Orion responded.

Stephan watched her soften a little for Orion's sympathy. Stephan on the other hand had enough cold loosing feeling in the tip of his nose. "You've been informed of the goings ons. I'm going to see what the book says," Stephan said, crawling back down the hatch. Orion and Diana stood alone holding each other in the chill night air. The moon blurred with the moving of a helicopter.

"Look, Diana, You and Woten have a lot of history," Orion said, his caring voice shivered with a hint of fear.

"History that sent me here instead of central," Diana continued still fuming.

"I'm sure that's not it at all," he said, her bitterness rubbing off on him slightly. He caught himself and returned his caring smile. He lifted her head to look into her golden eyes. "But I'm glad it is. We never would've met. Never gotten to know each other."

"Do we?" she asked, her face distorted with her impending dread. "Look, there are things you don't know. Things I have to tell you, should have told you. If what that thing in the basement said is true then…" Diana was about to tell him everything she never said only to have her words stolen by the return of the helicopter. This time it hovered over them. The wind sent their clothes fluttering. The water sprayed out in thin needles that cut at their legs.

"Let's get this over with!" Woten's voice boomed over the chopper, he jumped the rest of the way, landing hard on the dam with combat boots and fatigues. Three black clad soldiers followed him from the helicopter floating in the air behind him. One was a black winged angel, her raven colored hair fluttering savagely from the wind of the helicopter blades. The other was a man, with short blonde hair, scuffed with night vision goggles He hovered over the water two feet from the ground. The third was a raven struggling against the helicopter's wild air. Woten's grey hair batted against his face, and he swept it away from his good eye, dull blue. His other Eye was covered by a patch in the path of a savage looking scar.

His broad mouth was wide in a brave grin. Diana bowed her head submissively before looking back at him stiffly.

"Where do you want to start?" Diana asked, professionally, as the helicopter flew away to the real landing deck. "Anubis' report or the open book?"

"First I'd like to see our daughter," Woten's voice boomed like thunder shaking the ground they stood on. Orion looked back at Diana who refused to meet his gaze. Diana let out a gasp then lowered her head all hope gone.

"Right this way."

Orion stood with mouth open as she led Woten past him and down the hatch. The three soldiers followed them. Orion tried to ask what Woten was talking about but all that escaped him was short loud exhales "Wha… Wha…"

Inside, forgetting Orion, Woten turned to his soldiers. "Hermes, go to the book, learn all you can and report back to me. Hugin, Munin, find Anubis and this cop and locate me immediately following the briefing. Find out all you can about what they know."

Three short nods and his soldiers moved on, Hermes looking focused on Diana intently before departing to their chosen course. Diana turned to Woten after Hermes left. "Still having others do your work, Woten?"

"It's the most effective way. Third person view allows me to see what both first and second miss," he said. All he would have to do when they return is a touch and he would know all that transpired when they left him. He smiled at the efficiency. Diana led him to the dungeon and he focused on her. He smiled broadly at her. His good eye scanned over her making his smile widen. She was still beautiful after all these years. His hand went down for a quick feel but Diana's voice stopped the attack.

"I see you have Hermes in central now," she made small talk not turning back to reprimand him. Her stern voice said it all. He was more powerful by far, but she wasn't without power herself. He thought better of it and retracted his advancement.

"Yes, it seems to be a meeting ground for your former lovers," he responded sharply.

"When I heard you were coming my initial reaction was that you would take control of the north western sector and force me out of the loop. Was I right in this reaction?" Diana asked, tentatively.

"Diana, this is business. I'm not here to take over but to give extra aid. For what its worth you've done a superb job with North and Central America. Consider us only support," he assured.

"And I call the shots?" she asked, not believing his empty promises.

"Of course." She found it hard to grasp and couldn't help but doubt Woten's intentions. There wasn't time to question him further. They were at the cell.

"Hello, Atone. You've grown," he said, awkwardly. She raised her head staring out menacingly in the dark.

"Another visitor, I must be popular. Are you here to torture or talk, it seems to be all anyone here is good at," she barked bitterly.

"She has your sharp tongue, Woten."

"Who are you people? Why do you talk like you know me?" She shouted, shaking against her bindings.

"Are you sure it's her, Woten?" Diana asked, trying to ignore Atone completely. "Could there be some mistake?"

Woten moved his eye patch from his left eye to reveal the empty socket beneath, directly exposing the soul that swirled smoky red inside it. "It is her. I'm sure of it."

"She said she wanted to warn God of something. Some conspiracy," Diana informed.

"Well we can't be sure of that. There is no trust with her yet," he said back, replacing his eye patch.

"What do you suggest?" Diana inquired.

"Nothing yet. Let's get the other facts first. But if my insight is correct the book will shine some light on this," Woten contemplated almost to himself.

Atone yelped to the darkness. "Hey, I'm right here. Quit talking about me like I'm not."

Chapter 18

The makeshift survivors camp was being moved to ironically enough my school, Frankie thought to herself. The POE officer next to her had other thoughts. Sam thought this was a strategic place with thick wooden doors, metal bar gates down every hall that could be closed for safety, thick brick walls and high windows. It was an old boarding school back when the focus of school was a prison rather than learning. It was an imposing and well defendable choice. The Biology Lab and Chemistry lab were chosen as the main rooms in that there were metal gates on either side and the two rooms were joined together by a rest room accessible exclusively from these rooms. Also, since the biology lab had its own refrigeration, short term food supplies could be stored.

None of this crossed Frankie's mind. She looked through the crowd to see any faces that were recognizable to her. There was the old guy from the corner store. A few skater punk kids she recognized from school but didn't know personally. Was that it, she thought? All these lives and there was nothing. She had no ties to any of these people. She felt alone, deeply alone surrounded by strangers. She looked outside through the chemistry door to see two POE officers leading two other guys in security guard uniforms, to the math classroom past the metal gates. One of the two security guards had a real bad limp moving much slower than the rest and getting help only from the other officer. One of the POE officers noticed her and turned to face her. Removing his helmet he revealed himself to be Uthgar.

"Sad isn't it," he said to her on the other side of the doorway.

"Excuse me?" she asked, surprised that an authority figure noticed her.

"This entire city worth of people, reduced to two rooms in a public school," Uthgar clarified. Frankie nodded her head toward the math class.

"What's with those guys?" she asked.

"Hm… Oh, those two. Security guards from the hospital," Uthgar answered.

"Why are they over there?"

"One got shot. To make sure the world isn't infected we're keeping him under quarantine," he explained.

"That one looks kind of like Uncle Bryce," she said, before the door was closed. She saw him look up and wave. Before she could react the door was shut and guards stood in front of it. She looked up at Uthgar and opened her mouth to speak when Heinrich's voice was heard over the basic mumble of the amassed people, calling for his daughter. Frankie looked back over her shoulder on instinct seeing him searching through the crowd.

"Your father?" Uthgar asked, pointing at him.

"Unfortunately," she retorted.

"Want to calm his nerves?" Uthgar asked. She looked over her shoulder and nodded against her typical desire. He led her back to her father.

"Frankie. Stay close to me," he said, taking hold of her wrist.

"Relax Dad, I'm not a preschooler," she snapped, but stepped closer to him for safety.

"Under this circumstance humor me O.K.?" he asked. He wouldn't let her go if she said no, however so the question was pointless.

"Sure, Dad," Frankie said. Uthgar let go of her other hand and Heinrich turned his attention to him.

"Is there any word on Rebecca?" Heinrich asked, worried.

"Or my mom?" Frankie added.

Uthgar fidgeted with one foot. "Officially no. Unofficially, someone was picked up and is being held at POE HQ. Whether or not your Rebecca is this person I can't say? I'm not important enough for that information." Uthgar scanned the room to find a way out of this. He saw Poseidon talking to Yuri and Sam. "Now if you'll excuse me."

Uthgar maneuvered through the crowd to reach the inner circle of POE officers. "…and they're calling everyone from lieutenant up back to base. Sam, keep an eye on this place. Yuri you'll come with me. Uthgar, you stay here, set up the perimeter with Sam. Also set up a hunting team to spread out and take back some territory."

"Understood."

"I leave the men in your hands, Uthgar. Come on Yuri." Poseidon and Yuri turned to leave Uthgar. Uthgar let a growling sigh escape his mouth as he rounded up some of the basic soldiers.

"You, you and you follow me. Sam, set up two men to patrol the halls. I want nothing in this building without a heart beat got it?" Uthgar ordered. His commanding voice sent the men to their various tasks without question.

"Yes, Sir."

Frankie, watching from the crowd, got the basic understanding of what the soldiers were doing. Since the orders were simple and precise, she returned her attention to the crowd. She saw the blonde woman still holding the boy in her arms.

"Mrs. Murdock?" she asked. She was a friend of her moms and lived in the same cul-de-sac. Frankie looked around hoping to find her mother somewhere near by. Seeing one without the other was unsettling, especially with the current situation.

Atone

"Frankie?" she said, recognizing her through the gothic punk clothes and makeup. She looked up at Heinrich disapprovingly. He looked back at her, the zombie problem to prominent for either to voice their distaste for the other. Frankie broke the uneasy silence making them both feel selfish.

"Where's my mom? Have you seen my mom?" Frankie asked, cursing herself for sounding so much like a little child. The look in Mrs. Murdock's face was enough. She looked down; not wanting to look in those eyes, fearing that in some way she would transfer with a glance the wretched end of her mother to Frankie. Her eyes found others, Aaron, another neighbor, stared at her, never blinking, never smiling, not even a sign of breathing. Frankie felt the hair rise on her arms and stared back at the boy in Mrs. Murdock's arms. She sidestepped to see if he would do something. His eyes rolled to follow her, without any other movement. There was seriously something wrong with him now. Before, he was a carefree youth, now he was an emotionless void. She felt a piece of herself agree.

Chapter 19

Atone heard the heavy, quick footfalls of a man in a hurry coming toward her. "Oh goody, another one," she hissed with nothing else to do but dangle there helpless.

"You know I don't understand you," he said, angrily, as if having a conversation with a slacking employee. "What power you have over them. Have they forgotten what their purpose is? Have they forgotten that you're a threat? A devil? That we're supposed to kill creatures like you? I don't know what you did to them; devil, but they forget why we're here."

"So why are you here?" she asked, with a disinterested defiance that she knew would get her proverbially slapped. She could practically hear him smile with the thought of what he wanted to do.

"I'm here to do my Job," he said, raising his gun, the only part of him to pierce through the shadow, becoming visible to her. She barely had time to see the spark of light on the barrel before it blurred from the smoke of a fired bullet. Her heart spiraled upward into her throat, suffocating her. She could only close her eyes tightly and squirm as the bullet rocketed closer. She heard the impact and felt herself falling with a splash, the stagnant water forcing itself down her throat, pushing her heart painfully back in place where it beat rapidly. She gasped, trying to expel the tainted water.

Adrenaline coursed through her and she rose hacking violently. Water splashed wildly as she fought against the deep muck and struggled, panicking, to regain her balance. Orion, on dry land was unlocking the door; she backpedaled through the water to hide under the massive gears away from him. He crouched down at the water's edge. She spat, her water mixed with words. "So what are you going to do now, make a game of killing me?"

"I'm not here to kill you, that is, until you give me reason to," he hissed through his clenched teeth.

"How can I be sure?" she asked, from her hiding place disbelieving.

"Because the powers that be have decided your intentions are to be tested. I'm supposed to supervise you," he chewed the words disgusted by the taste. He clenched his stomach as it churned violently.

"Tested, how?" she asked, peeking out between two teeth of the gears.

"There is something somewhere in the WDO compound. Your test is to go in and kill it," he grumbled, not feeling like playing this game. Her very presence made him physically sick. It was his own personal curse. "Its all bogus if you ask me. In reality your mother and father don't want to admit their baby girl grew up to be a filthy fucking Devil."

"My what? You expect me to believe that?" She swam out and saw him standing at the edge of the muck, his gun, held loosely, was aimed at the ground. She swam tentatively over to him and began to emerge from the dirty liquid where a rusty metal ladder plunged into the dirty water.

"You know everyone expects you to be some prophecy made real. They all overlook the fact that you're a monster," Orion said. Her eyes dared to look up as she felt the cold steel pressed against the center of her forehead, right along the hairline. She knew he wanted to pull the trigger. She knew also he wouldn't, not without provocation. There was something more his confused emotions wouldn't tell her. Or maybe she just wasn't reading them right. Having a gun to your head can tend to make that happen, she thought. He waited several seconds before holstering his gun. "A monster that shouldn't be allowed to live. Hurry up. Name's Orion by the way."

He let her finish getting out of the muck. He led her to several corridors the last leading to an underground garage. There several different teams were preparing to go on their own tests, she assumed her eyes catching the attention of nearly all in the room. They all scowled suspiciously at her except for one in a brown suit, which looked confused, standing next to a Jackal headed man. She could see him voice the words "Rebecca Van Ness" even though she couldn't here him. Another man, definitely human, came over to her. "It really is an honor and a privilege to meet you, Atone. My name is Stephan Marquette. I would like to welcome you to our team. That is of course if you are the penitent angel."

"Calm down, Stephan, you're drooling," Orion grumbled.

"Hardly. It's nice someone seems happy to see me," she said, giving a glare to Orion's bitter comments and overall rudeness.

"Only because he doesn't know any better," Orion mumbled dryly under his breath, getting into the driver side of his car.

"What's everyone else doing?" she asked, but heard Orion before Stephan could speak.

"This is a paramilitary operation. There is no need for you to know. Stephan?" he yelled his name to make sure his friend didn't divulge information to an enemy. He started the car and revved it up. "And get in will you? The sooner I'm done with you the better."

She turned her attention to the car. Unlike the monstrous armored vehicles this was more or less an older model Buick. On closer inspection she recognized the 4" by 4" armor plates incorporated into the panels. The grill was modified to protect the engine and was also guarded by several small armor plates. She slipped inside the back driver's side door coming face to face with a black clad stealth operative. Weird goggles, hoses and wires of a strange breathing apparatus accompanied stranger gadgets that made the person appear more like some alien creature than a human being. She couldn't help but tense as she reluctantly finished entering the car. It, for lack of better definition, simply stared at her. She looked away at the other soldiers, with their streamline, lupine-headed outfits, sleek and sexy. She looked back at the freak next to her and wondered why he didn't get the same gear. What was under the solid black, body bag suit that concealed any real features? Orion looked back and saw her staring at the thing in the back seat.

"Oh, sorry. Should have told you about Hugin. He… is coming with," he finished finding no way to explain him easily.

"Hugin?" she asked. "I'm Rebecca, or Atone, which ever. Nice to meet you?" she asked, holding out a hand. He looked at it then her, his head jerking like a bird at every movement. Its head cocked to the side and a high wordless noise escaped its mouth. The awkward moment was broken by the sound of Orion's voice. A stray feather poked out at an odd angle from Hugin's collar.

"What do you think you are doing?" Atone and Hugin both turned their attention toward him, then Stephan who tried to take the passenger side.

"I'm coming with you," Stephan answered adjusting his glasses.

"Under who's command?" Orion asked, forcefully.

"The book said she was something special. As the keeper of the book…" He fidgeted with his hands trying his best to avoid Orion's direct gaze.

"You are not coming," Orion commanded firmly.

"I cannot let you go off and kill her. Not if she is as important as it says." Stephan grew bolder, strengthening his resolve.

"You're a librarian, Stephan. You are not made for field ops." Orion tore down his defenses.

"I don't care. I'm going."

"My orders are to observe the penitent one on the mission. Nothing further," he said, sarcastically. "Those are my orders Stephan."

"Even so…" Stephan started. Atone felt his resolve slipping. She felt her own worth through him, and felt sorry for his own weakness and false hope.

"I follow my orders," Orion continued.

"Not all the time," Stephan answered before thinking. His eyes widened before Orion could even respond.

"What's that supposed to mean?" Orion snapped. Stephan began to sweat and stutter.

"Only, that if you always followed orders you wouldn't be here." His voice grew high pitched and squeaky.

"You little bastard."

"Don't you see? That's why she's so important. If she's the penitent and she succeeds then you, Anubis, Poseidon, Diana, all of you would be given a chance to return to him. 'The fallen would be judged on the eve of the penitent's sacrifice'…"

"My what?" Atone interjected.

"…Those that repent will rejoin God. Those that remain evil will be destroyed."

"Are things always like this? So tense?" She turned, being so overlooked by Orion and Stephan, to face Hugin. It looked back at her without giving her a response. She looked back at the others, Orion and Stephan locked in a stare down. Their eyes fighting an epic battle all their own. The ninth beat of the heart was interrupted by a calm quiet sound from Orion.

"I understand your concern, Stephan. I give you my word to God himself, Atone will come back, unharmed if at all possible. Just because I don't like the mission doesn't mean I won't follow through. I will report what occurs and then if the information warrants upper management to approve removal, then I will act. I promise I will not kill her without an order from Diana."

Stephan remained frozen for a moment then looked back at Atone and Hugin. Atone felt like saying it would be O.K. even if it wasn't just to resolve the situation but she couldn't. Stephan looked to pitiful, his scrawny untrained body unfit for where they were headed, yet his resolve to keep her safe was admirable even if it was only for her to be sacrificed later. Despite the fact that his unskilled body would end up a shield if he went she wanted him with in some small way.

She was glad, however, when he closed the door from the outside. "Good," Orion said, looking back. "If there are no other stops or interruptions let's get this done."

The car revved again at Orion's encouraging. The lights illuminated several special features of the car not found in your average performance models. Rockets, Guns, amphibious adaptation, flame throwers all marked on small icons on a row of buttons along with others she couldn't identify by simple pictures. She felt it best not to get too nosey.

A helicopter could be heard but not seen as they left the garage. A massive armored vehicle crushed the ground behind them but they were faster and quickly lost sight of the other soldier's vehicle. Several blocks passed silently. It wasn't until they were out of the city proper that she began to speak.

"You said my mom and dad, before. What were you talking about?" Atone asked, curiosity at last taking over. He huffed turning the corner.

"Just what I said, your mother and father want you safe… in my opinion of course," he said, looking in the rear view mirror at Hugin. "Are you getting this? I hope so. I want her to know."

"So my mom and dad, the heavenly bodies that created me, breaking Gods commandment to do so, are here now?" she asked, not really wanting to know. But the conversation was starting to peak her interest. "And why would that change anything? They gave me up so easily the first time."

"I, apparently, wasn't high enough on the totem pole to even know about you until now." Atone studied him letting his emotions bleed into her own. In that she could find a certain similarity between them.

"You feel you should have been informed since you are, or thought you were, more important in her life?" she asked, grasping at the threads she gathered. His stern face grew even more harsh but he wouldn't reply. "She probably thought you would have a hard time with it and didn't want to put something like that in the way of your relationship. Thoughtless, true, but it wasn't a deliberate act against you."

"Shut up already," Orion growled low in his throat.

"Jeez, I'm just trying to help," she murmured turning her attention to the outside world. It looked like one might expect from any other day. The only difference was a couple of smashed cars, a few patches of fire here and there and the overwhelming emptiness of a city without people. Since they left the heart of the city blocks ago there wasn't even that much carnage on these suburban streets. Buildings gave way to trees and hills. The road twisted like a snake passing a bog of some sort then straightened passing the last crossroads before the WDO HQ. A fuel truck blocked one road, the car it collided with seen in the ditch on the other side of the crossroads.

Passing it they drove into the lot of the WDO building. There, the first thing they saw was the cop car of Erwin Marks. Zombies could be seen patrolling the perimeter preparing for the POE agent's attack. Orion was running through tactical options using the car as their stronghold. He drove to park near the trunk of the cop car, boxing Atone in. Orion then turned to her and said, "There might be some useful gear in the trunk. Try to pop it open. Watch for any movement from them, Hugin."

Orion and Hugin drew guns and rolled the windows down about an inch and a half. Atone tried the hatch with little effect. Orion grew impatient. "Just pop the hatch, damn it, what's taking so long?"

"How?" Atone barked. Orion made a face of disgust, daring to look away from the shambling horde.

"I don't know. Be resourceful," he barked at her loudly.

"Resourceful," Atone repeated thinking. Her claws grew feral, knuckles and fingers growing thorny, punching her fingers around the lock. She dug savagely through the sharp metal. The sound of twisting metal accompanied the agonizing pain of her flesh carving free from the bone. She restrained the urge to scream, not giving him the satisfaction. She wrenched it free from the rest of the car and through the lock into the front seat at him.

The trunk rose freely and she was greeted to the stench of decay and the barrel of a shotgun inches from her face. She could see the glimmer of the slug at the far end ready to fire. Instinct sent her hand in a swath in front of her, moving the barrel aside at the last moment. The heat of the shot burned the scales on the back of her hand. The shot was followed by a ringing silence.

Hugin slumped in his seat face pressed across the glass leaving an arch of red as his strength left him. A tear gas canister was flung into the car. Atone took hold of the gunman's arm and climbed out of the window. She leapt, twisting around the arm to land on the raised trunk lid. Her weight sent it down in a hurry, severing the malicious limb from the rest of the zombie ambusher. The driver side door opened, Orion tumbling out, blindly crawling away. In the wake of the destruction the horde shambled forward. Leaping from the cop car trunk to the armored one's roof, she took the shotgun, still in the mummified hand, with her. She twisted through the air, keeping her face on the trunk. It sprung open, the furious grasping claw and snapping teeth of the zombie quickly rising toward her. Within moments and shots the zombie fell dead again, the trunk of the cop car its new coffin.

The horde of zombies, though slow began to close them in. Atone grabbed Orion aiding him in their escape. There was no movement from Hugin's side of the car just his bleeding head pressed against the window. If they were going to make it, they would have to leave, now.

Retreating on foot to the crossroads, Orion could finally see for himself, eyes red and puffy from the tears. Atone checked on him. "Do zombies usually do that kind of thing?" she asked, when she gathered that he could function on his own.

"No. The demon we're hunting controls them somehow."

"A demon? And they only sent three of us to stop it? Do they not like you or something?" She howled furiously and dumbfounded.

"Compared to the alternative…" He flustered. "If they had the men to spare we wouldn't have to. Let's just say there is a lot going on right now."

"Some leader. Us against an entire army of undead and your alpha plan is to go for the main entrance," she chastised him bitterly.

"I was evaluating the situation," he snapped back. "To find a better way to proceed."

"Is that why I'm on this team?" she asked, spitting on the ground.

"What?" He hissed, trying to clear his eyes as more tears welled up.

"The demon. Is that why I'm on this team… use me to take out a demon?"

"It… Diana thought it was the best way to test your loyalties." Orion was yelling now no longer interested in the debate. "To see if your noble quest was genuine. And it's still a team; Hugin will be around soon enough. When God cursed us to walk the Earth until judgment day, he meant it."

"So that would be a yes? Or no? Kind of?" Atone tried to gain one straight answer.

"Yes," he finally conceded.

"Then let me try to storm the castle, All right?" She cocked his gun. Orion's eyes widened and he checked himself noticing now his absent weapon. "Relax. You can have it back. I'm just going to check out our new ride."

Orion rose as she began checking the now compact car. Pieces of it made a trial of broken metal and glass all the way to the grill of the gas truck. Orion followed the pieces to Atone examining the mutilated vehicle. He looked at her confused.

"That's not going anywhere." She looked back at him bitterly, checking the driver to make sure dead stayed dead. He waited for some information but when none came he had no choice. "So what are you planning to do?"

Chapter 20

The WDO building laid quiet, its occupants at their positions unflinching, unmoving. The walls of the immense structure were blurred with a thin fog of morning, the sun shining on the upward most slivers of treetops. All was peaceful until the noise broke the silence. Birds scattered from the eminent doom as the gas truck barreled over the drive and through the wall of the building, zombies reduced to red mist from the impact with machine to decay. Sparks lit the darkness as the protective metal shell of the trucks body scrapped along the cement bricks. The vehicle became hard to steer as the floors of the abandoned building began to give way.

Atone didn't seem to care as she drove demolition style through the place. Rebecca on the other hand was screaming in her mind trickling through and forcing it from Atone's mouth. "What the Hell are you doing? Your going to get me killed!"

"When the time comes, trust me. If you want to live then trust me," Atone said, comforting her.

391

Atone

"Trust you? This is a tanker full of gas, an incinerator on wheels. We're going to get burned alive."

"Trust me. It worked for Achilles, It worked for Isis. I'm almost sure I can do it too," Atone said, annoyed.

"What the Hell are you talking about…? Oh my God!" she screamed as the floor gave way completely. Like vertical dominoes, one collapsed on to the next. After the seventh floor gave way the tanker finally ignited, Zombie wails silenced by the roar of fire. Rebecca began to scream trying in vain to take control of her body. Atone held her back and prepared for impact. The truck ruptured spewing out a wave of flaming gas splashing across the walls of the last floor. The flames roared upward to escape the pit. Rebecca shattered the windshield, cradled in the broken glass a moment before tumbling out to the heart of the inferno. Flames ate away her flesh. She covered her ears, deafened by her own screams. Atone focused back inside her mind and tried to console her.

"It's all right. I wish you could understand that. Don't be afraid." Rebecca didn't listen as she seemed to burn eternal, though only a few minutes was required for her mortal coil to depart. The pain subsided with the absence of a body. The scream ended in a weak trailing moan.

"Am I dead?" Rebecca asked, meekly after a moment.

"No, as I was trying to explain," Atone answered harshly.

"Well forgive me if I don't know anything about Isis or Achilles," she said, then noticed that the voice wasn't inside of her. She looked around. Crawling like a serpent through the air was a dark purple swirl of light.

"It would seem you don't know anything about anything," the purple light spoke. Rebecca gasped twisting away only to find herself a pale green wisp of light. There was a silence as the two lights wandered around the building. Then Rebecca broke the silence.

"So what's going on?" She demanded tentatively.

"Your soul is exposed. Your mortal shell is removed," Atone answered simply.

"Doesn't that mean dead?" she asked, again.

"Well that is the most common way for this to occur, but there are other ways," Atone explained.

"O.K. I'll try to understand," she said, following the devil's soul upward through the compound. "What are other ways?" The faint grey souls of zombies cluttered the floor of subbasement 11.

"Immortality for starters," she said, simply, slithering through the burning wreckage. "Be grateful. Most people don't get this for free. Since we've shared souls some of me is in you. A little bit of my powers and being, enough to make you survive the crash at any rate. That is as long as nothing destroys your soul while it's exposed like this." Rebecca watched as Atone collected grey sparks from the corpses. "I've heard people offer just about everything they have for such services."

"Immortality?" Rebecca said, confused. Watching Atone harvesting the grey sparks of life, she had to divert from her original line of questioning. "What are you doing now?"

"Collecting souls," she answered. "Could you find something hard, like a hammer or something?"

Atone

At a loss Rebecca looked through her decimated surroundings her eyes settling on a drop forged pipe wrench, the plastic tool box it was in melted away to expose it.

"Over here," she called.

"Well pick it up," Atone said, not looking back to see.

"How? I'm a swirling ball of light."

"Are you sure?" Atone said, sifting through the debris. It appeared to be something of a restroom. She found one piece of small mirror that survived the fire. "Skin can lie, Miss Van Ness. But a soul will always show true." She angled the mirror to Rebecca. The person she saw in the reflection looked like her but yet subtly different. Like the version of herself she saw in dreams. The reflective form touched her face and Rebecca found her own face touched. Reaching out to the pipe wrench she watched as her glowing body took on the form the reflection contained. Atone continued to talk through her mystified discovery. "Most people's souls look human enough, like the mind's eye version of themselves. Some people look like animals. Some… Hah, some look worse than any nightmare you can imagine." Atone began pounding the collected souls into a form.

"What are you doing now?"

"Soul forging. I am making these souls, pretty pathetic as they are, into something useful, like weapons for fighting this demon," she stated. She began to make tiny daggers and passed them to Rebecca as she made more. "Consider yourself lucky. I may need you fully functional," she said, taking the collection of knives back from Rebecca, spreading them out like a fan then folding them back into a stack. "Get ready."

The fires of the WDO building were dying down as they approached what would be the secret room on subbasement 11. The heat departing, their souls began to generate a new skin around them. The exposed soul was now a light through a half-transparent shell. The dark red glow of something evil radiated from the room. The demon Asmodius waited, his heap of zombie throne now faded to a less grand seat of moaning ghosts patch worked together. His soul like theirs barely concealed in a see through skin.

"You have come, forsaken angel. You have come as the book foretold," a powerful voice responded to their approach.

"Why does everyone keep talking about this book? Chosen sacrifice? I'm getting tired of people hinting at things!" Atone shouted, cutting him off. "Like I'm supposed to know what they're talking about."

"They tell you only what they want you to know," Asmodius said, his contempt obvious. "I am here to tell you what you need to know."

"Why? Why tell us anything? We came here to kill you," Rebecca interrupted.

"A bold mission to be sure. A mission you will not fulfill," he spoke unafraid.

"Oh, really? Why so confident?" Atone growled baring her teeth. She fingered the daggers fanning them out again, ready for anything.

"I am confident because I have ghouls in every major city throughout North and Central America. The only thing keeping them at bay is me. Is that incentive enough to talk and listen?" He answered with the air of superiority oozing from his freshly made skin.

"So talk. What's with this book?" Atone asked, fanning the blades closed again and easing out of a ready stance. He nodded smiling at her submission.

"Before Isis was abducted, dragged deep into the Abyss she wrote two books. Knowing her fate, each book could not be read unless they were both read at the same time. One she made a gift to a mortal, a Sophia Demarco. Her descendents protected the first book of prophecy. The second was taken with her into Hell. Before she left Sophia she said never to open the book. Sophia didn't, giving likewise this warning to her descendents. But some time in her lineage the book was opened. I was fortunate enough to have the book at the time. I learned about you. About what you were going to achieve. Then I was attacked, Beelzebub tortured me for information and took the book, but whoever was on the other side had closed it and he was not given access to the knowledge. I made myself resolved in finding you and telling you what you were meant to achieve."

"Why would Beelzebub do this?"

"Don't tell me you were taken in by his nice guy façade," Asmodius said, with a wicked smile running across his transparent face. "Well it doesn't matter."

"The POE said that my sacrifice would allow the fallen the chance of forgiveness," Atone said, skeptically. "Isn't this what POE and The Order want?"

"Yes, but there are other things you need to know. The what, by now you've figured out. The how… Now that's what you need guidance on. Think, what was it that made you fall in the first place?"

"Hey, if you have all this information why don't you spill it instead of asking me these useless questions?" She snapped at him hackles rising and hair bristling. Rebecca stopped looking at her in surprise and fear.

"Very well. As you may have surmised your very presence in this world pulls apocalypse ever closer. You will need to leave it therefore, the sooner the better. Your efforts at a low profile have been commendable so far, but you'll need to find a way to heaven if you will fulfill you're…" There was a noise as some debris gave way above; a black oddly garbed form set a thin red beam, visible in the smoke and dust, to the still visible soul of Asmodius. Atone turned to pin point it and saw the shot fired. Her head turned back, following the bullet. When she saw Asmodius again he lay on the ground, life essence oozing from the soul, the freshly formed shell cracking like a thin, early winter ice. Asmodius reached up to take hold of her, in a burst of speed, drawing her down with him, bringing her close. Words unheard between them were spoken, Rebecca too confused to react. The attack was too quick, too precise to react to. Then her thoughts went to his warning. He had ghouls in every city. She wondered if it was even possible before the silence of the scene was broken by yelling. She was astonished to realize it was her voice, from her mouth.

"God damn it Hugin, what the fuck were you thinking? Do you have any idea what you've done?" The odd movements twisted the barely human's attention to her. She got the sense of confusion like a dog staring blankly with head cocked to the side. "Yeah, I'm talking to you!"

Atone took Asmodius's hand and laid it back on top of his now lightless form. She stepped up to Rebecca placing a hand on her back. "It's O.K. Rebecca. We'll deal with it. Let's just get out of here for now."

They clawed their way through the wreckage, aided by their only partially substantial bodies near weightlessness. Hugin squawked harshly then jumped into the air, becoming a dark shadow of a bird in flight. When they reached the top Orion and Hugin were waiting. Rebecca stood mouth gaping open. Hugin's body, condensed and covered in feathers, began to build in size, growing larger and awkward as it convulsed and jerked. The jerking marked Hugin's transformation into a human inside his black uniform. Rebecca froze at the sight of Hugin turn from a raven back into the form of a man.

"You're separate now. Good. I'd almost feel bad about killing a helpless human," Orion taunted with his gun on the ready. Hugin squawked something at him, hand on his own gun.

"We've got bigger problems then me right now thanks to trigger happy Freak Boy," Atone growled struggling on the edge of the WDO pit. Orion held his hand out to Rebecca leaving Atone to continue her struggle.

"You can tell them all about it. I've given Stephan my word," he said, holstering his pistol. "Now we're getting out of here."

Chapter 21

Sally Parker left her body and her name with Asmodius. With Birdie's body Sally Parker became Necristina. At the mouth of a cave in Nevada, Necristina watched. The horde of undead swarmed the Appolyon cave defended by the jackal headed POE agents. The distraction was not what she anticipated but she utilized it by blending in and staying at the back of the crowd. She stayed close to see but with enough distance to avoid the rapidly firing motion active machine guns. She watched as Winter Blue entered the cave and saw the call from a POE agent inside that sent two more POE agents inside after him. They carried on them the scent like Asmodius minus the decay. As Asmodius suspected the distraction would not be effective for Winter Blue. He was right to send back up.

It would soon be time for her to play her part. The soldiers were falling back deeper into the cave mouth. She watched as they laid down suppressive fire while another team moved the motion active machine gun back, further into the cave. The horde of undead was overwhelming them. When they retreated into the cave with the motion controlled guns it was time for her to advance. This would get her into the cave, and further her objective. Getting close enough in the line, she took a few shots to the chest. She tumbled backward to avoid any damage to her all-important skull. Her claws tore at her forehead, doing enough damage so that she would not look suspicious if they investigated the bodies before laying still. Now it was time to wait.

Chapter 22

"…That's all thanks to wonder guns over here." Atone burst into the office of Diana, Head of POE's northwestern division both her and her human twin naked. Only Rebecca seemed concerned. "He took out the Demon keeping them in control."

"What is the meaning of this?" Diana hissed at the sudden disturbance. She scowled at all of the people that entered her domain uninvited.

"As much as it pains me, Diana," Orion interjected, hand in front of him palm up in an attempt to calm her. "…and believe me it does, I have to agree with Atone. Hugin took the shot without knowing all the facts."

Hugin made a bizarre, alien noise, which Diana seemed to half understand. She looked up fiercely at Atone. "Your task was to stop him," she chastised. "You hesitated…"

"That's Bull shit!" Atone cut her off. "I was fully prepared to take him out but with every major city housing sleeper cells of zombies I thought that would be a bad idea."

Hugin again made a strange noise. This time Diana hissed at him. "A bluff? You risk my territory calling a bluff?" Diana made an unnatural noise of anguish, which she quickly reigned in, composing herself. "I don't have time for this."

A call from Munin's receiver reached through the air to seize control of the room but it was not Munin's soft female voice that spoke. On the other side of the machine came the rough, strong, dominating boom of Woten's voice. "Main threat removed at Demon gate Gamma. Zombies a threat at perimeter in mop up phase…" Woten's voice, after a long pause, came back trembling. "Munin's dead."

"Dead? What do you mean, dead?" Diana questioned baring her teeth, long like fangs, toward the communicator.

"She's not with us anymore. It's been over an hour with out any sign of her coming back," he explained. Diana was going to ask for verification but Woten continued to speak. "Shall we rendezvous with Poseidon after clean up?"

"Why would the undead follow them to the gates if they were not under control?" she asked herself. Rebecca spoke up.

"Maybe they were waiting there," Rebecca said, meekly getting an angry look from the group.

Diana shook her head. Something wasn't right here. She thought of the best contingency and relayed it to Woten. "Forego clean up. Spread out on Seek and destroy with intent to penetrate the city limits. Leave a few men to patrol the gates in case of second attack.

"And Munin?" Woten asked, voice trembling at her name.

"Bring her in when all this is over if she hasn't come back yet."

"Yes, Diana," Woten said, then turned to Kali. "You choose five others to make two teams of three. One team guards while the other patrols."

"Yes, Woten," she said, heading past the piles of death with the rest of the men, moving the base camp from the inside of the cave to the mouth. The bodies sat in heaps behind them. Necristina used the heavy foot of a soldier to turn her head without to much suspicion; her never closed eyes saw that soldiers were bringing up the motion sensitive machine guns back to the mouth of the cave. They disconnected the motion tracking equipment to use them manually.

She lingered until the angry one called Kali led the troop to their patrol then she marched on quietly into the cavern. Following the rocky tunnel it began to form straight block like edges. A few fires fed from natural gas lines replaced the backlight of the spot lights at the mouth. Still it was dim travel and she stumbled around uneven rock. She fell face first into a large room missing an unexpected set of steps. Looking up a shocked face stared back at her greeting her unexpectedly. She shrieked despite herself at the sight of the angel on the ground. Cowering in fear she slipped in the cracks of the one natural, uncarved wall remaining. Her eyes moved from the angel only once to see Winter Blue's unmoving and thoroughly dead corpse run through by some sort of Spear. A metal bladed device once used for carving the straight edges out of the stone was forcibly driven through the angel, a gaping hole carved from where her sternum would be. The metal was dulled by the drying of her blood.

"I thought I heard something," there came a voice from behind. She shifted closer to herself, hiding further in the crevice as the soldiers marched in. They patrolled the room; their feet walking past her hiding place. One of the soldiers had a flashlight that began to trace a slow path along the floor heading for her. She shifted even closer to herself to hide from the light but it still came. Pinned under rocks there was little else she could do against their guns if they noticed her. Her eyes forced tightly shut as the gunfire began. But it was too quiet and it was coming from behind her toward the mouth of the cave. Another volley sounded and the men ran from the chamber to help their friends.

Slithering from under her rock she noticed the strips of flesh that the rocks carved from her body, a weakness of the numbing effects of death. Her fear of the angel subsided and she set to work. Any noise was covered by Kali's war cry and the sound of firing guns. She clawed at the lock with no effect, before hefting up the heavy bladed staff and hacking it free. Now only two heavy doors stood between her and the completion of her mission. She looked at the angel on the floor, as if in its death it warned her of what lie beyond. No, she said to herself. She had to, it was her goal. She had to be a good Queen if she wanted to stay that way. She looked back at the dark tunnel leading to the combat behind. Then she stepped cautiously to the door. Prying the doors apart she was greeted by warmth and the taste of salt greeted her.

Atone

A great clamoring could be heard as shadows marched from the red haze. Soldiers marched through the red light beyond the door, filling the room around her. Strong demonic forces were all around her. One began to speak. "Our time is at hand. At last our liberation has come." Necristina watched crouched over the angel as the machine gun stopped. The speaker again spoke. "Fear not, little one. More shall come and we will take this land. Your reward shall be great."

They marched on, leaving her alone in the room with the dead angel.

Chapter 23

Clashing weapons and the sound of gunfire mutated by the reverberations through the cave until it was the sound of one continuous roar. Then there was a single shot and a wail. The cave was again restored to silence. It did not last as heavy, angry footfalls echoed through the cave. Kali the demon slayer walked down the cave passage her pale blue skin coated with blood and her four arms covered in gore. She tore it away with an irritated growl.

Kali marched into the main chamber wiping her forehead free of blood and sweat to investigate the room. The two massive stone doors, ornately carved with warring angels now stood open and the red glow illuminated the fog and ash that billowed outward. Munin lay crumpled in a heap her chest carved open, a dead girl with no head rested near her. The girl's body was torn into small pieces by gunfire; stress of the undead's lack of elasticity and self preservation sense. Kali gave a disgusted snort as her heavy boot kicked the body angrily. It flopped awkwardly, just simple dead weight.

"Your prize for your stupidity," Kali growled. She turned her attention to the soldiers filling up the room behind her. "That was just a taste of what is to come, people. If we don't get this door closed now we'll be facing twenty times that much. She watched the man with the urge to smile at the call for her talents. She suppressed it to show the seriousness of the situation to the men in her charge. She kept the open gate in the corner of her eye, ever watching for the unexpected. She pointed to one with a radio receiver. "You call Woten, report the situation. The rest of you help me close this gate."

Silence responded to her save for the whistling wind from the chambers depth. "Soldier, report…" She stopped seeing the soldiers change, twisting like marionettes from their straight and ready stance of attention. She instinctively fell back a pace and felt the presence that accompanied the hiss behind her.

As she turned to face it the soldiers opened fire. Bullets tore savagely through her ancient flesh shattering bone and puncturing organs. Kali's body felt like fire as the pain and shock took over. "I am… undone," she said, as the soldiers reloaded. She wasn't dead, there was still a chance, she thought, but there was too much damage for her to move. She looked up from the ground refusing to go down for good, but it was a struggle just to stay on her knees. She tried to move her arms but there was no way to. She saw one of her arms quivering on the ground in front of her, twitching only by some fleeting nerves sending their final messages.

Laughter from the men echoed in the chamber followed by one majestic voice down the red-lit hall. She dared to look back again. The sound of more gunfire drowned all other noise. She was beyond feeling. Her eyes penetrated the black cloud of smoke to see another set of eyes watching her. Finally her body collapsed from insurmountable injuries.

"Bael," she gasped in a noiseless cry. She tried to be afraid. She let the darkness envelop her, felt her soul worm free. It was too late for fear to bother her now. It was her problem no longer. The darkness burned away to a beckon of blinding light. "So bright..," she gasped, finding only the weakest voice. A smile crossed her face as the light faded from her eyes.

She was dead. Bael ignored the men to favor the other dead in the room, namely Munin. "So an angel can die. How lucky for you, little one." The men now slumped over like the undead themselves. Bael stooped down over her. His massive form of black smoke undulated into itself to form a solid, tangible demon. He leaned down stroking her hair the very touch from him making the skin and hair feel violated. He studied her inquisitively. "Very clever little one, but you may need help with those stitches."

Munin's body rose uneasily. Her hands protectively held in the skull of an imposter with the help of loose stitches. Necristina carefully turned her head to look at him innocently smiling. "If you don't mind?"

Bael's laughter rumbled through the cave like a small earthquake. With a wave of his hand one of the soldiers assisted her. With greatest care the officer tightened the strings, pulling the skin tighter, to hug the bone underneath. Bael supervised his puppet as it worked. "Lovely choice, though. I may have more use for you."

"And who claims they may have use for me?" she asked, her deadened nerves concealing the fear she felt in her never beating heart.

"I am Bael of the Diablonians," he answered proudly, with the noblest of bows extending a smoke black clawed hand and offering it to her. "And who am I claiming the use of?"

"Necristina," she said, accepting his claw with cautious hesitation. He watched her like a hungry cat at the fish bowl. His lips curled back in a wretched smile. He made a quick move to bite her hand, his claws like iron holding her. She struggled to free herself and he laughed at the attempt. His toothy grin hovered over her hand. His lips rolled out to kiss the clammy flesh. He held her for a moment, her skin still trying to pull free from his grasp. She stumbled to catch herself when he finally freed her hand, getting another sinister laugh. She covered her scorn with a nod of her head.

"Well Bael, I already have a master. Asmodius," she bowed slightly with the faintest of smiles, taking a step back purposefully angled toward the door.

"Then report to him and tell him that I will remember his greatness," Bael said, bowing very slightly in turn.

"I shall." She bowed again and backed from the room getting a riotous laughter from the demon's puppets as she left. Her mind tried to grasp just what it was that she brought to this world. Asmodius would explain everything, she

convinced herself. Bael's eyes followed her as
she left them. As she backed out through the
cave the men drew their weapons. Bael's
laughter chased her from the cave. With a wave
of his hand his men resumed their slumped, near
lifeless stance. His black body puffed outward
turning again to the safety of the intangible.

Chapter 24

The school's halls were disturbed by the periodical burst of gunfire from the stationary machine guns. Sitting next to the machine guns were their hardware. POE's technology incorporated the lack of heat with movement so that an innocent human would be safe to pass by without getting riddled with bullets. No one in the hall had the luxury to avoid gunfire, nor the logic to realize they were being hit. Inside Uthgar watched by a monitor. It was easy enough to hack into the schools already existing monitors. Heinrich stepped up to stand next to him Frankie in tow.

"It's like they're testing us," Uthgar said, noticing the Psychiatrist step forward. "Look. See all of them, here? Yet they only send one or two in at a time. They attack consistently so that we can't go and reload like they're just waiting for the machine to run out of bullets."

"You've kept us safe this far. If that happens we'll simply make the most of it," Heinrich said, not knowing what else to say that would make the situation sound any better.

"I've been reviewing our position on the blue prints. We don't have time to wait for them to give up." Uthgar's voice grew to a growl of frustration.

"What are you saying?" Heinrich asked.

"I need someone to get to the roof. The walls are too thick to get a signal to HQ. We have to get back up but the only way to get to the roof safely is to go through the air duct."

"I'll go," Heinrich volunteered.

"What?" Uthgar said, for the first time taking his eyes from the monitors.

"I'll do it, just tell me what you need me to do," Heinrich said, again.

"Your bravery is appreciated," Uthgar said. His gaze slipped downward. He choked up and struggled to clear his throat before speaking again. "But you are too big to fit in the ducts."

"So why are you…?" Heinrich said, realizing that Uthgar's down cast gaze fell not to the floor but to his daughter. His hand shot out and caught Francine's arm clutching her toward him tightly.

"Please understand…" Uthgar tried to explain.

"No," Heinrich denounced him.

"Be reasonable," Uthgar spoke softly, tired and secretly agreeing with her father.

"There has to be…" Heinrich continued to argue.

"There isn't. Only the boy there, Aaron, is thin enough other than her and she's the only one that can still think properly. I need that. She's our best hope. Only she can save us all. You're a logical man, Dr. Gordon. Think about what I'm asking you."

There was a long silence. Then Francine walked to Uthgar, eyes on Heinrich. Heinrich raised his clenched hand finding only her coat. "Dad, I'm going to go."

"Francine, please. You don't have to," Heinrich pleaded.

"Yes I do," Frankie said, hiding her shaking arms behind her back.

"She'll have a radio. I'll talk her through everything. I can make her as safe as humanly possible," Uthgar tried to console him. He was a military man and he could easily enforce his verdict but he would prefer a peaceful resolve.

"Trust me. Dad, I'll be O.K.," Frankie encouraged.

"Where is your proof?" Heinrich asked, his eyes began to blur.

"We're running out of time," Uthgar said.

"Go," he said, turning his back on her his head bowing. He cupped his hands over his face as he sat down.

"I love you, Dad," Francine said, following Uthgar and Sam to the grates.

"Here are the keys. You'll need them to open the gates and the door to the roof," Sam said, handing her a set of keys. She reached out from the grates to take them and then she was gone. All their ties to her now were through the communicator outfitted with an earpiece. "O.K. testing, testing, say something Frankie."

"Something Frankie," she said, shimmying through the air duct. Uthgar smiled on the other side.

"Good girl. The duct will fork ahead. You'll want to turn right. It will cross but you'll want to keep going straight."

"They're patrolling the hall," Heinrich said, pointing at a group of zombies stumbling through the corridor.

"You'll want to wait until its safe. There are some zombies outside. I'll give you the heads up when it's clear," Uthgar said, watching from the monitor.

"O.K. I'm at the vent out. I see zombies," she whispered. "Hold on I've got a plan."

"Frankie, NO. Safety…" Heinrich said, taking the microphone from Uthgar.

"I'm being safe, Henry," she snapped. "This will distract them." She twisted around to another exit several rooms away at the end of the hall. Banging the grate free she shrunk back in and waited.

"Smart," Uthgar breathed watching the room in the monitor. Frankie waited until the first undead appeared before shimmying out of sight. This did two things. For one it lured the zombies away from where she wanted to be and second it gave her a rough idea how much time she would have before they were onto her. Slithering back to her destination, it was cleared of hazards and she was able to bypass the masses.

"Good. Now you'll have to get through one gate and then left to…" Sam said, wrestling the microphone from Heinrich.

"I know how to get to the roof," she hissed back.

"O.K. but there aren't any cameras in that hall. I won't be able to give you a heads up," Uthgar said, through a second earpiece. Frankie walked silently through the halls "There is one little problem I can tell you," he began and she poked her head inspecting either angle. To the right was two metal bar gates. There was no need for a key; a huge hole was torn through the gate.

As she began to turn to the left she heard the high wailing of a call to arms. No need to verify the sound, she raced and slid through the whole in the gate, only then turning to face the mob. The first tried to enter after her and she opened the gate, closing the whole around its neck. A wet gurgle accompanied the beheaded body's thump to the ground. As quickly as she opened it she closed it again using the decapitated body to plug the hole. This bought little time as they had to fight through one of their own. She dug through the keys finding one marked for the gates.

"There should only be one key for all the gates but the doors are all different," Uthgar said. She tried desperately to ignore the clawing and moaning as she worked the key into the lock. With a reaffirming click she breathed a sigh of relief. The emaciated hand came down, clamping tightly to her shoulder her relief warped into a scream as she twisted around in her shirt. One of the undead hands forced itself through the gate to reach her. Now facing it she recoiled as it carved itself in half in its attempts to devour her. A metal bar dug into its shoulder cutting through rotted flesh, its own desire for her flesh breaking its bones. She fought against her own restricting clothing pulling free from a large patch of it, already slightly torn by the POE officers earlier. She fell away from the devilish sight landing hard on her backside, free from the freakish beast. She closed the second gate behind her locking it. The zombie still wriggled onward carved in half.

"There's a problem," she called into the communicator.

Atone

"Its O.K.," Sam said.

"But they're blocking the way upstairs," she said, wondering through the art department. "Should I go out the front door?"

"No! There's to much activity out there. Try to lure them somewhere else," Sam ordered.

"Say again I can't here you?" Frankie asked, as the radio signal began to break up. This wing appeared to be, at least for now, free of ghoulish zombies.

"…Go that why it's…" Sam said, broken up by the thick walls.

"O.K.," she answered navigating the school toward the front door.

"No! I said, No!" Sam called out unheard.

As she drifted through the vacant school the dim light of day silhouetted horrid shadows through the halls. The sound of the undead struggling through the metal gate, the occasional sound of machine gun fire the constant moans of the damned and the very rare crackle of radio waves masked any sound she may have made.

As she approached the exit to the school the sound of the gate giving way echoed down the hall. She inched toward the door eyes down the hall behind her. A raspy hard breathing caught her ears and she turned to see the undead sentinels stationed at the doors to the outside world. Shambling slowly was only a way to reserve power. As she got too close to them they burst into a quick, surprising speed. The words from the radio spurred her on. "Get out of there! Get out of there!"

She burst into a run. She raced down the hall to a wall of zombies divided on either side. As she passed them their greater instinct took precedent and they gave chase. Running blindly a thought forced its way through the fear. Why didn't they try to cut her off? As she reached the gate in her path she found the answer.

The mounted machine gun revealed itself with a panning motion, like a salute. The sound of gears whirring into motion warned her of the louder noise to come. Stopping instantly, her momentum sent her sliding forward on her knees toward the turret. A sharp unexpected intake of breath was joined by the scream of bullets. Her arms folded up in front of her in a feeble attempt to shield herself. Bullets whizzed past her, clawing her hair in stray tuffs as they continued harmlessly beyond her. She froze as it continued to fire; she could hear the moans, turned to whispers by the loud gun's wrath.

Then the clicking of the gun, free of ammunition, made her stop the scream she didn't realize she started. Looking up she lowered her arms raising her gaze to see the gun still going uselessly. She whirled behind to see the zombies, more dead than usual. Heinrich stepped out to see her. "That was very unsafe. Frankie."

"I'm in one piece, Dad," she said to him before the hand came down. A zombie from the heap pulled its way up, mouth open wide for attack. She pulled back, adrenaline kicking in. She hoisted the massive gun from the stand and brought it down hard across its face. Frankie's breath came ragged. The radio crackled to life.

"Please don't break the equipment," Sam said, painfully.

"Sorry, Sam," she said, dropping it aside. Her eyes searched the halls for anything left moving. Uthgar stood next to Heinrich guns ready. He called in the few remaining soldiers to reload the machine.

"Get that thing loaded quickly," he ordered before turning to Frankie. "Good work.

You lured them all out, that should buy us enough time to get it reloaded. Now, go, hurry. That won't stop them for long."

"I'm O.K., You know, thanks for asking," she said, bitterly, darting back off toward the stairs leading to the roof. Uthgar smiled.

"You have quiet an impressive daughter, Dr. Gordon."

Chapter 25

When Necristina was leaving Las Vegas she had second thoughts about what she had done. Now, as she entered Preston, Colorado, those nagging doubts became full-blown anxiety. Questions plagued her, why did she do it being the most prominent in her mind. She reached the WDO compound and saw it still smoking from the fire before she grasped the full extent of her manipulations. Charred to ash with only a few beams remaining, the once imposing and impressive structure had died and turned to bone. It was only then that she realized the absence of Asmodius in her mind. Even in her freedom he had controlled her.

She was a ghost among the decimated remains. She flexed the wings at her back, but without skill could only slowly, awkwardly drift, searching through the ruins of the compound. It began to snow gently, the slightest of snow, frosting the landscape.

She continued her search, pushing herself to move quicker. There, untouched by fire, unmarked by death's vile effects, was Asmodius's true demonic form. His chest resembled broken glass, a gaping hole in his chest marking his death. Clawing her way through the warped metal beams and collapsed floorboards, with inhuman fervor she unleashed her rage on the dead form. Her clawed zombie hands fought against the demon carcass.

"Even in my freedom you controlled me. You manipulated me. I was never free, you bastard," she cried out to nothing assaulting his flesh with her hands. After her rage passed she kneeled over him at a loss without his mind control telling her how to feel. She heard the distinct wails of unchecked dead.

"And what now?" she asked, in a whisper. Finding a pipe wrench near his corpse she picked it up half hesitating. "You will give me your secrets, my King. Give me your secrets!" She screamed. With a sudden and terrifying burst of speed and power the pipe wrench made a sick crack, dull and wet, as it smashed through his skull. Several more strikes followed until little skull was left to protect the brain. Clawing madly she picked through the fragments, devouring the inhuman brain. Its oily fluid marked a macabre path along Necristina's chin and slid down her neck, pooling at the clavicle briefly before streaming between her breasts, staining her black shirt. After the savage devouring she felt only the emptiness in her mind where Asmodius once dwelled. "I will no longer be controlled. Do you hear?" She roared to the night. "I'm free!"

Her war cry was cut short by the pain, the first physical pain she's endured since death. A sick green glow burned through her stomach glowing, floating globules burned up her veins and soon she clutched her chest as they reached her heart.

Her hands clawed at her flesh trying to stop the toxic burning but her grasping, tearing of flesh could not stop it. The light, burning the heart, shot straight with one muscular beat through the arteries along the neck and into the brain. An unnatural wail tore free from her throat. Her eyes clenched closed in pain. When they opened again they glowed with a balefire green.

Chapter 26

Orion and Rebecca entered the library. Rebecca wore a soft pink furry sweater and a grey blue skirt that was a tad to tight and small for her tastes that she got from Diana's personal clothes. Stephan was quickly clamoring down the sliding ladders. Atone followed behind him, her thoughts drifting to what Asmodius said about her being on this plane of existence. Orion huffed, loudly, the noise forming words. "You said you found something?"

"Yes. Something indeed," he said, with a wide grin. He looked at Rebecca his smile fading only slightly, pride shifting effortlessly to something else. "You look… different, Rebecca," he said, smoothly scanning her from head to toe and back again.

"Yeah there are two of us now," Atone growled.

"I don't think that's what he's referring to," Orion barked then turned to reign in Stephan's attention. "What is your discovery?"

"What? Oh right." He squeezed past them to use the desk behind them. "My discovery." An old hand bound and battered book slammed carelessly to the desktop its binding huffing out a cloud of dust. "I was looking for some information about this new Zombie situation when I remembered some studies in the 18th century. Now these actual documents didn't really go anywhere as far as helping me figure stuff out but then I found this." Stephan rambled on, all the while flipping through the pages of the old tome. Eventually his frantic flipping of pages found the revelation in question. Toward the back of the book there was a pressed letter with several loose notes folded with it.

"So what's all this about?" Atone grumbled.

"These notes discuss… Well here let me read it," he said, putting on rubber gloves and gently unfolding the parchment. Then he began to read.

"My dear Lucida, having only been in Idolstadt a short while, I have the most dreaded of news. Do you remember young Victor from days of youth passed? Though you my not recall him as friendly as myself I find him here in the most wretched of states. I have taken it upon myself to care for my friend though I know nothing of the medical profession. I have also noted to write his family though I dare not express the extent of his madness. His half-mad ravings seemed at first merely impossible ramblings of a crazed mind. Alas, however, as I was cleansing his room of his once loved equipment his journal revealed at least the plausibility if not truth of his fevered mind. I have not the mind for such a mystery but only wish my friend well. His lunacy or his truth I leave to you, as you are no doubt of a mind to unravel it to its core. I ask only that you take care as young Frankenstein is a friend and I pray, be merciful in your findings so as not to display his faults to the public. I'm positive that whatever he did was done for the greatest of good intention and am sad he now suffers for it.

"Alas He suffers fits again; I must rush this letter to its end. Your dearest, H- Clerval."

"So what's that mean?" Rebecca asked, disoriented. "You're telling me Frankenstein exists now, too? What's next, Bigfoot, leprechauns, aliens? Politicians that actually care?"

"I'm not saying anything of the kind. Only that the research was real, we have proof of that right here." Stephan explained. Atone folded her arms in front of herself her brow forming on angry V.

"So get to the point," she said, tapping her feet with her eyes fixed sternly on Stephan.

"I am. I've carefully scanned these notes into Natalie so we wouldn't have to handle them too much. She's really been helpful. And smart. To think a computer program burned a copy of itself to escape the WDO building when Erwin wanted the security footage. I've never seen self-preservation in a program. Think about it. We may have to redefine what makes up a soul. She's very special,"

"Thank you Stephan," she said, from down the hall. Stephan moved the group to Natalie's console. Rebecca rolled her eyes rephrasing her previous statement about what would be next.

"She made filtering through the unrelated notes a breeze. Natalie, what have you found?" Stephan continued.

"Nothing is confirmed, since we don't have a recent study but the…" The 3D female computer program said, with a friendly grin.

"Quit beating around the bush and just get to the damn point!" Atone snapped. The group looking at her indicated the severity of her unleashed anger and she tried to pull it back

and calm down, eying Orion's gun. "Sorry. I…
I've got a lot on my mind right now."

"The pathogen known to create Zombies
is three fold. The starting Pathogen or version
1.0 is internal and it is caused by the bite and
alters the body, mostly the brain. It also causes
thin tendrils to form at the base of the skull,
which we believe they use when necessary to
repair the spinal column and appendages. By
stretching past the injured area they bypass the
damaged part to use what is still good like a
backup muscle. That's why even the most
mutilated body seems to dance around. Version
1.1 is an air born pathogen external to the body.
This relays experiences collectively, a collective
subconscious if you will, from one zombie to
the next. Its like an upgrade, but these upgrades
go obsolete quickly that's why they get dumber
the farther away they are from each other."

"They're just not getting new
information fast enough," Stephan added.

"Then there is the major pathogen,
Version 1.2. As Dr. Frankenstein related in his
notes and WDO proved with Rodger Xaphan,
pathogen 1 can regain a form of sentience. It's
not a true transformation but rather a computer
like program of the subject's former life."

"Wait a minute. What do you mean?" Rebecca asked.

"Version 1.0 affects several areas of the brain, one of them being memory. These memories can be switched by version 1.1 transferring or down loading, if you please, version 1.2. This isn't the real you, but the pathogen's concept of you based on the memories it learns and that is reprogrammed back into target zombie. But wait, there's more. A subtle telepathy can be gained by someone with version 1.2, since their mind will still receive version 1.1 and be cognitive to understand what it's getting. This in turn gives them control over the undead version 1.0 because the version 1.2 zombies can relay what information it wants. It could even in theory tell version 1.1 to change version 1.0 to 1.2."

"So that is how Kara was made?" Orion asked.

"No. Kara was effected by Excleozine. This destroys the part of the brain that Version 1.0 and 1.1 need to survive forcing it to evolve into what we will call Pathogen 2.0. It does this to survive off of other parts of the brain. Private Rodger Xaphan, as he claimed was much like you; hence the Excleozine damage was repaired, unlike a normal person. Being a demon made no real difference except for repairing the brain damage. No. There was something proving crucial to Victor Frankenstein centuries prior."

"Something that activated version 1.2?" Rebecca asked, Atone sat back bidding her time.

"Yes, Private Rodger Xaphan suffered from a rare heredity disease known as Mastiffson's disease. The medication required a drug experimental at the time called norzateen X. This was Frankenstein's secret."

"So why did WDO overlook it?" Rebecca inquired.

"Because Norzateen X is used so frequently in medicines usually listed as other inactive ingredients. One in ten people have trace amounts of it in their system. The reason it showed itself in Private Rodger Xaphan was the quantity."

"I'm a little lost," Rebecca admitted confused. "What does that mean for us?"

"It means that their former lives may not be completely lost," Stephan said. He readied his next words when the scream of the alarm made all noise muted. A rotating red light went off by the door attracting all their attentions to it.

"What's going on, Stephan?" Rebecca asked, instinctively taking his side. Before he got to answer Diana's voice over took the intercom.

"Report to docking bay immediately! Report to docking bay immediately!" Diana ordered, calling out loudly.

Rebecca, Stephan, Atone and Orion began to run down the curved hall to the underground garage. When they arrived, Hugin was waiting. He looked unnaturally at them, head cocked to the side and crouched down to one hand. A sharp raspy gurgle escaped his face apparatus. A voice began to emerge from the machine attachment making up its face but it was Diana's voice. "We have a distress call at the survivor camp. I need you, Orion, to take Atone for reinforcements."

"There are only two of us," Orion grumbled.

"That's why your mission is only to get them out," Diana explained through Hugin, here voice demanding.

"Wait," Atone interrupted. "What makes you think you can tell me what to do? I've got bigger issues."

"We had a deal, Atone," Orion continued his grumbling. "You got Asmodius; I take you to see Heinrich."

"You don't get it. All of this started when I got here," Atone explained. "If I can get this done quickly I can stop all of this."

"Don't get full of yourself, Atone," Orion said, pushing past her to ready the helicopter. "This has been going on for years."

Diana's voice began to again emerge from the freaks mouth. "We don't have time for this, Atone. I haven't heard from Woten or Hermes in over an hour. I have received word from nearly all local chapters of a massive spread of this problem. Simply put we don't have the manpower. I'm asking you for your help."

"Fine," she said, after a long pause. "We sort this out later, but I want information on all this prophecy crap you've uncovered, no lies, no games. If I'm a pawn in some end all chess game I want to know."

Silence filled the room, only the sound of dripping occasionally from the cracks seemed to echo through the halls. Then the sound of a rewinding recording emanated from Hugin. It began to play back and Atone waited with Orion, Rebecca and Stephan to here the playback. Heavy breathing reached their ears.

"Hello main office. Come in main office. This is George Washington's High. We are over run. Repeat, we are over run. Send help. We need…" The sound of Frankie's voice was cut short by the sound of a collapsing door and zombie wails. "Oh come on. Go to Hell you bastards!" The moans crackled quietly, growing louder. Then they were joined with Frankie's scream. Then an unearthly wail of epic proportions deafened the room. Then the receiver went dead with an ear-piercing scream of dying electronics mixed with static.

"Frankie?" Atone and Rebecca gasped. Atone kept Rebecca from racing to the nearest vehicle, before looking at Hugin in place of Diana. "Fine I'll go but we're going to square this up when I get back."

"Take the helicopter. The land may be compromised," Diana advised.

439

Atone

"Whatever! Let's just do this," Atone hissed.

"Rebecca everything's going to be fine. Relax," Diana heard Atone say to the girl from Hugin's head set. She took off her head set and walked to a large mirror poking half way out of a small chest. She paced in front of it looking at it and at the same time taking in the whole room. It was a habit she developed when she had a lot on her mind. It was her way of finding a different perspective.

"Atone. You may seem self-serving but in the end you can't escape the truth. You have a heart," she smirked to herself before catching the reflection of the computer monitor on her desk. Levity was short lived as she saw more of the screen, a map of North America, Ignited into red patches. Each patch represented a city; each city marked in red was a dead zone, labeled because no word was received from them in under an hour. "My territory is dying."

The phone began to ring and she picked up without hesitation. "Yes this is head of North America, POE agency." The voice on the other end seemed urgent, forcing her to compose herself. "No. It is bad but… Yes… most appreciated, Morrigan, but I think the best thing you can do for us is reinforce the Panama Canal.

Yes, Mexico has similarly fallen. Honestly it may be too late for us. No, tell them that North America is contaminated and that no one gets through. We may not be lost yet but there is very little options left… No. I'm not going to declare North America forsaken. Not yet. Thank you for your concern. Good day, Morrigan, and thanks again."

Diana scowled as her hands changed the screen with a few key strokes. She drew up the revealed prophecy of Stephan's book. Her eyes scanned over the screen reading them. She sighed. "How can I give you answers I don't have, my daughter?"

Chapter 27

The Helicopter rose from the concealed base quickly cutting through the air to reach George Washington's High school. The city laid barren, empty. One prone body lay on the roof, torn clothes fluttering in the swirling winds of the propellers.

"Oh God, Frankie," Rebecca said, leaning out of the open side to get a better look, Atone grabbed hold of Rebecca's coat, another pilfered piece of Diana's clothes, and pulling her back in.

"Wait, she's moving," Orion said, from the pilot seat. The form clutched at the tattered clothes as she rose to her feet. Struggling with her clothes with one hand she used her free hand to wave. The helicopter landed forcing Frankie to seek refuge at the roofs door or be battered by savage cutting wind.

Atone and Rebecca got off racing over to her. Atone caught hold of Rebecca holding her back. Atone motioned for Rebecca to wait then advanced toward Frankie, her hand clutching one of the zombie blades. "Frankie? What's up?"

"Who… Who are you?" she asked, over the beating wind. The helicopter stayed running in case of an emergency retreat.

Atone scanned over Frankie's body, looking for any sign of infection. Confident on her purity, Atone eased up and motioned for Rebecca to come over. "I'm Rebecca's inner demon."

"Well do have a problem with clothes?" Frankie said, as Rebecca came over. Frankie saw her approach and turned to face her. "Rebecca?" she asked, finally raising herself from the corner. A segment of her shirt was torn away leaving the left front side exposed, Frankie pulling the right side over to maintain her decency. "Is that you?"

"Yes, it's me. What did they do to you?" Rebecca said, holding her protectively.

"They only finished what those jerk offs started," she said, pointing to the helicopter. "They tore my shirt when they checked us for bites. The zombies just finished the job. Then they broke the radio."

"Where are they now?" Atone asked, looking into the stairway down into the building, blades at the ready.

443

Atone

"They were about to kill me. I was done for. Then this God awful wail started and they all backed off, just leaving me here. The one on me had me in his clutches and just dropped me, and the communicator got broke. From then on I don't remember anything," Frankie said, excitedly to Rebecca.

"Probably knocked out, how's your head?" Rebecca said, checking the swelling at her temple. Frankie felt it and winced. A tear forced its way from her eye by the pain.

"Where are the others?" Atone asked, turning Frankie's head physically to face her.

"I can tell you where they were. If they're still there I don't know," she said, trembling, with her eyes locked into the empty void of Atone's eyes.

"Then let's go," Rebecca said, taking off her coat and giving it to Frankie. The flap of heavy fabric broke the paralyzing stare and Atone quickly looked away.

"Yes, let's," Atone huffed gesturing Frankie to lead, her gaze focused down to the ground.

Atone

"Hey Stephan, Does Frankenstein say anything about God Awful Wails?" She called back through the radio.

"Frankenstein?" Frankie asked, looking at Rebecca and Atone, eyes refusing to look at the devil directly.

"Long story," Atone said, as they descended down the stairs to the survivor base.

"We should really get some clothes for you. You might disturb the normals," Frankie suggested cautiously checking around the corner.

Chapter 28

Gary Farwell screamed. His cold, lifeless body writhed on the floor of the machine shop. A vague memory began to trickle through his revived mind and he stumbled with a lame leg to the window. He looked around noticing a town population sign across the street.

"Daytonville? What?" he asked the darkness, a lone light over the window. He was drawn to it, his mind trying to find the reason why he was here. He saw his face in the reflection of the window made mirror by the dark of night outside. He began to cry, his fingers numbly touching his face. He checked himself. His left arm hung loose, caused by an axe head, handle broken, which was lodged tight into his shoulder. He moved his fingers and flexed his muscles to find that although awkward he could still work the oddly angled arm. His hand trembled as he tried to remove the axe head to no avail. His right leg ended in a stump a few inches above the ankle. Loose thoughts and vague memories began to eat away his weak mind. His hand reached out at his stump leg, remembering. He began to cry again. "Martha."

Atone

Welcome, Gary. You are probably unclear as to what's going on. I can make sense of it all," a voice drifted through the corridor. Gary followed the sound through the darkness. When a light switched on two of the bulbs shattered from the surge of energy. This left one lone bulb turned on to light the room by itself. Two zombies, chained, stumbled mindlessly toward him. He screamed again but they continued to paw out at the end of their chain. Realizing that they could not reach him, he looked past them down the chains to their source. He saw an angel or former one, skin turned pale blue-green and grey. Small ruptures formed at her joints due to the lack of elasticity. A red streak stained a patch of flesh from her lower lip to beyond her black, stained shirt, marking her neck and cleavage.

"Who are you?" he asked her, his voice hoarse and cracking with some internal damage.

"I am Necristina, your Queen. I set you free from your wretched, mindless state, but we are not truly free, Gary. We have all done some heinous and atrocious acts when we became what we are. We are the damned but this does not mean it has to stay that way."

Atone

"What are you talking about?" he asked, panning over the rest of the undead lingering in the machine shop.

"Demons have entered this world. Their portal lay in a cave in Nevada. We must stop them. If we can destroy this portal we should be able to undo this dark event. Of course I can't make you, which is why I give you this choice. Join us, help us destroy this abominable construction or I can return you to the mindless, oblivious monster that you once were," she said, waving her hand to the shriveled corpse of her father snapping at his chain. "The choice is yours."

"That's really not much of a choice," Gary said, taking another step away from the horrid zombies. His chest rose and fell with a deep intentional breath. "What must I do?"

Chapter 29

Poseidon tried to brace himself as the helicopter came crashing down. He heard Woten and Hermes trying to find out what hit them when they were returning for Kali and the other troops. Erwin, his wolfish, monstrous half man form held on protectively to one survivor they rescued from Reno. "What happened?"

"Kara?" Anubis asked, looking for a phantom form of her.

"Negative, it was a blast of fire or something from below," Woten shouted over the whistle of wind. They hit the ground, the impact snapping the helicopter in half.

Poseidon watched as the girl and Erwin were sucked out to be lost by the sand and rocks of the desert, kicked up by the rolling wreckage. The second impact sent him toppling the other way as the front of the helicopter hit face first. Anubis was nowhere to be seen but the shattered glass of the windshield cut fiercely at Hermes' flesh. Woten tired to break free as the console began to crackle. Woten seemed muted as he shouted orders to him.

Atone

"Get out of here. It's going to blow."

Poseidon was in a fog. He must have hit his head in the crash but instincts sent him scrambling awkwardly from the wreckage. Soon the cabin ignited and the sound tore away what little hearing he had left. The blast sent him flying through the air, tumbling to a stop at a shallow gully. He could tell more bones broke in the fall. But he breathed, and that counted for more since immortality seemed a revoked privilege.

He didn't hear the heavy, confident footfalls of the enemy that attacked them. He lay there, unable to move. As his hearing slowly returned he heard more feet approaching. He heard their leader give a sinister laughter, encouraging his minions to enjoy this moment.

"Now my dear Poseidon, Your life will join your friends in oblivion," a demon boasted. Poseidon looked around recognizing him.

"Lihatiel," Poseidon said, the sand in his throat making a rough growl. He sneered at the torn apart body of the demon taunting him. "You're looking well."

Lihatiel smiled a savage, toothy grin that was anything but happy. He shifted his mutilated spine for better balance, likewise adjusting his attitude. With a sigh his sneer returned to a smile. "Focalar, he's all yours."

Focalar drew back his bow. The arrow looked like it was formed of bone and carved into a screaming Gargoyle. Poseidon turned to face it, eyes narrowed into slits of Hate. The arrow flew, piercing into him, a surge of blood rushed out from the wound. It poured from it and from his mouth shortly after, a violent surge slowing to a weak flow. A wail echoed through the desert, Thousands of voices strong. The demons searched the horizon, Cosmacrater pointing toward the disturbance. The demons headed toward it, assembling their forces. Meanwhile, on the hill overlooking the demon horde the marching of undead filled the desert, a slow and rhythmic battle march. Stopping in sight of the demons forces they bellowed their wailing war cry again. Some of the lower demon officers trembled looking nervously between to the horde of undead and the iron will of their superiors.

Anubis crawled from the sundered back half of the helicopter, pushing aside a twisted metal frame to witness the standoff. After the third wail Cosmacrater had enough.

"Destroy!" He cried out, his one voice however powerful finding it hard to push through the undying reverberations. The armies charged forward colliding in a deafening thunderclap. A series of laughter trickled through the battle as explosions, cannon and gunfire started from the side of undead.

The demon army was at a loss for only a moment before centralizing their attacks on the biggest threats. Those demons unlucky enough to get hit by the initial attack fell still in death. Anubis noticed a division in the undead ranks and followed the collection that branched off to the mouth of the cave. A small collection of bodies, both undead and demon, both now dead in the motionless sense, were scattered across the sand and rock. He reached the gate to see the undead finishing their valiant task. They laced a string of explosives throughout the room around the Appolyon gate. Anubis' eyes widened both from the dark and from their missions.

"No, don't do that," Anubis cried out taking them unaware. He pushed a group back trying to reach them. "If that's destroyed they'll be trapped here. They won't be able to go back to Hell."

Out of the corner of his eye, Anubis noticed the zombie, nearly just a skeleton, with a slack jaw, frozen in place his thumb pressing down a detonator. It was too late. The bomb was now armed. Anubis saw the illumination of the timer along the gate's open mouth. He made a step in to try and deactivate it.

"How much time is there?" Anubis yelled at him. "How much time to deactivate the bomb?" Undead scattered past him. The old bones with the detonator pushed him away waving his hand with a look of despair in his remaining eye. His lower jaw still hanging now proven to be disconnected, one side only connected by shriveled muscle. Anubis saw the light of another indicator blink then another. The optional lights were dwindling quickly. Three then two, Anubis turned to run seeing the light of the cave mouth before the bombs went off. Anubis learned to fly, his back banging against the caves ceiling and scrapped along it. He was fired like a bullet landing in a dusty cloud on the desert ground.

The dead rose and though Anubis took a fighting stance he knew he wouldn't be able to take them all. He was already injured. A zombie was carrying a surplus of weapons and a zombie with an axe head in his shoulder took a rifle from him to aim it at the wolf headed former God. The axe headed zombie spoke, his voice strained but strong. "You will explain yourself to our Queen."

Anubis looked over at the battle. Though several demons fell they, like the dead, rose again. Anubis saw a few unlucky ones still remain dead. They must have departed from their body and returned to Hell before the gate was destroyed. Anubis looked at the axe head zombie, clearly in charge. "You're not getting an upper hand in that fight."

"Those are cannon fodder, the mindless. This is not your concern, move," he said, disgusted as he looked over at the battle. His flesh around his mouth curled into a sneer as he kicked at the dusty desert ground.

"You're the boss," Anubis said, succumbing to the long march to their base.

Once the immediate danger of the demonic battle was well past them, the undead bound a kerchief over Anubis' eyes. He didn't feel the need to explain to them that his sense of smell was even better than his eyesight. That didn't matter once they entered the sewers. Curling up his nose he tried to breathe through his mouth only to taste the filth instead. Still it was a little better and with a wretched face he continued on. When he was brought to a sudden stop he realized he let his mind wander, his thoughts turning to a better time where he was with his wife and children. Back when he was married and his wife didn't know what he was. The memory of his divorce was cut short by the stop and he wobbled blindly trying to find out which way best to lean so as not to fall. His ears, still blissfully unaffected could pick up the axe head zombie talking to someone else.

"My lady, the destruction of the portal did nothing to help us. It only made things worse," the zombie with the axe head in his shoulder relayed the information. Anubis was somewhat surprised when the voice that answered him was not a woman.

"Who's this stranger, Gary?" A man spoke harshly to the axe head zombie, Anubis couldn't tell if it was anger or the passage of time over the fragile undead body.

"We're not sure. He tried to stop the bomb."

"And he still lives?" He hissed.

"He said destroying the gate would trap those demons here. He was right but was too late in informing us." Gary said, his voice growing grim.

Atone

"Damn you, Asmodius," a woman's voice shouted. Lyrical in its anger, Anubis had the faintest memory of hearing a voice like that before. "Even in your death you manipulate me." There was a moment of silence filled with far off whispers that Anubis could not make out. Anubis waited trying to hear what his surroundings were like, drips of water and echoing whispers told him large pipes or a drainage ditch. His deciphering ears caught their words shattering the image of the place around him. "Remove his blindfold."

"No. Wait." Anubis recognized with full clarity of the voice now. The blindfold slipped harmlessly away. The horrid mockery of his former associate revealed itself to him. "Munin?"

"I assure you, creature, only her body remains. I am Necristina," the undead woman in Munin's skin spoke a hint of noble bearing showing through her rotting shell's gestures and presentation.

"So Necristina, What do you plan to do now?" Anubis spat the words. His stomach turned, watching one of the POE agents used in such a way.

"That rests on you, new comer. You seem to know what's going on, at least more so than a normal man, you will tell us all you know," she demanded softly.

"And why would I do that?" he asked, his voice a growl, he hunched down instinctively preparing to pounce.

"We are damned but perhaps some peace can yet be obtained if we try to right our wrongs."

"Well you've done a bang up job so far," he growled back. She glared at him a spark of rage in her eyes fading quickly and returning to her diplomatic guise.

"We could always extract it by force," she said, using her bony fingers to crack open the skull of the chained zombie next to her father. The zombie writhed in pain before dying for good, its remaining life faded away. She turned her attention to Gary. "Of course such a decision requires thought; give our guest the finest suite."

Gary nodded, then he and his squad drove Anubis onward with the barrels of their guns. Anubis struggled shouting back at her while he was forced away. "It was you, wasn't it? You opened the gate. You destroyed it! What side are you really on?"

Necristina watched his shadow struggling as he was pushed further away. Once the "Throne room" was cleared of her guest along with most of her undead army, she slumped in her throne, grateful for her deadened nerves. No one would see her weak.

Chapter 30

Heinrich sat on the floor, legs folded up in front of him. The back of a desk and chair combo concealed him from the group of survivors. He ran his hands through his hair and fumbled absently at his glasses. His teeth locked tight in anger and fear.

Sam, the man in charge of patrols, emerged into the room, leading two men in security outfits. One was limping. They were in the middle of the conversation when Heinrich's ears perked up. "…if they know we're here then this is the one place we shouldn't be."

"Bryce?" Heinrich asked, looking at him through tear reddened eyes. "What are you doing in a security outfit?"

"Long story. Heinrich, I thought I heard you in here." Bryce scanned over him. "You look like shit."

"Yeah," Heinrich grumbled under his breath. His thoughts drifting back to Frankie and the last message from the communicator.

"Worried about your girl?" he asked, with all the seriousness he could muster. The look did worse for Heinrich than if it was Bryce's usual goofy one.

"How could I let her go?" Heinrich asked, half surprised when the words were heard out loud. Bryce hobbled up to him. Heinrich sat back down behind his school desk fortress. Bryce had more trouble, his injured leg sticking out awkwardly as he slumped down to join him.

"Funny thing about kids, huh? You spend your whole life trying to get rid of them and when they have to go you try everything in your power to stop them," Bryce said. Heinrich dwelled on his words, a confused and angered look dancing across his wounded face. Bryce shook his head. "I guess under this situation it's a little different."

"How could I let her go? I should've stopped her, or something." Heinrich's voice broke and he stopped unable to continue.

"Hey. I don't want to hear talk like that. You were there, by the radio. She got the message out. Help is coming. Besides, Frankie's razor's edge sharp, you'll see. You give her too little credit. Just because the radio is dead doesn't mean she is."

"Could we stop talking about it? If she survived she would have been down here by now," Heinrich said, looking at his friend, his eyes pleading for mercy.

"IF she survived? Oh you of little faith," he said, looking over the desks to see Frankie enter with Rebecca Van Ness and some other woman with red skin dressed in a sexy cheer leader outfit, torn open in back to reveal bony stubs on her shoulders. He looked confused and back at Heinrich. His countenance quickly changed back. "I saw what was outside. When that wicked weird wail echoed through here they all took off," Bryce explained.

"Yeah, to join the feast," Heinrich sobbed loudly.

Bryce saw the three women heading for the desk and chair bunker alerted by the sound. "Whatever. So what would you say if you had one last chance to tell her how you feel?"

"I'd say I love you. I don't want anything bad to happen to you. I want to keep you safe. Protect you from all this crazy shit that's out there. But now she'll never know."

"Well you just told her. So she does," Bryce said, with a wicked smile pointing over Heinrich's shoulder.

"Dad?" Frankie said. He turned toward the voice; his blood shot eyes distorting, at first, what he saw. Bryce, with the awkward family moment making him feel strange, shifted his attention to Rebecca.

"Hey, little miss crazy. How's it going? It seems your premature release was well timed cause that hospital… *Pllt*!" He made a farting noise with his mouth, waving his fanned fingers across his throat then finishing the hand gesture by holding it out for her to shake. "My name's Bryce. I like jazz, and poetry and a slow shuffling walk through undead infested streets in the middle of the night. I don't believe we've had the pleasure…"

"Heinrich, who is this guy?" Rebecca said, taking a cautious step back. Bryce's smile widened.

"This Is Bryce. I had him… He works, worked, at the hospital. Bryce, meet, Rebecca and…" Heinrich introduced then paused looking at Atone with a strange familiarity.

"Oh, and I'm her alter ego. My name is Atone," Atone said, accepting Bryce's extended hand.

"And what a stunning Alter ego you are. How exotic. I'd probably be a little more surprised if it wasn't for blood loss and the strange developments outside, you know."

"Actually, I do." She smiled and Heinrich found himself growl despite himself. Bryce caught it as did Atone. She smiled back at him as Bryce kissed her hand. "See he knows how to treat a lady."

"Only for a weekend," Heinrich murmured, looking at Rebecca and back at Atone. Very similar in appearance it was easy however to distinguish them. It was Atone's eyes that told him who it was he was starting to… But no she's a… He struggled against his feelings, too many of them at once making it hard to sort out. Bryce slapped him across the shoulder in mock anger, his smile never fading from his face.

"Ouch. That's a cold one, friend," Bryce said. "Are we a little jealous?"

Heinrich opened his mouth to speak but didn't know how to respond. Atone saw his frustration and for a change she wasn't sure if she liked it.

"See I told you I was possessed," Rebecca said, feeling overlooked by the men in the room. A touch of green glowed in her eyes.

"Come on, the helicopter is on the roof. We're getting everyone out of here," Atone said, trying now to avoid both of them. She slithered over to Sam trying to seem useful by helping survivors organize their exodus. She felt a stirring in her chest. It was familiar, dangerous and ill advised. She refused to accept these feelings. Heinrich was a mold of clay to manipulate, how did she let this happen, she thought. Simple, she resolved to herself, it didn't happen.

Once getting to the helicopter and the passengers were aboard, Sam radioed. "Hello, HQ. This is Sam. We're loading up the survivors now. Can we expect demolition?"

"That's a negative. Away team alpha and gamma have not yet responded. I will not deploy until I know where they are either in the positive or in the negative," Diana crackled from the receiver. In a blur of speed the communicator was out of his hand claimed by the devil in front of him.

Atone

"Just so we're clear. You haven't forgotten about me?" Atone hissed

"The information we have is right here and waiting for you," a tired voice said over the communicator.

"Good," she said. Sam reached for the communicator and she kept it from him. He went for it and she drew him in close. Her talons dug into his back, catching him off guard. He froze, wild eyed, any movement threatening his life as she held him. "Now what's this about demolitions?"

"Standard procedure. In outbreaks of this scale we blow up the infected area to reduce spreading. Since Zombies stay were the food is they tend to linger around their homes, hunting grounds, really. Even after everyone's dead they wait days, even weeks before moving on. That's when we blow the place," he explained, sweating despite the cold.

"Thank you," she said, smiling. She handed him his communicator and removing her claws. "Finally someone who will give me a straight answer. I like you."

Chapter 31

Anubis sat in his room, thinking how much better prison cells at the jail were. The stench of the sewers played mind games with his senses until they were so confused as to be rendered useless. With only his eyes and ears still worth anything he surveyed his predicament. Sounds of the undead seemed to echo from all around but no exact locations could be determined. For all he knew there could be just a handful in a small room making a lot of noise. No, he thought, with the forces he saw earlier he knew his honored hostess had the manpower to cover every inch of this place if she so desired.

He decided to focus instead to the one thing he could rely on, and that was the one undead that sat mere inches from him, watching him out of the corner of his eye. He was relatively in tact for being a zombie. His eyes seemed small white dots, poking out of the shadows from their place in the sunken sockets, concealed further from the low brim of the police hat. The rest of his uniform was pressed and neat, everything in its order. All but the muck, turning crusty, as it dried to his pant legs and boots.

"Surprised, Louis?" Anubis said, as he caught the flicker in the cop's eyes on him again. "You can look at me directly, you know."

"So Paul, how are the wife and kids?" he asked, jovially. His smile was forced and Louis did not turn to face his friend.

"Is this why she had you watch me? She figured a friend of the force might ease my mind?" Anubis asked, gruffly, in his man form he still towered over Louis as they sat together.

"I have to hand it to you, Paul, I would never have guessed," Louis continued on.

"Guessed what? That I'm not human?" Anubis had to laugh despite the sorrow in his friends dead eyes. "I hate to break it to you pal, but you aren't either."

"Did Nicole know?" Louis asked, for the first time looking directly at Anubis. Anubis shook his head making Louis's eyes widen. "Christ, man, she had two boys by you."

"Shit, Louis, You act like you've never been deep undercover. No one, NO ONE knows, that's the point," Anubis growled. There was a silence, both non-men looked away from each other, letting a thin steady drip of a leaking pipe occupy their attention. When the silence was broken Louis was the cause.

"So what are they, huh? You're sons… Are… Do they take after their father's side of the family?"

"Yes," Anubis said, not taking his eyes from the bead of water making ripples in puddle underneath the pipe. A thought crossed his mind suddenly. "Nicole. Is she…" He leapt to his feet. On instinct Louis drew his gun and bared his teeth, a strange inner rebellion of Technological conditioning versus the zombie's primal nature. Anubis slowed his reaction seeing his friend's reaction. "Do you know if she's all right? Is she one of you?"

"I don't think so. There are a lot of 'us' though." He bit the last part of his words feeling somehow judged by his former friend. The muscles of Anubis tensed, his heart beating rapidly only to realize there was nowhere to go, no way to find anything here. He settled back down, trying to calm his nerves. She's alright, He thought, unless I find out otherwise.

"So why are you watching me?" he asked, finally, putting the thought aside.

Atone

"I remember why I became a police officer. I wanted to help people. So many bad things happen, it's nice to know that someone was looking out for you and I wanted to be that someone. Necristina's not bad, Paul. I guess I chose to work for her because she at least tries to do the right thing with our situation. She's trying to do good for all of us." Anubis found himself nodding patting Louis's shoulder then Gary, axe head glittering, returned.

"Necristina wishes to see you," he said, motioning to follow him with a quick jerk of his hand. Anubis nodded again. He had time to think about a lot of things but he still wasn't sure just what they wanted him for.

Chapter 32

Atone hit the door hard making it slam against the wall in its swing. "Now we get answers, mom," she growled. Diana turned to face her, oblivious to her dramatic entrance. Her eye lids drooped, nearly closed. She motioned indifferently to the stack of papers on the desk.

"That is all the information we have for you," she said, the last few words mutilated by a stifled yawn. Atone scooped up the stack of papers reading quickly through them.

"That's it?" She threw them aside. They scattered noisily before floating slowly to the ground. The duration of their falling only seemed to fuel her anger more. "This is bull shit. This is nothing!"

"You wanted to see it. That's all of it. It's all just teasers and hints but no real information," Diana said, withdrawn.

"That's crap. You're hiding something." Atone spat the words.

"I'm barely conscious I'm not hiding anything," Diana said, then drank deeply from an energy drink to prolong her wakefulness. It was interrupted by a harsh cough. A look of confusion darted across her face as she swallowed down the germs. She cleared her throat and started again. "I've been waiting for some word on the away team."

"Don't change the subject!" Atone shouted angrily baring her teeth.

I wasn't aware there was more of the subject to discuss," Diana said, eyes half-closed watching her daughter.

"Then what about this?" Atone said, producing an ornately carved, golden puzzle box shaped like a pyramid. The sight forced Diana's drowsiness to retreat. She could be tired later. She reached out for the box to examine it but Atone pulled the puzzle box away catching her wrist with her talons. She could feel the heat of a slight fever. "What does this have to do with me?"

"Where did you get that?" Diana asked, now eyes wide-awake.

"Answer me!" She shouted shoving Diana back. Diana pulled herself up and looked at Atone looming over her.

"It's a seal, one of thirteen locks," she said, getting to her feet. Diana kept her back turned trying not to give in to her desire for retaliation. "Locks to prevent what you so plainly started."

"So this, all of this, is my fault?" Atone challenged.

"You are the herald of the end, yes," Diana said, with a sneer.

"Then I suggest you cooperate. You obviously know more than you let on. Tell me what I need to do to resolve this quickly," Atone said, the power in her voice turning to hopeful pleading.

"Why? Do you want it all to end so badly?" Diana asked, kicking the seal from Atone's hand, flipping around to catch it, drew the gun from the out box on the desk and aimed it at Atone.

"End? I don't want this world to end. I'm trying to stop all this from happening. Why are you resisting me?" Atone challenged again.

"Because you're trying to stop something that's supposed to happen," Diana shouted back at her.

"And you're O.K. with this? You're just going to stop. After all you've tried to do. You're giving up now because I'm here?" Atone shook her head in disbelief.

"No. I'm not O.K. with it!" Diana said. "I've spent my entire condemned life protecting this world from the likes of you, preventing these things from happening. Then finding out it was all for this!" she said, pulling the last sheet still sitting in the printer tray, tucking the seal in her inner coat pocket. She handed the sheet to Atone, never lowering her gun. Atone read the page, And Diana quoted a line of it. "And her Death shall herald the end of this life."

"I'm supposed to do this? I don't want this. That's what I'm trying to stop. Everything I'm trying to do…" Atone tried to explain. With the things going on since her arrival she found less and less chance to deny it.

"You see. You see, now."

"No," Atone said, looking up at her mother in caged rage.

"You are your father's daughter. Stubborn to the last," Diana chastised.

"When did you loose faith, mother?" Atone asked, through clenched teeth.

"How dare you?" Diana flared, pulling the hammer back on the gun.

"Oh, I dare. You don't get it do you? All of this work to think this is going to stop me." The rest of Atone's words were squelched by the firing of a gun. She stumbled and looked back, eyes flaring a violent fire practically smoking from her sockets. Her wound crackled a blue spark from her soul. She hissed stepping toward her. "What do you think I've been trying to do?"

"Why don't you tell me?" she asked, pointing the gun to the seal instead. Atone froze, and then slowly took a step back.

"Look around you. Look at what's all happening. There's only one thing in existence capable of fixing this. The sooner I can get to..."

"Why you? What makes you so special?"

"I don't know but I'm ready to do whatever it takes to stop this," Atone said, her voice trying to be calm. Her eyes darted back from pyramid to Diana and back again.

"Even if it means your own death?" Diana asked. Atone couldn't answer. "Maybe it's your turn to look around. All of this dying is on your head. How much more must this world go through before you accept it? I know how you fell, Atone. Are you ready to accept your fate, daughter, and how, how can we put our faith in a devil like you?"

"I wasn't aware you wanted more mayhem and death, Mom. The longer that trinket sits unopened the more chaos ensues. You'll either have to trust me or watch everything you've tried to protect turn to dust."

"You still don't get it. I've tried to stop the end of the world. I've been unwittingly trying to stop God from following through with his plan to destroy the Earth. I have kept the world safe for three millennium, fighting off demons, witches, werewolves, zombies, upstart demihumans and everything else you can imagine. Now I'm supposed to just let it happen because God gave the O.K.?" Atone didn't listen to her as she turned to walk away leaving Diana to her thoughts.

Atone

Atone was not happy. What was she going to do? Well there was the temptation of a Dr Gordon. Atone took a seat on a bench somewhere between the library and the garage. The bench looked like it was abducted from the park. She resumed her thinking. If Diana was going to jerk her chain by not unlocking the seal she would need another way. Heinrich, though a great diversion could not likely help her in finding that other way. That and she was already getting too familiar with him. She didn't want emotional attachments and wondered, suspiciously if her feelings were even hers or his emotions lashing back at her. Her thoughts were interrupted by Heinrich walking cautiously down the hallway.

"You look lost in thought," he said, taking a seat next to her. "Anything important?"

"No, just you," she teased, but without the heart to make it sound playful.

"Ouch," he said, clutching his chest.

"I didn't mean it that way. I need help," Atone said, slouching in her defeat.

"These aren't really my business hours or conditions but I'll try to manage."

Atone

"The longer I'm here the worse this world is going to get. Not a good sign since the first week opened with vampires, mental patients and finished with a massive zombie invasion. Now I found a way to finish my mission but Diana, the head of a secret paramilitary organization and my mother took the only solid piece of the puzzle away not that I could get it open anyway. Now I have to find a different way to get to heaven," Atone rambled letting her thoughts tumble out of her mouth. "Are you following all of this?"

"Let's see. Shitty world gets worse until you can reach heaven and finish your mission."

"Yes," she said.

"Gee, that's a tough one. Get baptized?" he asked.

"No. I've already explained that to Frankie," she answered slumping hopelessly in her seat covering her face in her hands. Heinrich stroked her absently along the spine between the boney wing stumps. Her head jerked upward at the soft welcome touch, his warm hands confusing her feelings even more. The soothing motion created a tingling desire deep within her. Heinrich, lost in thought was unaware of her arousal or the purring from her throat.

"Hmm. Well you said you don't know how to unlock it. Maybe what you should do is learn more about this puzzle piece while you think of something else. Do research. Find out how it works, that's what I would do in this situation." When he turned to look at her he saw glazed white, almost silver eyes peering at him hungrily. She pounced on him pushing him back. He braced himself steady with his free hand as she kissed him roughly, trying savagely to devour his affection. With finding his resistances slacken she eased her assault, allowing him a chance to kiss back. Slowly her senses returned as she remembered Natalie, probably bored out of her mind, alone in the library computer.

"That's it," she exclaimed pulling back. She looked at Heinrich confused, eager and at a loss. "Research. Your right. Thanks," she said, kissing him again, without the force or passion. She rose to go to the library. "Sorry about all that. I know the rules… No temptation and what not. I just got carried away."

"I suppose a little temptation is good," he said, composing himself. Everything but his voice would have convinced her. "After all without temptation there wouldn't be something to overcome."

She left, her mind stuck on the word. Overcome. Was that how he perceived her? She wondered. The more she tried to forget about it the more it seemed to gnaw away at her subconscious, until by the time she reached the library she had her claws balled into fists her teeth clenched.

She pressed the button to the computer watching the screen flicker to life. Soon Natalie peered out at her from the other side of the screen. "Good morning, Ms. Atone," she said, cheerily. It didn't last long. The background grew darker, foreboding as her mood mimicked sadness. "You don't look happy. What's wrong?"

"It's nothing really, Natalie."

"Well what can I do for you today?"

"I need some information on 13 holy seals. I had one that looked like a pyramid, if that helps at all. I need to know what they do and how they work if you can do that, please." She blinked off the screen filtering through codes and streams of files.

"Certainly, Ms. Atone." Atone smiled feeling that at least now progress was being made. Heinrich was right.

Atone

Chapter 33

Lihatiel chuckled as they fortified the disassembled gateway. He didn't even mind that he was set upon to do the brunt of the work. Looking over his shoulder, made easy with his broken bones he saw Cosmacrater and Focalar returning from reconnaissance. Cosmacrater had maps folded up in his hand. In his free hand he carried a case of modern beverage, the sight of this and the blood marked grocery bags Focalar carried made the rest of the demon assembly hoot and cheer.

"Finally no more soul sucking damned to dine on," one guy rooted, getting a chuckle from those nearest him.

"Real food. Compared to Hell's menu this'll be like sweet ambrosia," another creature gurgled. Lihatiel said nothing, finishing his fortifications. Though not that many demons made it through the gate, the assembly seemed strong. Lihatiel didn't bother with a head count, he wasn't a leader any more, but even so he knew over forty at least were here. A handful of demons hauled corpses of mindless dead, propping them up, sometimes with the use of wires and string to intimidate any one unfortunate enough to try to interfere. Some just did it out of a perverse necrophilia or love of the sick and bizarre. Regardless of the motives, Lihatiel thought, the effect worked. Probably because they would actually follow through with any threat their morbid puppets suggested. As the demons consumed their supplies, Cosmacrater and Focalar dove deep in the maps looking for the best defendable areas and the most likely to fall under attack. As their meal was in its last stages Cosmacrater stepped over to them.

"Zalzion, I want you to select five of the best eyes to watch along this ridge here. The rest I want working on living quarters and making this our base for now with shifts patrolling through here," Cosmacrater said, pointing out sites on the map. Zalzion growled.

"Who said you were giving orders? Not all of us…" Zalzion's voice boomed. Before he could finish Focalar had an arrow to his chest. "Now what are you going to do with that, Order Dog?"

"That really depends on you, Diablonian," Cosmacrater said. "We've waited a long time for this day but we need a defendable base at this gate to stay here. If you have suggestions I'd be more than happy to hear them but we need someone to lead."

"Why you?" Zalzion challenged.

"Because I'm the best for the job," Cosmacrater said, simply.

"Go on and shoot, bitch. Won't do you any good. You saw what happens now that the gates down." Zalzion taunted. "I lead this Diablonian unit and I say once at odds always at odds. We don't take orders from The Order."

Focalar looked over at Cosmacrater with a frown. Cosmacrater nodded and the arrow fired lodging half way through Zalzion's chest. Zalzion winced for only a moment. "That's it? I told you nothing was…"

"Don't try to remove it," Focalar advised flatly as Zalzion pulled at the arrow.

"Still trying to give orders. Well in that your…" The arrow burned his hand, his flesh flaking off, continuing on as the heat scorched away the mortal coil, revealing his exposed soul. Zalzion screamed. "Get this off! Get it off!" He screamed. His men the Diablonians stepped forward to help him.

"Stay where you are," ordered Cosmacrater. The Diablonians looked back at Cosmacrater then Zalzion, most froze and a few even stepped away from Zalzion.

"Help me," Zalzion squealed. "Are you not Diablonians?" They looked back at Cosmacrater who eyed them sternly. "Grenizel? Michedael? Manchez?" Zalzion exclaimed seeing his brother in the crowd. "Manchez? Help me, please, my brother."

Manchez took a step to aid his brother eying Cosmacrater then Focalar who stood still, his business done. Stepping back he reached out to Zalzion. "What can I do for you, Zalzion?"

"Remove this arrow. It burns," Zalzion squealed. Manchez reached out cautiously looked for some trigger or trick to the magic arrow.

"Don't remove that arrow," Focalar warned.

"Please," Zalzion pleaded. Manchez wiped sweat from his palms. Taking in a deep breath he pulled the arrow. It was stuck. He pulled harder making Zalzion squirm.

"It's not stuck it's anchored. Hooked in somehow," Manchez tried to explain.

"Push it through," Zalzion gasped. Manchez tried to push it and his work paid off, forcing it through. As the arrowhead escaped the soul the finned blades opened. Manchez heard it and stopped but it was too late. The explosion was silent, a myriad of thin needles shredding apart Zalzion's soul with ease. Cosmacrater and Focalar barely flinched as a few stray needles cut them. Manchez at ground zero was slashed to ribbons. He collapsed lying on the ground. Cosmacrater stood over him.

"Congratulations, you just killed a superior officer. Manchez was it? Who are the five best eyes you have?"

"Michedael... Ferial, Muriel, Grenizel... But the best would have to be Bara Kasha."

"If your name was called, go along that ridge and keep your eyes open for attack." Cosmacrater sunk his fingers into Manchez's fresh wounds and hoisted him up to his feet. Focalar stood behind him, fingers on the notch and bowstring, ready to fire another arrow if necessary. "Now, Manchez, name two of your best fighters."

"Aboris, he's good for tactics and melee. Carmichael, he's good at… He's just that good."

"Step forward, please," Cosmacrater beckoned. Aboris stepped from the crowd Carmichael lingered a moment, judging Cosmacrater and Focalar's abilities before proceeding to the circle.

"That good, huh? That is quite a recommendation. It makes me wonder what exactly you can do." Cosmacrater said, inches from his head. Carmichael seemed confident enough as he stood there not smiling, with judgment in his eyes.

"Fire your arrow, Focalar," Carmichael said, without taking his eyes from Cosmacrater, waving a finger to have Focalar aim at him. The slightest sign of enjoyment slipped past his steely demeanor.

"Cosmacrater?" Focalar asked. Cosmacrater studied him intensely to find some clue, some betrayal of self that would explain the desire for Focalar to shoot him.

"Focalar fire your arrow." Cosmacrater nodded, though he was confused. He would be dead or 'that good' in seconds. They would find out which. The bow sung as the arrow flew. In a flash Cosmacrater was airborne the air pushed out of his lungs by the impact of nothing. No, Cosmacrater thought, Carmichaels hand was out aimed at him. He flew backward through the air. He saw the arrow home in on its target, then stall and fly back toward Focalar.

Focalar saw what appeared to be Carmichael grasping the arrow in mid path and sending it back at him. He tried to move as the arrow whistled toward him. Forceful bursts of air made any move Focalar made fruitless in effect holding him in place. He had nothing to do, nowhere to go as the arrow flew closer. He refused to close his eyes; it was simply his time to go. He was out witted, out skilled. The arrow hovered in front of him before collapsing to the ground.

The roaring wind faded. Cosmacrater hit the ground. He picked himself up from the desert sand, dusting himself off. As he walked back to the group, satisfied with his dust off and Carmichael's skill, he began to clap. "Impressive. Taking two of The Orders top on and not only surviving but gaining the upper hand in less than three seconds. If we had more men of your caliber... but regardless I see Manchez's boast was well founded. I am curious. Why didn't you stop us when we made a display of your superior?"

"Because he was wrong," Carmichael said, simply. "It is imperative to work together."

"Well Carmichael, I'm glad you see it that way. Aboris and Manchez come here. I have a special mission for you three…"

Chapter 34

Anubis instructed his men, men of course being a loose term. This wasn't the first army of the dead that he ruled, far from it. He was old and had done many things before seeing true power. He was a demigod once. He was well known for manipulating the dead. He wasn't good enough for heaven because of his tampering with the natural order, nor was he bad enough for Hell. He lingered here on earth. He was then little more than a dream. But then the angels fell and the Princes of Earth were formed. It was then he saw the chance for light to his darkness. Now his time had come. But what of his sons or their mother, he thought. When he, or if he, returned to the POE agency he would have to find out.

The quickest way to freedom is to give them what they want.

"…Now intense heat or mystical effects can reveal your main target. Since Mystic effects are uncommon at best and most likely unavailable we stick to heat. Scorch away their mortal seeming and you'll see a glowing light. This light can seem like a hideous beast, a pretty damsel or a simple glowing ball or anything else. The point is it is the true self. The soul. When this is visible they are vulnerable."

"Strike the soul, kill the demon," the assembly chanted.

"Rule two. If you can not kill the soul keep them from resurrection. When a demon dies it shuts down. In a normal situation they would go to Hell on their defeat. But when the gate was destroyed the soul will instead sit in a body awaiting resurrection. That's pretty much what happens in Hell too, since there is nowhere else to go. It's a special kind of torture all its own. This resurrection ability is kept secret by the generals, the most powerful demons. Taking the head denies the resurrector the raw material's needed to do their work."

"Keep them dead, take the head," the assembly chanted.

"Rule three…" He began seeing commotion above, near Necristina's assembly. "Gary, take over." He weaved his way through the assembly as Gary took his spot and continued the instruction. Anubis took the stairs along the wall to the balcony to reach them. On the other side of the balcony, Necristina's chief science officers worked steadily on replicating the odd mummification rituals, dissecting the process he explained to them to find the scientific cause. Necristina was eager to master this technology. Her skin was already a dark purple and grey. Her water-logged skin took in the moisture around her making her bloat. Her wings were nearly boned, a few die-hard feathers hanging on desperately as the skin beneath them decayed. This wasn't what Anubis was interested in. He was focused more on the zombie that drew her attention from the researchers.

"Louis and Riley were lost in the fight but we found them," Anubis heard as he reached them. "They've squirreled themselves away. There's a cave in the Rockies but they won't let us explain. They're like animals," the stranger said, focused now on Anubis.

"And their mother?" Anubis asked.

"Riley thought he saw something resembling a woman. But he was cut down trying to get a closer look. That's when they attacked."

"What did you expect? They're my sons," Anubis said, proudly.

"Your instructions have been most appreciated, Anubis. I only hope they will work," Necristina said, her voice diplomatic but clearly upset at being interrupted.

"That remains on you and your men. Just because you now know how to stop them doesn't mean they'll make it easy for you to do so. We still need more. We need to get in touch with my agency."

"We've been over this before," Necristina sighed, looking hotly at the jackal headed man.

"And I've expressed my concerns to you about the body count. More soldiers of your army will die."

"We are supposed to die," she exclaimed. "We aren't natural. We're not supposed to exist."

"If you weren't supposed to exist then you wouldn't, but regardless of any personal views is it really what you owe them? Think of them. Besides what if you fail and all this retaliation is for nothing. You lose and they win." Anubis saw that his words were getting through to her. He also saw the anger boiling inside of her. He bowed his head submissively, and chose his next words carefully. "I'm sorry I didn't mean... Look I do understand. It is your crime you wish to repair. All I'm asking is that you meet with Diana. She runs the organization. She can help you."

"I will consider your words, Councilor Anubis," she said, dismissively. He suppressed a growl as he stormed off. As he reached the front of the assembly a blow horn carried Necristina's voice after him.

"Gary Farwell, report to the main office." Gary passed the torch back to Anubis, before returning to the side of his Queen. "Gary, I have a special mission for you."

Chapter 35

"I have finished the research you requested. Though activation seemed a bit cryptic at best I did manage to uncover some information," Natalie said, hiding behind open windows.

"Can you print it?" Atone asked, with a sigh, the events of the last couple of days starting to get to her.

"Sure thing, Atone," she said, with a smile as the printer came to life. After the calculation the screen informed her that it would take 27 pages. This was going to be a while. Footsteps caught her attention and she slithered from her chair squeezing close to the book shelf. She peered over the edge but couldn't see anything. A flash of someone passed, too quick to identify. She risked a look back at the printer. Only three pages sat complete in the tray. She heard Orion and Stephan's voices as they headed toward her. They worked for Diana; they may try to stop her. They were only talking at the moment. She slipped into the shadow snatching the seven pages that were finished. They were near them now; she slipped around the bookshelf to the other side watching them and the computer through the shelving.

"Natalie, what's up?" Stephan asked. Orion clutched his stomach feeling himself sicken. He looked around.

"I was just printing out some old archive information. I thought it would be a good idea since some of the hard copies are old and fragile. This way you can organize information better."

"Oh, smart thinking," he said, looking over. "Hm, Cairo."

A red alarm went off at the top of the door, Atone dropping down instinctively. In moments a page was heard over the loud speaker. It was Diana's voice. "The books open again. Stephan, report immediately."

Stephan and Orion headed for the door, Orion stopped, trying to pinpoint the cause of his sickening feeling. Atone Crouched even lower in the shadows. He glanced back at the printer before heading out the door. When they left she returned to Natalie.

"Thanks for helping me…" Atone began.

"No problem, Atone. My creator had me lie all the time," she smiled back.

"Yeah, mine too," Atone said, without a smile.

"There. All done. If you could fill the paper feed tray I would be glad to print out some convincing archive information," Natalie offered.

"Thanks Natalie, you've been really helpful," Atone said, trying to figure out how to show her gratitude to an image on a screen.

"There is one more thing. You will want to think of an alibi," Natalie said, winking at her.

"What do you mean?" Atone asked, looking up from the pages she thumbed through.

"Stephan left with a sheet of your read out. They'll probably put two and two together soon enough. But don't tell me anything. The more I know the worse it will be."

"Understood. Good bye," Atone said, leaving. She saw Diana scanning over a page as she took it from Stephan. Orion's back was to her in the doorway. Her voice increased in volume. Atone darted down the hallway before they figured it out. She navigated the corridors her mind divided on avoiding Diana and on finding an alibi. She heard the door to the library open with a bang. She raced through the hall checking random doors, as she worked her way to the survivor's encampment.

Orion could be heard, heavy footfalls behind her. She took the doorknob. The footsteps were closer. She turned it. It was locked. She saw his shadow, he was getting too close. She tried another. The door was stuck. Orion came into view. He was looking away. She pushed through. She was safe. There was a sound of something falling and a pained moan. She watched through the door. He was coming. She looked in to find Rebecca on the floor, getting up, her eyes focused on Atone, surprised. Heinrich sat in a chair near her at the head of a couch. Atone looked flustered her cheeks growing a darker shade of red. "Hi."

The door pulled away behind her and she staggered to support herself. Orion had come. "There you are, Atone. Diana would like a word with you."

"In a minute, Mr. Orion, Sir. We're in the middle of group," Heinrich said, catching the brief pleading look in her eyes before they fell to the ground.

"Oh, really?" he asked, studying them. Then he turned to leave. "I'm sure this can wait until you are done. She'll be in her office when you're ready."

"No problem. No doubt going to yell at me some more," Atone grumbled, getting back on her feet.

"Maybe. Not my problem. I've delivered my message," he said, queasy. He left quickly not bothering to close the door. She breathed out.

"Now what, prey tell did I just get involved in?" Heinrich asked, setting down his notebook.

"Just me being me I guess," she smirked.

"And does it have anything to do with this puzzle piece you were talking about?" he continued on.

"Only all of it."

"Want to talk about it?" He gestured to a seat.

"Not really. Like you said, I'm just an obstacle to overcome," Atone said. Heinrich sighed turning to Rebecca.

"I'll have to cut this session short, Ms. Van Ness."

"Don't bother. You don't owe me anything, you don't have to keep helping me, and you certainly don't need to clear your busy schedule," Atone growled at him taking him by surprise.

"And you don't have to save me or my daughter, you don't have to stop some cosmic conspiracy and you certainly don't have to tempt me," he said, softly.

"On that note," Rebecca said, squeezing past Atone still blocking the doorway. "I'm leaving. Since no body seems to care. I think that Stephan guy's into me anyway. At least I'd like him to be. Later." Rebecca left leaving the two alone.

"Why are we doing this?" Atone asked, as Heinrich motioned for her to take the couch. She set her papers near it on the floor and took the seat. "I don't see why you should have feelings for me or why I should be upset by it. I mean, I'm leaving soon to never come back. It would be better if you didn't."

"What about you?" he asked.

"What about me?" she countered.

"Would it be better for you not to care about anyone, so you wouldn't feel guilty if you fail?"

"You sound like Axael. Now I'm not only an obstacle but I'm a cold heartless obstacle. Oh, yes. I can see how that's a lot better," she said, getting up only to feel his gentle but firm hand on her shoulder ease her back into the seat.

"What I meant was it would be easier but it is not possible. A cold heartless person wouldn't go out of their way to do for me what you did. But you're right. I don't have to do anything for you just like you don't have to do anything for me. I know that. But I do, because I think maybe it's the right thing. I've been thinking about it a lot lately. I think maybe that's what you need."

"So what are you trying to say?"

"I'm saying you don't have to tempt me, because I'm already tempted. I know you didn't do it on purpose," Heinrich said, with a soft smile.

"Do you? How can you be so sure?" She challenged.

"If you did then why would you resist it now? No. I may be wrong. Maybe you did in some way manipulate me. But it doesn't really matter. What matters is that I want these feelings to be real. I think deep down you do too."

She listened to his words, realizing for the first time that it wasn't about her at all. He needed her. "Heinrich, I'm not sure."

She was cut short by his lips, on hers. She didn't resist him. His hands ran along her skin and scales, making her quiver. He moved over her. Atone closed her eyes as Heinrich's hands traced the inside of her leg. "Axael" she gasped making him retreat. Her eyes fluttered open at the absence of his touch. "I'm sorry."

"Axael. Who is that? You've mentioned that twice since coming in."

"I'd better go," Atone huffed fixing her clothes. Heinrich tried to stop her but she escaped him, leaving him with a bitter taste of her real love on his lips. She ran to Diana's office tears struggling to escape her eyes. She stopped outside Diana's office trying hard to restrain her self before entering. Inside Diana looked at the monitor. A smell of decay greeted her and she noticed a shadowed form in a seat back to the door. Diana covered her face discreetly as she searched information on the monitor. Atone spoke up when Diana didn't look up to greet her. "Look if this is about the seals you can stop right there. I don't need anymore hassle."

Diana took a long time to respond her voice ragged from harsh coughing. "I'm sorry Atone. I didn't mean to pin all this on you as I'm sure it seemed I did. But I'm still worried that doing the right thing now may make you do the wrong things all over again," she said, weakly. Atone was about to say something anything to shift the subject away from her demise, when she saw the pyramid and sheet print out sitting near the desk.

"But you're right also. Time is running out. If you linger here it's only going to make things worse. The truth is we don't know what any of this really means for everything else," she chuckled. "It's just a bunch of cryptic questions rather than real answers. I don't even know if I'm supposed to help you or be against you."

"So what are you going to do?"

"Make you an offer. Oh, I'm sorry. You haven't been introduced. This is Gary Farwell. He has some interesting information." The chair in front of her swiveled back to reveal Farwell, the air of silent compliance was radiating from him, as well as the reek of death.

"Yeah," she said, at Gary then focused back at Diana. "So what's this deal, mom," she snapped bitterly.

"The gates of Hell have been destroyed, Ms. Atone." Gary began. "Help us rebuild the gate so we may drive back the devilish forces. They can't be killed easily as there is no way for their evil to return to Hell," he continued Diana trying to stop him from the Evil, Devilish, and Hell Gary adamantly detested. "We came across Anubis, your associate; in our battle but if we really want to undo our mistake we first must send the… them back."

"Do this for us," Diana began when Gary stopped, "and I'll give you back the seal."

"No," Atone said, flatly.

"What? I shouldn't be so surprised since you are…" Diana started.

"I mean no, I won't do it just to get the seal," Atone said.

"So you're getting greedy?" Diana asked, her face sneering.

"I need to get to heaven. I don't know what I'll do when I get there but if I fix this gate for you then you get me there," Atone demanded.

"Fair enough," Diana conceded.

"I'll need a lot of building materials, a place for heat and forging and then…" Atone continued.

"Yes, yes whatever you need."

"I'm not sure you're aware of what building material I need. I'll need armies, one to hold off the demons that leaked through and another to sacrifice, for said building material."

Atone

"Oh, my God!" Diana gasped horrified and disgusted at such a request. The zombie, Gary, didn't seem at all phased.

"I'm sure our Queen realized the importance of sacrifice," Gary said, without any hint of surprise or disgust.

"That's very noble Mr. Farwell, but it would take…" She paused for a moment figuring out the magnitude of the task they offered her. "…nearly 3000 men if not more all making one structure to cover something that power level."

"This is nothing. We have more than that ready to swarm this dam right now," he said, and then added quickly as he saw Diana's look of surprise turn his way. "That is only if things go poorly. We are nationwide."

"Yes. Well," Atone said, trying to come up with something to convince them of the bad idea. Finding no other option she replied, "Yes. I agree."

Diana looked back at her and Atone could feel Diana's nerves tense and her heart rate increasing as she lied. "Then afterwards we will find a way for you to go to heaven."

"I accept," she said, knowing full well that something was wrong. She needed to think. She took her leave and headed for the room were Heinrich was giving psychiatric help. As she neared the refugee encampment there was a lot of commotion. Several survivors were eager to leave the dam hearing word of their new ambassador. She saw Heinrich and Rebecca among them.

"What are you guys up to?" she asked.

"We're going top side, checking out the city, make sure it's as safe as it seems," Rebecca said, pulling her attention from the commotion around them to her devil twin.

"Should you, really? I mean wait for the POE to O.K. it first," Atone said, protectively.

"It was their idea to send out a few civilians with armed escorts to salvage the city for supplies. It's like legal looting. We're only going to find stuff for now but eventually we should be able to stay. Once we know its all clear we'll be able to rebuild civilization," Rebecca said.

"Oh and you left this in my office. Interesting stuff. Especially page 5," Heinrich added handing her the pages.

Atone

"We'll be back before too long,"
Rebecca said, over her shoulder as she left with
Heinrich.

Chapter 36

Atone entered that room taking a seat, and stretching out on the couch. She knew Diana would betray her somehow. Her mind tried to wrap around an idea of how to get out of it. She began thumbing through the papers, scanning over them for any thing that jumped out and screamed in her face. On page five an ornate disk with a gem in the center, red as fire, did the next best thing. It was known as the Beacon of God. Atone scanned farther down the page to see the Pyramid. This one was known as Blessed Liberator.

"It's the wrong artifact," she said, to herself in a whisper. She sat aside her pondering to pay close attention for the Beacon of God. "It was made into a necklace in 1879, for the Lady De Leona an Heiress to a railroad tycoon. She was slain by banditos who took the necklace. The necklace was never reclaimed. Juan Salvador, the only Bandit captured kept the secret of the Beacon of God taking it to his grave. That's just great," she thought aloud. The seal she needed was lost somewhere in the Mexican desert if it wasn't smelted down for bullets. She read a little more but her mind already wondered to what she was gong to do about that Gate and her mother's lies. She closed her eyes to think about what course of action to take.

Stephan came down the hall gasping for air. He saw the door open and pushed his way in. "Atone, thank God… I've been looking… all over… for you."

"What is it, Stephan, you look…" she said, waking up abruptly. She looked at the clock and saw that several hours had passed.

"It's Heinrich and Rebecca." His face was sullen. She felt her heart sink, fear creeping into her. She followed him without hesitation.

Stephan led her quickly to the top side emerging into the middle of the city. The cold rain splashed across her cheek and arms trying to cool her rage, cool her hate, as Heinrich's body was being returned to the head quarters. Rebecca, though alive, was severally mangled by whoever did this. Heinrich was dead. Her mind froze up her body. She wanted to lash out. She wanted to cry out a tortured angry wail. She wanted to kill all those that let this happen. She did nothing. Her arms reached out wanting desperately to hold him but refusing, as if not touching him would prove in some strange way that his fate was still in question rather than a cold hard reality. In a bolt she was in a full run, roaring with the storm, crying with the rain. Orion looked up as she ran past, then back at Stephan.

"Shouldn't we…" Stephan began to ask him. Orion looked off. His hands busied themselves by playing the surveillance tape. He saw his men walking through the foggy, frosty morning toward the local mall. He watched his men turn against each other fighting themselves as mind-controlled beasts. The mind controlled survivors then set about raping Rebecca over and over again. Orion wanted to look away but had to watch to find any sign of who did this to his men. Then he saw, briefly, a black collection of smoke in the corner. "There," he exclaimed pointing at the screen then rewound the tape. "That strange fog was present the entire time my men were possessed."

"I said, shouldn't we go after Atone?" Stephan asked.

"Give her some time," Orion said, in mock concern. If all went well she would draw out the culprit and who knows, maybe it would take her out, saving him the trouble.

She ran the ground beneath her turning to mud. The sky turned dark and blurred by rain. She said something in the dark cursing his name and wanting him there. She wanted an explanation. The tombstones pushed through the muddy wet soil forming jagged rows of stone teeth across the slick ground. Her step skidded sending her tumbling to her knees sliding into the stone. Her ribs cracked, the air driven from her lungs. She pushed herself back from the stone, sitting down in the cold mud. Her palms sinking in the muck, her stomach heaving, she added vomit to the sludge. She could feel a rumble down below the shifting earth. She looked up eyes burning red and swollen to see the black Mercedes drive by then slow to a stop. The back, driver's side door opened and Stephan Marquette stepped out.

"Atone. Please, come in out of the rain. I'll take you home." Atone could feel her rage fade to loss at last breaking down to tears.

"Home." She put her hands on the headstone to steady herself as she raised. With a gasp she felt a presence as she touched it. She looked down reading the words. "Candice Marcos. Candice?"

She looked around for Nathaniel too, feeling him here.

"Rebecca, are you coming?"

Atone

"The devil you know. I'll get to you first," she whispered. "Vengeance will be mine."

"Rebecca," Stephan called.

"I'm coming," she called, then speaking to the stone. "I'll be back for you tonight." She went to the Mercedes and entered with Stephan and Orion.

"Do you want to talk about it?" Stephan asked.

"Please just let me have some time alone," Atone answered, turning to the window, her arms held around her.

"I'm afraid I can't do that," Stephan said, holding up one of the fallen soldier's recording devices. "Orion thinks you might know the thing that got to his men, since you are… what you are…"

"A devil? Let me see the footage then," she said, with a huff. She watched the men corrupted. She let out a gasp, her eyes crying with the death of Heinrich. She watched Rebecca's violation in a strange way a defilement to her as well. She sobbed realizing that she suffered. It was real. The recording unable to carry with it the emotional essence, she knew these feelings to be her own. "That voice."

"What?"

"Turn up the volume."

After Rebecca collapsed deep into her own mind, growing silent, Stephan raised the volume surprised to hear laughter.

"Do you know who that is?"

"It's Bael. He killed me once before. This is really bad." Stephan shut off the recorder quickly. Atone, surprised, let out another gasp. The car came to a stop and she looked up to see that they were back at the base. Stephan opened the door and crawled out rushing over to her side and opening her door.

"I'm sorry you had to watch that. Of course Orion probably needs information on this Bael. I should probably go and check the library. I should check on Rebecca first."

"I'll go. Let me talk to her. I'll let her know you're concerned."

Atone

Atone walked to the hospital room waiting, trying to figure out how to proceed. She opened the door to see the Curtain drawn. A shadow along it moved back and forth, a thin laughter slipping past it.

"Rebecca?"

She heard a sniffle and saw the movement stop. "Hello, Atone."

"I guess it would seem kind of stupid to ask how you are doing, huh?" she asked, feeling the emotion crawling under her skin. She fought against it to reach the curtain.

"It's kind of ironic isn't it, Atone?" Rebecca started as Atone opened the curtain. Atone saw Atone's wrists lashed violently her hands still clutching the knife etching into the skin. "Giving immortality to a suicide is a pretty cruel joke."

"Rebecca I…"

"Just go away."

"Rebecca, this…"

"I said go!" She screamed Atone taking to a battle stance. She dodged the knife and went against lunging at her in response. She walked to the doorway leaving Rebecca to return to her sobbing laughter.

"Stephan wanted to come down. I told him no. It was probably for the best. When you get things straight I'll let him visit."

It was nightfall; the rain was still falling when she exited the hatch to the top of the dam. She slunk back into the city, rain and darkness concealing her escape. She pulled the hood of her confiscated windbreaker tighter, trying to protect her head from the cold wind. It didn't take long for her to arrive at the cemetery.

"First we'll get Mercy, and then find Longing," she hissed. Her weapons sat six feet under her, waiting for its master to return. The thought of Heinrich's death and the violation of Rebecca encompassed her mind as she clawed savagely at the ground. Rage and hopelessness filled her growing stronger with every fist full of wet ground. It was nearly daybreak when her claws struck wood.

"Candice," Atone sighed, sweeping the dirt from the casket. Mud stuck to her fingers in clumps as she shook to free them. "I'm so sorry."

Atone

She pulled at the lid ready for the smell of decay. The smell was more like rich earth, too much time passing after her death. Her shriveled, dried husk looked up at her, eyes sunken in. The dried skin drank thirstily at the rain, soft splotches replacing brittle, dusty flesh. Atone pushed gently at the stomach caving it in and reaching up toward the head. She could grasp the essence and began to pull. Candice jerked and writhed, a loud low moan escaping the corpse that intensified to an agonizing scream.

"Even now I hurt you. I'm sorry," she pleaded removing Mercy from the corpse. Taking it in her hands she clawed her way to the surface. She slipped on the soft soil twisting her ankle with a loud snap. Looking at her wound she heard the subtle ping of rain hitting metal. Glancing toward the sound she saw the freshly washed gleam of metal, curved and round. She clawed at the object, the hollowed grave starting to fill with water. A loud sucking sound released the metal object from the ground.

"Nathaniel," she said, looking at a small ornate urn. "They were buried together, so close yet so apart." She unscrewed the lid reaching in to grasp the soul. The metal crushed and bent as the gleam of the shining blade emerged. "Longing."

Atone

"I made a promise a long time ago. I can give you half of that promise now." Atone rose from the grave taking off the windbreaker she had worn. She took Mercy and Longing to the nearest mud puddle and rinsed them off wrapping them up in the windbreaker. She snuck through the night getting back to the base. She slipped back into the hatch at the dam and reentered the base.

"I see you're feeling better, Atone," Orion growled from the darkness of a doorway.

"Orion?"

"I'm not here to intervene." Orion rose from his shadow toward her. "Let's get something straight here. If I didn't trust Stephan's convictions I would snuff you out right now. But he thinks your part of some greater purpose." In a quick swipe while Atone was trying not to sprinkle mud everywhere, Orion took the windbreaker and opened it. "What a beautiful treasure."

"They're not complete," Atone said, taking them back. "I made them a promise."

"You're keeping your word?" Orion asked in disbelief, stepping back in the door to retrieve something. "Here is a present for you."

Atone opened it to find an ornate Hammer and a blood red cloak. She looked back at Orion.

"For what its worth I am sorry about Heinrich."

"That hammer is a… was a gift from one of your father's friends. He had it among his things. I thought you should have something of his," Diana said, coming out of the room with him. By the look of things she had awakened them in her passing. She could feel Diana's heart pained by the information of Woten's death by Anubis.

"Thank you," Atone said.

"No need," she retorted taking Orion and leading him back inside. "And I know you're going to try to get vengeance. Rebecca wanted us to apologize to you. Good luck."

Her body shook at the words. She took her weapons to the dungeon room, where she was first introduced to the POE organization, to avoid bothering people with too much noise. Even so she retrieved a CD player and turned it up to conceal any noises she may make. She thought of the hate, the pain and the rage she felt and dealt in her life as she combined the two weapons into one. The pain she once shared when first she formed them was now a sweet pain of unity in agony reunited in suffering. As she merged Longing and Mercy a strange comfort took over her, knowing in her agony a chance for hope. The weapon took on the pattern of Damascus. She formed the weapon into two blades on opposite ends united by a long flexible pole. A thin prong lined the back of the blades on either end. She studied her weapon quizzically. "I shall call you Gemini. Now is the time, Gemini, serve me well."

She rested most of the day then woke up to practice. Watching the daylight sun fade to the dim light of the moon, she slammed the blade down, flexing the pole down to double over it. The tension repelled her and launched her toward the grate above the dungeon. In a swipe she cut it open and she flew through the opening, weapon in tow. It was time to hunt Bael.

The sound of a deep bass beat rumbled the air well before she reached the nightclub. As she grew closer she felt it shake through her body. On a different night she may have enjoyed the vibration through her but not now. She was on a mission. Now it aided her death march, echoing through the emptiness in the pit of her stomach. She stayed along the wall, following the alley path until she was at the edge. She could feel him inside. Two bouncers guarded the door. She tried to slow her savagely beating heart. She bolted from the shadows. She eased on the tension, the blades extending from either hand until they scratched the ground as she ran. In a fatal leap she spun through the air blades outward, pole along her back. The bouncers hit the ground when she did. Only she remained in one piece.

The door gave way easier then she anticipated. Looking around no one seemed to notice the disturbance outside. She held her cape close concealing Gemini underneath, looped and linked together with it's tines. The pounding music made all the nearest sounds evaporate. She couldn't depend on sound, or emotion, since all of these puppets shared his. Navigating the crowd she reached the middle of the dancehall. It wasn't long before the familiar voice was heard. It came from above as she saw a possessed zombie hanging upside down from the rafters.

"Bael."

"You remember. I'm touched." She felt his words dripping into her mind. "I thought to much time on this plane would have befuddled your little brain."

"So you killed Heinrich, and tortured Rebecca." Atone looked at the puppet that talked to her at the time. Atone looked around and saw the crowd closing in around her. The partiers stopped dancing all looking at her.

"You know me so well. I had to see how much of you there was left. I'm glad you still have your spirit." Bael hissed carelessly falling to the dance floor in a crumpled mess. In a brief moment the partiers were freed looking around confused. Bael caught their fragile minds again and resumed his conversation. The crowd parted to allow the mangled host to rise to his broken legs, a macabre marionette of shattered bones still working.

"How did you do it, Atone? How did you make it so... Permanent. How did you escape Hell? Come on, give it up."

"All I will give you is death. You and all your puppets." The cape parted as she unlinked the Gemini and let the tension lash the blades out at the possessed bodies. They straightened out shredding through the nearest throngs of the dance hall including Bael's host body. It offered little resistance. The black inky smoke freed itself from the corpse, entering another.

"Bold words, Atone. How hard are you willing to fight to make it true?" The music stopped for a moment. As the new beat began the fighting commenced. The song was fast, savage, and brutal. It was the perfect song for the chaotic dance of blades, brains and blood. She would have to kill them all. An empath, she quickly realized there was nothing here to save.

Springing and twisting she carved through the dance floor but regardless of how well trained she was the masses would eventually overwhelm her. Holding on to the prongs she swirled through the crowd. Soon she was over run. Hands pawed harshly all around her. One of the faces in the crowd spoke.

"Impressive as always," Bael said, through a half rotted face mere inches from her. "But I've killed you once. I'll do it again." Atone just looked at him smiling. This seemed to anger him more. "What? Your little plot is about to end, why are you smiling?"

"You should know Bael. I always have a trick up my sleeve," Atone stated releasing the Gemini. The tension from the cable sent the blades straightening outward again clearing the masses. The look on Bael's face made her smile broaden. This trick wouldn't last for long. She sprung over the bar, swinging Gemini one handed like a pole arm. Standing on the bar she hacked through the masses but soon they would overwhelm her again. Nothing she tried lasted long, as they changed their tactics to match hers. She turned her attention to the bar, hacking violently at the liquor. Slashing the tip across the brick wall a spark ignited the bar. There was no way of fighting him now. If she would ever beat him she had to follow her orders and rebuild that gate. The fires burned around her. Slamming the Gemini down she pole-vaulted through the night club, landing on the window high above the club. Bael and his minions roasted below. She smashed through the glass and escaped the burning building. Landing blade down she launched herself away, insuring that her retreat could not be followed.

She retreated, wrapping Gemini around herself and interlocking the prongs of each weapon to hold it together to form a metallic circle. She cursed herself for being unable to gain a victory over the Diablonians most feared warrior. She returned to the dam ashamed.

Chapter 37

Atone worked feverishly on the gate as Gary stepped up to her. Anubis had returned and was leading the army that would defend them while this gate was being made. For reasons of security the gate was being built at the foot of the dam, for the dam to be flooded after words concealing the construction. He walked carefully over the ridge of rocks and scaffolding to where Atone worked.

"I know it is hard for you right now, Atone." Gary tried to comfort her. "Heinrich was a good man. I'm sure his soul isn't trapped in his body unable to get out."

"If that's your way of saying he isn't in Hell then thank you, if you're just trying to make small talk then you are one disturbed zombie bastard."

"Progress seems to be going smoothly," he said, looking down at the half formed gate zombies pooled together in half forged states, bound to the same rough-hewn structure. All the while they droned on the mantra she had taught them. She wiped the sweat from her brow rising out of her seat.

"It is. They hardly feel a thing which makes working with them very easy, for me."

She slid down the side of the dam to resume her work after the meager break. He took the longer way down. "There doesn't seem to be any sign of the demons yet." Gary noted as they reunited.

"There will be. This mantra strikes cords with every fallen. They're getting agitated, really, really pissed off. They can't pinpoint the vibrations. Not until the last mantra. All they know is something somewhere is making quite a dent in their plans," she had to yell back at him, the mantra 2,000 strong drowning out anything else.

"And when are you going to start that last mantra?"

"I should be able to finish this tomorrow. Which means tomorrow is going to be a really crazy day!"

"I'll get the preparations ready for our guests."

"Good."

Meanwhile below where Anubis led his division, Diana headed over to him.

"Anubis. It's good to see you again," she said flatly.

"And how is she doing?" he asked, looking back at the massive structure under construction behind him.

"I don't know. We may have to take her out," Diana said. Anubis shook, forced to do a double take at her words.

"What about the prophecy?" he asked.

"It's because of the prophecy. If she succeeds according to it, all of us, all existence is taken with her into oblivion to be reprocessed," Diana explained.

"And you think that means death, world wide?" he asked.

"What else could it mean?"

"Salvation. That's the optimistic way to see it," Anubis answered. "To be made anew. You seem to be forgetting something."

"Like what?" Diana demanded.

"The first line," Anubis said, smiling his lupine features at her.

"Excuse me?" She snapped.

"As God wishes one of his own shall rise again. As God wishes. It is really beyond us at this point. Isn't it? I mean wasn't it the whole point of POE to keep earth in accordance to God's wishes? Now God says things will be set right when she returns to him. Its something so large so grand that we can't fix it, that's why he will."

"And you believe this?" Diana asked. "You believe we'll be forgiven and everything will be set right when she returns to him?"

"It's the only real option, isn't it?" he asked, "We just have to have faith."

"Yes." Diana pondered the word, repeating it. "Faith."

Chapter 38

The undead lined the drained lake bed. The small dark red specks in the distance grew larger by the minute slowly revealing themselves as the demon army. Fifty thousand undead men joined the bakers dozen of remaining POE agents including Anubis, Orion, Hugin and Diana. Stephan was sheltered away with the refugees deep inside the dam.

Atone looked out from the scaffolding. The sun silhouetted the demonic forces. The mantra was molded like its material, into a vibrating hum. The once deafening humm was growing weak, a sign of the near completion.

"Almost done," she said to herself eying the crowd. The sound of the undead moan covered up the humm. But then the demon army's war cry soon drowned them out. The outlying zombies crumpled and fell, demonic forces desecrating them in their attack. Atone recognized Cosmacrater pointing to the gate. The demonic armies broke off into two divisions, one to attack the gate, the second to weed out the opposition. The undead numbers where no match for the demonic horde.

"There, the gate, destroy it." The horde charged forward, ignoring the remaining undead's feeble attempts to stop them. Anubis raced across the rocky ledge as a jackal making sure his undead army held the line.

Shifting back to his traditional onyx skinned human body and lupine head he began to speak. "Now, do it now!" He howled.

Hugin, flying the battlefield as a raven, relayed this to the undead army everywhere. Fire filled the dried lake bed scorching away their mortal coils. Cosmacrater screamed in agony.

Bael watched the tides of war worsen as he piggybacked through Gary. The fires cut the demonic army down. The more powerful demons managed to take over some of the torches, igniting the numbers of undead before their exposed souls were destroyed. The undead manned the remaining gas and fire as the POE officers took down their targets.

Gary slithered away with Bael taking control and leading him to the dam's control center. The demonic army would get a helping hand. Gauges and switches controlled the pressure of the river of one side and the amount passing through to the other. With the recent rain and short lasting snow it wouldn't take much to make this dam burst. The Bael possessed Gary went to work quickly hitting the switches watching the emergency lights go off. The sound of breaking pipes and walls made his undead host's face smile, ripping along the edges with coagulated blood running slowly from the wounds.

"And what do you think you are doing?" Rebecca asked taking him from surprise.

Outside The war raged on, a handful of demons surviving the fire. Atone heard the banging sound behind her. She turned to see the concrete wall heave. She bolted quickly as the wall ruptured. It spewed water. She raced against the ever-growing hole. The scaffolding shook making running hard as the water slammed into it. Water filled the lake, flooding away the demon, undead and POE agent corpses. Lihatiel took hold of the edge of the scaffolding, clawing his way up to the gate. The weak hum, told him there was still time. A winged bat like creature rose from the waters on slick bat like wings. Cosmacrater held tightly to his ankles. Anubis growled leaping from the ridge to dive on Cosmacrater's body, slashing and clawing.

Atone

On the scaffolding Atone struggled to escape. The broken demon corpse of Lihatiel moved unnaturally swift, cutting off her escape route.

"Atone. It's been a while." Lihatiel growled intercepting Atone as she fled.

"Lihatiel. How did you merit a resurrection?" She said, hanging on to the metal pipe of the remaining scaffolding as the center of it collapsed. Lihatiel was nearly pitched off, his claws holding tight. Atone tried to kick him nearly tumbling off herself.

"You weren't there to explain your treachery. Speaking of which I owe you something." He dove at her, with a growl. She swung violently, hanging on to the rocking pole with her legs to swing with Gemini. Lihatiel's battered and barely collected body shifting and wriggling to avoid her blades.

Orion pulled himself up along the filled lake. He saw Anubis and Cosmacrater fighting in mid air and Lihatiel overpowering Atone near the gate. He searched himself for a weapon and found none on him. On the ridge laid a dying demon barely clinging to life surrounded by a dozen sacrificial undead lambs. Its thin cheetah like body lay in the mud Bow still clutched in his hands, the quiver of arrows scorched and burned. Two arrows survived the intense heat. He looked over at his friend and then the devil woman he despised. Lihatiel would soon be victorious.

Rebecca twisted the axe head from Gary's shoulder driving it down through his head. A billowing smoke cloud rose from him as he slumped down. This fog like phantom entered into her body. Her eyes glowed green for a moment and she smiled.

In the refugee rooms, water began to trickle from the walls.

"I'm sure it's nothing." Bryce said, holding Frankie close as she examined the cracks. "I hear dams crack all the time to alleviate pressure. Yeah, that sounds good."

"Now, Atone. You will pay for what you've done to me," he growled tackling her to the ground. The flexible pole of Gemini worked against her as she tried to keep him away from her. She could barely hear the hum. Only a few seconds more.

"Over my dead body," she said, taking a zombie dagger from her waist, and throwing it. He batted it away effortlessly.

"Soon," he said, pulling the Gemini from her hand and kicking her hard in the face. As she lay there dazed he swung the Gemini up toward the Gate. In a whistle of noise the arrow plunged into his temple and out the other side. In a brilliant, devastating explosion Lihatiel's head turned to mist.

His body collapsed, disappearing. The humming was over. They had made it. Anubis was kicked free slamming into the rocky wall and tumbling to the water. Cosmacrater, injured, called out to his winged savior. "We're to late get us out of here."

"Not so easy," Anubis said, with his hands on a machine gun. Bobbing in the water he fired at the two escaping. In a scream of ammunition and death they fell to their watery grave.

"What's this?" Bael screamed, trying to jerk free from Rebecca's body. She took hold of him as the dam began to collapse.

"You can't have my body," Rebecca hissed through clenched teeth. "But we can die together," she said, taking hold of him as the bricks fell.

Atone

Water poured in torrents through the inside of the dam. People ran to the highest ground possible some in the back of the group having to swim. Bryce held Aaron on his shoulders trying to sludge his way through knee-deep water. "Frankie. Here," he called holding on to a ladder leading up to the hatch. He turned back to face Frankie and saw the crushing wave of death funneling down the halls toward them. He caught her hand before she could look around and set her on the highest rung of the latter he could reach. "Go up quickly. I'll be right behind you."

Aaron clutched onto him tightly as Frankie went up. "No. no. no," he cried.

Bryce pulled him free "You have to. Get out of here," he said, looking into Aaron's surprisingly tear filled eyes. Aaron saw the same look his father and then his mother gave him trying to save him from the zombie horde. "Go."

As his hands took hold of the later and feet scurried up it, Bryce was swept away from him by the raging current.

Atone rose unsteadily to her feet on the scaffolding. Diana revealed herself at the edge. The thin red dot of her scope marked the space at the center of Atone's collarbone. She shouted over the rushing water. "I'm sorry. I can't let you destroy this world."

"I have to do this. Don't you see? It's the only way to set things right," Atone called over the raging waters. They could hear the screams of innocent lives as the water began to flood the dam itself and the people inside. "Trust me; you'll have to trust me."

"How can I do that? How can I take you at your word?" The screams from inside grew louder. Diana turned tentatively to look back at the collapsing dam.

"There is no time. Use the seal. It can save them."

"This is a trick."

"No. If we don't act soon they're all going to die," Atone yelled. Diana began to lower her gun. Then the arrow pierced through her, blood covering her clothes and marking the water near her a diluted pink. Atone staggered teetering on the edge by the gate's mouth, feeling her mother's pain. Her gaze looked down to see the phantom wound only to find a gaping hole. She was hit after all. Atone and Diana turned to face their executioner. Orion held the bow in his off hand looking past her at

Diana. Atone turned back to see her mother astonished at the attack. She held her hands out toward Atone, the tears in her eyes swept quickly away by the torrents of water.

"No, I'm sorry," Diana gasped. Atone staggered and tried to right herself. Over balanced and weak she stumbled in the portal that sucked her in like a hungry mouth. She was gone only a ripple at the gate surface to indicate her passing.

Diana drew the pyramid from her pocket. She could feel the life inside fading. Her hands shook as she fingered it, unraveling the mystery in it. In a strange way she felt it had to be this way and that she was meant to activate this device. She had the comfortable feeling that she knew now what she was here for. Looking at Orion as he ran toward her she began to shimmer in a brilliant white light making Orion cover his eyes. In a blink she was gone, the screams with her.

Frankie clawed her way free of the wreckage looking down at the carnage and the water raging underneath her. Behind her Aaron followed emotionless once more. She turned and shouted down the hole at the raging water. There was a burst of light. The people with her scrambled to the rungs of the ladder before igniting brightly then disappearing. She was about to shout down for any sign from the others when the dam buckled under her. She instead turned to Aaron. "We have to get out of here. Now! This whole place is going to fall apart." They ran along the questionable footing between the two bodies of water falling to the ground on the banks as the dam crumbled into nothing. They looked down to see the glimmer of the demon gate not phased by the destruction, debris flowing harmlessly past it. A hand pushed free from the water, taking Frankie's arm pulling itself upward. Frankie screamed trying to pull free instead only helping the attacking arm to rise from the water. In a gasp Rebecca rose.

"Rebecca." Frankie called hugging her once she reached her feet. A few footfalls sounded behind them. A shining limousine drove up, the Queen of the undead emerging. They stopped to look at her. Orion stepped out soaked to the bone, dripping water all over the seats.

"It's over now," he said, holding his hand out and motioning for them to enter the limousine. "Let's get out of here."

Chapter 39

Atone awoke to the sting of salt in her wounds. She breathed deep feeling the burning harsh pain in her lungs. Immediately she began coughing savagely. She hissed out clutching her clawed hands to her chest. Opening her eyes she saw the feet of the Order around her, standing in the salty hills of Appolyon. "Oh, yeah. I remember. Appolyon Salt Fields."

"Well, well, whatever shall we do with you?" Lihatiel chuckled, twirling Gemini around dangerously. Atone searched herself, her mind slow on the pick up that she was looted on her arrival. Lihatiel's aim was true as it swung down to decapitate her. Cosmacrater caught the swing and jerked it free from him the blade wobbling mere inches from her tender neck.

"We take her with alive and unharmed," Cosmacrater ordered. Atone looked up with the vaguest of smiles. The look he shot her stole it from her face. "We'll leave all the harming to Lord Beelzebub."

"Now strip her and bind her," he ordered. The men leered at her, clawing eagerly as they removed fragments of her tattered clothing. Several claws dug too deeply in their desire to disrobe her. Small lacerations alone covered her now. Many men kept the trophy of clothes fragments, wearing them like a badge of honor.

"Now move," Cosmacrater said, pushing her on the back. She rose guarded at all sides by thick muscular Diablonians, their minds wiped clean and operating on the simplest function to guard her. Cosmacrater followed after her daggers close to her back.

Focalar waved a hand south. "You heard the man, forward march!" In moments her broken bones were bound and they carted her off toward Assaih.

"You don't want to be stopping me. There is something I have to do. The Order wants forgiveness. I can get that if you just let me go. The world is never going to get bett…" She tried to explain before being interrupted by Cosmacrater.

"Enough talk."

"Cosmacrater you have to…"

"I can very easily revoke my untouched policy. Do you care to continue?" Cosmacrater inquired. She stopped admitting defeat.

A roar was heard and Cosmacrater motioned for his men to stop. Focalar stepped up next to him without a sound. "An avalanche?"

"Harrowing beast?"

"No. Not in the salt fields."

"Then what?" Focalar asked in a whisper. The salt exploded upward. The order shielded their eyes to the burning salt. The sound of the deep, deafening wail made the braver men risk their eyes to see. Atone, unable to shield her eyes, squeezed them tight and scrambled for footing.

"A salt wyrm!" Focalar called watching the men scatter. He watched frozen for a moment taking in the horrific and awesome sight of the massive beast. The wide strong ribs where wrapped tightly in shriveled and emaciated hide. A wide mouth three men wide greeted them, smiling with jagged teeth at his prey, its head oversized to the starved and dehydrated body.

"Kill it," Cosmacrater shouted. Concolor, a low ranked soldier stared up. The mouth opened wide. He shivered. His breath drew in deep, eyes clamped shut. He felt the sting of blades puncturing his arms. He felt the wind as he rose. He couldn't take it. He screamed. A sharp alien scream echoed back at him. A scream he knew. "Poyag."

His eyes opened, stinging with salt as the strange bat like pet of Beelzebub flew high into the air. He looked down, the men below attacking. The four Diablonian guardsmen rushed forward, their boar like tusks biting deep into the beast. Their mouths shriveled tightly as the moisture was pulled from them by the salt. Focalar, his bow gone took to his sword. When the beast twisted around to swallow the Diablonians, Focalar's sword plunged deep into the eye. It swung the blind side around sending the men flying. Focalar screamed at his broken and dangling arm. His bow lay near his body where he fell.

The salt wyrm rolled using the massive body it possessed to crash down, the weight of it crushing three men to death. Lihatiel, quick on his feet, rushed over to Cosmacrater panting heavily. "They're not getting through. The hardened hide is impenetrable. It's only a matter of time before it kills us."

Concolor watched from his flying ride to see the wyrm's eye gazing up at it. The skin around the ribs tightened as it breathed deep, drinking up a large amount of the salt surrounding it. The salt sprayed upward. Concolor shielded himself. Poyag squawked bitterly, fluttering from the sudden blast. He screamed again as he collided into a dune.

"It thrives in salt," Cosmacrater ordered. His eyes turned skyward to see the darkening clouds above, the vague form of Berakas Debora above him. "Berakas Debora! Get the bastard!" Cosmacrater screamed over the wailing beast.

The massive storm formless yet powerful roared back at the beast. "There's not much for me to work with!" He boomed with a voice of thunder. He did not wait for a reply as he squeezed the moisture from his body. The water sizzled, hitting the salt treated leather hide. The salt wyrm screamed as its body softened.

"Now kill that thing," he ordered his men. They swarmed the beast, blades and fangs tearing it apart. It thrashed around sinking its teeth deep into Michedael's shoulder. His arm tore free at the shoulder as the wyrm rolled in its death throws.

Focalar rose and dusted the salt from his skin tearing his shirt into strips. He took hold of his broken arm and bound it. He took his sword and lined it along his broken arm, tying them together to use as a splint.

"Where is Atone?" Focalar asked, wincing. Poyag flew between Focalar and Cosmacrater in a black blur. A body fell from it, groaning as it hit the salt. Cosmacrater looked at the form, covered only in the white powder of their surroundings. He stepped up to her, hoisting her up to her feet. Poyag screeched in response to Cosmacrater's question.

"Now that wasn't very smart, Atone," Cosmacrater said, calmly. "You've already destroyed what little amount of trust you've managed to establish."

"We should kill her now and avoid any more chances of escape," Lihatiel demanded. A few of the demons among them shouted their agreements. One even went so far as to rush forward to attack. A dagger sunk into the fleshy meat of the palm and he recoiled from Cosmacrater's strike.

"No," he said, looking at the men. He looked forward to see the ridges of the salt wyrm's ribs rising up behind them. "Form a circle around the beast."

As the order moved to obey Cosmacrater, he turned to face Atone. "Atone, what you did was bad. I want you to pay. I also want you to realize that I alone keep these men from killing you and worse. You will be taught a lesson." He handed her a dagger and nudged her toward the circle and the beast within. Still leaving her tied. "Cut free one of the ribs. This will be your punishment."

She looked back only to be struck and roll toward the remains. The rainwater was already absorbed by the salt. Her hands still tied behind her back, she turned to face the crowd, the beast behind her. She sunk the dagger into the flesh when the first crack of the whip cut the flesh above her right breast. She screamed but quickly regained her composure.

Another crack of the whip stung the tender flesh of her left. By the third, the underside of her thigh began to bleed. With a scream she fell to sitting on the salt. It sizzled as it sucked the water from her blood. In a moment she was back up, carving madly. Cosmacrater turned away to let the men have their fun.

Atone

"Focalar, you are in charge. Make sure they don't do anything permanent," he said, then headed south to scout the trail.

BOOK THREE: Reunion

Chapter 1

Atone awoke to a gentle rocking, her eyes resisting her will to open. The gruff voice of her captors reached her, riding on the scorching wave of heat. A sharp blow to her chest made her rocking anything but gentle. Her eyes snapped open in surprise to see Lihatiel along side her. He sneered, his eyes lost on his evil plots, most likely against her. She felt her side start to bleed and saw what he stuck her with. He coiled up Gemini around his broken body.

He opened his mouth beyond the laws of nature but Cosmacrater, somewhere near her feet barked an order for him. His wide monstrous mouth reduced to normal and he reached out to press against her now opened side. She winced as she felt her cracked rib break.

"I have no intention of letting you reach Beelzebub, Atone. Justice will be mine."

"Lihatiel, don't make me tell you again," Cosmacrater ordered.

"Soon, Atone," he said, falling back to join his superiors. Atone looked from her entwined imprisonment to see the order guards carrying her by the long hard rib of the salt wyrm. Lihatiel's talents where unmistakable, the coarse swine like Diablonians set mindlessly to their mission of leading her to her fate. She cast her eyes down sympathetically shedding a tear for them. With Lihatiel's talent for eating the minds of others the swine were beyond feeling. The Order thought it best seeing the Diablonians as only feeling hatred and thinking of torture, which is why it puzzled her that only some Diablonians were so affected. Looking out to what little of the crowd she could see she found four Diablonians unhindered by the lack of a mind. Perhaps the Orders policies were in question since the trip top side, she thought. Her guards could feel nothing and think of nothing. She tested the ropes and winced as they cut into her wrists. Her hands were tied together, with the massive pole between them. The few moments of earth life made it that much harder on her to return to the sweltering heat, and savage terrain. She tried to look behind her, where the majority of her captors were, but found it hard to see around her own body. Her legs, tied like her hands, blocked most of the view but she saw the booming storm and the cloud formed body of Berakas Debora. She could make out Cosmacrater and… Lillith? She thought. She thought also of calling to her friend but if she was a captive she didn't want to make it worse on her.

Weaponless, immobilized and surrounded she could only think of a way to pull off another escape. She thought about just letting them take her to Beelzebub. He was always reasonable especially since he had a hard time distinguishing lies and truths, not an easy thing to do in the realm of lies and with her empathy curse she should be able to manipulate the situation.

But Beelzebub wasn't known to allow error and betrayal, both of which Lihatiel probably filled him in on. Regardless how much she may have reason to rise against him, Lihatiel was her superior. She looked around disoriented at first by the upside down world she now found herself a part of. They were passing the ruins of the Fortress of Sheol. This meant that there was much more ground between here and Beelzebub's massive Palace, giving her weeks to think.

As night approached the demon hunting party drew to a halt. A burned building foundation, unable to completely stop smoking in the intense heat served as their base for the darkest hours. Atone was set down by a crackling purple light. It took her a moment to realize where she was. A massive bat like creature the order called Poyag, landed near her flipping the sign and she saw the word 'As--dius's' facing her, the 'mo' blackened and dark and the 'As' flickering.

"The rocky foundation and remaining stone pillars will make a good perimeter for camp. Everyone set up," Cosmacrater ordered. Lihatiel looked over, still scheming. He watched as Cosmacrater talked to Focalar, which then instructed the mind wiped boars to put Atone into the dog kennels that for one reason or another survived the fire they left the last time they were here. Cosmacrater again spoke up as the other demons readied camp. "Our prize will be in the dog kennel. I want four teams, two on and two off. The two teams on will take turns guarding the kennel and searching perimeter. The two off will…"

Lihatiel watched as the teams unfolded, waiting to see who would join his. The names were called and he found himself in charge of one. Michedael, one of the Diablonians with leathery bat wings and large ears of the bat added to the boar like features was in his team along with Concolor, a pale order member with thin needle like teeth and long black hair and Berakas Debora the living storm. Berakas he knew well enough. A former angel of wind, like Carmichael, he wasn't nearly as talented. He did have a skill that Carmichael seemed to lack that of weather control. Always looking for unusual advantages the storm cloud body made him both powerful and weak. Lihatiel shook his head thinking to himself about the foolery of others. Not having a body was quite a benefit here, though many craved to have a substantial form. Maybe he could use that, he thought.

He stopped thinking of his own men and looked at the leaders of the other teams. Of course there was Cosmacrater and Focalar, the fourth being led by Lillith. The team working on the same shift as Lihatiel was Focalar. This was a foolish move on Cosmacrater's part. Lillith was not very popular with the men, gaining such a high rank in such a short time. Lihatiel gave a grimace as Lillith passed by to find her soldiers.

His mind went back to Focalar since he would be the biggest obstacle to his plot. I will simply have to find a way, he thought to himself. If Atone was allowed to return she would twist Beelzebub's ear to get off this. Knowing her she would probably make it even worse by making him seem like the evil one. This matter was simple, he thought, she would have to die.

Atone

Lihatiel came to the first step of his plot and moved over to the Diablonians where Michedael lingered with his colleagues. He extended his emaciated hand to the Diablonian.

"Looks like we are both on watch together," he said, as Michedael eyed him wearily. His voice wormed its way deep into his ear. Michedael grunted a bare minimal acknowledgement to his presence. Lihatiel looked out toward the darkening horizon as the other Diablonians filtered off. He pretended not to note the dismissive tone. "It's a shame really. Marching you all to your doom like this."

There was a deep breath span for silence before Michedael spoke. "What are you saying, Friend?"

"Nothing, nothing…" Lihatiel stated then slowly, continued, "It's not like you can do anything about it since they divided you all up. It's not like you are going to fight us three to one."

"Do anything about what?" Michedael eyed Concolor and Berakas as they grew near. Lihatiel saw them also and quickened his conversation.

"Well we are going to the order's territory. What would they do to you there?"

"But we work with Cosmacrater now."

"On Earth the deal was to work with each other. That is true, but we are not on Earth anymore. And think about it. He took three of your best men and sent them on a fool's errand. This tipped the balance of power even greater into his control. Now you are going blindly to your death? I just think that's sad. Really." Concolor set one meaty claw atop the hard stone ridge pulling himself up to the hill overlooking the camp. Time was dwindling quickly. Lihatiel spoke no more but Michedael's reply confirmed that his devious words were hitting home.

"What would we be able to do? As you say we are outnumbered and each one of us Diablonians are on different teams."

"Organize somehow. That's what I would do."

"But Focalar... What he did to Zalzion."

"Cosmacrater is a man that saves his face from his men. He wouldn't deny you if you spoke diplomatically in front of his men. If you explain your concerns and provide a reason to escape your fate he couldn't let you down. Not while even now you are under his protection. Of course there is a chance it wouldn't work but it's the only option I see for you."

"But I am not diplomatic. I am a simple scout," Michedael confessed. Lihatiel snorted a restrained laugh.

"That's too bad. I used to lead an entire battalion of men before the battle of the Sheol fortress. Diplomacy was crucial for that task let me tell you," Lihatiel led him on, waiting for Michedael to take the bait. Concolor and Berakas took their place within the team. "Good, we are all here. Let's start this slow dance."

As they began their patrol Michedael leaned next to the zombiefied ear of Lihatiel. "Would you help us be diplomatic?"

"I'm sure we could work out something, positive in fact," Lihatiel said, with a sickly over wide grin. Phase 1 was near completion.

Chapter 2

"And that is why we no longer feel obligated or comfortable following you. We bare no malice and hope that we may part on good terms," Michedael finished looking nervously through the crowd to find Lihatiel. Cosmacrater's voice drew his attention back before he could locate his advocate.

"Well I regret your choices though you are certainly allowed to make them. No doubt you feel that your concerns are genuine." He paused, thinking. Lihatiel couldn't help but smile. Cosmacrater looked at Focalar who had his bow ready, and then to Lillith who rhythmically wobbled back and forth to her own music. She turned and smiled at him oblivious to the events at hand. He turned his attention back to Focalar and shook his head in the negative. "Permission granted. It was a pleasure working with you. I certainly wish you the best that this place has to offer and the guarantee that no one will hinder your leaving. I promise you."

"Thank you, Sir." Michedael bowed. Lihatiel found himself near Concolor and watched. The least understood in his team he waited for some sign or clue to what he could use against him. It was not long for an exploitable trait to be found.

"We will move out within the hour. Focalar, Lillith with me," he said, drawing the inner circle, minus Lihatiel, into his tent.

"What makes her so great?" He breathed deceptively to himself, loud enough for only Concolor to hear. Lihatiel knew his look well.

"What did you say?" he asked, turning with cautious skeptical eyes.

"Nothing, nothing at all, Concolor," Lihatiel said, timidly. The assembly dissembled to tear down the camp's series of tents. Lihatiel's tent was near to Concolor not unintentionally. Lihatiel shifted his mood shedding the old like a serpent skin. He put on his best jester's smile "So how long have you been in the outfit?"

"Eighty years or so," Concolor reported with pride. "472 years I've been with Beelzebub and the order."

"That's a long time," Lihatiel said, with mock interest. "600 rounded down for me. Though I've only been with you guys recently." Lihatiel kept the conversation merry, waiting for the time to twist it to his will. Concolor surprised him by twisting it first.

"That's what I don't get. Cosmacrater's a decent guy by and by, and yet a neonate like Lillith gets into the inner circle. What gives?"

"I hear you, Buddy," Lihatiel said, finishing the folding of his simple tent and daydreaming of the time he had an entire castle to his control. "I wonder how many of us feel the same way."

"No one is willing to do anything about it. They are all afraid of Focalar. He doesn't waver from Cosmacrater's will."

"Well Focalar is on the same watch shift as us. Do you think he would listen to reason?"

"Not at all." Concolor finished packing his rucksack and slung it over his shoulder in silence. He looked over at Lihatiel and saw him deep in thought. "What's up?"

"Just thinking," Lihatiel said, letting his guise slip. This quickly came to his attention and he smiled back falsely to Concolor.

"Plotting if I've heard of you correctly," Concolor grimaced.

"Sometimes it's the best, the only way, to improve your situation."

"I don't want any part of it, whatever it is," he said. Hearing the order to march they began to navigate toward the bulk of the Order's masses.

"You said yourself what Cosmacrater's done isn't right." Lihatiel argued upset that he was so quickly banned before his plan was ever addressed.

"Still…"

"Who better to change things for the better than us?" Lihatiel teased Concolor's already wavering judgment.

"But Focalar..."

"Hence the plotting. We can't go against Cosmacrater head on. This would be a delicate plan if we're ever going to improve things around here without anyone getting hurt."

"No one gets hurt?" Concolor asked, in disbelief.

"Well, maybe Lillith… and Atone but they are an outsider and a traitor. Sacrificing them would be worth it."

"Still, I don't think this scheme of yours is the right thing to do."

"Not like you've heard it yet but it isn't," Lihatiel confided. "But what power do you have over the situation right now? We get told to do bad, despicable things all the time from higher up the chain. But if you were higher up then some good could be done," Lihatiel explained. He would sweat if he could. If he let Concolor slip from his mischievous clutches then it would not only be over for his plots but his pathetic life as well. One whisper to Cosmacrater and it would be his undoing. He looked over at him and they locked gazes. Concolor broke his gaze to look around. No one seemed interested that they were to the side of the marching order rather than in it, nor did anyone seem aware of their discussion. He returned to Lihatiel.

"And no one gets hurt?"

"Not a single, loyal order member."

"What did you have in mind?" Concolor said, as the storm cloud built over them. It

settled over them stopping just overhead.
Lihatiel looked up to see Berakas Debora's half
formed body, the corrosive, corruptive drops of
rain dripping down from him onto Lihatiel and
Concolor. The cloud looked down at him
rumbling in laughter at Lihatiel's surprised look.
Its mouth opened making Lihatiel cower in fear.

"You foolish schemer, Lihatiel,
whatever shall we do about this?"

Chapter 3

The course, thorn laced ropes dug deep into Atone's wrists and forelegs making blood soak them and make her slip within them. This only helped in cutting her own flesh more and she struggled with the tears forcing them to stay within her eyes. Seeing from this blurred scope she watched from the mouth of the cave, an unnerving sense of dread worming its way into her skin. She remembered the last time she was here. It was the last time she saw Axael, dead and imprisoned in a savage living vineyard. The thought of him made the tears start to fall and she sniffled, unable to dry her eyes. She let them fall even welcomed the pain from the thorn lined rope, in some way sharing the pain that he suffered when he died here.

Her brainless boar faced guardsmen heard Cosmacrater's orders and dropped her thoughtlessly and uncaringly to the ground with a loud thud. The scorched and jagged stones dug into her back tearing up her naked, exposed flesh. Her tears and blood made the thick layer of ash around the sharp spikes of stone teeth turn to a thick grey/pink paste. The pain and blood loss made her mind began to swim. Focalar rushed over and checked her quickly and carefully freeing her from the harsh earth that bit into her.

"Careful, Lummox," Focalar hissed inspecting her body like a skilled mortician performing an autopsy. "Cosmacrater wants her back in one piece." He held a finger up in front of the boar man's face to make sure he understood. His other hand forcefully restrained its head to focus on the one raised finger. "One."

Atone knew what he was feeling and it was anything but mercy and compassion. Still the gentle touch cleaning her wounds was a small comfort. In the haze of her blood loss her mind faded to a more peaceful time on a flowered garden. A gentle, warm breeze ruffled her dress and pushed her lightly over as she flowed with it. She looked through the Brown Eyed Suzanne's and the wild grown Snap Dragons, to watch Bast sun bathing on a large marble stone a hawthorn bush shading her face. A marching troop of Houris led a band of newly released souls through the garden in a tour showing the lay of the land. There she saw Zopheal with a young charge, Axael. They were so beautiful, the Houris. They were the angelic beauties whose job dwelt on the satisfaction of the newly arrived souls though some say they were the spies of God to, using their shape shifting gifts to go places a normal angel couldn't. They entertained, skilled in the arts of romance and music, playful games and other social niceties. They are even taught the arts of seduction and carnal fulfillment. She prowled toward them imitating Bast as she had so many times before when Ptah stepped lightly on her delicately arched back.

"Hey, Ptah… master. What are you doing?"

"Shouldn't you answer that question, Little one?"

"I want to see the Houris. They are so exotic. Strange. I find them interesting. What are they doing with the dead below? Could I do that?"

"Do not concern yourselves with them…"

"But…" Atone huffed.

"Their way is not ours, sweet one of God. Angels are not to love each other that way."

"But why? Are we not the same? Why can they with the dead?"

"Because the dead are compatible in tool only. There is no release. Besides…" He smiled letting her up. "They are Houris. We do not sleep with the dead. Do not dwell on tainting yourself in this way. Get back to your practices."

"What are we learning about today?" she asked, smiling wide to match Ptah's grin as he smiled from her words. "Is it fun?"

"Perhaps. Look over there. I think Bast has relaxed for quite long enough…" he said.

Axael heard the disturbance, looking up from the caravan to see the Akia playing a little prank on each other, or rather the reaction that resulted from one. He saw the souls of old and young alike all in awe of him. Wanting him for companionship. An old woman's grandson, a youth's best friend. Whatever they wanted. But he didn't feel right. It wasn't right to lie to them. Their loved ones were not here. They would never be here. Heaven would not be so sweet without them, and the lie remained. Zopheal took to the lie well. Zopheal lost himself in other people's memories of who he should be many times and Axael used this opportunity to leave.

Atone

"Gregory, Gregory where are you going?"

"I'm not Gregory, Linda. I'm not your little boy. Sorry for deceiving you but I think the truth will hurt you less in the end. He was a rotten kid that did many evil things but your devotion to him was blinding. He will never rest his head in our plentiful fields or eat in our glorious banquet halls. I am sorry for him, but not for you who lived the righteous life of love and mercy," he said. The old lady's lip began to quiver, her eyes tearing up. With a crack her aged hand struck harshly across his jaw making his youthful boyish neck twist sharply to the left. Turning back to face her, his eyes were unchanged. "Go in peace and enjoy the bounty that is for the righteous." Then he turned, wings growing and took flight.

"When you get down here little sparrow I will eat you," Bast growled with a sinister smile. Atone was almost convinced that the threat was in jest. Still she wasn't leaving the grand Oak. Ptah, too busy laughing in his plot to aid her or talk Bast down was of no use to her now. Bast stalked around the base of her tree.

"Come up here then if you are so eager for a meal."

"So you can fly away, little sparrow? I may get distracted in my climbing and fail to see where you take refuge."

"All talk, Bast."

"I'll think of something," she purred, prowling again the base of the tree. Atone leaned back relaxing. She almost dozed off when the leaves began to shudder.

"What the Hell is that thing?" growled Concolor falling back with the rest of his unit. Focalar gave cover with a new bow procured by one of the lesser officers. Poyag and Cosmacrater tried to pull Atone free from the massive plant, so that they could join the rest of the company in safety. Poyag's razor claws cut the vines free making room for twice the amount to take hold again. Cosmacrater took hold of the bone rib trying to wrestle it away. This proved even more foolish as the vines twisted around him.

"Cosmacrater!" Focalar shouted trying to take aim as he disappeared in the mass. He dared not take a shot and ordered the remaining men to retreat. Poyag could not take flight in time and was bound fast, his more fragile bat like bones crackling loudly as the vines broke them apart. "Fall back. Retreat. Let the beast take the day before we all die. Lillith get away from there."

Focalar rushed her, scooping her up in one arm, jabbing the plant with a single arrow in his free hand to buy them some precious seconds. From a safe vantage he watched as the beast absorbed Atone, the boar men grunts and their captain Cosmacrater, taking them into their new cavernous tomb. Focalar lowered Lillith down bowing his head to the death of his master. Lillith seized his leg desperate for his compassionate touch again. He raised his bow in honor firing a stray arrow high overhead signaling a respectful silence from the crowd.

Atone looked over to the rattling leaves of the majestic oak as it stopped. Sliding farther along the limb she looked back once more to the stillness. Looking down she saw no sign of Bast. Atone slithered even farther from the base of the tree sweat beginning to bead up on her delicate tanned skin. "Bast, look it was Ptah's idea, really. I just…"

"It's O.K.," the voice came from the tree leaves but it wasn't of Bast. It parted only enough to show the nervous visage of a young boy.

"What are you doing here?" she asked, lowering her voice to a whisper concealed by a wind rattled collection of leaves. He dared to emerge from his hiding space enough to get close to her. For her part she returned toward the closeness of the sturdy trunk. "Ptah says I'm not to be with you. That it is not the Akia way to love. How can it be your way then if we are both angels?"

"You are an Akia. Of all Gods creations you most assuredly need love, wouldn't you?" he asked, leaning into her. Then realizing his place he slipped back. "I mean you create all that is, how can you do so without love?"

"They are things. What does love have to do with it?"

"Love… Are you simple?" he asked, crunching up his face in his best attempt at anger. "Do you not feel anything for what you have made?"

"I feel gratitude. Satisfaction and I want the best things for them. I feel sad when I see what the humans do to them. But not love."

"Couldn't that be called love? That's what love is."

"But Ptah says it is foolish to love because some day you will watch them all wither away and die. Everything fades to dust, the dooms day watchers see to it. So what's the point?" she asked. She could feel his emotions but they were so alien to her that she felt heady and lost. She found a single emotional strain within them and she picked at it. She focused on it alone as he tried to find a way to explain it. She felt pity in him pity for her and she grew angry.

"Why do you feel this for me? Why does your heart beat with sympathy pains for my well-being? You are feeling incorrectly, Sir."

"Axael. And I feel. There is no denying it. How can you live without love? What enjoyment can there be without it."

"I can live just fine. How come you make it seem so important?" she asked, spreading her wings. "Your strange, Axael. Ptah was right about your kind. Good day," she said, flapping her wings and taking flight. From the air she heard the faintest whisper blown words on the wind.

"I will teach you of love and then you will understand."

Atone

Cosmacrater's skin grew harder, resisting the vicious vines attempts to strangle. A tremor began to shake deep within him and his skin crackled and broke. The newly thickened stone like skin expelled outward tearing the plant to lifeless patches in a ground-shattering explosion. The Cave mouth blasted outward, adding its own stones to the mix. Cosmacrater's men scrambled for refuge as the burning stones plummeted down.

"Cosmacrater," Focalar called over the crashing of stones. "Please tell me this is your doing." Focalar drew an arrow and readied for attack. The dust and smoke settled to show a burning bush charging out toward him. His fletching was pulled to his ear in a moment ready to fire when the plant stumbled and collapsed. Cosmacrater tossed the remaining plant aside, fingering the rapidly healing wounds on his skin. He eyed Focalar and his ready arrow.

"I wouldn't recommend it, my friend," he said, sternly and the weapon was at once eased.

"Cosmacrater. You survived I thought for surely."

"No time. We make camp here. Check on Atone. Now."

"At once," he replied entering the cave. He found Atone strewn aside with savage burn marks and twisting vines tangled around her. "Hang in there Atone. We want you alive."

As he studied the body he found bone scattered across the cavern floor. Even with his untrained senses he could feel the righteousness radiating from them. He checked Atone curiously for any missing parts. "Their not yours," he uttered in her general direction. He heard Lihatiel stepping up behind him, felt the Gemini ready in his hand. Lihatiel was three paces away and getting closer. Focalar pivoted the bow and arrow, the point trained in an instant on Lihatiel's throat ready to fire.

"Look for the rest of these bones. Set them up in a pile over there then inform Cosmacrater. Quickly, before night fall," he said, ignoring Lihatiel's confused and cowering form to attend to his patient. Listening to Atone mutter in her own twisted dreams as he worked he shivered.

"Axael. You will teach me love… but in love there is sacrifice. The end of love… Death," she rambled on and an unfamiliar and

Atone

nervous tingle made him look again at the pile
of bones assembling.

Chapter: 4

Cosmacrater sat on an ornate if simple chair carved from stained bone. A map lay spread out across a matching table with a trail of hatch marks marking their progress. By the X's on the map only 2 camps remained counting their stay at the cave mouth before they would reach the massive chitin palace of flies.

Cosmacrater looked up at the movement of Concolor twitching. "What is your concern, Concolor?" He said, impatiently making the lesser demon shriek just with the infliction in his voice. Concolor babbled for a moment before forming words that Cosmacrater could understand.

"It's the men, Sir. Rumors are starting."

"Rumors? Of what?" He grumbled, agitated.

"A possible deception," Concolor continued the words Lihatiel fed to him.

"By who?"

"By you, Sir. You and the new comer, Lillith."

"That's absurd," Cosmacrater scoffed, motioning him away and returning to his maps. When he didn't hear the flap to his tent rise and fall he looked up. His angry retaliation was muted by the seriousness in the lesser demon's features, even as he stood there shaking.

"That may be but they still talk and they have their reasons to," Concolor continued his conviction growing.

"Namely?"

"Well…" Concolor stammered. "Like who she is, Sir. She is a friend of the prisoner and this combined with the fact that she only recently joined us and already leads a unit."

"She's been given the better soldiers for a reason," Cosmacrater announced then muttered a confession under his breath. "Besides there's not really any uses for her outside the bedroom."

"But they speak of this as well. She has the best men. They wonder why." He trembled readying his final plot. "The other half may know the reasons, Cosmacrater, but our side does not. They are forced to make guesses with their conspiring minds. Accusations. Since your unit and hers are never apart it makes the camp seem separated."

"So what do you suggest?"

"Mix up the units," Concolor said, after a sufficient pause to warrant spontaneity. "You could watch one night with our unit. While Focalar watches Lillith."

"Break up the alleged conspirators," Cosmacrater said, growing quiet. Lihatiel entered bringing in the bones of Axael. Lihatiel looked over and seemed surprised.

"Concolor? Aren't we on duty soon, why aren't you ready?"

"Silence, Lihatiel. Concolor and I are discussing the trip back. Ready the others and take your place."

"Of course, Sir," he said, watching him angrily as he left. When he was confident that Lihatiel was not in earshot he snapped his eyes to Concolor. "This sounds like a wise decision. Thank you for the heads up. There are two nights left before arriving at the Fortress of Flies. Tonight I will watch with Lihatiel. Tomorrow Lillith will. This seems best. Inform your unit leader and send Focalar in. I have some other things to discuss."

Concolor slithered from the room instantly. Focalar was not hard to find, supervising Atone's imprisonment. Concolor told him of Cosmacrater's orders before returning to Lihatiel's side.

Focalar felt the eyes on him as he entered the tent and turned to glare at Concolor who darted his eyes elsewhere. With a harsh snort of air he entered.

"It's done. Tomorrow night we will have our chance," Concolor said, afraid of being overheard. Lihatiel glanced nervously to Atone who still slumbered, lost in dream.

"Tomorrow? Why not tonight? We are running out of time."

"I couldn't force the issue. I think he was already getting suspicious. Are you sure it has to be this way? This is the only way your scheming can find?"

"Our scheming. And yes. It has to be. Tomorrow night we will set things right. Now look watchful damn it." Lihatiel sighed deeply,

taking a deep breath and then hissing the air out.
"She's slept enough. Time to wake her."

With a savage blow to a wound to her
side, Atone surged violently.

Chapter: 5

Lihatiel watched from the sandy dune. Behind him was the jagged, hungry mountain range containing the massive cavern system they left behind several hours ago? Here the heat was far worse than the fortress of Sheol or the Appolyon salt fields. The sweat beads from his body had long since evaporated away the last of his moisture leaving him a thirsty husk, marching through a field of similarly dried husks. Even Berakas with his stormy body looked shriveled and weak. The meager rain he managed to summon dissipated before even touching the ground. Now there was barely a cloud to sustain him.

Lihatiel watched Focalar scouting through the sandy terrain to find a safe place to set up camp. Here everything starved even the land itself. There was always the fear of being sucked down into its depth and drained for what little remained within from the outside world. Even safe rock outcroppings turned out to be giant beetles or alien stone goliaths ready to crush you. There were no oasis, no plant protected watering holes, only dead heat as far as the eye could see. From here these eyes could see the massive shell of an insect, bent and formed to become the castle they hurried to. The Fortress of Flies. A massive structure from here in one day's hard marching they would actually be at its gate. Looking at the lay out of their surroundings and seeing the O.K. from Cosmacrater, Lihatiel had to agree that this was the best place to camp. Lihatiel took to his marching watching where Lillith put Atone for safekeeping. Atone was snuggly settled into a rocky crag outcropping overlooking the bulk of the camp that lay in a deep valley. 3 hours into his march the rustle and bustle of the men in the valley died down. An hour later Lihatiel and his men grew closer to his goals. By the time they realized it there would be no time to stop it. Atone would be dead and he would be on top once more.

Lillith camped with the prisoner, babbling on and on about all the cute guys like a giddy schoolgirl. Atone tried in vain to keep Lillith's attention long enough to convince her into helping her escape. The other guard, since Poyag's untimely and most beneficial death, was a demon by the name Garson. A long time enemy of Asmodius's affiliates he was all too happy to join their ranks when Cosmacrater told them about the traitor and that Asmodius was involved. Only by circumstance he received his revenge. Lihatiel thought about this. If only he had given him more consideration when he first met Garson there may have been some way to manipulate him.

This was decided against watching how fondly he worked with Lillith. Lihatiel gave one last look down to the encampment. Berakas Debora floated up behind him. Lihatiel didn't bother to turn around. "We take out Garson."

"Are you sure this is the only way?" Concolor addressed from the side startling Lihatiel. He cursed his nerves before replying.

"Now is not the time, Concolor. We strike now before it's too late."

"Right," he said, unconvinced. "Of course."

They slithered from their roost on the dune to head to the rocky crag.

"Ho there!" Garson boomed, his voice powerful but slurred by orc-like tusks protruding from his lower jaw. His thick muscled arms entwined around each other over his broad barrel chest. "Oh, you guys!" Stubby workman fingers scratched at the thick bristles that grew from the green skin on the back of his arm.

"Yes, it's just us." Lihatiel slithered smoothly. "All clear on our end. You?"

"Prisoner's still here. I think Lillith's been torturing her a little though."

"No harm there," Lihatiel chuckled working diligently to keep him talking. Concolor headed around him. In a flurry of motion Garson struck. Concolor let out a shriek from the shadows dropping his sword as a razor edged quill dug into his throat. Concolor held it, trying to stop the bleeding it caused. His skin began to form spider web cracks his mortal seeming flaking away.

"What treachery is this?" Garson yelled waving a quill lined arm at Lihatiel.

"I had nothing to do with this. I swear," Lihatiel pleaded tossing everything down and prostrating himself. It was a gesture he knew well. It was a gesture he found the most revolting act. Garson noted the pitiful creature and turned to deal with the traitor Concolor. No sooner than Lihatiel attacked.

Drawing the Gemini from the ground he leaped at Garson. Then the earth began to moan. Lihatiel fell to the ground his head toppling from his shoulders. It landed propped to gaze down at the horrors that befell the camp in the valley. A great sucking maw drew in the sand. The men scrambled toward the rocks for safety. He heard Concolor's scream of agony but couldn't turn to face him. His headless body crawled after his head blindly. Garson cleaned his blade laughing at the spectacle. A bolt of lightning resounded behind Lihatiel as his hands found his head.

"You will have to do better than that, Storm creature," Garson roared.

"I will." The desert wind sucking downward lashed at their clothes pulling Berakas from his mark. A steady stream of electricity crackled the earth next to Garson sending shards of glass sand scattering into him. Garson coughed breathing in the sand and staggered to safety. He tumbled unsteadily over into the hungry earth. Berakas fought against the wind using his own in an attempt to save himself. Lihatiel held fast to his head angling it to see Lillith and Atone held safely in the stone.

"The men are coming, Lihatiel," Berakas called before he slipped and got sucked farther. Concolor, soul fusing a new seeming took refuge quickly, his body textured by the sand and glass.

"Berakas, we must go after Lillith. Quickly," Lihatiel called even as the cloud was sucked away. He looked back to see Concolor crawling in his torment toward them. Lihatiel felt the sand storm grow more intense. Lillith and Atone seemed so deceptively close but it seemed ages before he could reach them, fighting the sand as it swallowed itself. He caught Concolor and shoved him back nearly sending him over the edge. "Go and stall the others, I will finish things here."

"What's going on?" Lillith said, walking freely in the savage wind as if in a gentle breeze. Lihatiel studied her. He must strike now.

The sucking force and downward pulling wind disappeared, the sudden absence sent him fall to the ground. Lillith laughed at him, his head rolling toward her. She scooped it up and looked at him. "Do you want to play with us?"

"Indeed I do, my dear." He smiled as his jaw distended. With a vicious intake of air he felt her soul and struggled to suck it free from its shell. He felt her tears, her body shivering in an attempt to keep it. Lillith shrieked collapsing to the ground in a heap.

His head rolled to see the survivors talking to Concolor. There would be no time for error as he saw the swift punishment. Concolor hit the ground and was tethered just as quickly. Lihatiel's undying hands worked busily to tie up Lillith just to be convincing before it grabbed his head and rushed over to Atone returning Gemini to his hand.

"Get your hands off me, you bastard!" She hissed. Struggling as his hands worked with the ropes around her arms and legs. He looked back to see Focalar advancing. He liberated one arm. Good, he thought, now the rest of her.

"Look. We are in a lot of trouble. I'm willing to let bygones be bygones to save my hide."

"Bygones, You devoured my mind and made me your slave. Don't act like…"

"Yes, I'm a villain. I have no problem with that. If saving you means saving me than I'm all for it. Get over it."

"What's your deal? Afraid of what I might say?"

"I heard you mumbling about your angel, Atone. I believe what you said about destiny. And when we found that angel body…"

"What angel body?"

"The one we found at the crossroads. At the mouth of the cave."

"Axael? You found him?"

"Found him and left him. But I remember what you said when we captured you. Now I'm giving you a chance to follow through."

She fell to the ground as the last leg was freed. She studied him quizzically before seeing Focalar coming up. She went to speak when Lihatiel pushed her aside. "There is no time. Go get out of here."

Focalar was distracted, studying Lillith's motionless shell. Taking hold of Gemini she cracked the blade down using the tension to propel herself upward. Rocketing through the air she bought herself some distance to the cursing of Lihatiel. She saw Focalar ready his bow when Cosmacrater stopped him. From the air she saw what remained of the army. Aside from Lihatiel, Focalar, Cosmacrater and Lillith, only one other remained.

Lihatiel smiled his most evil smile as Focalar approached. Everything was falling into place, even after the disaster. Lihatiel forced his face to remain serious, even wretched, as he walked back toward Focalar and the husk of Lillith.

"Lihatiel, Explain yourself!" Focalar demanded. Concolor was dragged along at his feet, thumping along the rocks. He was about to speak when Lillith's mindless blank state looked back at him eagerly and began rocking back and forth repeating the word helpless over and over again. He knew she shouldn't be able to do anything. His confidence quickly dissipated leaving him with a bumbling rambling in an attempt to restore the odds he thought he had.

"Lillith was trying to help the prisoner escape. As we were passing by we noticed and tried to stop it."

Lillith erupted from her repeating to blurt out violently. "Hello. I'm all tied up. This is the part where you fuck me."

"IS this true, Lillith. What Lihatiel said, that is?"

"Not really." She fussed trying to remove her clothing while tied. Focalar stepped inches from her face, forcing her eyes to only see him in an attempt to reign in her stray thoughts.

"Focus, Lillith."

"He was the one who was trying to save her," she explained. "I couldn't stop them in time. Forgive me. Please don't beat me," she pleaded, her posturing suggesting her desire for the opposite. She got a strange look from Focalar for her efforts.

"How typical a deception. Of course she's going to try to blame me. But think, Focalar. Why would I save her? She's her friend. I was slain by her. Who has a better reason to help her here?" Cosmacrater stepped up toward the rest of the group taking all four by surprise.

"Where will she be, Lihatiel?" Cosmacrater commanded, his skin taking on a cracked earth pattern.

"Cosmacrater I swear I did nothing… or are you so blinded with lust for her…"

"Silence, Lihatiel. I've known of your plot since the capture. I'm surprised you hadn't noticed," he said, throwing an object from a sack to the ground in front of him. Lihatiel dared to remove his gaze from his master long enough to see what it was. The decapitated head of Michedael stared lifelessly from the ground. "His punishment will be more severe when we return home. Death is not an option for him or for you. Now speak."

Lihatiel felt the tip of an arrow at his temple and his own will crack. He returned his eyes to Cosmacrater's with a grim smile. "How did you do this, Lillith? How did you reject my mastery of undoing? Very well. I'll talk."

Chapter: 6

Atone used the springing ability of Gemini to gain as much ground as she could stomach. Soon she would be up the dangerous stone rock face to plunge into the depths. If she could just find Axael's bones and enter Sheol before Cosmacrater can reach her she would be safe. This would be a huge if. She looked down from her perch to see what remained of Cosmacrater's forces beginning their treacherous climb. She quickly looked away instead focusing on the rough mountain she perched upon. She nursed her shoulder, a deep red welt began to swell and turn purple where Gemini cracked against her skin. She held Gemini, still quivering from the last hard impact, and looked up to the remaining climb. Her thin barbed claws began to dig their way into the rock and climb slowly upward. Her thoughts drifted to what started it all. Find Axael and return him to Zopheal. How hard could it have been, Hmmm? she asked herself. How quickly it all got out of hand. She thought about what Heinrich said, remembering when he asked her why she wanted to warn God. This started as a simple search and rescue and escalated to a cosmic conspiracy with her as the number one pawn. She thought about apocalypse and if what she started ended with her returning to this place. Maybe it would be better to just stay here and leave the rest of the world to its own end.

She ended her thought as she reached the mouth of the cave. She looked down to find her pursuers having trouble at the base of the mountain. This was good. It might even give her enough time to sort everything out. Wasting no more time on thinking she turned and darted into the cave.

Meanwhile, several yards straight down Cosmacrater and his men made their way. Tedious fingers worked diligently, seeking out the safest way to climb. There progress was constantly hindered by the always-hazardous footing and loose stone. Twice now he fell several yards and a third threatened to be soon in coming.

"Easy, Concolor. That edge looks tricky," Cosmacrater advised.

"I've got it," he replied undaunted. The sound of his voice was enough to make the stones pull free. His screams where masked by the cascading stones, his body churned to bloody scraps by the rocks falling with him. Soon his body twisted unrestrained through the air bouncing with a slosh across the jagged rocks below, coating the rock face and the sand at the foot of the cliff a rich, dark red.

Cosmacrater cursed silently to himself looking over at who remained. Lihatiel was in the lead and Lillith following Cosmacrater. Focalar was ahead of Cosmacrater by an arms length. Cosmacrater surveyed the best course of action when he saw the massive builder falling toward them all. It fell in silent ambush breaking free and succeeding in avoiding a warning bounce. Lihatiel and Focalar didn't see it. His voice range out quickly, the boulder growing in size as it grew ever closer. "Lihatiel, look out!" He called grabbing Focalar and pulling him from the rock face and into the relative safety out of the car sized stone's path.

He heard the impact of stone hitting stone with flesh and bone in between and knew without looking that Lihatiel was too late. Focalar dangled helplessly from Cosmacrater's grasp as the mammoth stone rolled by. Focalar looked up at his captor.

"You saved my…" Focalar's words were cut short as the massive boulder rolled back up the mountain crushing him. Crater held on astonished. In Focalar's painful flailing Cosmacrater was wrenched free from his meager hold on the cliff. He fought against a scream as he saw the earth coming ever closer, ever faster. Instinctively he closed his eyes and held his arms across in front of him.

The boulder again changed course and fell after him. Hearing the start of an avalanche he had to look back. He looked from falling stone to rising earth and went back to closing his eyes.

"Barbellos, I'm sorry," he began speaking in a whisper. After several minutes of nothing he opened his eyes. Cosmacrater found himself suspended somehow between the falling rock and rising earth. Time and motion seemed to have stopped. His mind tried to grasp what was happening when he heard the clicking heels against stone.

"Yes my love." Her voice was soft and kind in his ears. He opened his eyes and tried to turn. He knew she was there though he couldn't see her. He struggled watching for a glimpse, a fleeting image of her. "For what it's worth I'm sorry you got caught up in this."

"You killed my men," he said, his mind still rattled by his soon demise. She took a firm hold of him and pulled him free from his fall, setting him up to a safer handhold.

"I am sorry," she said. Her eyes widened like a reprimanded child.

"I should be grateful for your skill at time control but I have to wonder: Why are you here?" he asked, confused. He wondered if he should be mad that she slaughtered his men or grateful that she didn't let him join them.

"I am here to protect the chosen," Barbellos said, holding him close as time resumed. The rock smashed into the blood-coated ground. Shrapnel scattered across the desert plain.

"You mean Atone. Look we all pretty much know who she is," he grumbled. "But she still has to…" His words were cut off by her lips pressed firmly against his. A savage screaming echoed in his head. Time and space collided by their embrace and he saw all that was, in this exact moment of time, on every plane and every place.

He pushed her off. She coughed roughly, hiding speckles of blood in her hand. Cosmacrater rushed over to her as she stumbled, catching her. He gasped feeling now her clammy cold skin and seeing her pale green complexion.

Atone

"She wasn't the only option was she?" he asked, feeling something suspicious in himself. Something he didn't realize before.

"The world is dying Cosmacrater. If she doesn't succeed the whole universe ends."

"That doesn't make any sense. If her presence insures apocalypse then how can she save the world?"

"It is the one injury that can only be cured by the one that struck the blow," she said, before returning to her hacking cough. He held her tight, pulling her robe closer trying to warm her chilling flesh. Her icy hand reached out to touch his face. "She was cast out after the flood. Now she must do it again only this time make the right choice for the right reasons."

"I don't understand. What are you saying?" Cosmacrater asked, frustrated. Barbellos smiled.

"Poor, Cosmacrater. You always were a simple fool, my love," she began coughing again. He held her until the savage convulsions stopped.

"We need to get you out of here. There has to be a way to save you."

"No!" She demanded violently, her voice taking him by surprise. "A plague spreads through out heaven. There is nowhere else to go. It is my time. At least let me do this in the manner I see fit."

"Wow you guys talk a lot," Lillith said, dangling upside down precariously from her place on the ledge. Both of them looked over at her.

"How long have you been listening?" Barbellos asked, her voice shaking. Cosmacrater instinctively drew himself away. "You should be frozen in time right now."

"I've only been listening since the rocks went mad and you pulled him from his fall."

"You are an interesting one, aren't you?" Barbellos asked, concealing yet another cough with her tarnished hand.

"I'm nothing," Lillith said, with a grimace.

"Indeed. You found a winner here, Cosmacrater."

"I'm glad you approve," he said, his sharp sarcasm fading to sympathy as she went again into a savage fit. "Use your powers. Can't you go back to when you weren't infected?"

"No it's my time to go."

"What about protecting the chosen then? Isn't it more important than screwing up the time line?"

"You still haven't figured it out yet have you?"

"Well why don't you just tell me?" he asked, fuming. He stomped past her to continue his climb. After several minutes and only a few yards to show for it he froze, shaking. "God wants the world destroyed?" he asked. When he looked down he saw nothing lying in the space Barbellos occupied.

The trek up seemed to take mere moments. When his hands clasped the stones he felt the fingers taking hold of his wrists. Jerking away he slipped only to again be captured and a familiar laughter echoing down, the dangerous stone mountain face. He looked up to see Barbellos pulling him to the relative safety of the cave mouth. Lillith's babble could be heard from inside the cave mouth but could not be seen.

As Cosmacrater rose he noticed the once restored Barbellos already start again to corrupt and sicken. "That's not exactly right. Always going for the straight and easy answer."

"Wiping out a world, despite what others may say, is not easy," Cosmacrater said, straight faced.

"The world runs off several balances and counter balances; life and death, good and evil, right and wrong, you and me. God's tools to control these counter balances are War, Famine, Disease and the Beasts of the Earth," Barbellos explained, stepping in place behind him as he looked for Lillith.

"Revelations 6:8, the four horsemen," he noted as they walked through the cave.

"This is what God uses to control the balances," she continued to explain only a breath between them as she followed closely.

"So? What of it?" he shrugged shivering as his shoulder rubbed up against her. She was soft but hot to the touch, even in these torrid temperatures.

"These tools are used to keep the world balanced. But when God needs to change something he goes at odds with these tools and they run amok trying to repair everything. Atone is a key that is required for God to again regain control."

"Two things, why would God need to change things and when did he loose control?"

"Haven't you been paying attention? In the beginning there was only God. But God saw problems develop. He needed to change the world; he made the demigods and destroyed the tower of Babel. That was the first change. God couldn't interact directly with the world. It just didn't work."

"The first time he destroyed the world."

"Changed, please. The world is still here. Humans are still here. You don't remember that time except in stories. It was when you were made," she said, stumbling. He scooped her up and walked for the both of them. "But the world again became flawed over time. The demigods forgot the origin of their birth. What happened next was a series of Apocalypses. Ragnorak. Those demigods that repented where returned to God as his angels. Those that did not repent where cast aside as Demons. A handful of fallen were allowed to remain to supervise the Earth."

"The second time he des… changed the world."

"Then there was Noah's flood and the nephilim," she coughed. They were growing close, the darkness of the cave showing the first signs of red, ominous light to guide them to the crossroads. "That was the third. But then some of the angels for one reason or another turned against God. Why?"

"Because we were evil," he said, simply.

"NO. Not then. The concept of Evil had not yet developed until after the fourth end times." She shuddered, a chill creeping into her skin despite the scorching heat. Her eyes grew heavy and closed. "So why?"

"Because, God…" Cosmacrater thought, thinking about her words and the topic at hand. "Changed… by making a dualistic world, splitting it into Evil and Good?"

He felt her clammy corpse like skin against his flesh. Her closed eyes winced in pain though a smile forced itself to dance across her face. "The fourth change."

"So? Now what?"

Atone

"Now here comes the fifth change," Barbellos said, her voice growing weaker. Cosmacrater had to set her down and lean his ear close to her mouth to hear. "All of these changes were prophesized well in advance all of these mechanisms put in place before they could even grasp they're importance. Her parents union, her expulsion from God, even you and me having this discussion. It must come to pass."

"You said they and they're? If she doesn't make it... is there..." He tried to ask when her trembling hand took firm hold of him with such a surprising strength that he couldn't free himself. Her body went into convulsions jerking violently as blood poured from her mouth. Her skin began to sizzle and tear as she entered her death throws. "No, Barbellos. Fight it. Live. Live!" He cried struggling to draw her from the edge. He struggled in vain, tears falling to the ground to make an ignited stream along the cracked stone floor. "NO!"

His sobbing concealed Atones advance as she leapt toward him Gemini in full swing.

Chapter 7

The Gemini struck the stone in Cosmacrater's hand making sparks fly at the impact. Atone pushed against it until she was inches from his face. The force made both his hands struggle to keep the weapon at bay.

"Where is Axael's body?" Atone growled snapping at his face.

Cosmacrater bowed as he freed his hand sending her spinning away. His hand took the pack from his back and pulled the string making it empty while flying out at her. She shifted to a battle stance as the bones scattered. She shrieked as the bones fell out. She scrambled to capture them. "He is here, Atone. He is as safe as he can be here."

She clutched the bones close to her keeping her eyes on Cosmacrater. When she saw that he stayed crouched low to the ground weeping she risked her eyes free from him to see what he mourned over. There she saw Barbellos set along the ground carefully, even lovingly aside. "Who was she? What did you do?"

Atone

What did I do?" Cosmacrater growled lunging half-heartedly toward her in checked rage. "What I did? A plaque spreads through Heaven as we speak. The Earth is falling apart. Humanity is dying and God is helpless. All because of you and you have the nerve to ask me what I've done!" Cosmacrater drew his knives ready to fight her then and there. Atone dropped the bones to take hold of Gemini again. Cosmacrater's foot tripped over Barbellos and he saw her again in his downward fall. Atone dove ready to strike. Her heart began to ache, feeling a deep well of loss and regret as Cosmacrater stooped over the angel. She held the Gemini at his throat. "What I did?" he began, all his rage gone. "I loved her. That's what I did."

She eased her weapon away and he got up from the ground taking a seat next to his love. Atone crouched down next to him, here eyes uncontrollably leaking. "So who is this angel to you? What have you done?" Cosmacrater asked, picking up one of Axael's bones carefully.

She let out a weak laugh twisting Gemini around her passively locking it in place with the prongs. "By the sound of it He was to me what she was to you. As for what I've done… I've brought death to the world," she said, her tears becoming her own.

"Not necessarily," he said after a long, contemplative silence. "You are really just a tool. Wait, that's a bad way to start. Your actions are predetermined. Sure it looks bad but the up side is that this is put into place to insure Gods control of the world. You're suffering and toil is merely a process for God to change the world and restore balance."

"So what your saying is that Axael died because God want to change the world, Your angel died because God thinks this world is wrong, Heinrich, all of those people on Earth , had to die so that God can come out looking good, like he didn't make a mistake? So that people don't remember all the horrible things that happened, just because he wanted to do something different?" he heard the anger in her voice rise. Cosmacrater fingered a knife absently in case she decided to take it out on him.

"Well I wasn't going to say it that way," he said, trying to calm her down.

"And what? I'm just a pawn. A puppet! He's playing around with all my feelings, all this pain and suffering and they don't even matter. For all I know if I'm such a tool the feelings I have are all because he puts them there. Why, Cosmacrater? Why does he make me feel these things? If I'm a tool what good are emotions?" Atone ranted. Cosmacrater reached out to her and she jerked her way free from his hand. When she turned to face him her eyes shimmered, pulsing light like a warning. Cosmacrater took a step nervously as the light darkened around her.

"Atone. I know your upset…"

"Upset? Upset? I am far from upset. He thinks he can use me? After he threw me out! Fuck Him! I am not a tool. I'm not going to do his bidding. If you care so much why don't you do it? And if you see our maker before you die you can tell him that he fucked up when he thought he could still manipulate me with this," she said, holding Axael's skull out toward him for him to see. The sound of more people coming made Atone sink farther in the shadows, her hand reaching to her chest. She doubled over in pain from the raw sensation of something tearing its way deep within her. Cosmacrater reached out to her as she groaned, her harsh voice mixing with blood, bile and half-digested food. "Stay back!" She shouted inching farther before collapsing to her hands and knees. She could feel the blood burning inside if her, flowing along the savagely torn flesh of her esophagus. The pain was so much that she almost overlooked the glittering crystal in the vomited gore in front of her. She took hold of it, ignoring the vile refuse.

"Atone. I know you're…"

"You know nothing, Cosmacrater. If he thinks I'm going to play his game he should've never counted on a devil!" With a vicious downward throw the crystal shattered. In a flash she was gone. Cosmacrater returned to Barbellos standing beside her before the noise of someone approaching caught his attention.

"Cosmacrater!" Lillith called tossing a chewed demonic arm aside to run up to him. She hugged him forcefully nearly knocking him over his deceased angel. He hugged her back more to steady his balance than for comfort or revelry. His eyes found the hand she discarded and tried quickly to forget the familiar ring of the order sheathed around the finger. "What do we do now?"

"We find Asmodius, Lillith," Cosmacrater said, holding her closer now so that he didn't have to look at the hand or the body at his feet. "And I'm going to need your help."

Atone

Beelzebub's heavy hoofed feet sank into the arid desert. His multifaceted eyes scanned the heights of the rocky cliff facing. His metallic dragon fly wings created a whirlwind as he prepared to take flight when his eyes saw the fragments of Cosmacrater's soldiers.

"Whatever happened here?" Beelzebub spoke to himself. From the sundered bodies a skull battered and wretched rolled awkwardly in the wind. Beelzebub stopped his assent and his massive fluttering wings to retrieve it. "State your progress, Lihatiel!"

"The girl is on the move."

"Is there something I should know?"

"Probably," the crippled head laughed. Beelzebub squatted to sit on a massive rock.

"How long have we waited, Lihatiel? How long have we been together?"

"Ages my lord. But worry not. She is the one, I swear it. Soon it is time to act," Lihatiel said, smiling or rather in an attempt to smile. Beelzebub saw this and chuckled.

"You alone know what it is I really crave. And if what you say is true then we should get ready," he said, switching the skin covered skull to his other hand. Beelzebub's face crunched up at the gore on his now free hand. "There is only one problem. I can't have you coming with me looking like that."

"What did you have in mind?"

"You'll like it. I've designed it myself. I think you've more than earned it with what you've had to endure," he said, his deep heavy voice soothing and tender. Lihatiel gurgled.

"You are too kind, my lord."

Chapter 8

Atone collapsed in a wave of pain, hatred, lust and a myriad of other sinister emotions. The room she appeared in was thick with such raw emotion that Atone could only see blurred shadows. Her body jerked spasmodically to force what little remained in her stomach from her injured esophagus and out onto the floor of the new establishment of Cronos. She quivered violently trying to inch away from a flood of emotion drowning her, without a place to retreat to. Witnesses on impulse kicked and struck her as she wailed for the suffering around her. She struggled to focus her mind to push out the emotions that forcibly entered her open mind. Perhaps if she was not so emotional before arriving here, she began to think through the emotions that were not her own. She tried to focus on the conversation that she had with Cosmacrater before arriving here. The emotions fought against her attempts to control her.

"Atone?" Naamah said, in disbelief from her seat at the bar. She rose and fought her way to the curled and defenseless creature. One demon struggling to take the metal bar wrapped around her body. Naamah kicked him hard in the temple making blood squirt from his eyes and mouth. At that the others inched back allowing her to pick up the nude body. "I didn't expect to see you again. Things didn't go too well then I take it."

Atone, grasping for something in the sea of hate and fear, found a little piece of emotion unique, compassionate, and took hold tightly struggling against the vile tide. Naamah faltered in her pace as Atone hugged her tightly feeling their bodies pressed against each other. Naamah couldn't resist a smile at the touch. She quickly reined it in changing it into a sneer and snapped back at the crowd.

"You know the rules. All of you. This is a safe haven." The words lashed out like the sting of a whip forcing them all to retreat to their prior affairs. "She's under the attention of the house and is the moment she arrived. Another attack like this and you'll be banned from this place. Now shape up." She turned back to safer ground walking past the marching procession of damned waiting to be bought and sold like cattle to the horde for whatever sick and twisted desires they may wish to unleash.

Naamah led Atone away kicking open a door by the bar and entering the shadows inside to climb a spiraling staircase. Nudging open another door high on the top she entered her room. It was small and sparsely filled. A queen sized bed with wine colored canopy curtains and a small chest of drawers at its foot next to the door where all that shared the shadows depth. The only light seemed to radiate from a fist sized whole above the center of the bed washing it in red. Naamah pulled back the semi transparent curtain and set Atone on the hard mattress. Atone felt herself drawn from the depraved emotion by this alien one.

Naamah watched over Atone helpless in front of her. She ran a hand soothingly across her trembling skin. She couldn't help but feel her desire awaken something deep within her as she studied Atone's naked form covered only with a coiled up weapon. She reached out to remove it allowing Atone to get more comfortable. Claws caught her in a flash. Naamah jerked back instinctively. Atone's claws dug deep as she pulled Naamah close.

"Atone," she said, surprised, realizing that she was straddled over her. "I realize what this must look like but really I was only…"

"It's O.K.," she said, weakly. "I know." Axael's skull rolled from the bed as she shifted position. She let Naamah's hands continue their work at freeing Gemini from around her. Her talons reduced to simple claws freeing one of Naamah's arms to set the Gemini aside. Atone's mind still waded in the fading emotions below. She focused on Naamah's to clear her mind. She felt her concern and maternal feeling trying to control her deep-seated cravings and lust.

Naamah fought against her own emotions freeing her eyes from Atone's red and sweat-laden skin to face away, looking at the foot locker at the end of the bed. "We should get you some new clothes," she tried to turn toward the locker only to have her attention jerked back to Atone and her claws still in one of her arms.

"No. Not yet. Just let me rest, please," Atone panted raising Naamah's deeper emotion. Naamah froze as Atone caressed her leg, her abdomen and then pulling her closer to cup her buttocks. With a squeeze she evoked a squeal from deep within Naamah's throat. Atone released Naamah's arm and used her free hand to tease Naamah, running her claws up and down her spine. Her claws stripped the shirt free from her like husk from corn.

"Are you feeling all right? This doesn't seem like you?"

"I feel alright. You've felt for yourself haven't you?" she asked, sitting up and wrapping her arms tightly around her, enveloping her. Naamah's breathing rate increased, growing more ragged with each hard exhale.

"Is this really happening?" She gasped as Atone's hand ran between her legs, feeling her heat through the pants fabric.

"What do you think?"

Atone gently pulled her down to lay with her, then climbed over her, dominating Naamah. Atone pulled Naamah's pants free feeling a wave of helplessness and a hint of fear with her lust that tasted sweet to the empath. "This is real. This is real," Naamah panted in pleasurable surprise as Atone's fingers found their way inside of her. Atone's mind flickering back to Cosmacrater. What is real, she thought to herself.

Naamah moaned, deep and guttural her eyes clouding over with lust. Atone smiled outwardly hiding in the emotion Naamah fed her. But deep in the back of her mind she couldn't hide from what she knew. She felt Naamah's fingers join hers then abandon them to venture to Atone's womanhood. It was Atone's turn to gasp. She turned her head to see Axael peering out from the darkness his empty sockets staring at them, watching. Her eyes closed tight. When she opened them Naamah was there. She locked her gaze on her, forcing herself into the waves of lust using Naamah's cravings to force out anything else. Atone felt a growl rumble loose from her throat. Her eyes grew wide with surprise realizing it was her growl, her passion. The emotions radiating from Naamah crawled under her skin and became a part of her. They became her own and flowed back through Naamah building ever stronger. "I will be no one's puppet."

She threw herself onto Naamah, their lust building to uncharted heights and she became her soul focus, her only thought. Damn them all. If they are all puppets then damn them.

Naamah's face contorted in ecstasy, Atone drinking it in and letting it overwhelm her. Naamah began to squirm, fighting her own craving for release, the pleasure too much to contain. Atone felt the surge of lust in tandem with the waves of ecstatic juices that pumped, hot, from Naamah. She quivered free of Atone's kneading fingers.

Exhausted, she laid there every touch to sensitive to withstand. Atone laid with her eyes wide open. Naamah's afterglow, at first all consuming, became slowly transparent fading to thoughts of the world dying. Atone curled up around her partner desperately. She tried to hold on to any other feelings rather than her own guilt and rage.

"Naamah, I…" Cronos said, entering the room. "Oh."

"Cronos…"

"We'll talk later… Get some rest," he said, breaking his stare and saw the skull watching him. It unsettled him. He struggled with its blank gaze for a moment, Atone eying him suspiciously from over Naamah's shoulder. He felt her eyes on him and looked back. "Right, I'll be… somewhere else," he said, closing the door.

Chapter 9

Several days have passed since Atone arrived at Asmodius II's. Atone sat in bed, the skull of her angel at her feet, her chains, procured by Marcolf, coiled around her arms. Her borrowed thin white nightgown was made transparent with sweat. She stared unblinking into the sockets of Axael's skull, the two of them locked in a test of wills. Naamah slept near her, content and for a brief moment happy. Atone made no sign of acknowledging her as Naamah curled up along her, purring in her sleep. She was lost in the dark nothingness of her angel's eyes.

"So how much of this is destiny?" She narrowed her eyes staring back at him. "You? Her? Is this blinking eye timed to a log in his consciousness?" she asked, his unblinking unwavering face still and lifeless.

There, she felt that there was almost some emotion in his hollow bones, a voice in the back of her mind speaking, repeating one single word that she couldn't grasp.

In a fit she sent her heel to his face sending it clattering across the room. She was sorry for it instantly and chased after the rolling skull. She searched the skull for any signs of chips or cracks, refusing to part with any more of him. After insuring his undamaged state she cradled him lovingly under her arm.

"How long have we been together?" she asked, guarded. She added with a smirk, "or apart?" The ruckus of the demonic horde and tortured souls died down though the first blood red rays of morning were still far off. "Was all of that just a plot of his?" She risked setting the skull aside only long enough to get some of Naamah's clothes, a black sequin dress with an open back, before retrieving it and carrying it downstairs peering out to the bar from the shadows. She watched Marcolf merrily conversing with someone concealed in the other room. She lurked in the doorway taking a seat at the foot of the stairs. "How much of my emotions are not my own?"

"An interesting question," a voice, powerful and strong, called out from the shadows behind her. "Especially for something like us." Cronos emerged from the shadows.

"Cronos, it's nice to see you."

"Likewise, Atone. It's been a while," he said, placing a hand on hers. He retrieved a hammer from his belt and handed it over. "Here is your hammer, Atone. You still, by the sound of it, need help finding things."

"I'm not looking for anything," she retorted, taking the hammer from his massive grasp.

"A purpose is a thing. Answers are things. Both I can help you with a whole lot better than running to the bed of Naamah and hiding from your problems."

"Why do you care what I do?" Atone asked, with a growl.

"I care? Why do I care? For a savior and a herald of doom you're dense."

"Cronos…" She growled.

"Do you honestly think I wouldn't be interested in what you do? What you do affects us all," Cronos said, calmly explaining.

"What I do? I'm just a puppet. Why don't you just make me do it? That's what he does," she said, pointing up.

"If that's what you wish to think."

"If I'm wrong than why am I destined for this and prophesied for that?" She set the skull aside and covered her face with her hands, muffling her sigh. "I never wanted to be the herald of apocalypse or the savior of demons or the Cosmic Catalyst."

I may have been destined to help you or I may have been destined to slay you. I made a choice to be your friend. Whether I was destined or not is really not an issue," he said, picking up the skull. Atone's heart squeezed painfully tight and beat violently. Cronos spoke to the skull. "I think she's looking at this from the wrong set of eyes."

Atone snatched the skull back from him guarding it possessively. "I am in no mood, Cronos." She curled around it in a protective ball. Marcolf's conversation was at an end and the other side of it walked past the door, pausing before walking on. Through the whole moment she watched the stranger, but her empathy felt the eyes of Cronos on her.

Marcolf turned to see her and she instinctively looked away. Cronos backed up looking at the door. "I suppose it's none of my business. Not my problem," he said, turning to walk toward the door. She felt like calling out for him to finish what he so harshly hinted at but her pride choked her throat. He looked over his shoulder and began to speak. "Except…"

Atone jumped from the stair as he turned back to look over her shoulder. "That whatever you choose affects us all."

He exited the half open door closing behind him leaving Atone in a meager sliver of light. She jumped from the stairs taking hold of the doorknob. Swinging the door open the emotions again overwhelmed her. She doubled over as though hit by a massive fist. She felt her head pound and her stomach lurch aided by the smell of blood, semen and rot. Those still in the room paid her little attention. Marcolf cleaned his glasses while the various demons enjoyed their "table dances." There was little that remained of the term except the name. These private parties of carnage and violation created pools of emotion creating traumatic islands throughout the room. She inched back into the darkness to regain her focus, build her resolve.

There she saw Cronos talking to the shrouded man that Marcolf was talking to earlier. He was already at the far end of the room unaffected by the islands of emotion between them. She started slowly, one careful foot over the other. A drunken reveler was arguing physically with another, sending a stunned and drunken demon into her. Drunk off his intoxication she was unable to avoid the collision. She shrieked stumbling forward into the booth were a demon was raping a woman while skinning the flesh from her, back to front.

She screamed at the pain of the barbed phallus cutting groves into her tender and private flesh. She felt the skin carved from her own back and writhed around in pain. She kicked wildly trying to free herself from him, at the same time feeling the sick pleasures of the rapist. Atone threw up in her mouth choking on the screams in time to the woman's. Her clawed hands fought to shield her spine. The indifference of the demon mixed with his basic arousal made the physical and emotional trauma to the tortured girl that much worse. Atone scrambled for safety unwittingly entering another emotional pocket.

A woman set up in a device like a vertical rack was slowly being pulled apart limb from limb, a band of gambling Diablonians taking bets on which limb will pull free first. Atone's limbs popped from their sockets and she collapsed to the floor. Broken and in pain she tried to worm her way free. She laughed against the woman's pain even as she felt it feeling the demon patrons. To make things worse one of them, a shape changer, took the likeness of her lover and struggled against them to "Save" her. The women's mind caught his gaze and had a flicker of hope. Atone focused solely on that sensation, freeing herself from the torment. Atone was crying unhindered now her vision blurring with the complex mixtures of emotion that her body was forced to endure.

Another pocket of emotion, one step closer to Cronos. A legionnaire, disguised as a young girl's father forced his way upon her. Atone felt the lust of the father and the betrayal of the daughter in one. "Why daddy, Why? Don't do this? It isn't right?" Atone sobbed. Laughing wickedly a moment later. She felt his fingers groping her. She sobbed at the betrayal and yet yearned in some ill placed loyalty to please her father. She crawled on her hands and knees in some sick ways wanting to stay.

Atone was crawling now every molecule of her being struggling against her desire to give up. She felt dizzy in the dueling emotions. As she crawled her way to the next table her heart beat savagely expecting the worst. What she found was the warted skin of Cronos.

"And here she is. I knew you would come," he said, oblivious to her pain. But it wasn't her pain, she thought. She forced herself to dwell on this calming her own emotions down. "Not stellar or anything but she got here despite her drawback."

"And why did I come here?" she asked, still too exhausted to ask her real question. After a few gasps and calming nerves she continued. "You said I should look at this differently. How do you suppose I do that?"

"First of all I said see it through another set of eyes," Cronos corrected. "Secondly, I think it rude that you haven't said hello to my guest and close friend."

Atone looked from Cronos to the creature beside him. She stumbled over the chairs, falling backward again toward the emotional sea. "Death?" She gasped cowering on the floor. Her eyes pulled away from the skull face under the robe to return to Cronos. "Destined to slay. You're going to…"

"Have to apologize for your less than flattering reaction to my old friend. I'm sorry, Astanphaus."

"It's quite alright, Cronos. Most react in such a way. Atone trembled until her gaze fell to Axael whose skull sat on the table where she must have dropped it in her attempt to escape. Astanphaus saw it as well and reached out for it.

Atone

Before his long bone fingers could wrap around the skull Atone snatched it back standing by the table. "I was going to inquire about that skull. Where did you get it? It's such a strange thing to dote on like you do. Who was it if you don't mind me asking?"

She opened her mouth to speak but then stepped back again. "You are Death. You should be able to get those answers…"

"Normally yes, but if you don't mind I would like a closer look," he said, hand extended outward for the skull. Atone tried to think logically. On one hand it's Death, not someone you want to be friends with, but on the other hand he may be able to uncover something that would help her move on. With a sneer she set the skull into his hand and took a seat next to Cronos. She watched trying to hide her eagerness as Death clutched the skull and turned it in his hands studying. His bony brow seemed to bend in frustration and he set it down. Gnashing his teeth Death rose from his seat.

"What is it, Astanphaus?" Cronos asked, half rising as well. Astanphaus pointed condemningly at the skull on the table.

"This is not something for me to deal with. It is beyond me."

"It can't be," Atone cried out before she could help it. She squeaked as Death glared at her bitterly.

Cronos patted her hand and said with his voice calm and relaxed. "It can be if he's still alive."

"Regardless there is no need for me." Death bowed to the large froggish demon. "I'm sorry I couldn't be of any further use in this."

"It's quite alright and thank you, old friend."

The skeleton face seemed to smile, not difficult given the natural design of a skull. It wrapped the hood closer around his head as he made his way to the door. He clutched it closed as a gust of wind lashed violently at his tattered robe from the now open door. He turned in their direction one last time to wave a boney claw. If he said anything there was no sound due to the yowling tempest of the outside world. A moment later he was gone. Two bodyguards of Cronos struggled with the doors, trying to close them. Cronos and Atone sat silently mulling over the revelation. When Cronos spoke Atone gasped, surprised.

"Sorry to hear about your angel, Atone. I invited Astanphaus here to maybe dig up a little insight or guiding light."

Atone rose, noticing that the room was now empty save for one grizzled old demon keeping Marcolf company at the bar. She paced the room, still avoiding the remnant auras from the booths and tables as she searched her mind.

"Israfel," she breathed, remembering his prophecy. "Israfel will be the first to die. Angels, demons, devils, none of us can die until he does. Axael's in this prison of bone forever?"

"It doesn't sound that bad," Marcolf commented and Atone looked up not realizing that she spoke out loud.

"Not that bad? Have you ever been in your own dead body?" Atone snapped, her eyes red from her tears earlier adding a harshness to her face that took Marcolf aback. "I was dead once. You are left unable to see, hear, taste, feel and smell. Any thought of despair or hope or anything else stripped away as soon as it's perceived. Not being anything? That is true Hell."

She turned and weaved the floor quickly, sobbing all the way. Cronos watched her leave, heading back up to Naamah's room. The bar room rippled once she left and Asmodius approaching Cronos at his table after appearing from the very air.

"Should I…" Cronos started but Asmodius cut him off.

"No. Let her figure out her own path," he said, patting Cronos on his shoulder. "Besides I have a plan."

Chapter 10

Naamah Stirred in her slumber finding Atone sitting at the edge her legs pulled close in front of her. "How come you are always awake?" she asked, with her eyes still closed. "You need to rest."

Atone stroked Naamah's hair to sooth her. Naamah nuzzled her nose to Atone's skin absently kissing her hip. Atone smiled down at her in case she opened her eyes. "Soon. Right now I've got a lot on my mind."

Naamah wormed her arms around Atone's waist and pulled herself closer to her possessively before dosing back off. Atone took comfort in Naamah's feelings of complete safety and peace. Her own feelings began to corrupt it. She felt deceitful. Atone's arm dropped down naturally following the curve of Naamah's back. Atone's eyes, long since adjusted to the windowless room's darkness, watched the skull that sat on the footlocker.

"How come I can't feel you? How come it took someone else to let me know what torment you've found?" She thought. Some of what she thought must have escaped her lips because she heard Naamah mumble. She thought back to the battlefield when the fortress of Sheol fell. When she died everything was stripped away, even her thoughts, almost before they could be had. She didn't want that for him.

She felt Naamah stir again and stretched out to lie beside her. Instinctively Naamah entwined herself around her like a second skin and Atone let her, too tired to know if she was worth the comfort, and security of being with someone, that Naamah had to offer. She had to leave, she decided. The best she could do now is to give Naamah tonight.

Her eyes closed without her intention and remained that way. Then, as so many times before, her mind drifted to the cliff. The wind howled its contempt to her warning her of what it was she was about to do. She dove heedless of the warnings the wind screamed, heedless of the many cries of the angels above, heedless even of the cries of her love, Axael. Axael flew after her. In a jerk she was pulled back. Axael held her wings in a tight grip.

"Don't do this," he cried.

"Don't stop me," she hissed. She drew his weapon severing her wings in one savage swipe. Wingless her body plummeted faster.

Her rocky doom waited eagerly for the impact that grew ever nearer. She felt the wind claw at her face as she fell, lashing tears from her eyes and reddening her skin tearing away patches of her fine scales. She could feel Axael screaming wanting desperately to follow her. It was the last free thing she would hear. She hit the jagged stones below and her bones shattered, breaking through the skin.

She was dead. Her mind struggled to hold on to anything even the last echoing scream of Axael trying to stop her. Her feelings bled away with her senses and she was lost to the abyss. She became nothing. She was beyond nothing.

This was her first death. There she was emotionless, sensation less, lost in the never-ending erosion of her own soul. She felt only the absence.

When next she opened her eyes she saw Beelzebub's bullish face and heard the buzzing of his dragon fly wings.

"Welcome, daughter of desertion."

"I feel… Pain… Axael, why… The echo…"

"I can take those feelings of pain away. Join me, serve me and all the horrid memories that brought you here will be forgotten." Beelzebub comforted her in his thick muscled arms. "Do you want that? Do you want peace?"

"Yes," she sobbed in a moment. Beelzebub motioned for Lihatiel. His thick black hair was separated into braids clamped tight with gold rings.

"This will only hurt for a moment, pretty one," he said, touching her face lightly with the boney spikes along the back of his hand. His mouth opened and unhinged like a snake, and she felt her very memories stripped away, eaten away like a worm chewing through her mind. She tried to fight but it was already too late. His feasting left her weak and as her memories became his she knew her secrets became his to keep. Atone found something worse than oblivion as Lihatiel became her keeper. He used her, that night and many nights thereafter, his boned exoskeleton and armor forcing itself into her, breaking her as he feasted on both mind and body. It cut her deep within and then was stripped away, leaving only an unexplained anguish. He fed off her memories like a parasite and her body like a letch. She felt her empathic bond feeding off those around her replacing the thoughts and memories that Lihatiel devoured after the long nights of sexual and mental torture. When he feasted on her ability to Soul forge, Lihatiel hid it from Beelzebub. It was from his own mind that she learned of it. Dishonesty breeds dishonesty. She suffered, forging for him during the day, locked away in his tower, and tortured by him in the darkest hours of night.

She found her opening and struck deep, letting her soul forged creation out to report to Beelzebub. It was many nights before the marching of Beelzebub's main forces was heard coming. She did not here the entire conversation but Beelzebub's powerful voice could be heard arguing with Lihatiel's cowardly one. That night both of them came to her tower and Beelzebub forced Lihatiel to return what he stole.

Lihatiel's jaw opened wide spewing out many tiny razor edged bugs that dug painfully into her skin and into her mind. She remembered, each memory bringing with it a special kind of torture and longing. She spent many days crying but Beelzebub made sure that Lihatiel and his army left her alone. A soul forger was a rare treasure not to be treated poorly. It was weeks before she returned from her tower and was allowed to see Beelzebub in person. He sat on his grandiose dragon carved throne. On the ivory table in front of him sat an archaic treasure that he pondered over barely acknowledging that she was there until she spoke. He pulled his eyes from the book and smiled strangely at her, her mind telling her that it was an unfamiliar gesture.

"I'm glad you are well," he said, the book constantly distracting him. "I'm afraid I have a mission for you if you are ready."

"I would like to begin paying the debt I owe you, Beelzebub."

"Lihatiel is escorting this book to the Fortress of Sheol. I want you to accompany his troops."

"Lihatiel, but…"

"Understand this, Atone. This book is very important to our cause. Within it is a way to undo the great suffering that we endure. Somewhere within its pages there is a prophecy that explains how a second judgment is coming. Remember our cause, Atone. We may be damned but that does not mean we are not a part of God's plan. I need this book safe until we are able to find a way to plead our case to God once more. An army alone is not enough. I need weapons and armor to equip these soldiers. That is why I want you… No. I need you to go. Do this not only for me but for everyone down here trying to redeem themselves."

"I will go with Lihatiel. I will do what you ask."

She awoke to the sounds of Naamah walking around the room getting dressed. "It's nice to see you sleep again." She kissed her on the forehead and then the mouth. "I'll be back in a moment. Rest well."

"Wait. There is something I need to say." Atone stopped her. She couldn't wait any longer. It was time to finish this.

Chapter 11

"You're leaving me? You can't do this!" Naamah shouted. Atone stood in front of her knowing that the tears in Naamah's eyes would not fall in front of her.

"I have to finish this, Naamah," Atone tried to explain, fitting into one of Naamah's more wing digit friendly outfits. She turned to smile back at her getting a sharp stabbing pain of anger in return. She ignored it. "Besides, I'm not leaving you. You could come with me."

"Do you know where we are? This isn't Sheol, Assaih or even Camael. Asmodius had us rebuild at the mouth of Gehenna. Gehenna! It is only the second most dangerous place in Hell. It is known for its four-way war over a door back to heaven. Not some place to just trot through."

Atone stopped listening when she said, "...door to heaven." She looked at Naamah taking the skull from the footlocker and pointed it at Naamah to replace her finger. "We are going. Whether you are or not is up to you."

She took a bag from the footlocker and put Axael's skull inside along with a spare set of clothes. The outfit she wore made a low almost unheard wail of she twisted and moved with a trickle of its agony bleeding into Atone's subconscious. "Are you coming or not?"

"You're crazy. Crazy!" Naamah shouted back. Atone walked past her and down the stairs to the main room. She stopped at the door, trying to steal her nerves. She opened the door and felt her stomach lurch and her heart twist inside her chest. She stood there several moments, wide eyed, scanning the room for a weak spot. The two booths along the wall had only a single patron. She edged her way toward the bar to Marcolf who smiled back at her.

"Anything today, Atone?"

"No. Nothing for me, thank you," she said, taking half a seat. "Any sign of Asmodius. He hasn't come back yet?"

"Not to my knowledge I'm afraid."

"Right. What of Astanphaus?"

"He's around somewhere. He said he would say goodbye to Cronos before he departed, which he has yet to do."

"Good. Thank you," she said, sliding from her seat and following the bar to the far wall, lingering in the dark to avoid stronger emotions. A tortured soul made a break for it slamming into her before the demon's captured her. Steely knives carved flesh away, Atone falling to the ground feeling her own flesh carved loose. She cried out loud clawing at her own flesh. She jerked spasmodically trying to liberate her skin from the myriad of daggers. She screamed clutching her sides trying to protect injuries that didn't exist on her.

When Atone was able to open her eyes she saw Naamah staring back at her. "How do you expect to beat Israfel if you can't even cross a room?" Naamah asked, sitting on top of her pinning her arms down to keep Atone from struggling. The emotions were too much for her and her body stopped moving, no recollection in her eyes.

"Stop this!" She looked out into the crowd. A ripple formed and Asmodius appeared. The pools of horrors evaporating, his complex illusions no longer required.

"Take her back to your room. She is not ready," he ordered, not interested in his peons petty complaints.

"Stop this or I'll…" Naamah threatened her hands balling up into fists with no real power to do anything else.

"You are in no position to bargain, Naamah. Your sister can attest to that," Asmodius said, his voice growing ragged with annoyance.

"You bastard."

"I could just as easily punish you," Asmodius said, all of his civility bleeding away to show the real monster beneath. "I would watch what you say!"

Naamah cowered and carefully scooped Atone up, carrying her to the darkness of her room. She could feel Asmodius watching her and knew that if it was not for keeping Atone satisfied she would easily find her way to the chopping block. She had to comply. There was no way out of this. There was no way to free herself from him. In the dark one single salty tear ran down her face.

Chapter 12

"Why are you keeping me here?" Atone growled pacing the floor feeling the moaning boards invade the faint shadows of her mind. Emotions crowded in around her pushing their way toward her. Naamah sat on the bed, tears streaking down her face.

"I'm not," she sobbed for the 40th time.

"I wish I could tell you…" Atone said. The words and voice were alien to her, making Naamah cringe cursing her own mind for thinking.

"Atone!" Naamah cried leaping from the bed to Atone's side as she staggered. Atone seized her, claws sinking into her flesh screaming from the pain in Naamah's place. Her eyes were wild, panicked, tears cutting them into a sore painful red.

"What is this that's happening to me?" she asked, her eyes flickering from a myriad of colors and hues, each color a person each person reflecting their pain. "I can feel everyone. What is this place? This pain? You have to get me out of here!"

Atone

"I can't. Asmodius is too…" She stopped watching as Atone crumpled weak in her arms her weight dragging them both to the ground. "I will. Just give me some time."

Naamah pulled herself free from her and escaped into the darkness leaving Atone alone with everyone else. Cautiously she walked down to the bar looking back and forth for him, she breathed a sigh of relief when he didn't appear. She went for the door to find it opening already. Ducking behind it as it opened she waited to see Cronos helping a dismantled Agrat carefully to another chamber in the house. Her sneer turned to concern and hatred at once, concern for her sister and hatred for Asmodius. Cronos caught her gaze and looked at her, a flicker of pain in his own eyes. She looked at Agrat. Pieces were torn from her flesh, thin purple ridges through her skin marked the passages of several flesh-eating worms. Her eyes were only empty blood clotted sockets barely concealed through a thin wrap of gauze. She dangled limp over the shoulder of Cronos with broken limbs unusable and atrophied from lack of use. Bones were set, broken and set again making countless lumps under her body. Naamah moved to speak but saw the inch thick metal rod driven through her ears. Cronos faltered in his steps making Agrat moan strangely, maggots falling from her tongueless mouth. It was then that his presence was felt.

"I heard what you said. You wouldn't be trying to trick me or betray me, are you?"

"I had to tell her something. She's getting suspicious."

"I see, Naamah. Very well then, do your job and keep her occupied. This may work better for us. It could give her something to strive for… Just remember that I'm always watching."

"How could I forget?"

"Good. There are some new people at table 7. One is out of her mind. Go see what they want."

"Sure. Yeah," Naamah said, using the option to free herself from his presence. She went to Marcolf knocking over the drink he just poured, much to the angst of a serpentine legionnaire. "Marcolf?"

"Naamah, Astanphaus was here," Marcolf said, pouring her and the upset serpent a new drink. She slid it away.

Atone

"So?"

"Atone was asking about him earlier," he explained flustered at her shortness. "He said to inform her that he will stay here for two days if she wanted him for anything," Marcolf said. Naamah left Marcolf with the angry legionnaire. She took several steps away before returning and taking the glass he poured her before.

She turned to head to table 7, her mind struggling against what her mouth and hand did. She gave up the fight and drank the rest of the glass. Through the bottom of the glass she saw a familiar face that made her choke on the rest of her booze. "Lillith is that you?"

She was answered by a squeal and a violent, passionate hug. "Naamah!"

"You!" She condemned pointing at Cosmacrater. "You burned Asmodius's!"

"My name is Cosmacrater. I am still looking for your friend."

"You and what army?"

Lillith began to speak but Cosmacrater stopped her with a squeeze to her thigh. "I am no longer in the order."

Atone

"Yet you still look for her," Naamah said, suspicious of him. Lillith got excited jumping up and down. "What, Lil?"

"We found Faust. He's not a big jerk now. He's a good horse waiting outside."

"Really? We should probably check on him. This isn't the best place to leave anything alone," Naamah said, ushering them toward the door. Asmodius had less control outside and she would have a better chance of talking safely there.

They reached the exit without further conversation and motioned for the guards to open the door. The wind sent Cosmacrater and Naamah back staggering. Lillith walked unaffected laughing at their struggles. Once outside they clung to her using her to keep from blowing away. The ground was a stripped and barren plain. A mountain worth of weapons, bodies and debris from endless battles collected against the side of a real mountain until the stone surface could no longer be seen. They followed Lillith to the mountain face finding the cave mouth to Camael. In the safety of the cave and with the roaring wind muted Naamah could find her voice.

"What do you want with Atone?" She began quickly ignoring the waiting steed.

"A religious experience," Lillith said, chuckling.

"Well I'm not really sure. Barbel... An angel had charged me with protecting her, to make sure that what she must do gets done."

"How noble. How can I know this isn't a trick that you'll wave in an army as soon as there is proof she's here?" Naamah demanded.

"Barbellos died for this, and..." Cosmacrater began loosing patience.

"What's with the two of you? You sound like she does. You two are way to close to the other side. I would be concerned about that if I were you."

"Is she here or not?" Cosmacrater demanded. Naamah waited trying to read his mind. Eventually she caved in. She wasn't capable of dealing with this herself and she needed help, even if it proved to be an Order trap.

"Yes. Asmodius is doing something to her. If we don't get her out of here soon all this destiny you two speak of is over," she confirmed.

"We'll need to hurry then," Cosmacrater began. Before he could make a strategy Naamah stopped him.

"Yes but going against Asmodius is dangerous. You'll see things that aren't there and be oblivious to the things that are right in front of you."

"I won't," Lillith said, rubbing up against Faust to feel his fur against her skin. Naamah and Cosmacrater turned to face her. She stopped, feeling their eyes on her quizzically. "What?"

Chapter 13

"Alright, Lillith you can do this," she said to herself. She walked across the dusty plain to the small cottage. The scent of decay lingered in the air and she sniffled in an attempt to cleanse her nostrils. Her mind flickered absently. "No. I Must stay focused on… something."

"Getting Atone, Lillith!" Naamah shouted against the wind, dodging debris. Lillith turned to see Naamah hiding behind a rock, bones littering the ground in front of it.

"Atone's in there?" Lillith said, pointing toward the tiny house.

"Yes!" Naamah called out. "On the third floor," she said, her eyes drifting to massive tower, like a black needle pointing to the sky.

Lillith looked over at the one story cottage. "Third story? In there? Is that even possible?"

"Listen!" Naamah growled then tried hard to restrain herself clenching her hands into fists. "Just go in and get her, O.K."

"Whatever," she said, going back to the cottage.

"Are you sure this is going to work? She's mental," Naamah said to Cosmacrater before noticing herself alone in the cave. "Cosmacrater?"

He reappeared at the mouth of the cave His eyes squinting to see through the blowing dust. "I think I've found a way out of here but I'll need your help. Follow me," he said, before leaving her sight again.

Her heart beat hard in her chest. She knew Asmodius was well trained in the arts of illusion and wished that she had some way of knowing if the man calling to her was really Cosmacrater. She froze searching for any trick, any ripple that might reveal some deception. She saw Lillith carrying a body from the massive black tower.

"That has to be an illusion. There is no way that Lillith could have gotten her that quickly," she thought to herself. "She must have been captured. Knowing her she told them everything. She bolted from the cave after Cosmacrater, trying not to be seen by the figure leaving the hideous nightmare building.

"Where is she going?" Lillith said, weighed down by Atone. She shifted her over her shoulder trying to find some way to make it easier and changed her course to follow her.

"I found this boat," Cosmacrater said, working on the ropes that secured it against the wind. "I think its Death's. Help me with these ropes. Those damnable souls won't let go of the anchor."

"We're stealing Death's boat? Are you insane? Do you know what he'll do when he catches us?" she asked.

"Look, quit being so negative. We want this thing wrapped up quick, right? Death's boat can go anywhere. We can use it to sail right into that gate."

"No. Before I follow you tell me one thing," she said, looking for a way to prove that it was indeed Cosmacrater. "Why are you suddenly so concerned about doing the right thing?"

"If we don't then everything goes to oblivion. We might deserve this fate, but there are things out there that deserve better. Now help me."

Atone

Lillith turned the corner and watched as Cosmacrater and Naamah worked against the waves to liberate the small sailing vessel.

"I've got her. She didn't make it easy," Lillith said, readjusting her captive on her shoulder, her side slick with Atone's sweat. "She wouldn't let go of this skull and this metal bar digs into my shoulder," she said, standing at the waters edge next to the boat.

"Alright. Bring her over," Cosmacrater called before Naamah could stop him.

"Stop, Thief!" Astanphaus said, following Cronos and Asmodius. "You're taking my boat."

"Lillith listen to me. Bring Atone back here," Cronos said. Lillith turned to see Cronos.

"Cronos," she smiled waving excitedly, nearly dropping Atone. She turned and took a step toward him.

"Lillith, no. Bring Atone over here," Naamah called to her sister. Lillith turned to look back at her.

"Oh, right," she said. Stepping toward the boat.

"She needs our help. She isn't ready to fulfill her destiny," Cronos bellowed. Lillith turned back her face turned into a puzzled mask of confusion. "Let us help her."

"Don't listen to him Lil. He only wants to stop her. They only want to hurt her," Naamah warned. Lillith stepped back not taking her eyes from Cronos.

"Where is Agrat? Where is my sister?" Lillith said, looking around.

"She's inside. She wants to see you," Asmodius said. Lillith smiled and took a pace toward them before Naamah could stop her.

"She can't see you Lil. They tortured her. They dismembered her. They'll do the same to you," Naamah called after her sternly.

"Stop it! You're confusing me," she cried out stopping and sitting on the dirt covering her ears Atone slung over her.

"Enough of this," Astanphaus roared. An undulating vibration escaped his throat and the dead in the river began to lash the boat violently sending Cosmacrater falling out. "Minions of Death arise. Arise, my boatmen."

Atone

Cosmacrater on the dock staggered looking back to see several warped skeletal minions rise from the depths of the ship.

He grabbed Lillith and Atone as Cronos and Asmodius rushed them throwing her onto the boat. Drawing his daggers he severed the last cord keeping the boat ashore. "Take her and go."

"Now my minions, at…" His command was cut short by the dagger penetrating the Adam's apple imbedding itself through the vertebrates. The dead shuffled aimlessly, the boat rocking back and forth. In a lunge Cosmacrater was overtaken by Cronos, Asmodius rushing past them to get to the boat.

"Come on Dead guys… Boatmen, row." Naamah called trying to activate Death's minions. Their only response was to blink lifeless without expressions.

"Boatmen, set sail." Naamah looked back to see Asmodius on the docks gaining ground. Soon he would be upon them and she would be punished for her transgressions.

Boatmen, onward… to distant shores," Atone spoke in her stupor again in a voice not

her own. The ship lurched forward and
Asmodius dove toward the moving boat.

"You can't take her. She isn't…" An
explosion propelled him off the mark sending
him into the corpse rich streams of the river
Styx. Bits of stone and flesh, ablaze by an inner
fire tore hunks into the side of the boat. The
dead boatmen continued to row unaffected.
Naamah brought Atone and Lillith down to the
lower deck.

"No. You don't understand. You
can't…" Asmodius called after the ship as the
undead souls clawed at him. "Get off me…" he
cried as he was pulled under. Angry hands took
hold of him. Damned souls pulled him down
into their crushing depth. He struggled not to
drink of the pure forgetful waters of Styx. He
struggled in vain to swim to shore, all the while
battling the undead. Astanphaus watched as
Asmodius was pulled down. Soon not even a
sign of struggling disturbed the river surface. He
turned his attention to Cronos and Cosmacrater
and gasped at what he saw. He tried to pull the
lodged knife free preparing for the battle ahead.

From the sundered body of Cronos
Cosmacrater emerged, his soul glowing
brightly. He turned to see the ship setting sail.
"God speed, girls."

Atone

A boned hand swung out after him, fingers piercing him threw his exposed soul before his outer layer could reform from the explosion. "You helped them escape," Astanphaus choked out liberating the knife finally in his other hand. "You will pay for aiding them."

Cosmacrater smiled forcibly through the pain. "Not so fast, Death. Let's cut a deal. How about a horse? You'd look pretty bad ass on one of those, what do you think?"

Chapter 14.

"The gate's up ahead," Naamah said, crouched low, with Atone who was still lost in a catatonic state, poking her head from below deck. Lillith watched the vessel as it sailed on by the power of the boatmen. "Atone. Atone come on wake up."

Atone moaned feeling the mindless and desperate souls in the water, the soldiers on the shore and the drone like boatmen in their own special Hell. Lillith smiled, the light of heaven shining on her from the gate above. "It's so beautiful. I've never been here before."

"Lillith get below deck. The last thing we want to happen is to be spotted by the angels when we pass through. This is very important. If they see that we took Death's boat we are going to be attacked instantly."

"I'm not going down there it's all wet and it stinks," she said.

"There's… O.K., I'll play with you if you come down here."

"OOO… Do you promise?"

"Yes. I swear by my right eye."

"The pretty one?"

"Yeah. It's all yours if I break my promise."

"Deal," she said, jumping below deck. Instantly her hands began to roam over Naamah's body feeling the soft flesh through her clothing.

Naamah let her caressing and loving bites go unhindered her eyes watching Atone shivering in cold sweats. A searing bright light washed over them and lingered on their retinas. Atone's breathing calmed down and the sound of birds and animals could be heard. Naamah let out a sigh.

"Come on Naamah. Play with me. You promised," she said, grabbing Naamah's hand and slapping it across her own face. When she got no response she grew angrier. "Play with me, damn it!"

Naamah's eyes scanned the lower deck and found the taskmaster's station. She took hold of her forcibly and dragged her to the restraints, smiling wickedly as she listened to Lillith's eager giggling. In a strange way she

missed her sister's innocent if warped presence.
She tied her to the wall, using the shackles
provided by the ship. Lillith squirmed until her
tattered skirt was hiding nothing then spread her
legs wide as she could.

"You've made a mess, Lillith. You've
been a bad girl. I'm going to leave you here to
think about what you've done."

"Yes," she breathed weakly. Naamah
left her waiting there, fighting the urge to peek
outside. She heard Lillith waiting for her return.
Several moments passed and she could hear
Lillith calling to her desperately. She tried to
push her out of her mind.

Naamah peeked her head out from the
lower deck and scanned the horizon. "Dear
God," she gasped running back down. She took
hold of Atone and shook her violently. "Come
on, Atone. It's time to snap out of it."

With no response from Atone she
lowered her down and quickly paced the boat to
where she left Lillith. With a quick jerk she
pulled the bindings free and Lillith hit the
ground. "Lillith come up here, quickly. Bring
Atone."

Atone

Naamah walked back upstairs and boldly emerged to witness the carnage full well. The water, The Guff, flowed with fragmented, unprepared souls waiting to be born. Serene and peaceful. Only when her eyes made it to the shore did the world change. Bodies lay strewn across the tranquil fields and lush gardens of heavens beautiful landscape. Her eyes filled with tears. "In Hell at least we had heaven to show us what was right. What are we supposed to do now?"

Lillith lugged Atone up and plopped her carelessly onto the deck.

"Lillith, careful," Naamah said, scornfully. Lillith scowled back.

"You don't have time for me anymore," she fussed. "All you care about is her now." Lillith held Atone up looking at her for something special. "I say we eat her."

"No, she's not getting eaten."

"She's nothing special," Lillith cried pulling the body over to the edge. She looked into Atone's lifeless eyes with a scowl. Her face turned to crazed joy her mouth open wide as if about to laugh. "Bye, bye," she said, sweetly, dropping her over the edge. Naamah, distracted by the carnage was slow in her reaction.

"Lillith? Where is Atone?"

"She's gone now. She went away," Lillith said, with a twinkle in her eyes. The water swallowed her, drawing her down. Naamah ran to the back of the boat looking over the edge at the endless waves. "Lillith what have you done? Atone!" Her eyes scanned the waters but could not find any sign of the fallen angel. She breathed under her breath, "We're doomed."

Atone, lost in others oblivion swam through the darkening pool, a spiral twisting downward. She prepared herself for it, for the nothingness. A part of her even welcomed it, to be in the absence with Axael. Her fingers, nearly forgotten, felt around for his skull.

"Axael?" She cried out surrounded by nothing.

"Atone. There will be time for that later," a voice called.

"Who...?" Atone asked, hearing the voice moments before it was stripped from her.

Only the faintest memory of someone speaking guided her.

"You need to know," it began before oblivion captured it. "You need to feel."

She opened her mind, without resistance expanding outward for the memory of the voice. She could feel the speaker out there and headed toward it. Finding a shore emerge from the darkness she walked onto it. She focused on anything, everything that there was around her. Slowly oblivion became existence. A voice became a person.

"Mother?" she asked, seeing Diana watching her. Diana smiled at the word.

"I'm sorry my child. I'm sorry that you have to do this, I'm sorry that I was blind to what you had to do. But I am here now, to help you. Come," she said, leading her into a cave. Atone hesitated and felt oblivion welcoming her from behind. She shook it off trying to run from it only to invite it in further. "That won't work, Atone. It's not you. Feel yourself."

"What is my own feeling?"

"If you don't know that then I can't help you."

Atone

"My destiny?"

In a moment she found herself facing Cosmacrater being tortured by reflections of his own men. She cringed feeling the pain and the warped pleasure of Asmodius. She began to feel oblivion creep back into her as the emotions consumed her.

"Stop it. They are not your own. You are not them and theirs is not yours. Use it; do not let it destroy you."

"How?" She began as Diana disappeared destroyed by oblivion. Atone let the feelings wash over her, welcomed them in. Swimming in them she felt Diana again at her side.

"Expand it farther."

"What are we here for…?" she asked, then found what all this was about. She saw the pain and hate warped around a thin, frail truth of the real feelings, an emotion protected.

"Cosmacrater, Asmodius…"

"You see it. You see the truth hidden from them by their own emotion."

Atone

"What is this thing?" Atone asked, feeling the core of their hearts. "Asmodius did it all to help, to teach. He tried to show me this… He tried to show me what you show me now."

"What of Cosmacrater?" Diana said, neither confirming nor denying her statement.

"He's a martyr. He does what is right, He… Still serves…"

"A sacrifice of heaven, like you. Do you begin to see?"

"Like me?" she asked, turning to see Diana only to find a reflection of herself. Hands clasped tightly against her skull and in that link they saw the truth within her. Her mind drifted to all the events that brought her here. She saw echoes of the time when she fell, when she took Zopheal's offer, when she reached earth among others.

"What do you see?" Diana said, a disembodied voice watching over her.

"I see myself," she said, watching. Her voice was withdrawn as she analyzed the scenes visible in front of her. "Moments in time."

"Look closer."

Atone

There, she saw it. Over every choice there was a phantom of herself and others, each phantom a choice not taken.

"Do you see it now?"

"Things I didn't do," she said, quietly. Then her mind flushed back to her and Cosmacrater in the cave. "I chose this destiny by my actions. I made this my destiny."

"There is only one thing that can truly be yours," she heard a man's voice from behind.

"Axael?" she asked, the illusion falling away. She found herself on the cliff overlooking the crashing waves. "You're alive," she said, then stopped, taking a step back, knowing her words were not true. She saw the dark sundering formlessness of oblivion stripping him apart as he spoke. Her empathy was at such height that this was him in oblivion reaching out to her, reaching out to the only thing left to reach out to. "Your actions are all that you can really call your own. Your actions led to beginning all of this. My actions tried to stop you, to spare you. I didn't want you to have to go through this."

"I understand. I can let go now," she said, feeling the skull tumble from her hands. The urge to grab at it again bit against her mind and she fought the urge to swim deeper to follow after it. She felt the soft moist shore and clammy flesh of an oblivious angel, its desperation reaching out to here. Opening her eyes she saw a field of death, all begging for release, for a way free from this never-ending nothingness. Her eyes grew wet and she forced the tears at bay. She knew at last what she needed to do.

Chapter 15

Atone walked the perfect earth and flowering vegetation avoiding the larger masses of decaying angels, trapped in their own husks. Their faint pleading auras where now roaring wails of desire as she made her way east. Finding Zopheal was a moot point now. Everything was worse than dead here. If she wanted to end all their suffering in one powerful swoop she needed to find Israfel quickly, which meant entering Eden, the only totally pristine area left. It was here that the Archangels dwell though even they do not go to the heart of the garden. No one since Adam was cast out for feeding off the forbidden tree ventured to the tree of knowledge, the first tree. This site, more than any other in heaven, would warrant their protection. The Norse referred to it as Yggdrasil. She wondered what happened to her father as she made her way to the tree. Would he be here, like her mother was or did he in some way continue to survive in the zombie controlled North America. She stepped up to the tree and, as she expected saw Israfel. He was strapped to it, ready to defend at least this before his death.

Atone

"I felt you from a mile away," she said, barely getting a bob from his head. His eyes rolled in a feeble attempt to view her. She stepped up to him, feeling the hatred he bore her. Some of that hatred was legitimate, as she did represent a rebel to God's forces. She appreciated this in a small way. What made her sneer was the hatred he bore her for bringing him to ruin, for destroying what he would have made, a perfect world.

"Then finish it," he said, his hands struggling to bring the horn carved trumpet from his side to his lips. She leaned up against the tree to help him in his task. The feeble and broken reverberations, a frail and pathetic sound, did the image of a majestic trumpet hailing the apocalypse no justice at all. But she smiled, even leaning down to kiss him on the forehead. She slumped, her hand falling through the bark as the tree rotted under her touch. The tree, corrupted by her touch, crumbled and collapsed. Atone shrieked despite her bravado and avoided the brunt of the debris. Israfel sunk into it falling into the decayed plant with a moist, rotten thump. After her initial surprise she stepped up standing by him. She showed no sign of caring that the first tree died at her touch. She crouched over the angel and dusted the decay from him.

"I came here for revenge. I wanted to hate you so much. You plotted to kill me, blocked our chances to redeem ourselves in God's eyes and because of you Axael is in an undying prison, just like the rest of them. I have every reason to hate you. But I don't. I know now why you did all of this. God has all but disappeared. Nobody sees him anywhere. Nobody knows what he's doing or why, like we are all left to our own devices. Only our actions reflect any real, tangible difference. That was what you were going to do? You were going to take a stand, to be the God of action that the world could follow. To be the God that isn't vague and cryptic. But you forget something. There already is a God like that. God is all things. He is everything. He is every angel, demigod and demon. He is every rock and tree, He is all the hate the fear the love and the sorrow. You can never truly be without God. You can't become something apart from him. Those who try end up like all of them," she said, waving at the bodies littering the ground behind her. "Hollow and lost, trapped in their own shell. What I do is not for me. I don't bare you any malice. Not anymore. In a way I want you to take comfort. Your destiny will come to pass. This better world will come," she finished then steeled her resolve. She swung hard, and with that one powerful move decapitated him.

Atone

Silence followed. She felt nothing. There were only far and distant emotions including a trace of Naamah and Lillith to the south.

After the murder she backed away watching as the dying vegetation spread from the sacrifice. Tears flowed freely from her eyes and for the first time since her fall they were all hers. She sobbed with out the will to stop. The dry shriveled blades of tall grass crumbled as her tears fell upon them. Soon the ground grew moist under her.

Chapter 16

Naamah sailed the boat to the Throne's many palaces. This massive structure outshined anything Hell had to offer. The doors to the giant palisade were torn free and left sitting cock eyed along side the massive opening.

"Something's wrong here. The Dominions and the Thrones should have some better protection. Could it be? Has even the mighty Thrones and Dominions failed?" Naamah asked, leaving Death's ship adrift in a small eddy that kept rocking it gently toward the shore. She walked up cautiously eyes ever weary. She turned back to see the grass behind them dying. She grabbed Lillith and rushed in as the grass withered rapidly at their heels. They looked out from the large elaborately decorated floors to the rotting vegetation outside. "What has happened here?"

"How would I know?" Lillith grumbled. "You always overlook me. Everything I do you think is strange and stupid. What makes you think I know what's going on now?"

"Are you alright?" Naamah asked.

"No. You won't play with me and you're always mean to me," she said.

"Look, we're under a lot of bad and dangerous things right now. We don't really have the time to…"

"Naamah, look," Lillith said, pointing at the massive barricade still in place even with the gargantuan doors torn loose.

"If they had it barricaded then what came in here?" Naamah asked, her eyes still scanning the dark depths inside. "What is still here?"

"Atone?" Lillith asked. Naamah's heart fluttered but she suppressed it with logic.

"Atone wouldn't have the capacity for something like this," Naamah spoke out at barely a whisper. The echo that reported back made her muscles tighten. "Lillith. Say absolutely nothing, understand? We don't want any attention, understand?"

"Yes... I mean..." She giggled and mouthed silently the word, "Yes."

"Good," Naamah mouthed back and darted back and forth through the massive structure a few yards at a time from hiding place to hiding place. Lillith followed diligently after her without a sound.

Minutes seemed like hours as their hearts jumped at every noise and fluttering stray bird. Eventually they reached the golden and radiant First Throne. Seven in total, like princes, dwelled in this kingdom-sized castle. The radiant room was an overwhelming beauty to behold. Naamah froze, taken aback. Her body trembled with unworthiness as she beheld the immaculate splendor. It was Lillith who reacted by seeing the first Throne's body cut open and strewn aside.

"He's dead."

"What?" Naamah said, shaking herself free from the vision to witness what Lillith spoke of. The thin, porcelain skin was marred by a harsh jagged slash through the midsection and again through the neck. A blade remained driven through him the tip splintered and broken. It was a sure sign of the obvious; a corrupt and evil presence was here.

"What would have done something so horrible?" Naamah asked. She heard the rustling of something and turned in time to see the walls crawling with insects. She caught Lillith and began to run, the crawling bugs swarming after them. "Run, Lillith."

"Bugs, like the Order."

"But the order wouldn't…" she asked.

"Who… Oh, the little whores from the night club?" A voice came from the mass of insects coming in behind them. Naamah dared to turn and see what spoke. The horde of insects parted to reveal Lihatiel, a new powerful body replacing the old and undead. Thick crimson armor, like that of harlequin beetle, guarded him. Only his undead head, visible within a massive multifaceted eye, reflected the origin of the beast. "What brings you here?"

"He's distracting us while they try to surround us. Let's move," Naamah shouted. Naamah and Lillith returned to their running. Lihatiel's savage laughter echoed through the sacred halls before the clattering of beetles drowned it out. They turned the corner halting in her tracks as two massive, stone-skinned mantis statues began to move. Their mantis shaped bodies reached out slashing at him. Naamah dove down. The blades cut deep into her arm. She rolled between them. They hissed, tentacle tongues lashed out at the blood on the ground. Naamah dove onto one, digging her fingers under the hard stone skin by the base of his neck and head. It whirred angrily fighting her. It toppled her, blindly slashing at her as she rolled through the air.

"What the fuck!" She screamed at the beast's head still in her hand. She threw the lifeless, twitching mantis head backwards, seeing the swarm of fist sized insects closing in on them. The headless mantis swung blindly, insect juices pumping outward from its long, now headless neck. Its blades swung out for Lillith who froze looking at her impending doom. "Lillith!" Naamah screamed. The bladed arm swung. Its blade sunk deep. Lillith opened her eyes seeing the blade driven into the claw of the other mantis. There was no time. Naamah tackled her as the free blade swung down at her. Now behind the mantis they watched in horror as they slaughtered each other. They turned again to see a golden angelic female statue smiling downward at them from 30 feet above. She was surrounded by lush green foliage as yet untouched by the corruption outside. The room was illuminated by a massive ornate sky roof.

"Naamah we have to move." Lillith pulled at her.

"I… Know…Her…" She spoke trying to remember what it was she looked at.

"No time," Lillith said, pointing skyward. The light began to darken by a massive collection of insects. Lillith pulled her toward a door, the first group of bugs starting to claim it. "We have to get out of here."

"No," Lillith hissed pulling back with such force that Lillith was nearly jerked from her feet. "This way," she said, pushing through the foliage, the soft radiant green leaves crumbling to dry and crisp brown before crumbling to dust. Naamah felt a shiver run through her as she wondered how she knew about the door at the statues base. The bugs crowded in around them their wings creating whirls of leaves behind them. The door behind the statue jammed. The bugs rushed for them. Tiny insect mandibles bit hard. Lillith screamed flailing. There was a rumble underneath them then nothing. Naamah and Lillith scratched at the walls as they fell. Only a few insects remained with their mandibles bit into their skin. Clawing at the walls proved fruitless so they slaughtered the remaining bugs. Dust flew up around them as they hit a lush, downy bed with a thump.

Naamah rose to her feet looking around. "I know this place. Lillith," she said, turning. Lillith lay unmoving on the bed. Naamah stepped back to her leaning over her. "Lillith? Lillith!"

Lillith jumped up in a flash throwing her over on to the bed jumping onto her. Her mouth kissed her hard. "Come on. Be with me," she growled kissing her with bruising force. Naamah pushed her off.

"Lillith," she struggled through pressed lips. She fought for air and a chance to speak. "Lillith, no. I'm not… Not here. It doesn't feel right. There is… someone else."

"So you're not going to play with me?" Lillith asked, her voice trembling.

"Do you want the eye now?" Naamah said, flatly.

"No. I want my Naamah back," Lillith shouted running away from her crying. Naamah felt the urge to chase after her but hesitated. She didn't understand yet how she knew, but this passage only led to one thing. If she could only remember, she cursed herself. Either way she would find Lillith there and hopefully by then have something to say to her that wouldn't hurt.

She struggled with her mind trying to pry away what was hidden inside. If only she could remember… but she couldn't. Damn Styx water, she cursed to herself. She reached the end of the underground passage and saw a bright brilliant light blinding her darkness-adjusted eyes. The sky, an eternal sunset of blues, purples and reds, greeted her and she saw a grandiose chariot decorated with carvings of beautiful angels romancing each other. Ahead of her was 36 statues made of fire. Each flaming statue had four expansive wings and four massive heads.

"The Hayyoth," she gasped. Her mind pulled back toward the chariot. She walked up to it running her hands along the relief of two female angels entwined in a loving and passionate kiss. She walked to the front of the carriage climbing up onto the bench. She looked around at the controls, her hands feeling the soft leather and metal plated lines. At her feet she saw an engraving. "Shekinah," she said, reaching out to feel it. A hard lump formed into her heart and she clutched at it her eyes growing moist. Her fingers touched her eyes, and she pulled them away to see them wet with tears. As she studied her hands reaching through her memory to find the source of her pain a splash of red fell into her palm.

She turned to see a form fall onto her. She rose, throwing it off. "Oh, God… No,"

Naamah sobbed. Lillith lay torn asunder at her feet. She tried to back up in the driver seat and felt the sharp jagged claws at her back keeping her from falling backwards out of it.

"'God, no.' How very astute," the rumbling voice growled from behind her. "She couldn't make these beasts move." His claws broke the flesh and she felt the sting of his poison in her veins. "I hope you do better."

Chapter 17

"Naamah!" Atone called out feeling fear push beyond her sorrow. Atone jumped to her feet feeling the ground beneath her feet grow soggy and wet. She turned back and saw the edge of the Guff, The primordial soup of new souls and old ones recycled, mixed and formed into their next new life, growing closer. Her heart jumped into her throat and mutated a scream from it. She back peddled away not taking her eyes from the water's edge. The water had a powerful way of slowly breaking up a soul, defining it into a usable material for new life. Its counterpart, the river Styx, was known for the corrupt and dark power of obliterating a soul piece by piece but where the water of Styx tore apart and destroyed, the watery souls in the guff retained their individual essence to mix it and blend it into a new and unique entity when the time was right for the reforming.

"Don't worry," the voice came again as the water washed around her, surrounding her on all sides. The wave refused to touch her, and she remained a prisoner in it. "It is only the souls coming home but it is not your time, just yet."

"God?"

"Is it really so hard to believe that you have to ask it rather than say it. Should it not be obvious? You know what I am."

"It's been so long."

"No. I was always with you. Even as you denied seeing me I was there all the time," the voice said, bubbling from the waters of the guff. "But I apologize. I hear that I am unknowable and confusing. I am sorry you didn't know."

"What did you need me for? You are God. Why…? Why make me go through all of this?"

The wave turned into a collection of galaxies and planets swirling with seeming aimlessness through the cosmos. "Look at this world, Atone. Is it not beautiful? Does not everything in it strive to make this perfect?"

"Perfect? Crime is everywhere. Demons corrupt innocence into villains…"

The planets seemed to turn collectively to face her, to watch only her. "Why am I here? If the world was going as intended I would not have anything left over to form a body. You say this world is corrupt. Of course. It is everything as I am everything. This exists because this life needs to balance death. This makes the world a better place."

"How can you say this, God?"

"Without evil, good means nothing. Without change nothing can grow, without a challenge nothing will strive to better itself. I ask you, am I not all things? What exists without me? Even Armageddon is a part of me."

"So all of this was for nothing. You are just going to let everything die."

The waters returned. "No. You didn't waste your time. You wanted to stop this. You were right to return but wrong in thinking I could change things. These moments are inevitable. I see now why I have reformed. All I want is to be a part of everything. But in that everything I am nothing. Until something like this, like you happens. I know what you have done, and why. But these lives within me... man have fooled himself into thinking that I serve him. I am all and serve myself, which is everything. He separates himself from the world around him and from me. He has put himself above me."

"Above you?" Atone asked, confused. "But millions of people follow you in a myriad of different ways."

"They follow what they choose, forget what they disagree with and warp what is not right by them until it fits to their will. I am all. And as all I was unaware of this treachery. I am the Guff and the soul of all created things. I was lost in being everything, I became nothing. This is my paradox: if I am all things and am nothing at the same time then how can anything exist? I needed you to understand this. I am sorry it had to be you. But there is much work to do now that I have returned."

"What are you going to do?" Atone asked, nervously, beginning to see the whole picture at last.

"You wanted this apocalypse to end? What should we do?"

Atone froze, not expecting a question from the omnipresent one. Her mind searched to what she really wanted. "The demons are either to sick to survive, or unable to redeem themselves because of dogma and holy guardians. Good angels are being used as puppets by their superiors who are themselves corrupt. Humans seem oblivious to all of this as they try to find what is right to do, or follow their evil schemes to the grave." She saw the aquatic face of God contemplating from the swirling mass. The water swirled and spread in a vivid smiling swish back at her.

"Each man or woman will have their own share of Demons and Angels. In this no human will have the same way of believing. The time of community is at an end. With the world growing it becomes Global and the word of God changes from unify to tolerate. In their diversity and individuality a new sense of Unity is born. Each man or woman will have their own share of demons and angels and through the actions of each man and woman their angels and demons will be judged. Likewise by the balance of their angels and demons the human shall be judged. Thus the deeds of a good man will speak well of the demons in their next life, the deeds of an evil man will weigh down the angels in its. In this way a demon can find redemption and guilty angels shall be vanquished. Is this not a suitable idea, Beelzebub?" The waters spoke, a wave twisting upward to face the flying chariot barreling through the air toward it led by 36 burning Hayyoth.

"I will have your dominion. I have grown powerful. The time for the true end is here!" Beelzebub roared as he burst from the chariot, making it veer awkwardly from the sky.

"Beelzebub?" Atone cried. She saw his twisted visage a powerful, muscular bull mixed with the features of a dragonfly. She felt his hatred and rage like a fist to the stomach. She staggered back physically hurt. "Stop. He is giving…" She shouted. She peeled away the layers of emotion to find the one true inner emotion, which struck her like an arrow. In her pain her eyes were opened. "You never intended to be saved? You were going to take over! You used the order this whole time?" She went on instinct to stop him when her heightened emotions found Naamah, struggling in the plummeting carriage. Her fear made Atone's own heart beat rapidly. As the chariot collided with the waters of the Guff her feelings evaporated.

"Naamah!" Atone cried out diving in after her heedless of the waters power. She saw Naamah her essence already beginning to strip slowly away. She could feel her own existence begin to fade, her own fear making her swim that much faster. The wave engulfed Beelzebub the essence of millions crushing in around him, flowing through his nose and down his throat. He thrashed violently unable to injure the ever-flowing waters. Atone swam with ease, aided by

Beelzebub's wasted thrashing. Soon she reached
the wreckage. Naamah drifted unconscious. She
swam up and took hold of her carefully. The
essence of their souls mixed, tender and soluble
and she swam for ground above the rising
waters. In her rush to safety her mind
overlooked Lihatiel as he rose from the
wreckage and swam after her.

Beelzebub thrashed violently and
gnashed his teeth trying to hurt the water around
him. It was futile. Atone looked through the
water searching for some safe ground. There. In
the distance she could see a small island. She
swam hard, Naamah light in the airy waters of
the Guff, aided onward by Beelzebub's
thrashing. As she reached the shore, Naamah
came to resting on grassy hill. Atone looked
around and saw where they were. Her heart
ached at the sight of it. It was the cliff face she
revisited so often in her dreams. In the depths
behind her she could feel Lihatiel swimming
closer.

"I found you, Atone," she said, weakly,
the Guff's mystic waters working on her. "I
found myself. And for the first time I can feel
you as you feel me."

"Naamah…" Atone started before being
pulled back to the Guff's watery depth. Their

souls tore apart leaving traces of each other in them. Atone screamed at the pain of their separation. Lihatiel was to fast for her and she was pulled down with the incredible force of his insect strength. The Guff flowed into her and ended the noise. She whirled around, fighting. Lihatiel pulled her down.

"I cannot let you stop Beelzebub's true agenda. Did it never occur to you why he kept me around? His plan was to exploit you from the beginning. He kept me as a watchdog to end your miserable life once you started the end times. Now I have my time. You will die," Lihatiel roared. He held her in her claws crushing violently. Her ribs broke. Her body, malleable by the Guff's mystic waters, yielded easily to his hardened pincers. She screamed, choking on the waters. The pincer squeezed Gemini to its maximum tension, the crushing force battling the tension of the metal coil. Atone screamed pulling her hand free, stripping away her own skin to liberate it. She drew her hammer slamming it into gigantic claw's joint. The claw opened, pain vibrating through Lihatiel's core. Gemini released severing the pincer in half. Atone took the advantage. She captured her weapon and dove toward the beast. Lihatiel captured her in another claw pulling her toward his clattering mandibles. She grew disoriented as the Guff began to shuffle loose her mortal seeming. She felt Lihatiel's claw squeezing her soul, killing her. She dug the Gemini into the pincer severing the muscle inside. The beast's head rolled back roaring in pain and Atone dove toward his open mouth. His beetle like head lowered, his multifaceted eye searching for her. His Eye caught a myriad of images as her hammer shattered the lenses. Claws flailed madly clawing at its blinded eye. She felt the razor tipped edges of the two middle legs shaving off pieces of her, stealing small fragments of her inner being. Lihatiel's head sat in the insectoid brain mass. Her chains coiled out, entwining around what little remained of her former controller. The insect roared in pain the claws lashing around the opened skull. Atone dove to strike. Her hammer swung down to crush the soul. A bladed arm drove through her. Her soul shivered the deadly blow stealing her revenge.

"Not now. Not when I was so close." Atone took hold of the claw. She swung her hammer, the blade tipped leg cracking. "If I go… Then we both go… together," she said, growing weak. Her strikes breaking free the leg. She collapsed to her knees as the leg pulled free. The light within her began to fade, her soul bleeding into the Guff even as it died. Must go on, she thought. She held on to the broken leg using it to rise up.

Atone

"I die knowing my mission is complete," Lihatiel said, as the bladed leg punctured through his skull. Atone surrendered to her doom, the waters shedding her soul like a serpent's skin.

Her mind returned to the cliff her memory warped by the power of the Guff. Her mind noticed something wrong but was unable to remember this memory as Naamah set her down on the rock ledge, doting over her.

"You saved me, Atone, by giving me a piece of yourself. Now I save you by giving it back," Atone expanded her feelings, groggy at first. Her soul tried to remember the restored pieces of themselves. She rose unsteadily helped by Naamah. The smile was short lived as she saw the fear in Naamah's eyes.

A thick black muscular fist took hold of her leg tight. Beelzebub wrapped his massive paws around her, crushing her. She couldn't breath. Her vision faded. Her newly restored body was too weak for this. The pressure around her was too intense. She could hear the bones in her leg popping. She tried to scream as they broke pushing through her flesh into the hide of Beelzebub.

"Back away, High and Mighty or I crush your little tool," he growled with a smile back at God.

"As you wish," he said. The water flowed from them both pooling into one tight form and appearing as a young boy. Beelzebub laughed. Atone felt heavy by the sudden lack of water. The hold on her leg became more intense as her body dangled upside down awkwardly.

"You are weak old man. I'll kill your tool anyway," he said. The tightening muscles of Beelzebub's arms slacked for a moment. She knew that only one chance would be afforded. Atone's eyes settled on the thin metal pole with twin blades on either end.

"I'm sorry," Atone cried, Her hands reaching out to the blade.

"Don't apologize, Atone. There is no need."

"...I didn't see the truth earlier. I just want to know one thing?" She twisted in his hands.

Beelzebub growled looking at her. "What is that, Meat?"

"Was it the whole time?" She spoke. She struggled against his hold her fingertips barely touching the metal bladed edge. "Or did you actually believe it once?"

Beelzebub growled swinging her up in the air. Gemini flickered at her fingernails before falling to the ground. Beelzebub kicked it up blade raised skyward. She screamed as Gemini was pulled farther away. Beelzebub swung downward to impale her. Her body hit the spike hard. Beelzebub raised his massive arm to swing again when Gemini recoiled back. Atone held onto it as it snapped angrily. Gemini's blades thrashed like coiled lightning across his skin cutting his hands free from his arms. Beelzebub screamed succumbing to the pain for only an instance. Atone hobbled trying to run from him on broken legs. Beelzebub's screams turned to laughter as his hands flowed back as a swarm of insects.

"I will get to you soon enough, little Soul forger. But first I will be rid of you," he said, looking at the little boy. His hand reached out swarming around the small youthful boy.

"If you want to be free of me I will grant it," the boy said, slowly closing his eyes. Atone looked back seeing Beelzebub fade to nothing in an instant. Atone didn't even have time to shriek when it happened. When the boy opened his eyes it was over. He floated without movement to Atone smiling with a hint of sorrow in his eye.

"Now it is almost time," he said, and in a moment they were back on the ledge. Atone could feel her wings restored and her broken legs made anew. Naamah was there, bedecked in jewels, the image of a queen incarnate. The boy shifted and changed to a female image parallel to Naamah's, her long brown hair dangling down toward her ankles. Naamah smiled letting the tears fall freely.

"God…"

"Shekinah. I have waited so long," she said, kissing her, lovingly. Shekinah wept uncontrollably. It was then Atone saw what God really was.

"You couldn't be with her unless the world itself changed," Atone exclaimed. God turned back and smiled.

"Though I do not have to be in this form it pleases Shekinah. I have you to thank for this," she said. "Now there is only one thing left to do. Do you remember the last thing you did for me before the fall?"

"Noah's flood. But why? You have her back."

"No. As I promised it will not be as before, but I cannot change this world as long as man still holds to a Hating God. I will not make you do this. But the world needs a cleansing. The old must be washed away to allow the evolved to thrive. To allow this world to truly see peace."

"I understand," she said, "but what of Axael? You got what you wanted. The world will get what it needs…"

Naamah stopped God from speaking and walked over to kiss Atone softly on her closed eyes. "As much as I wanted our love to be real, there was always someone else. You had your angel lover, and I had mine. He's waiting for you, right here."

Atone reached out with her empathy, feeling him, fragmented and whole at the same time, drifting in and out through other souls throughout the Guff, among souls like him.

She opened her eyes again and saw the Guff raging underneath her. She could feel Axael somewhere out there.

Atone

She felt the first splash of rain across her cheek echoing her own desire. She watched as the torrential waters brought the guff to overflowing. The waters rose, flowing into the chambers of the damned where once she dwelled. She could barely feel the faint phantom of human life being washed by the rains. The rain came so hard that it washed away the illusion they built in front of their own eyes. The truth was revealed with each splashing drop. The waters rose all around her, rising up to her chest and still further. She felt her soul unraveling at the washing waves. Her heart beat once in fear as the water rose over her head. She swam in its waves seeking her lover at last. She jerked unexpected. Something held her fast. She twisted around. What hindered her? She felt Gemini pulling at her through the water. She released it watching as the metallic weapon began to break apart to reveal Nathaniel and Candice still entwined and clinging to each other desperately amid the waves.

Her body washed away, her soul shed off in layers leaving only the thin, true strand, her core like a true shot arrow. Through the murk of the watery depth she saw, and felt what she longed for. She swam for it binding with it. They were together. They became a single echoing cord. The sound of a tear splashing in the surface of a still pond echoed through them.

Atone

"You found me," Axael said, in essence
rather than words.

"I found myself in you," Atone
responded. "We can finally be together."

"Forever."

Public Service
Announcement

We've discussed a lot of things in this book. We at Scavenger's Publication wish it known that Domestic violence is a serious problem and though we feel it necessary to emphasize certain atrocities, both in the netherworld and in the physical one, we do not in any way promote this kind of activity.

If you suspect a loved one of being abused talk to them about it. Listen to what they have to say. With tact, ask direct questions about their situation. Explain that domestic abuse is a crime. Explain that abuse is not the victims fault and that violence often escalates. Emphasize that help is available whenever they need it. Protection can be provided by the law/courts and through domestic abuse programs. Help identify resources, build there self esteem and just be there for emotional support. Don't give up on someone you know to be in an abusive relationship. Abuse is taught, or conditioned, and ending it will have to be conditioned as well. Don't get frustrated. Talk to them and follow up once in a while. An end to abuse does not necessarily mean an end to the relationship. The abuser, like the abused, is conditioned. Programs can help the abuser stop.

If you are a victim of abuse here are some things you can do. Have an escape plan and avoid kitchens or rooms with weapons. Know somewhere safe and secret to go (a motel, a friend's house, or a shelter). Teach children what to do and say in case of emergency (call 911, give address and information to dispatcher or police, etc.) Store a bag with spare keys, ID, important papers, phone numbers, money and clothes at a friend's house. If you are not sure that what you experience is abuse then look out for these signs: Pushing, throwing, tripping, slapping, hitting, punching, kicking, choking, shaking, assault with a weapon, burning or freezing, throwing things, threatening, intimidating, Destroying personal property, violence to animals (in front of or to control partner), name calling, shaming, mocking, criticizing, isolation from friends and family, blaming, convincing victim that they can not make it or are worthless without other, forcing partner to participate in unwanted, unsafe and/or degrading sex, forcing someone to view or participate in pornography, stalking, monitoring phone calls and computer use, using hidden cameras to control partner, harassing friends and loved ones for information on victim, threatening violence toward victim's loved ones, taking/denying access to personal possessions, withholding economic resources, denying food, clothes, medication or shelter, denying the victim the right to work or pursue a career, use of religious beliefs against them, preventing or denying practice of religious beliefs, Fear of spouse or partner, not being allowed to discuss certain topics sensitive to partner, fear of death from partner, using their children to manipulate the victim, emotional numbness- desensitized to situations, threatening victim with self mutilation or committing suicide, denial of phone use, excessive possessiveness or jealousy of victim, putting victim in "house arrest" or preventing them from being gone from the house longer than a set amount of time, denying them access to certain places or events like a friends house, or a family get together, checking up on victim frequently when he/she is gone, use of degrading words and acts, neglecting your needs or ignoring your existence, blaming you for there violence, sexism, objectifying, considering you property.

IF YOU ARE IN AN ABUSIVE
RELATIONSHIP GET HELP
Contact the National Domestic Violence Hotline at 1-800-799- SAFE (7233)
or contact them online at www.NDVH.org.
The National Domestic Violence Hotline website also has local listings of domestic abuse programs, or browse the internet for local sites like S.A.F.E. house in Nevada (can be contacted

at www.safehousenv.org or their 24 hour hotline 702-564-3227. They can also be reached for counseling and advocating purposes at 702-451-4203

Lastly, if you are a survivor of domestic abuse speak out and tell your story. Show someone being abused that there are others like themselves and that there is life after abuse. It may be the final push a victim needs to seek help. Thank you for giving us this brief chance to express a concern in the community and thank you for reading our books.

www.ingramcontent.com/pod-product-compliance
Lightning Source LLC
Chambersburg PA
CBHW032249020726
47495CB00001B/26